THE COLLECTED STORIES OF NOEL BLAKISTON

This volume contains stories
from the following collections
originally published by Chapman and Hall

Canon James 1951
Men of Letters 1955
The Lecture 1961
That Thoughtful Boy 1965
and from *The Cornhill* (Summer 1969)

THE COLLECTED STORIES OF NOEL BLAKISTON

CONSTABLE
LONDON

First published in Great Britain 1977
by Constable and Company Limited
10 Orange Street London WC2H 7EG

ISBN 0 09 461540 3

Set in Photon Baskerville 10pt
Printed and bound in Great Britain by
REDWOOD BURN LIMITED
Trowbridge & Esher

Contents

Contents

From That Thoughtful Boy and other stories

From The Cornhill (Summer 1969)

Acknowledgement is made by the author to the following journals, in which various stories which comprise this volume originally appeared: *Cornhill Magazine; English Story; Harper's Bazaar; New Statesman and Nation; Penguin New Writing; World Review; Réforme; Winter's Tales; Pick of Today's Short Stories*.

Introduction

The stories here reproduced have been out of print for a long time. Several of them were written thirty or more years ago, and even at the time of writing some of them were describing a world of which few vestiges remained, the world of my boyhood memories before or during the First World War.

In the matter of language a modern reader will soon be aware of an archaic flavour. Youthful expressions such as 'By Jove!', 'pater', or 'ripping', are to be found alongside the adult but no less obsolete 'My aunt!' or 'My hat!'. The writing is further dated by echoes of the Bible, which may well puzzle today's reader.

Meanwhile the faithful descriptions of the social hierarchy that existed thirty, forty, fifty, sixty, years ago, may astonish him. He must simply accept it as a fact that when I was a boy rustics would touch their cap to squire or parson. Servants were then so called and the word 'sir' was widely in use.

No attempt, in this reprinting, has, of course, been made to modernise the script, but history has moved so fast in my lifetime that even the stories that were written about contemporary life in the forties, fifties, or sixties, may also now in various respects seem to belong to a distant age.

This publication has been made from the four volumes of stories, *Canon James* 1951, *Men of Letters* 1955, *The Lecture* 1961 and *That Thoughtful Boy* 1965. Five items have been dropped and one has been added, *The Regans*, which was published in the *Cornhill Magazine*, Summer 1969.

Canon James

Canon James had the feeling that he was marking time, while all the fascinating people he had been with moved onwards. He was soon left alone, and so he came to consciousness. It was always a surprise to wake and find that he was not dead yet. Not that that would be uninteresting. It was fascinating either way.

He turned over and looked towards the door where the boy who had just called him was standing hopefully. Behind the boy, in the half-open door, were other children's faces.

'Can I watch you dressing, sir?'

'Why, of course, Raymond.'

The boy banged the door in his sisters' faces.

'By Jove you're decent, sir.'

He walked over to the dressing table and began to examine Canon James's collar. He took a folding ruler out of his pocket.

'By Jove, your collar's high, sir. It's four-tenths of an inch higher than pater's. By Jove!'

Canon James reflected that the diversity of styles of clerical neckwear was indeed remarkable, varying as they did from the high and stiff to those limp and shallow apologies for a collar which the Roman Catholics wore. On the whole probably the higher the collar the lower the church. No—he thought of his colleagues—yes, no—evidently there would be a good many exceptions to whatever generalisations one made. He must get the subject up. He must start assembling data. It was worth a monograph. Who, by the way, had invented the clerical collar?

Being of a philosophic and contemplative nature, Canon James had trained himself to put a certain check on the meditative impulse and to wrestle with facts. Otherwise, he knew, he all too easily went off into a dream and began seeing things from outside. And that was too exciting. He must postpone that. He must keep himself busy. He was like a man in love, who has a delightful evening of love ahead of him, which he tries, all day, continually to push from the forefront of his thoughts.

'I suppose you'll be working in the church again to-day?' said Raymond.

'Yes, I must try to finish to-day.'

'By Jove, you must be clever to be able to read those old books. I say, I've got to go down to the village on my bike after breakfast, on business. Is there anything you'd like me to get you at the shop?'

Canon James was shaving.

'I don't think so, my boy, thank you very much.' And then, as Raymond seemed disappointed, 'What do they sell?'

'Oh, all kinds of things, like bread and stamps and jam and ripping thongs you can make slings with. I had one but it got bust.'

'I'd like a thong.'

'By Jove, would you really, sir? What do you want it for?'

'A present for you, to make a new sling with.'

'By Jove, you're awfully decent, sir.'

Meanwhile Raymond's father, the Rev. John Dixon, was passing the time until his venerable guest came down to breakfast by strolling round the lawn. It was a delicious rather misty morning in the middle of May that held the promise of great heat. Not a breath of wind disturbed the massive shapes of the beeches which had just now attained their full splendour of proportion and had not yet lost the bloom of youth. A giant hand had been brushing the leaves of all the trees. It had brushed the chestnut blossom upwards against the leaves, and brushed the may blossom downwards until it looked like white or pink paint upset over the tree. The hedges had suddenly grown so thick that you could no longer see the church from the garden. You could not even see old Croft's cottage. Only from the upper windows of the rectory could you see the church or any houses. At one end of the lawn Mr Dixon was wooed by the sweet scent of lilac, at the other by the drowsier odour of the may blossom. The birds called to him. The lovely morning offered itself to him without reserve. But Mr Dixon did not respond.

He was put out. He had been disappointed. He had so looked forward to this visit of Canon James. Was not the old man acknowledged to have one of the best brains in the diocese? What a treat it was going to be to have him under his roof for nearly a week! Weeks, months, went by during which his only company was practically illiterate. And now, for several days, he was to have an intellectual man all to himself! Mr Dixon was not one of those clergymen who never read a serious book again once they have passed their ordination examinations. He had made it a rule to read six or seven deep books, carefully, each year; and he was able to look back on a resolution faithfully kept. But somehow, as the years went by, he seemed to receive less and less profit from what he read. He had thought that when he buried himself in this remote country parish he would probably expand his programme of reading. He would become a regular scholar. Well, he had had the time certainly, no lack of that. But nothing had come of his plans. It was the stimulus that was lacking, the sense of purpose, the *terminus ad quem*. For he very rarely had the luck to meet anyone with whom he could discuss the theological books he read. He very rarely met anyone he wished to impress with his learning, and he no longer got any satisfaction from impressing himself. He was not now called upon to pass examinations on his reading. All the subsidiary motives for study seemed to have gone. Only the main motive, interest in the subject, remained. And it is a virile mind that can so plod on with zest, alone, year in, year out, through stiff books. Mr Dixon's mind had lately begun to wilt, he knew it.

And then had come the prospect of Canon James's visit, arousing him from his lethargy. The notes he had been desultorily jotting down on Rolf's *Prolegomena* suddenly seemed worth making. It was the book of the moment. Everyone was reading it. That is to say, perhaps ten or a dozen of the better brains in the diocese would be reading it, Canon James among them. The Rev. John Dixon decided to master that book before the Canon came, to have it at his finger-tips. What interesting discussions they would have together, walking slowly round the lawn or sitting in the study, discussions in which he would hold his own with his distinguished guest. The prospect fired him with intellectual vigour. He began to feel himself again.

His acquaintance with the Canon had been slight, but they had met each other on several occasions, and when Canon James had made some inquiry about the church registers, he had boldly suggested that the Canon should come and stay and look at them for himself.

'Quite right,' said Canon James, 'it is much better for me to go to them than for them to come to me. I sometimes have them sent to me to work on, but it is much better and safer to move them as little as possible. Then I will come to you the third week in May. How kind of you! I shall look forward to it. I think you and your wife will find me a harmless guest.'

And so Canon James had arrived on Monday and now it was Friday, and somehow Mr Dixon felt disappointed. He felt that he and Canon James had not got to grips with each other. Who was to blame? Well, quite honestly he did not think he could reproach himself, unless perhaps for having expected too much from an old man. But no—and there was the galling part of it. The old boy still had plenty to give. It was his method of giving—promiscuous, irrational, uncritical—that seemed to Mr Dixon so wrong and wasteful. The Canon seemed to have no sense of the hierarchies of life, of the great distance that separates scholars from non-scholars, men from women, adults from children, even human beings from animals. He gave himself to all and sundry. He mixed the talk proper to one level indiscriminately with that of another. He talked to Mr Dixon about flowers and boys' clothes. He talked to Mrs Dixon—yes, Mrs Dixon—about Rolf! He had brought the subject up at tea-time, if you please, when the table was full of women and children. He told them about the rise of monotheism in ancient Egypt. He certainly did it very well. He made it picturesque and awoke their interest. Mrs Dixon asked him several questions. He held his audience. But—pearls before swine!

'John never talks to me about these deep things, do you, John?' said Mrs Dixon, at which her husband looked uncomfortable, and when Canon James said afterwards 'What an intelligent woman, your wife,' the compliment found no echo in Mr Dixon. For one of the many matters on which he had made up his mind once for all was that of his wife's intelligence. She was hopelessly ignorant. Women were. It was not their fault perhaps. They simply had not got the education. You could not talk about deep things to them. You should not try to bring deep things into everyday life anyhow.

But it was not merely his failure to establish a scholar's *camaderie* with Canon James, to the exclusion of the rest of the household, that Mr Dixon found unsatisfactory. His guest slipped through his fingers at every turn. He seemed to have no idea that there was such a thing as wasting time. Children, for instance. It was delightful to have them about the place, certainly. No home is a home without their happy laughter. And one wants to have their love rather than their fear or distrust. But they must be kept at a distance. It is all the more fun for them to be played with by grown-ups, if it is only done for short periods and at specified times. One does not enter into their amusements as though they were one's own. Ten minutes at most and one disengages oneself. Mr Dixon's children had soon found that they could be like leeches upon Canon James . . .

And then, the lower classes. Mr Dixon was no snob, but really one must have some standards. Gardeners and people like that—one smiled benevolently at them and asked them some pertinent question about their work and left them with another genial smile, confident that one had their trust and respect. Sometimes, no doubt, they would bring out some amusing dialect word, and they certainly had a kind of shrewdness of their own, these country people. But old Croft, simple old Croft, who could hardly write his own name, might have been one of the Wise Men from the way Canon James hung on his lips. For nearly forty minutes yesterday evening Mr Dixon from the study window had watched them talking. 'He told me all about his wife's last illness,' explained Canon James. 'Fascinating! Fascinating! Her last words were "Don't be long George," but he has survived her nearly twenty years. He said "We didn't come into the world together, so I suppose we couldn't hope to go out of it together.' Wasn't that a beautiful thing to say? Beautiful! Beautiful!' Mr Dixon could not work up much enthusiasm about old Croft's *obiter dicta.*

And then there was that man who drove the butcher's van. Really! Did Canons stand half an hour by the back door talking to the man who drove the butcher's van?

But it was not merely to human beings that Canon James gave himself so indiscriminately. He was just as bad with animals and with inanimate things. Did adults fill their pockets with a lot of clanking stones? True, he was something of a scientist. But scratching a pig's back with the tip of a walking stick for fully twenty minutes was not science. It was simply frittering away time and he seemed to have no idea that one way of spending time was better than another. And perhaps most incomprehensible of all to Mr Dixon was the work which had brought him here, the copying of fatuous old lists of names. Surely an unworthy occupation for a man of James's intelligence? No wonder he had the reputation in the diocese of not having made the most of himself. He seemed to Mr Dixon to have no sense of the urgency and solemnity of the spiritual life, indeed to be quite unable to distinguish between it and ordinary life, and to have no sense of death. Mr Dixon looked at his watch, a thing which he, like many of those who have not quite enough to do, did very frequently. Eight-forty. He went indoors to see if his guest was down yet to breakfast.

At least in his last reflection on Canon James he was quite wrong. The Canon had an ever-present sense of death. He never forgot it for a moment. Everything was dying all the time. Voices died on the instant, and the expressions of faces, and happy meals, and moments of time, and flies, and sunbeams, and people. It was a race for death. He lived each day, each hour, as if his last, unless he could remember to forget.

He did not tell Mr Dixon, but behind his host's chair at breakfast he saw an enormous waste. If he had moved in literary circles he would probably have thought of this, to him familiar, sight as 'deserts of vast eternity.' Actually he used to associate it with the wilderness of Beersheba, which he had once seen, nearly fifty years ago now, when he had stopped in Palestine on his way back from Australia. It was against this background of illimitable stony desert that he usually saw the person sitting opposite him at meals. He was conscious of a similar expanse behind his own chair. The feeling was not dull at all.

Nor, though Mr Dixon said to him as they walked down the drive after breakfast 'Doesn't it sometimes get rather dull?' did he ever find his work uncongenial. It was for its dullness that he had chosen it. It was the dullest work he could think of. (But even it let him down at times.) He had been at it now for the best part of half a century, copying, extracting, indexing, publishing, parochial registers of baptisms, marriages and funerals. There was hardly a village in the county whose registers he had not tackled. No other county in the kingdom could boast a similar antiquarian achievement. But how deadly dull, thought many people besides Mr Dixon. Yet to Canon James himself the registers had been like the bit of ground into which a mountaineer, overtaken by giddiness, buries his face to forget the surrounding void.

'The cleverest man in my diocese,' said the bishop as they passed Canon James on his bicycle one winter day on the wolds, 'and the idlest.' The chaplain looked out of the back window of the car at the bent cyclist, who was struggling uphill against the wind with a cussedness he could not help admiring. 'Hardly the idlest,' he said, pulling the rug more tightly round his knees. 'Well, perhaps not,' the bishop agreed. 'The most perverse, let us say.'

For his capacities were known in high quarters. His annual sermon in the cathedral was recognised as being in a class of its own. With the first of these sermons the dignitaries had realised that a new and quite individual voice was addressing them. The text had been an offhand little sentence from the first chapter of Genesis. 'He made the stars also.' A little item the Creator had almost forgotten! And Canon James proceeded to focus the imaginations of his hearers on to a period in the history of the universe, to which, though far the longest period, they were not in the habit of giving a thought, the period namely before the human race had even been dreamt of. Science was rare from the pulpit. His audience found it both restful and surprising. They looked forward to his next. And they reflected what a waste it was that such a man should be allowed to vegetate in a tiny out-of-the-way parish. They told him to his face that he was wasted on his little flock of rustics. 'But,' he protested, 'they seem to appreciate my efforts. I get very good congregations, considering the size of the place,' which was quite true. The people loved him for his piety and unaffected friendly interest in their concerns, and his sermons, with the simplest words, lifted them on a magic carpet beyond the horizon of their fields, over seas and deserts and continents, beyond the earth, beyond the stars. These wonderful weekly journeys through time and space became an indispensable part of their lives. Not that they seemed to reach anywhere. The further they went the further they seemed from any destination. But who wants a good fairy tale to come to an end? They were content to share their vicar's wonder and curiosity.

His texts were not always from the Bible, as when he preached from Johnson's 'If the world was to be created, why was it not created sooner?' His congregation watched the question drop like a pebble on the still surface of his mind, where it started other questions, question upon question expanding outwards until—well, for a quarter of an hour. He never preached for more. That gave them quite enough to think about.

Mr Dixon left him at the end of the drive but Raymond followed him to the stile and took his leave there.

'Now, I've got to leave you and go down to the village on business. But I'll fetch you, sir, for dinner at 12.45 from the church without fail as per. I won't let you down. I give you my word. By Jove! My word is as good as my bond. I say, you'll be able to watch me do some slinging before dinner. The yard pump's Goliath. Swish! By Jove! Good-bye for the present, sir.'

Canon James climbed the stile and began walking along the path to the church. Three big fields away from the rectory, the church was even further from the village. It had been planted away by itself among the fields. Few casual visitors came to it. Not one had come in this week during the hours that Canon James had spent sitting there at his work. Mr Dixon had suggested at first that the registers should be brought across to the rectory so that Canon James could work on them in the study, but the Canon had preferred the church. He liked the quiet of it. He liked its lonely position. He liked its cold stony smell after the heavily scented summer air.

'Dull indeed! My work dull! Well, suppose it is. Mayn't one have some respite? Ah, rue. That's interesting. *Thalictrum flavum*. So that grows here.' He brushed with his foot a fernlike leaf that was growing in the long grass. 'He thinks I waste my time. He does not understand.'

He walked on, humming, towards the church, carrying his seventy-five years as unconcernedly as a little bird its long Latin name.

A gentle breeze had got up and was turning the leaves of two poplars which grew one on each side of the gate. Before going into the church, he pottered about the churchyard looking at the attractive English stones. No Italian marble disfigured this burying place. The vicinity of a quarry accounted for a beautiful uniformity of stone colour. 'My word, what style!' he said to himself as he inspected the veteran regiment, every now and then going up to some particular slab to examine it closely, feeling a carved cherub with his hand or deciphering an old inscription. He inspected with a loving and professional eye. He knew about gravestones. His paper for the *Antiquaries* on the seventeenth-century stones in his rural deanery was a model of what such things should be. This churchyard, he reflected, was worth a monograph on its own. If only one had the time. Attractive stone, it was already warm to the touch. A pity one could not eat stone.

At length he went into the cool church. The registers were kept in a safe in the vestry. He used to bring them out and work on them at a table near the children's corner, which he first cleared of the visitors' book, the picture postcards of the church and the pamphlets of the missionary societies. He made two journeys to fetch the seven volumes. No bicycling and no carrying of heavy weights had been the doctor's orders ever since that day last autumn when he had fallen off his bicycle and lain panting on the roadside for half an hour. He must be careful of his heart.

Why, the church had had some visitors, who had written their names in the book. Yesterday's date. They must have come in the evening after Canon James had gone back to tea. He had a pang of regret that he had missed them and wondered what they had been like. *Names:* James Harris, Muriel Harris. *Address:* Sheffield. *Remarks:* 'Where is death's sting?' Was their 'remark' a cry of pleasure or of pain? Were they a contented old couple who were placidly awaiting their end, or a brother and sister who had inherited some lingering disease from which they prayed for release? Or were they a honeymoon couple on a tandem bicycle so dizzy with happiness that they would be happy to die? God bless them whoever they were.

He settled down to work at the registers. The oldest of these was a long narrow volume which began in 1561, a homely looking affair, in which the parchment folios were only approximately of the same dimensions as each other, and the stiffer, but still bendy, cover, of a thicker hide, was anything but rectangular. It smelled good, at least so Canon James thought. In places there were holes and knobbly imperfections in the coarse parchment and many of the pages bore a swirling pattern of whorls and eddies according to the grain of the skin. There was a place on the inside of the back of the cover where you could rub your finger against the bristles as against an unshaven chin. But it was in another and rather less primitive looking volume that he began working this morning. Nothing stirred in the church except his writing hand and his head that just moved as he looked from parchment to paper and back to parchment. After a while he looked up and out of the window. One of his oldest memories was looking from his seat in church at the trees outside in the wind. You felt that you were in a boat that seemed to be moving up a river, but actually it was not the boat that was moving, the boat was still and the river and banks went sailing by. Or you were in a train, standing still on the line, watching the trees and telegraph posts and stations go speeding past. You were the still point round which the world revolved.

In the church of his memories, as in this church, the windows of the aisles were not made of coloured glass. The little diamond-shaped panes were made of every variety of white glass, from a purely diaphanous to an almost opaque greenish yellow, and the leads bulged inwards and outwards, so that the trees looked different through every pane and underwent the most extraordinary contortions as you shifted your eye from one pane to the next. Once, when a little boy, he had fallen over into the pew in front, doing this during the Psalms.

How long had he been looking at those swaying poplars? Impossible to say. Come on, he must get on, or Raymond would be upon him. He turned over a page. Marriages, he read, 1663 April ye 14 Abednego Smythe to Sarah Harison. Abednego Smythe, the name was familiar, surely he had had him already? He looked back among the baptisms. Yes, there he was, Abednego Smithe 11Octo. 1641. And now he was getting married. Just here, two yards from where Canon James was sitting, he and Sarah had made their solemn promises. They used to sit perhaps in that pew there and stood singing there and knelt there mumbling responses. Think of it. Canon James could not restrain his imagination. He hunted on to the end of that register and began looking in the next. At last, found. Here they were. Burials, 1712 July 21 Abednego Smith; 1713 Jan. 2 Sarah Smyth, widdow. There was the whole story of them. And that other older book, just as it now was, with its bristles and knobbles, had been lying there in the church before either of them was born, and would go on lying there long after Canon James was dead, and Raymond was dead. Two centuries had gone by since the air had closed in on their voices, speaking, praying or singing. He thought of all the other voices that could no longer be heard in that church, and of all the voices that there had been anywhere, and of all noises whatever that had died since the beginning of the world and all the shapes and colours and all that everyone had ever felt or done or thought of—all seeming to roll itself into a ball which was a balloon receding at a great rate into the void until already it was only a speck. He stood up, his heart beating fast. 'By Jove!' he said, walking up the chancel, 'By Jove!' For some minutes he wandered round looking at mural monuments, trying to calm his excitement. Then he returned to his all too heady work. But he could not concentrate any more. At length he decided to give it up for the morning. He did not carry a watch, but thought it must be nearly time for Raymond to come. It seemed to him that he could easily carry all the registers back to the vestry in one journey. He piled them together and lifted them. His body gave a wrench, and they fell from his hands.

'Ah now! Now, at last. How intensely interesting! How absolutely fasci . . .' He staggered and fell forward on to the stone floor.

Raymond, sling in hand, was already on his way to the church. He had not failed. Had he not given his word?

Home Front

Hugh Palmer had been well brought up. He stood when ladies came into the room and opened the door for them when they went out. He took the cake that was nearest to him, left his plate clean, did not smoke in the bathroom and tried to make people who felt awkward feel at home. He was not a superior person. And, like the Roman sentry at Pompeii whose corpse is said to have been found standing stiffly to attention at his post, when the lava of domesticity flowed down towards him in an engulfing torrent, Hugh never for a moment thought of running away while there was still time. Or rather, such was his upbringing, he did not appear to think of it.

He had had a bad night. When he got in from Home Guard night operations at about half-past twelve he found Helen very sorry for herself. She was coughing, running at the nose and aching in the legs. 'I am starting 'flu,' she said. 'Oh, Hugh I am sorry.'

'Never mind,' he said, 'we'll manage. I'll get you some hot water to inhale with.'

He went down to the kitchen and switched the electric kettle on. I must remember to ring up the man to-morrow to come and see about the kettle, he said to himself. Like all the beastly modern inventions in this beastly modern house, the kettle was always going wrong. He was chilled to the bone. Some snow had got inside his gumboots early in the operations, and while Helen was inhaling he made himself some Bovril. No whisky in the house, no such luck, though the proprietor of The Bull had promised him half a bottle at the end of the week at sixteen shillings and sixpence.*

Helen had decided that he should sleep in the spare room to avoid infection, and had made up the bed there and put a hot-water bottle in it.

'How kind and thoughtful you are,' said Hugh. 'I hope you will be better in the morning. Good night, darling.' He felt too tired to do any more work and went to bed. His memorandum had to be ready the next afternoon, but he thought that if he worked on it in the train on the way up to London, and was lucky in not being interrupted during the morning, he should be able to finish it in good time. Anyhow, it was too late to start on it now. He fell asleep as he put his head on the

* A most excessive charge in 1943.

pillow.

At a quarter to two the siren went. Peter, who was seven years old, and Julia, who was four, slept across the landing. Peter was woken by the siren and was frightened and ran into Helen's bedroom.

'Can I come into your bed?'

'Please keep out of here,' said Helen.

'Come into my bed,' whispered Hugh from his door.

'Oh, are you in the spare room?' said Peter at the top of his voice. 'Why are you in the spare room?'

He banged the door of his mother's bedroom and came across to Hugh's room and got into his bed. Julia had been woken by the noise Peter made and came across to Hugh's room and got into the bed, too. This was fun for them, and the hot bodies wriggled and squirmed on either side of Hugh. He could remember what fun it must be for them. In fact it only seemed a few thousand light-years that separated him from sharing in their enjoyment of this midnight adventure. Presently the wriggling ceased and they were asleep again. The all-clear woke them.

Then Julia complained of ear-ache and began crying. She often suffered in this way, and Hugh knew what he was supposed to do. He got up and warmed a little oil and poured it into the ear, then put some cotton-wool in and then a pad of cotton-wool over the ear and a bandage round the head to keep it in place. Julia cried hard all the time.

'Shut up, Julia, you baby!' said Peter, and began kicking her. She cried louder.

'What's the matter?' called Helen from her room.

'Nothing,' said Hugh. 'It's only Julia's ear again. I'll manage.' He lifted Peter out of his bed.

'You're going back into your bed now,' said Hugh.

'Oh, can't I stay in your bed? I want to stay in your bed, I want to stay in your bed!'

He kicked and shouted as Hugh carried him across the landing and put him into his bed

'Now go to sleep, and shut up!' said Hugh, 'or I'll write and tell Father Christmas not to come to this house.' He went back to his room. Julia was moaning. Gradually the moaning became quieter. Then it stopped.

'I want a drink of water,' called Peter.

Hugh pretended not to hear.

'I want a drink of water.'

Hugh got up and fetched a drink of water.

'Now go to sleep,' he said.

'You won't really write to Father Christmas, will you?' said Peter, when he had got him into the room.

'Not if you go to sleep now at once.'

'I will,' said Peter.

'I'm sorry you're having such a rotten night,' called Helen.

'It's all right,' said Hugh, and went back to bed and thought about his memorandum. An hour later the house was woken by his alarm clock. The first thing he did when he got up was to go downstairs and switch on the kettle. During the next two hours he dressed, shaved and made and ate his breakfast, got the children up and dressed and saw them eat their breakfast and do their business. He would have liked to do his own, but there was not time, as he would have to go by foot instead of bicycle to the station on account of the thick snow. He took Helen's temperature, which was just under 101. It was not a case of having a doctor, she said. The worst would soon be over, she was sure. He took her up some tea. The coffee was finished. He must remember to get some more coffee in London. It was the only thing that dragged them up into the day.

They discussed the day ahead. The children should be able to find their own way to the corner where Mrs Eaton picked them up to take them to school. He must not forget to see that they took their house shoes. Then Mrs Harvey would be coming at ten. She stayed for two hours and would leave the lunch ready for the children. The afternoon would be rather a problem. Perhaps they could call on Mrs L., a neighbour, to come and put the children to bed. Helen promised to ring her up or get Mrs Harvey to ring her up.

'Don't attempt to stir out of bed yourself, darling, will you?' said Hugh.

'I promise. Good-bye, darling.'

Hugh saw the children into their overcoats. He saw that they had got their drawing-books and their house shoes in their satchels. He saw that they had both got clean handkerchiefs. Julia's ear-ache had gone, but he tied a woolly scarf round her head. It was perhaps unwise to send her to school at all. But at least it got her out of the house. He left them standing hand in hand in the hall ready to go.

'Now, when the big hand gets just there you're to start. Mrs Eaton will meet you at the usual place. When you get home you will find the key under the mat, and you'll find your dinner in the nursery. Don't go into your mother's room, will you? But you can talk to her from the landing. Try to be as quiet as you can, won't you, and look after Julia, won't you, Peter?'

'M'm.'

'My ear's started aching,' said Julia, as Hugh opened the door.

'Well, tell Mrs Eaton if it gets worse,' said Hugh, and saved himself as the French would say.

It was a ten-minute run to the station, in the dark, through the snow. Curse it, he thought, I have forgotten to leave a note for Mrs Harvey to ring up about that kettle. Still, as he stood on the platform, stamping his wet feet, among the business men waiting for the eight-seventeen, he felt that he had done a fairly good day's work. He felt about ready for bed. His head was beginning to ache.

Poor Helen. What a nuisance that she should get influenza just now, on top of everything. 'Everything' included the following facts: that their cook-general had left in the spring, shortly followed by the nurse; that both of these were quite irreplaceable; that even Mrs Harvey would not be able to come after the New Year; that Helen was expecting a baby in March; and that she had heard last week that her brother was missing. What a nuisance, thought Hugh, that to-night was his fire-watching night, which he would have to spend in the A.R.P. hut with that fellow Rogers. If he saw Colonel Houston-Wright, who was the village A.R.P. chief, and occasionally went up to town on this early train, he would ask him if he could be excused that night.

A car drove up to the station. It was the Houston-Wrights. Mrs Houston-Wright, who was a good deal younger than her retired colonel husband, always drove him to the station. I wonder where they get the petrol from? Hugh asked himself. He walked towards them.

'The very man I wanted to see,' said the Colonel. 'We can count on you for to-night, can't we? Old Rogers rang me up this morning to say he has rather a sore throat, and thinks it would be wiser to nurse it. I said I thought you'd be able to manage at the hut alone just for one night.'

'I'll manage,' said Hugh.

'How's your wife?' said Mrs Houston-Wright.

'I'm afraid she has 'flu.'

'Oh, I *am* sorry. You know, I must give you a serious talking to. I think your wife is an absolute saint. I think she does much too much. The last time I saw her I thought she looked frightfully tired. You really must look after her better, especially in her present condition. You mustn't let her do too much. You men would all be slave-drivers if we weak women gave you the chance.'

Any practical suggestions? Hugh wondered. Any offers of any kind? 'I'll do my best,' he said.

'Do you promise?' she said in a pleading, 'winning' voice.

One could guess you had an old husband, Hugh was thinking. 'I promise,' he said.

The train came in. It was crowded as usual, but the passengers squeezed together to make a seat for Hugh. He allowed himself to feel a glow of gratitude for the improvement in manners brought about by the war. It was the kind of glow that is got from a cheque one suspects of being a dud.

The people were letting the blinds up. The blackout was over. A little girl of about five years old was sitting in one of the corner seats and pulled her blind down again and let it go with a snap. She did this several times during the journey, but her mother did not seem to mind.

Hugh took out his memorandum. He had no elbow-room and could only just see to read in the half-light. But he must get on with the beastly thing as he had to produce it and expound it at a conference in the afternoon with the Minister himself and some big-wigs from the Air Ministry, and he had got to see the Under-Secretary at twelve o'clock, so he had not got very long to finish it.

'The Dispersal of Bomb-Load.' He read the title and began to skim through the pages he had written. The beastly thing. How he hated it! Hugh had not been one of those who welcomed the war as an escape from a dreary job, or a chance of seeing the world, or a welcome change from the pursuit of pleasure at an age when pleasure is beginning to pall. His job was not to him dreary. He loved it. He was a publisher.

Nor was he one of those people, in 1939, who went on with their lives as though nothing had happened. It seemed to him, in September of that year, an incontestable fact that something was happening. He was thirty-five at the time. Persuading his firm, much against its will, to release him, he tried to get into the Army. He received from the Army the kind of answer that would be given to an Italian costermonger who walked into the Turf Club and asked how one became a member.

At length, after a good many interviews and much wire-pulling, he got into the Ministry of Bombs. He hated ministries, he hated bombs. It seemed to him that he was not entirely failing to do his bit. Within six months he had made himself indispensable.

After five minutes the train stopped at a station. Two strapping A.T.S. got in. The people on the side opposite Hugh squeezed together and made room for one of them. If the mother took the little girl on her knee, there would be a seat also for the other. Hugh waited for a few seconds in the hope that this would happen. It did not, and he stood up and gave his seat to the other A.T. That put a stop to his getting on with his memorandum.

His headache was getting worse. Poor Helen. What a dirty trick to leave her alone like that! He would ring up Mrs Harvey during the morning and find out how things were going. Poor Helen, in that beastly house. They both loathed the place, and the stockbroker's garden suburb to which it belonged. The air raids had forced them out of London, and that was all they had been able to find. But rather than break up as a family they had stuck it now for three years. They tried to make the best of it. Surrey, they would say, must have been the loveliest county in England forty years ago, and once, just once, Helen had said that Woodlands Links Estate reminded her of the outskirts of Biarritz.

Hugh was holding the luggage rack with one hand. He put his other hand into his overcoat pocket, where he felt some letters. He had met the postman just outside his front door and pocketed his post. He took out one of the letters and opened it. It was a bill. Another, Income Tax. Another, a bill. Surely three, or at most four, guineas for looking at Julia's ear? She had only been twice, ten minutes the first visit, five the second. Seven and a half guineas! Really! There were still three or four letters in his pocket. He decided to open them later.

He looked round the carriage. In the desert of outspread newspapers there was one oasis, a French book, bent back on itself. The reader was sitting at the other side of the compartment, and Hugh could not see the title of the book. Still, his heart was warmed. How long would it be before he returned to civilisation and to the making of immortal books? Perhaps not more than a year now. And he remembered, too, with a glow of pleasurable anticipation that he might be getting back the *Goncourt Journal* any day now. In 1940 he had acquired this now quite unprocurable work and had been so self-sacrificing as to lend it, before he had read it himself, to Anthony Gilmour, who was then due to go abroad in the near future and promised to let Hugh have it back before he left. He went to Egypt without returning it. Now he was back and Hugh had met him in the street, and Anthony had promised without fail to post it to Hugh as soon as he went down to the country, where it was, in a few days. This was a treat to look forward to.

A word was knocking at the door of his consciousness, a word that woman had used. He let it in—saint. What had he or Helen got to do with saints in 1943? He thought of holy, lonely men, in bird-haunted caves or cells, at grips with fascinating temptations, and simply could not remember when he had last had a temptation worthy of the name.

His eye fell on the correspondence column of *The Times*, which was held out by one of the A.T.S. He began to read a letter which was entitled 'Population Decline. Another View.' The letter said that to have more than one child was wrong, to have more than two was positively criminal. All our ills are the result of over-population. Of course, if you like slums and bad housing, if you like the Great West Road and cars for all, if you want suburbia to embrace Wales and Cornwall, if you like the radio in every glade and the gramophone in the furthest backwater, if you like the sky to be obscured by aeroplanes and smoke from factory chimneys, if you like country houses to become schools, if you like tramps, outcasts, unemployed, and starving children, if you like hundreds and thousands of motor-cycles—then be fruitful and multiply, oh, bring forth abundantly!

Now come on, said Hugh to himself. Don't let yourself be distracted. Your time is valuable. Can't you think of something?

Peter had got to an age when he liked to be told stories. It seemed to Hugh that any child has a right to expect to be told stories. But sometimes when he came to say good night to Peter and Peter said 'Tell me a story,' he was too tired to think of anything at all. His brain simply would not work. If he could have something prepared beforehand, the merest outline, he would then be able to make a respectable story in the evening without effort. So he began to think of a story and within a minute fell into a half sleep, with his head resting on his outstretched arm. When he awoke they were at Waterloo.

'It's surprising the young men one sees not in uniform,' said one of the A.T.S. to the other, as, just in front of Hugh, they gave up their tickets.

Hugh became part of the stream of people making for the moving staircase. Then music began to come from the loudspeaker, and everything suddenly became different. He seemed to be floating, to feel his feet no longer, to be swept onwards with all these people, by an irresistible rhythm, in a gigantic ballet. All private responsibility had gone in a flash. Something had taken complete charge. No doubt they were all dead, all in heaven. Oh, God, make this go on for ever! O Lord, may I never reach the top of the moving staircase!

He walked from the underground station to his office. There was not much snow to be seen in London, at least not in the streets where it had all turned to slush. It was about twenty-five minutes past nine when he arrived at the Ministry. He glanced through the pile of letters on his desk, then got down to work on his memorandum. He would have liked to do what he had not had time to do before leaving home, but thought it wiser to get on with his work in peace before that ass Brock arrived. He would have time later on for that. His eyes had begun to feel as though they were hanging from his head on strings. He scribbled away at high speed.

After a time, a good time, his room companion came in. Ronnie Brock looked in the pink of health. Though he was well over forty, he looked a much younger man, and this well-preserved appearance, though no doubt it owed much to a comfortable private income, was also to some extent an achievement. For Ronnie Brock had always been most assiduous, and most successful, in avoiding all kinds of ageing activities.

'Not a letter,' he said, looking at his desk. 'Thank God!' And he opened *The Times* and began reading, with his feet against the fender. Every now and then he chuckled or ejaculated 'Hm,' 'Ah!' 'The swine!'

Hugh scribbled on.

At last Ronnie put down the paper and stood in front of the fire warming his behind.

'Damned good letter, that about over-population. Did you see it?'

Hugh did not answer.

'Then I'll read it,' said Ronnie.

'I saw it,' said Hugh.

'Well, isn't it just what I've always been saying? You'll bear me out over that, Hugo. I've said it again and again. Children are the curse of our age. They are the great wreckers of the good life. Marriage is bad enough, but children are the end, at least modern children. It was perhaps not so bad in the old days when parents kept their children at a distance and thrashed them twice a week. But your modern parent loves his children. He thinks they say such shrewd things. "Out of the mouths of babes and sucklings." Ugh! He thinks they are funny. Ugh! He allows them to wreck adult conversation. Do you know, I went down to stay with the Fosters last week-end—you won't believe it when I tell you that they actually have high tea! Yes, high tea, then bread and cheese for supper. "To fit in with the children." Surely that's the very end? I'll tell you, I came away really miserable from that happy household. Why? Because Arthur, who is one of my oldest friends, simply doesn't exist any more. He's not a man any more.

'Yes, one of the saddest things about middle age is the way one loses one's friends. Politics take some. Look at a man like Cuthy Stephens. Fifteen years ago he used to be great fun. You know him, don't you?'

'M'm.' Hugh's firm had published his *Regency Fanlights* in 1929, and his *Spain, our Shame* in 1938. 'Well, it was good-bye to him in the thirties, when, like so many previously superior people, he became left wing and political. Do you know, the last time I saw him, years ago now, he would insist upon talking about malnutrition. Which reminds me. It is time for elevenses.'

He unlocked a handsome mahogany cupboard which had followed him round in the frequent transfers that had disturbed his official life, and took out a biscuit tin, a half-bottle of wine and a wine-glass. Prewar gingerbreads came out of the tin and real claret out of the bottle.

'Lestage '25,' he said. 'Yes, '25 of all years, but very respectable, in my opinion.' He sucked the wine through his back teeth and held the glass up against the light. He explained how he had come by the wine and where one could still get wine, and at what price. 'Thank God I can still keep my head above beer!' he said. He then returned to his former theme. His eloquence did not demand an attentive audience.

'Politics are bad enough, but marriage is worse. At least there is no danger for Cuthy in that direction! And worst of all is children. These are the three great enemies.'

'And work?' murmured Hugh.

'And work, of course. I admit that that is an evil which some people are not in a position to avoid. I was only talking of those unnecessary evils which have been self-imposed. "Be fruitful and multiply," indeed! A disgusting motto. Fit for rabbits or rats or Jews. No, you won't find the fruits of the womb growing in my garden. You won't find a pram blocking my hall. No thanks!'

Hugh lifted his eyes back into place (In, vile jelly!), and read the sentence he had just written: 'If the weight of womb-load is then increased by three per cent, it will be found that the verticality of discharge has been increased by no less than seven per children.'

'I say, Ronnie, would you mind shutting up? I simply must finish this blasted thing.'

'All right. I'm sorry. I'm sorry. I am afraid I must disturb you. But then,' and he moved to the window and looked out at St James's Park, 'but then I'm the old-fashioned type of civil servant. Perhaps I am the last. I am told that I am an anachronism, that I went out with the last war. Perhaps I did. Anyhow, I shall go out with this. It's all up with the superior person this time.' He gazed sadly at the familiar view, then returned to the fire.

'And I'll tell you the root of the evil. It's the changed attitude towards women, it's the idealisation of the useful woman, the housefrau. Those terrible red hands! Don't you, in your heart of hearts, Hugo, ever dream of something white and soft, lying in bed, eating Turkish delight and reading Catulle Mendès? But I am old-fashioned. You see, I am an Edwardian born out of my time. Oh, I am sick of this present-day London. I'd give anything for a change!'

Hugh was putting through a telephone call to his home. It was a surprise when Helen answered. Mrs Harvey, she said, had not been able to come. She had sent a message to say that she had gone down with 'flu. But it was all right, said Helen; she would be able to manage. Unfortunately, Julia had been sent back from school because of her ear-ache, with a rather curt note asking that she should be kept at home till it was better. Mrs L. had been out when Helen had rung her up. Poor Helen! Hugh told her to go back to bed at once and he would be home as early as possible, probably on the five thirty-five.

'I think I'll take your tip and do a little private telephoning,' said Ronnie, as Hugh put up the receiver.

Hugh glanced at the clock and scribbled on. At last, at one minute to twelve, he finished and put down his pen. At last the beastly thing was finished, though not quite as well as he would have liked. Now he must go and see the Under-Secretary. He would have time during the luncheon interval to do what he had not yet done this morning.

Meanwhile, after various failures, Ronnie had made a satisfactory engagement for luncheon.

'I may be rather late back from lunch,' he said, as Hugh left the room.

Sir Herbert kept Hugh till twenty-past one, then told him that the afternoon's conference was fixed for two o'clock.

I must not fail to get that coffee, Hugh thought, then I'll have a sandwich at a snack-bar; then I should have time to do the other thing before the conference. He went back to his room and got his coat and then hurried up Whitehall towards Soho. His eyes were dangling by his feet. The pain was excruciating as they bounced on the pavement. Poor Helen! It can't have done her influenza any good getting up like that.

He felt the letters in his overcoat pocket and drew one out and read it as he went along. It was an airgraph, from Jack Bailey, of all people. It was a surprise to Hugh that Jack could write a letter at all. A wine merchant in peace-time and for the first two years of the war, he had been claimed by the Army in 1941 and was now in Italy.

> 'Dear Hugo,' it said. 'I had to send you a line from this place to wish you all the best because I've just found yours and Helen's signature in the visitors' book of the hotel of this place which is my billet. You spent three weeks here in April. D'you remember the place? I can only tell you that it's very *joyful*, if that helps. Rather too many bullets about for comfort and the wine is piss. Cheerio. Jack Bailey.'

Did Hugh remember Gioia della Valle? Does one generally forget honeymoons? In his mind's eye there was an indelible picture of that ancient village clinging to its castle on the hillock above the torrent that came down from a great arc of mountains and meandered through olive groves towards the sparkling sea. Almost precisely such was that Roman soldier's last view of this fair world. And now bullets were whizzing across the sacred valley. Providence chooses such places for violent death. For lingering death, the Woodlands Links Estate.

Hugh was kept waiting a little in the coffee-shop, and it was nearly a quarter to two as he took a seat at the snack-bar of a pub. In the mirror opposite he caught sight of his neighbour.

'Why, Cuthy!'

'Hugo!'

Cuthy was dressed like a fireman. He was holding his cap on his knee. His bald patch showed like a tonsure. He looked old, lined, mothy, a sad wreckage.

'That uniform suits you,' said Hugh.

Cuthy brightened up.

'Oh, do you think so?'

'Yes,' said Hugh, 'you look marvellous.'

Cuthy became animated. He told Hugh how he was hating this beastly war, how empty his life seemed, especially since Eddie had gone away, how all that he valued seemed to be going under. His values appeared to Hugh to be veering back towards fanlights.

'But tell me about yourself,' said Cuthy.

'There's nothing to tell. I just lead a humdrum life with Helen and the children.'

'Oh, but I envy you,' said Cuthy. 'If only I had some children! It's the only thing I really want. If only I had a background like you. I have no background.' His eyes were lonely and hungry.

'Envy me? No, you don't. Let me tell you.' And he told him, and, when he had rushed away, Cuthy felt that his own life was perhaps not so badly organised after all, and as he put on his fireman's cap and looked at himself in the mirror, he glowed to think that he was not yet on Beauty's shelf.

Hugh had just time to go back to his room and take his coat off before the conference, which lasted from two till ten past five. If I get away now, Hugh thought, as they rose from the table, I shall just be able to catch that train. But the Minister detained him, motioned him to a chair and offered him a cigarette. Sir Herbert also stayed behind.

'I have been asked,' said the Minister, 'whether we can spare anyone from this office from the senior administrative grade. The Prime Minister is anxious to find a few suitable people to send out to Southern Italy and Sicily to supervise the organisation of Amgot. This would probably not involve a very long stay there, but would mean a certain amount of travelling about. The idea would be for those who have had some years of administrative experience to show a fatherly interest in the organisation in its initial stages and give it a helping hand.'

The Minister's words were like Sabean odours to them that now are past Mozambic. Hugh's heart had begun to beat hard.

'Sir Herbert and I have been talking it over, and it seems to us that the only person we could spare is Brock. He is in your department, Palmer, I know, and of course I would not dream of depleting you if you think him indispensable. It is about that that I have wished to consult you. The fact, by the way, that he is a bachelor has, of course, influenced us. We should not feel that we were cutting any home ties in recommending that he should be sent out there. Now, the question is, do you think you can spare him?'

'. . . I . . . but I . . . Yes, I can spare him.'

'You don't seem very sure. I don't want to force your hand, Palmer. If you honestly don't think you can get on without him, don't hesitate to say so. Perhaps Sir Herbert and I have rather underestimated him. The decision is with you, Palmer.'

'Well . . . I . . . Let him go! Yes, let him go!'

'It seems rather like extracting a tooth. Are you sure you mean it? Very well. In recommending him I shall not fail to mention the high opinion in which he is held by his colleagues. Thank you, Palmer. Good night.'

Hugh caught the five fifty-eight by jumping into a moving carriage. The sirens were sounding and the guns were going. There was just standing room for him in the compartment. The hand which he had in his overcoat pocket felt two or three of his morning's letters still there unopened. With difficulty he drew out one and looked at the address. He recognised Anthony Gilmour's handwriting. His heart sank. It was a parcel, not a letter, that he should have been receiving from that quarter. He opened the letter and read:

'Dear Hugo,

I am afraid you will never speak to me again, but I may as well be honest with you and tell you that I have lost your *Goncourt Journal*. Hugo, I am *frightfully* sorry. I don't know what can have happened to it. But it seems to have disappeared when they moved my things down to the country while I was away. I have looked high and low, but there's no trace of it. What can I do to make it all right? I feel absolutely rotten about it.

Grovellingly yours,
Anthony.'

Hugh folded the letter and put it back in his pocket. 'B——r!' he said in a slow, clear voice. 'Oh b——r!'

Boy

'Leonard,' said his father, 'are you busy?'

Leonard lay sprawling on the study floor, browsing on an atlas. Some day, no doubt, he would go abroad. If he found somewhere particularly attractive he might even sojourn there and not return to the land of his fathers. Who could tell what he might not do when he grew up?

'Not specially,' he said. He turned and lay full length on his back, stretching his hands above his head as far as they would go. Though only fourteen he was already not far off six feet in height, or perhaps one should say in length, for he spent much of his time in a horizontal position. He gave a yawn and a groan. The yawn did not imply either fatigue or boredom, nor the groan pain. They were simply expressions of the infinite physical reserves of youth.

'Then will you take a note to Dr Postgate,' said Canon Barnes.

'All right,' said Leonard. He did not move at once, then with a sudden leap he was standing in front of the desk where his father was addressing an envelope to the Rev. Maxwell Postgate, D.D.

'When you get back,' said Canon Barnes, 'we might have a hand of piquet.'

Leonard took the note and went and fetched his bicycle from the woodshed where it was leaning against the derelict harmonium. It was a two-mile ride to the next village. He had once done it in six minutes forty-three seconds. You could free-wheel, if you wanted to, most of the first mile.

'Yo-o Hee-ho!' He roared the song of the Volga boatman as he pedalled hard down the hill. 'Yo-o Hee-ho!'

He came off his bicycle trying to turn in to Dr Postgate's drive without holding on to the handlebars. Dr Postgate was a liturgiologist. Leonard found him sitting in the dining-room, with a large old parchment tome open in front of him and various other open books littering the table.

'I have to work in here,' explained Dr Postgate. 'This is the only table in the house large enough for these big books. But it's not a very satisfactory arrangement. No sooner have I got them to clear the breakfast away than it seems to be time for them to start laying the lunch. They don't give me much peace. If you want to be a scholar, Leonard, don't be a poor country parson. The difficulties are too great.'

Still, thought Leonard, you don't have a bad life. Leonard was good at his books and had the makings of a scholar. He could feel the spell of that table with the open volumes.

'By the way, what *are* you going to be?' said Dr Postgate, glancing at the note Leonard had brought.

This was a question Leonard was always being asked.

'I don't know,' he said.

'Look at this,' said Dr Postgate. 'This is what you ought to be. A clever boy like you ought to go into the Diplomatic Service.' He held out a letter which he had received that morning, closely written on paper embossed with the Foreign Office stamp.

'That's from Sir Reginald Hayward. He is a great authority on Coptic liturgies. He and I have corresponded for years. That's the life for you. You travel all over the world, have a most interesting time, meet all the most interesting people. And all the while you have heaps of leisure for a hobby. Sir Reginald always writes to me on Foreign Office paper.'

'It sounds nice.'

'I expect you'd like some cider. Look in that cupboard, while I write an answer to your father's note.'

Leonard rode home at a leisurely pace. From time to time vapours from the cider surged up through his throat and nose deliciously.

'Yo-o Hee-ho!' he droned, and a thousand miles to Astrakhan. Leonard the travelled man, Leonard the man of the world. Sir Leonard. Sir Leonard Barnes, diplomat, in grey top hat, grey morning coat, sponge-bag trousers, white spats, eye-glass, cane with gold knob, smoking a long cigar, sauntering down a boulevard. A foreign countess, driving in an open carriage, would spot him and stop to exchange greetings, leaning towards him beneath her sunshade with a bewitching smile. She would laugh like a bell at the effortless witticisms with which, in her own language, he would greet her gay sallies, and, as she passed on, would toss him a rose saying 'For the most charming man in Europe—and the most enigmatic!'

He rode along at a leisurely boulevard rate between fields of uncut corn towards the clump of trees that hid the rectory and all but the stocky spire of his father's church. Turning into the rectory drive without holding on to the handlebars, he almost ran into Colonel Dobbs who was walking out.

'Hullo, Leonard.'

'Hullo, sir.'

'Back for the holidays?'

'Yes, I got back yesterday.'

'So did my boys. They've got some tennis on this afternoon. Would you like to come after lunch?'

'Thank you very much. I'd love to.'

'Good. Have a good term?'

'Quite decent.'

'Sorry to leave?'

'It was rather awful saying good-bye to everyone.' By which he probably meant no more than that the actual process of saying good-bye to people at his preparatory school had been embarrassing, embarrassment, rather than sorrow, at his age being the chief awful thing.

'Do you know what you're going to be yet? Colin and Richard both want to be professional cricketers.'

'I don't know. I might go into the Diplomatic Service.'

'That's not a bad idea. But I should go into the City if I were you. A clever boy like you ought to be able to make a lot of money. And you're good at games, aren't you?'

'Do they play games in the City?'

Colonel Dobbs laughed.

'Not exactly, but you'll find it a great advantage, I can assure you, in after life if you have been good at games. We English, rightly or wrongly, set such store on people who have learned to play the game.'

Colonel Dobbs looked at the tall boy, with the thoughtful face.

'Besides,' he went on, 'a young man ought to grow up in London. There's no other place where he can get the same experience of life. After all, every young fellow has got to sow his——'

Giving Leonard another friendly, man-to-man look, he realised that this boy was hardly older than his own Colin.

'——has got to grow up, yes to grow up,' he finished lamely. 'Well, we'll see you this afternoon. Good-bye.'

'Good-bye, sir.'

In the drive Leonard found the stump of a cigar that Colonel Dobbs had dropped. It was still smouldering. He put it in his pocket, went into the house to deliver the note and fetch a box of matches, then came out and found a pleasant place to recline, behind the arbutus, on the edge of the plantation, looking over the lawn.

Nobody watching, he reflected, would ever suppose that this was his first cigar. With easy assurance he let a thick cloud of smoke out of his mouth, then blew a hole through the middle of it. What was he going to be? Why did they all ask him that? As he turned it over in his mind, the question seemed to him rather insulting. The implication of it was that he did not yet exist. At some future date he would start to be. For the moment he was not. When he was old enough he would reach that period known as 'after-life'—not, by the way, to be confused with 'the after-life'—and then at last he could be said to exist. Life proper would only begin with 'after-life.'

Which all seemed quite contrary to the facts as he divined them to be. It seemed to him that he already unquestionably was. Indeed, his whole character was already there. True, it was still immature. But like an unripe apple, it was already fully formed. It lacked only the final colour. And he felt he could very well remember what he would be like in fifty years. No transmuting grief, no excess of joy, would have poured unpassable waters between his present and his future self. He looked across at Prebendary, Professor, Sir Leonard, Mr Justice, or even Viscount, Barnes, or possibly Len Barnes, the tramp, lying on the grass at the edge of a wood smoking some rich man's cigar stub. He looked across at the amused, good-natured face, and puffed smoke into it. Hullo, old chap.

The fact was, Leonard had not much ambition. With luck he might get through without having to be anything, though he did not quite see how.

It was not long before the wet stump would yield no more smoke. He got up and strolled through the plantation until, hearing a noise of tapping behind the churchyard wall, he went in by the wicket gate to see what was causing it. At first he saw no one, then, with a renewal of the tapping, he became aware of a man squatting in front of a white gravestone underneath the yew-tree over against the wall.

With reverent step Leonard threaded his way between the graves towards the man.

'Tread softly,' he murmured,

'Tread softly because you tread on my dreams.'

He had won the Recitation Prize again last term. Poetry was potty, really. He had never understood why some people made such a trouble about learning it.

Intent on his work, the man was not at once aware of Leonard watching him. He was cutting out some letters which he had already drawn in pencil, on the lower part of the upright marble slab. He had cut about half of them. AND OF ELLEN HIS WIFE WHO DEP—— Judging by the thinning brown hair on the top of the man's head Leonard deduced—the deductive method, my dear Watson—that his age must be about forty-seven. There were no flies on Detective Barnes.

Presently the man looked up.

'Hullo!'

'Hullo!'

Clean-shaven, blue eyes, medium build, accustomed to an out-of-door life, scar on back of left hand—from the transmitter in his hip pocket Leonard morsed the particulars through to the Yard.

The man laid down his chisel and wooden mallet and got up to stretch himself.

'It's rather a cramped position,' he said, 'working so low down.'

On the ground were a rubber mat he had been sitting on, and his tools and a paper bag with his lunch.

'It's a pretty churchyard,' he said, looking round, 'one of the prettiest in the county.'

'There are sixty-seven gravestones,' said Leonard, 'and two wooden ones.'

'Are there indeed? Well! What does the poet say—

'"Beneath those rugged elms, that yew tree's shade.

'"Where——"'

'"——Where heaves the turf",' said Leonard, '"in many a mouldering heap,

'"Each in his narrow cell for ever laid,

'"The rude forefathers of the hamlet sleep."'

'Bravo,' said the man, 'I see I have found a kindred spirit. Stay and talk to me while I get on.'

He sat down again on his mat and renewed his chipping.

'That looks fun,' said Leonard, 'can I do a bit?'

'No. I think not. You might spoil the whole thing. It's not as easy as it looks. Tell me about yourself. What are you going to be when you are grown up?'

'I don't know. I might go into the City.'

'The City! Why the City?'

'Oh, I don't know. I'd be amongst people who play the game.'

'"Play the game"!—in the City!—' The man looked at Leonard in astonishment, then went on with his work.

'Where are you at school?' he said presently.

Leonard named a famous public school.

'I'm not actually there yet,' he said. 'I go next term.'

'I once knew someone who went there.'

'Did he like it?'

'Very much indeed. He was blissfully happy. The days were simply not long enough. It's a school where, even if you are not much good at things—and he did not shine either at work or play—you can still have a very good time. There is the river of course, and he loved boats. He was always making things. He made a boat once, with the help of a lock-keeper he was friends with. Once from a field-day with the corps he brought back a lump of chalk from which he carved his housemaster's head. The old boy was very pleased with the likeness and put it on his mantelpiece.'

A bell sounded through the plantation.

'It is a very beautiful place, you know, with its old buildings and its meadows and running water everywhere and you are allowed a good deal of freedom there. It seemed perpetual summer, perpetual plunging off mown grass into warm water, or fielding in the deep with one eye on the game and the other on the sky and the trees and the river that could be seen smoothly moving behind the trunks of the trees, and strawberries and cream, and happy shower-baths and in the cool of the evening strolling round the cloisters making friendships that nothing, nothing, in life would sever. The little victim! He did not know his doom.'

Leonard could hear his father calling him.

'His doom?' he said, 'Why, what happened to him?'

'He had a very good position waiting for him—in the City.'

'I say,' said Leonard, 'I've got to go now. That's my lunch ready. Will you be here this afternoon? I'm supposed to be playing tennis, though. How late will you be here?'

'I shall stay to finish the job to-day. I shall not be done before six or half-past, I expect.'

'I'll be back before then,' said Leonard. 'Please don't go before I've come back. Good-bye for the present.'

Immediately after his luncheon Leonard bicycled up to the Hall for tennis. There were two or three other boys there besides the Dobbs boys, and some girls. Strenuous tennis was played without pause throughout the hot afternoon. The best set was that in which Colonel Dobbs and Colin Dobbs played against Colonel Dobbs' brother and Leonard. This was known as 'A men's four.' The latter couple won 7–5. The wool on the chest of Leonard's partner showed black through his shirt. He shook Leonard ceremoniously by the hand after the game and said 'Well done, partner, I always knew we'd wipe the floor with them.'

There was iced coffee for tea and cucumber sandwiches. After tea Leonard said he must be gone and took his leave.

Back in the churchyard, he found the man had nearly finished the job. He had put the lead into most of the letters. There were still a few to do. The process consisted in drilling two or three holes into the cavities of the letters that he had already chiselled out, in order the better to hold the lead. Then some lead was pushed into the letter with the fingers and hammered in with the mallet.

'Can I do the next letter?' said Leonard.

'All right.'

Doing as he had seen the man do, Leonard with scissors cut a thin slice off the sheet of lead and pressed it into the hollows of an italic E. He then hammered it well in. It overflowed the sides of the letter and these overflowing parts he scraped away with the chisel. It was delicious, the way you could do what you liked with the lead.

'Can I do the next letter too?'

'All right.'

And Leonard did the remaining letters.

'There,' said the man, who had a piece of sandpaper in his hand, 'now let me come. There's the cleaning up to be done.'

Leonard sat and watched him.

'Finish off about that boy you were telling me about,' he said.

'Oh yes. Where did we get to?'

'His doom.'

'Well, his uncle held out very good prospects for him in the family business. Only he must start at the bottom like anybody else. The question now had to be decided whether or not he should go to Oxford. It was clear that he would not be much of a scholar, and his elders inclined to the opinion that he would waste his time at the university. Still, the decision was left to him. He himself had very little idea what was involved. In the hope of receiving some heavenly guidance that would help him to make up his mind, he carved the words LONDON and OXFORD on a buttress of his school chapel. But the words said nothing to him. They were of equal length, and the vowels in each case added up to nought.

'At length his lack of will in the matter enabled his father to persuade him, without much difficulty, of the advantages of getting an early start in his career, and so, after a long summer holiday abroad, he found himself one day in an underground train bound for Mark Lane station. By the way, have you ever been to London?'

'Yes, once,' said Leonard, 'I saw the "Chamber of Horrors."'

'Ah!'

'And the Bloody Tower, and the rack and Guy Fawkes' signature after he had been tortured. It was lovely.'

'You saw only the loveliest things. It's not all lovely, as my hero soon found. There was nothing lovely at all in the subterranean morning approach to work, squashed in that condemned, despondent, multitude. There was nothing whatever attractive about the dark box, in which, for eight hours a day, he and seven other clerks did arithmetic. One day, not long after he had been there, an unusual patch of light appeared for a moment on his hand as he wrote. He traced it to a window on the other side of the narrow street, which must have caught this momentary flash of reflected sunlight from a window higher up on his side of the street. He remembered an old Italian picture he had seen called "The Annunciation" in which a golden thread of light came down into an Italian street and through a ground-floor window on to the forehead of the Virgin Mary, in a direct line from heaven. The fleeting patch of reflected sunlight, which had zigzagged its way down on to his hand, seemed to bear the tidings that he had seen the sky for the last time.

'He loathed the work. He had never been good at arithmetic. Three or four hours a week of it at school had always seemed quite enough. But now he did money sums all day. If it had been just the morning he might have been able to bear it. But immediately after lunch, when by all the laws of nature you change into flannels and go out into the fields, he had to return to his desk. He loathed the crowded eating places. Even the novelty of having a sandwich lunch among the sparrows in the little churchyard of St Rosemary Platanum wore off after the second or third time, and if he retired at sixty he calculated that there would be twelve thousand more lunches. He loathed the afternoon stuffiness of the room in which he worked. But most he loathed the hour when from lift and office and cellar the people flowed out again into the street and back towards the underground, and his thoughts turned wearily to pleasure, as to a duty, after the lost day. Does this bore you by the way?'

'It is very interesting indeed,' said Leonard.

'Well, after a while, in order to give him a little change, they allowed him to stand for an hour in the morning on the pavement outside the office. There was a little group of Old Etonians standing there. He and they had iron filings in their pockets. Sometimes the handful of iron filings of one of them was worth more per cent than his. Sometimes his handful was worth more than any of theirs, per cent. There they stood on the curb talking about money and iron filings. Far, far above, it may or may not have been jolly boating weather. On most days there was no way of telling, in that dark alley. Even this change in his routine seemed no sort of life to him.

'But he stuck it for nearly three years. Another year, perhaps, and he might never have got out. The iron filings were entering into his soul. He got out just in time. One morning, as he was being jostled forward in the crowd to work, he said to himself "No! I will not. Never again!" He turned about and pushed his way against the stream back into the underground, and so away. From that moment he went what would probably be called downhill. For him it was a delightful process, like water tumbling down over boulders until it finds a level where it can flow smoothly forwards. His father and uncle were furious with him, and when he persisted in his obstinate refusal to go back to business they told him that he could jolly well fend for himself. Which he did. He went from one thing to another until at last he found himself in the happiest job in the world.'

'Ah,' said Leonard, alert, 'What's that?'

The man had stood up and was contemplating his day's work:

AND OF ELLEN HIS WIFE WHO
DEPARTED THIS LIFE THE
1st MARCH FOLLOWING
'The Lord is my Shepherd'

'He became a sepulchral mason,' he said.

'Ah!'

Appearing satisfied with his work, the man packed up his tools. As he did so, he cut off a slice of lead for Leonard. Then he tied the tool-bag on to the back of his bicycle which was leaning by the gate and bade Leonard good-bye.

'Good-bye.'

Leonard walked slowly back through the plantation bending the lead in his fingers. Rather a nice man, that. He had been distinctly interesting. It was lucky that Leonard had met him and now knew about the City. Not that he had the kind of father who would ever expect him to go in for a job he did not care for.

As he came out of the plantation he saw his father, in his shirt sleeves, mowing the lawn on the further side of the copper beech. Under the tree was his deckchair and beside it on the grass the open book he had been reading. Leonard glanced at it. It was called *Galatians and the Modern World*. Presently his father would stop mowing the lawn and come over and say 'How about that game of piquet?' He would stop abruptly, the moment he was bored, in the middle of the lawn, and would probably leave the mowing machine out there all night. He was lucky in his father certainly. Those Dobbs boys were always being made to put things away. And his father was the only person who never asked him what he was going to be. Leonard lay down on the grass by the chair, and writhed and groaned in lethargic contentment as he looked up through the leaves at the sky, which was infinite, like his future, and clear and blue.

Honest-to-God

'What are the Psalms?'

Major Newman was struck by the question, which came across to him from the public bar. On most days of the year it would have made no impression on him whatever. But this particular Sunday evening was not quite like other evenings. Major Newman was alone. It is true that, corporeally, he was often alone. But this evening he was experiencing the unusual feeling of being alone in spirit. He had just seen his wife off by train to Scotland. It would be three weeks before he saw her again.

Their separations were rare. They were a devoted couple and did not like being apart. They gave each other so much. Mrs Newman was a garrulous and rather silly woman. But her husband thought her brilliant and was perfectly content to leave all the talking to her. She filled his life with words, which suited him very well. It saved him from thinking; while keeping pace with her chatter gave him the illusion of mental activity. No wonder he had come to find her indispensable. The stability of mind, which her company ensured, had even grown to be a thing in which he took pride. It enabled him to hold an opinion of himself which he found satisfactory. He believed himself to be straightforward, honest-to-God, English to the core. But perhaps only the last of these descriptions was always applicable.

Then, from time to time, she would go away, and the words would go out of his life, leaving an uncomfortable void. And then, willy nilly, thoughts would creep in. He would not be comfortable again until she came back.

After seeing her off on the train he decided to go into the White Hart and have a whisky before starting back on the fifteen-mile drive to his village. The wireless was on as he stood at the bar drinking.

'Oh turn that off, lady, for Christ's sake,' said a voice from the public bar. 'What is it? It's awful!'

'I'll turn it low,' the lady conceded. Some of her customers might be offended if she were to turn the wireless right off. 'That's a service,' she said, 'that's the Psalms.'

'What are the Psalms' The question came looming towards Frank Newman, like a close-up on the films. He could not turn his eyes away from its nakedness, its shameless unzipped modernity.

'The same again, please.'

He took his drink and sat down at a table to think about things. He was in no hurry. There was no reason why he should be home at any particular time this evening. He must think this thing out, at his leisure, here as well as anywhere else, to the subdued accompaniment of a church service. The only companions of his thoughts in the saloon bar were some flashy people sitting over the other side on a sofa. The women's nails were trowels dipped in blood.

'What are the Psalms?' Was it not incredible that such a question could be asked by an adult man in this Christian country, in this twentieth century? Supposing, thought Frank Newman, my father had heard an Englishman ask such a question, why, he would not have believed it possible. He would have thought the end of the world was coming. He would probably have had a fit.

And am I going to have a fit? No, frankly not, nowhere near. But then, my parents, in fact all that generation, took religion much more seriously than we do. One must move with the times. Still, even I cannot help being struck by someone not knowing what the Psalms are. The mere ignorance of it, the gap in general knowledge which it implies, is surely very surprising, quite apart from the question of whether the man is a Christian or not. And how does it strike you, Frank Newman? Is your feeling merely one of surprise, or is there some regret too? Are you entirely satisfied with having moved with the times? For this fact you must face. It is your generation that has made the break. From your father backwards there are hundreds of years of faith. From you onwards, Frank Newman, there is an entirely new age. History will look on your generation as the one that made the big change. It was you who threw things over. It was your generation that gave up going to church. How do you feel about it?

'The same again, please.'

Undoubtedly there is still a lot to be said for church even if one cannot take all the theology seriously nowadays. For one thing it is a brake on the speed of modern life. People attending a church service have at least got to stay in one place for a whole hour on end. The church tends to prevent people rushing about and worshipping speed. It is one of the few places nowadays where you can be quiet. Those churches in the city of London, for instance, he had been into one or two of them, surely they were a beneficent influence in the middle of all that material turmoil. You could not but be better after passing a few minutes in their coolness and quietness, quite apart from the question of whether you prayed or not when you went inside. And on the question of prayer Frank Newman would rather not be pressed.

Why not? Come on, face it. Your parents prayed until the day of their death. You prayed until you were sixteen. You have not taught your sons to pray at all. It is your generation, Frank Newman, that has made the break. You cannot say that your boys learn these things at school. What was 'Divinity' in your day has now sunk to being 'Religious Knowledge,' and no doubt will soon be a special subject like Spanish, or even an extra like Art. Your sons, having the benefit of an expensive education know what the Psalms are. It is doubtful whether your grandsons will know. Thanks to you.

'The same again, please.'

And then church is good for the singing. It is about the only place left where ordinary people still make their own music, still can join in. Even after all these years Major Newman would sometimes find himself humming or whistling 'Through the night of doubt and sorrow' or 'Our blest Redeemer ere he breathed,' and if he happened to think and identify the tune he would become wistful as he was taken back to the world of cricket bats and chapel and jolly shower baths and changing rooms. (Incidentally, what a lot of one's school life, looking back on it, seemed to have been spent changing one's clothes.) It was good to have tunes that linked one part of your life with another, good old tunes that remained the same and were always there, like the best kind of old friends, while you grew older. Undoubtedly there was a lot of good in all that, which even forty years' neglect could not quite kill.

And then there were the Prayer Book and the Bible. The Bible was grand stuff. Odd, unforgotten, phrases came up into his mind. The voice of the turtle is heard in our land. It must not be supposed that Major Newman was in the least literary. He was absolutely normal. Since he left school his life had been wholly free from literary experience. But this very freedom, this complete lack of later superimposition, had ensured that the ruins of his own expensive education were not obliterated. They were with him for life, his desultory collection of broken ornaments, his tiny Forum of literary fragments. The voice of the turtle is heard in our land.

I said, I will take heed unto my ways. Well, and what have you done about it, Frank Newman? You cannot pretend you have done much. During the first few months after you came to Wellby Hall you paid a few perfunctory visits to church. Then a disagreement with the parson about the boundary of a field gave you what you believed to be a very good reason for giving up church-going. You could not bear the man's voice either, and liked to think that you were actually right not to go to church if you felt like that about him. Yet, when he left and was succeeded by little Barlow, you did not change your ways, though you have nothing against Barlow and he has done his best to be pleasant to you. It can't be much fun, his job.

'The same again, please.'

In fact, now I think about it, I wonder he can go on at all. The fear of the Lord is the beginning of wisdom. Just who, in Wellby, from myself downwards, fears the Lord? Two or three old women perhaps. The rest of them are afraid of nothing at all, except perhaps of me. But what can I do about it? It's not my job, it's Barlow's. Now, be honest with yourself, you know very well you can do everything. They know it's Barlow's job, so they pay no attention to him. It's you they follow. Wellby is in many ways an old-fashioned village. It is one of the decreasing number of villages that are some way outside the tentacles of a town. It is a village with a squire, one of the decreasing number of villages in which the habits of one man can set a tone. You are that man. If you were to rally to the church you know you could bring them with you. You stay away, they stay away. It is in just such a place as Wellby that the rot can be stopped. In the towns it has gone too far.

And it must surely be stopped? Not that Major Newman personally would expect to gain much at his age from a revival of church-going on his part. But then, he had absorbed the essential benefits thereof when he was a boy. He had been able to live on capital all his life, on the capital his parents and their generation had saved for him. But what reserve of capital, he asked himself uncomfortably, was he handing on to the next generation? Had he put by anything, or had he passed his whole life spending? The facts stared him in the face. During his lifetime the principles of good behaviour had been allowed to lose their religious backing. Decency, modesty, self-restraint, sweet reasonableness, gentlemanly thoughtfulness, English uprightness, Christian tolerance, the Anglo-Christian spirit of fair play—these things no longer had that security behind them. How long would they last? How long would it be before the entire English nation consisted of vulgar outsiders like those people sitting over there, without tradition, without background, without breeding? Not long. Thanks to you, Frank Newman.

He stood up, and went to the bar, and had one last one which he drank standing. As he drank he made a resolution. Next Sunday he would go to church, as an experiment. It would be awkward and embarrassing. He would probably find he had forgotten when to kneel and when to stand. Still, he resolved. It needed some pluck to make this resolution. He felt rather good afterwards. Indeed, he had had a rather wonderful evening.

The time was just before six o'clock. The Rev. John Barlow was standing in the church porch looking out on the summer evening. In a moment the bell would start ringing. It would ring for ten minutes, there would then be ten minutes' silence, then it would ring for another ten minutes, then the service would begin. This long drawn-out method of summoning to prayer was the local tradition, which Mr Barlow had not liked to change though he often felt that its solemnity was sadly out of proportion to the occasion. Still, he must humour Jackson, the verger, who, he was painfully aware, would be most difficult to replace should he take offence and resign. And Jackson loved pulling that bell. It gave him a thirst, as Mr Barlow had more than once heard him explain, all too audibly, to members of the congregation who passed him on their way in to their seats.

The vicar looked towards his village. His parish consisted of what would once have been described as five hundred souls. A good many of his parishioners were visible to him as he stood at the porch. Several of them were working in the allotments, and he was looking at these when the bell began to ring. Did any of them stop working to go indoors and get ready for church? Did any of them pause a moment, bow the head and say their reverent *angelus*? Not they! The sound of the bell was meaningless to them, except in so far as it told them the time was six o'clock. It was the signal for Harry Cobb, the publican, to get up from his sofa and begin to think about shaving and putting on his Sunday suit and getting the place ready to open at seven.

A group of children was playing in the road and two older boys were showing how they could ride bicycles without holding the handlebars. Two men were standing fishing in the stream and from a pool lower down could be heard the shouts and laughter of a picnic party which was bathing. It was a delicious beautiful golden evening. The two or three owners of cars and motor bicycles in the village would be far away now, at the seaside probably. In a field the other side of the church young people were engaged in a game of rounders. A young couple were climbing over the stile from this field into the next. In the next field the hay had not yet been cut. It was deep and soft and yellow with lady's-bedstraw. Or, if you were modest, there was a broad, dry ditch on the further side of the field, shielded by an impenetrable hedge. Their shameless voices were distinctly audible to Mr Barlow, the vulgar giggling of the girl, the rude laughter of the boy as he helped her, rudely, over the stile.

An old woman came up the church path. Mr Barlow smiled at her as she passed him and went into the church. One, he counted. He remembered that two or three Christmases ago his mother had sent him as a present one of those instruments that officials in galleries or museums or other places of assembly sometimes carry in their hands to take statistics of attendance without involving the super-human mental strain of counting. Standing by the swing gates at the entrance they press the instrument—click—once for each person in the bank holiday crowd that surges past them. A crippled girl came up the path. She was plain, and not popular in the village, and could not play rounders. Two, counted Mr Barlow, without strain. He had never found much use for his mother's present.

The first bell ceased. Jackson came out from the tower, nodded familiarly at his vicar and went round the corner to relieve himself. His beer-laden breath made Mr Barlow wince. He must speak to the man about it again. But then, he had the impression that Jackson was only waiting to pick a quarrel and clear out. And without Jackson what would he do?

Looking at the fields had not given Mr Barlow much satisfaction. He looked towards the village. Was that any better? His eye travelled along the red roofs until it came to the Park and then along the beautiful old wall of Major Newman's vast kitchen garden, and then upwards to the chimney of the Hall peeping out among the elms. Ah, there was the evil, there was the real sore! There was his cardinal failure! What could he hope to do unless *they* were on his side? He was coxing a boat in which the stroke had failed to turn up. The other oarsmen would have rowed had there been a stroke, but in the circumstances they too had scratched. There he was, sitting at the end of an empty boat. And his eye wandered downwards till it came to the vicarage. Now there at least all was well, surely? No, not even there. The Rev. John Barlow could not even count on his own son. The boy was away at school at present, but had this been a Sunday evening in the holidays, Mr Barlow knew that his son would have been—in church? No—playing tennis with those boys up at the Hall. And he looked again at the chimneys in the elms, and his thoughts were far from charitable.

A rich car drew up on the road and some people got out. Talking and laughing they walked towards the churchyard gate. When they reached it, they stood looking up at the church. There were two ladies and two gentlemen, four cultured voices of a kind Mr Barlow did not often hear, in fact had only heard two or three times in his life. But he identified them immediately. He knew at once that these were the salt of the earth. Good heavens, and he had not got a sermon ready! One of the party appeared to be acting as a sort of guide. 'An early broach spire,' he heard the voice, 'the exact pair of Grumby . . . lancet windows . . . remarkable dog tooth moulding . . . reminds me of Moissac.' They sauntered up to the porch where they found themselves face to face with Mr Barlow. They smiled politely, but seemed embarrassed to find a clergyman standing in the porch of a church. At that moment, just as they were preparing to enter the church, the second bell began. The look of mild embarrassment on their faces suddenly became one of positive disturbance. Their manners had almost been at fault! 'Oh, is there a service?' they said, 'Oh, we are so sorry!' And they backed out apologetically like adults who have inadvertently intruded on a children's game.

'I'd like to have seen that interior,' Mr Barlow heard one of them say, as they walked away round the church, determined at least to see the outside. 'I keep forgetting it's Sunday.' 'Yes,' said one of the ladies, 'Sunday's a rotten day for seeing churches.'

Mr Barlow's immediate feeling was one of relief at not having to preach to those people. He did not usually preach at all on Sunday evenings, so small was the congregation. But in the event of there being visitors, he would of course have to give a sermon. Sermons were rather a trial to him at the best of times.

He looked out once more towards the village and the Hall. And then he saw the last thing in the world that he expected to see. A green door in the wall of the Hall garden opened and a man came through and began to walk across the field towards the church. He walked briskly and purposefully. Could it really be—good heavens it was—Major Newman, heading straight for the church. The vicar's agitation at first prevented him thinking, but when he perceived beyond all doubt that the striding figure was making for the church, was moreover, carrying a prayer book in his hand, he collected himself and managed to put some thoughts together for a sermon.

Major Newman passed through his ordeal successfully. He contrived to enter the church as unconcernedly as though it were a habit and took a seat in a pew about half-way up the right-hand side as though it were his own regular pew. By keeping a discreet look-out from the corner of his eyes on the movements of the half dozen other members of the congregation he contrived to sit, stand or kneel at the correct times, but moving to the next posture just a moment later than other people, giving an impression, each time, of absorption. He sang and responded visibly, if not audibly. When kneeling, he knelt. He did not just sit leaning forward. He wore an attentive and preoccupied expression of face during the lessons and the sermon, and refused to catch the eye of the crippled girl who stared at him without stopping throughout the service. He did not once look about him awkwardly. He did not look round at Jackson's all too audible 'Well I'm—!' when Mr Barlow walked towards the pulpit. He put a ten shilling note in the collection bag and did not acknowledge Jackson's 'Christ!' as he did so. On the whole he thought he put up a very decent show.

But his face, as he walked back across the field, had not that air of relief after trouble overcome which might have been expected. He was frowning, evidently absorbed in thought. That night he sat late at the library window, which was open on the lawn, turning over the pages of his Bible and his Prayer Book. It was a beautiful scented night out on the lawn, but for Major Newman a night of doubt and sorrow.

The next morning, after breakfast, he was standing on the steps lighting his pipe. Coming up the drive was the Rev. John Barlow. His face wore a radiance, a jubilation, that had not been seen there for many years.

'Good morning,' he said cheerfully, as he came up to Major Newman.

'Good morning.'

'I . . . hope you won't mind me coming to you like this, Major Newman . . . taking the bull by the horns at this hour of the morning. I . . . I was wondering whether I could persuade you to become our churchwarden?'

Major Newman did not answer at once. He puffed his pipe and frowned.

'If you hadn't come to see me, Barlow, I should have come to see you.'

The words were gratifying, but somehow the way they were said was not encouraging.

'I would have been delighted to see you, Major Newman. What was it you wanted to see me about?'

Major Newman took a puff at his pipe, then spoke. 'I owe you an explanation. I'm sorry, Barlow, I can't do it. It's no good. I can't go on with it. It would not be honest. You see, it's the Creed. I don't believe a word of it.'

'Oh, that doesn't matter,' Mr Barlow was about to say, but checked himself. He was so taken aback by what Major Newman had said that he could not think of what to say. Surely there must be some answer to such an objection. He tried to think, but the other was speaking again, and all the thinking seemed to have been already done. There was no muddle at all. The state of affairs was absolutely clear-cut, exactly defined, and quite hopeless.

Major Newman was not a fool. He had not said in his heart there is no God. If people are divided into those who believe, those who do not believe, and those who disbelieve, Frank Newman, English to the core, took the middle course. But unfortunately this middle course was, for practical purposes, not to be distinguished from the last course. He could not, could he, continue to come to church if he did not believe? It would be sheer hypocrisy, wouldn't it?

'I'm sorry, Barlow, that's how it stands. I can't see any way out of it. I must be honest, mustn't I?'

A much cleverer man than Mr Barlow might have been at a loss how to improvise an attack on such an impregnable position. As for Mr Barlow, no thoughts of any kind came into his head. After a few moments' silence, he looked up at Major Newman with a hurt expression, then turned and walked away slowly down the drive.

It was all Frank Newman could do not to call him back and unsay what he had just said. But he held firm, standing there on the ruins of his old school, his village, his regiment, England, the British Empire. All this, he reflected, would never have happened if Mary had not gone away.

Daphne

Daphne lay on her bed and took the receiver off the telephone, so that she might not be disturbed. Alone, and in peace, at last! She would have Daphne all to herself for the rest of the day if she chose. Unless, of course, he followed her home and lay like a dog on the mat outside the door waiting for her to open. The knowledge that such a course of action would certainly be considered by him made her already relent a little. But he would have the gumption not to follow her. He would realise that her abrupt departure was a way of telling him that she wanted to be alone. Of course he would have the gumption. And a wave of love came over her. Oh, he was the most perfect person in the world!

And yet . . . and yet . . . She had suddenly felt at the fair that she must escape and without saying a word to Michael or to any of the rest of the party she had slipped away and come home by bus. It was not the actual noises of the fair that she had found so exhausting. Those noises, loud though they were, had indeed a restful quality. In spite of amplifiers, they remained, like the various whizzing or oddly gyrating machines which an electric age had added to the *repertoire* of a fair, curiously old-fashioned. Perhaps because they were tethered, while most modern noises, like the noise of traffic, or aeroplanes, are moving and have no edge, no beginning and no end. It was from a sound that had no beginning and would go on into eternity that Daphne had fled, the sound of Michael's voice.

A soft and charming voice, a witty, happy, exuberant, sometimes slightly preposterous voice, a serious, commanding voice that spoke with authority on so many subjects, a wise, mature and sympathetic voice, an unpredictable, exciting, illuminating voice that continually seemed to be turning the light on in dark rooms, a hot, insinuating, irresistible, sincere voice that paid you the most exaggerated compliments and yet convinced you that they were true. Altogether a perfect voice—and yet . . . What was wrong with it? Nothing was wrong with it, that was what was wrong with it. And it would not stop. It wooed her relentlessly. For more than a month now it had been with her all her waking hours, and now it was about to take over the sleeping hours as well. To-night, she had thought, perhaps. Suddenly, at the eleventh hour, she had broken away from it.

Before going any further, while she could still speak, she must say her say. She must assert her right to a little privacy, a little ego. He must be made to see that her life had its own rhythm which was a good deal slower than his. Before they settled down to living side by side for ever and ever—which was, of course, what they were going to do—they must come to an understanding about the tempo of that life. She must insist on long blank periods which she would share with no one but herself. Otherwise, at this rate, she would soon cease to exist. Exist, that is, in her own imagination. For the person whom his love had called into such vibrant being was somebody in whom she only half believed. It was certainly not her familiar, lazy, lovely self.

The afternoon was very hot and she kicked the sheet off and lay there on her back with nothing on at all, her arms under her head on the pillow. Her large tabby cat, Rules, who was sitting on the dressing table, looked at her for some minutes, then stretched himself and let himself carefully down over the furniture and slowly—for it was very hot—walked towards the bed. He did not immediately jump up but stopped to bite an itching place in his tail, which led him on to biting several other places after which he licked the fur back into smoothness. He also tried to find how nearly he could lick the top of his head. He then sat upright, blinked, and shut his eyes as though for sleep. Opening them again, he looked about him, then jumped on the bed. With cautious tread he came alongside Daphne and stretching his nose towards her gave her a cold wet dab on the cheek. He sniffed about her, then rubbed his ears against her ribs. The delicious contact of fur and skin. He then put his front paws on her and pressed, first one, then the other, making her feel his claws just, just, as much as she could bear. It was too hot for him to continue this exercise for long and he looked about for the most comfortable place against her side to dispose himself for sleep. But as he brushed against her he apparently decided that their bodily contiguity would be too hot and jumped with a thud on to the floor and made his leisurely way back on to the dressing table where he trod carefully between the bottles back to his former position and there settled himself, yawned and closed his eyes upon the impenetrable privacy of his thoughts. How unlike a man, thought Daphne.

It was that relentless alertness of the man that she found so wearing, that unremitting consciousness. There was never a blank in which she could commune with her old self, that attractive humorous lazily expectant self whom she knew and loved so well, that drowsy imperturbable catlike self. As she lay on the bed she could see her face and most of her body in a long mirror. Hullo, Daphne darling, surely you and I still have our secrets? We are just watching all this going on, aren't we? And as things become even more intense and reach a climax, and after that as he and I work out our blissful life together and have children and eventually die, you and I will be watching all the time, won't we? The face of Daphne in the mirror smiled back at her, familiar and reassuring; yet between them was a trellis of exciting, unforgettable, slightly preposterous epithets with which Michael had covered that face. There had been a new one that morning, 'Virgilian.' Just what could that mean? Shutting her eyes, she fell suddenly asleep.

She slept for about an hour and when she awoke felt fresh and calm. With a yawn she stretched herself and lay on her side looking at the mirror. Rules, hearing her move, cocked one ear cautiously but did not trouble to open an eye. She began to stroke the golden down on her forearms. Attractive Daphne. She bit and chewed the soft skin in the angles of her elbows. There are not many parts of your body, when you come to think of it, that you can bite. Unlike Rules. She put the receiver back on the telephone.

Michael was always telling her what an animal she was. 'Creature' was his favourite word for her. You lovely creature, magnificent creature, also glorious, golden, glowing, subtle, unattainable, infinite, feline, proud, peerless, Olympian, echoing, mountainous, swift, tender, furry, creamy, crystal creature. They came flowing out, the epithets. Ambrosial creature—that had been a good one. Why doesn't he ring?

Virgilian. She had taken away a book off his shelves that morning to unravel the sense of the latest adjective. She looked at it now. On one side of the page was the Latin verse, on the other the English prose translation. There must be two or three words of English to every one word of Latin. The verse was printed in a larger type than the translation, with decent intervals between the lines and a spacious margin. Even with smaller type, smaller intervals and a smaller margin the English was only just able to squeeze itself into its allotted page. Looking at these adjacent pages, Daphne had the idea that this was how she and Michael must learn to live together. She the verse, he the prose. She the basic rhythm, the slow original beauty, the source of their life, he its voluble and busy interpretation.

She yawned again and stretched herself impatiently, then got up and sat on a stool in front of the long mirror where she admired herself from many angles and in many postures; from straight upright with a hollow in the small of the spine and head and shoulders held proudly back, to a forward droop with elbows on knees and hair over the face. Occasionally she would seem to forget herself then suddenly, with a swift startled look over her shoulder, take herself by surprise. At length she lay down again on the bed. Supposing he was hurt by her abrupt action?

'Rules,' she said.

The cat moved his ear, but did not open his eye.

'Rules,' she said again.

Again he moved his ear but still did not trouble to open his eye.

'Rules,' she said peremptorily. 'Why doesn't he ring?'

Meanwhile, about a mile away, Michael too was lying on a bed. She thinks, he said to himself, that it is still possible for her to stand back and take stock of the position. She thinks that she will remain the pursued for a long time yet, perhaps for ever. She does not dream how fatally soon our rôles will be reversed. She hardly yet realises that she has started on an irresistible downward motion. You might as well try to stop a sledge that has got well going downhill. The trouble, of course, is that though we are both going down the same hill we are going down on different sledges. It is always the way. My sledge has got started well before hers and, as it travels faster, will reach the bottom long before hers. If there must be a bottom always? Must there? Oh dear! Is there no hope ever that the road will lead downhill all the way?

Surely, this time, it is more than just an affair? That entirely depends on you, Michael. If the idea is firmly fixed in your mind that it is going on for ever and ever, then it will. If you trust to the events of the moment to make up your mind, then it won't. You can decide as well now as in a few weeks' or months' time. Yes, but if I could be quite sure that there would be always, always, something about her that I could not get at, something that I would never learn to pity . . . Am I feeble? Abnormal? A cad? Oh God, I love her.

The telephone rang. It was Daphne.

Lost Day

Sir Alison Whitehead stood in front of the crackling log-fire in his study, filling his pipe. He was dressed in an old tweed knickerbocker suit, the kind of suit a man cannot be persuaded to discard though he is told that it will soon be too shabby even to be sent to the jumble sale. On his feet he wore bedroom slippers. He had just had breakfast. Lighting his pipe, he looked round his bookshelves and out at the falling snow. My word, I'm happy, he said to himself and pulled his knickerbockers in front so that the hot tweed embraced the backs of his legs.

The day stretched ahead of him in uneventful bliss. It was in the uneventfulness that the bliss still mainly consisted. No one would try to get at him. No one would ask his opinion. He would not have to make any decisions. He would not have to give his mind to any matter unwillingly. Memoranda would not appear on his desk demanding his urgent attention. His attention could be given to just what he chose. Beyond certain well regulated domestic duties he had not an obligation in the world. This happy state of affairs, which had now lasted a fortnight, was still too good to be true.

Many of his colleagues, he had noticed, when the moment of retiring approached, began to take fright. That leisure to which they had professed to look forward so eagerly, became, when imminent, less attractive to them. They hung on past the moment when they might have retired. They hung on as long as they could. Not so, Sir Alison. Leisure had no terrors for him. It had indeed been his dream for forty years, a dream that became only more delightful as the prospect of its realisation came nearer. But, unlike the others, he had never spoken of his secret aspiration. He had never let the cat out of the bag. All were astonished therefore when, as soon as he was pensionable, punctually at sixty, he made off, shaking himself free from all entanglements. Not a committee, not a board meeting, not an inaugural address, should call him back. It was incredible. Everyone could have sworn that Whitehead would die in harness, Whitehead the conscientious, the dutiful, the indefatigable, the impeccable, the firm, the wise, the good—in a word, the indispensable. How would affairs be carried on without him? 'Give the younger men a chance!' he said. 'But I look on you as one of the younger men,' said the

Minister.

The compliment was not a hollow one, for as he stood warming his back at the fire Sir Alison did indeed feel young. His physical mechanism was in perfect order. He slept excellently. His appetite was splendid, he had just eaten a schoolboy's breakfast. His mind, meanwhile, was as alert and inquisitive as a boy's. What fun he was going to have, taking up his education again where he had left it, all those years ago, at Oxford. There they were on the shelves, the leisurely masterpieces, waiting for him, the *Aeneid*, the *Decline and Fall of the Roman Empire, The Anatomy of Melancholy, Gerusalemme Liberata, Arabia Deserta, Erasmus' Letters*. What fun it would be! With luck he still had a quarter of his life ahead of him.

He walked over to the window and gazed out at the snow. Happy sight! The fall was so thick that he could not even see the pergola at the near end of the lawn. His new house, lonely at any time, seemed more than ever remote as it was thus severed even from its own garden. Which, in Sir Alison's opinion, was all to the good. The fluttering cascade that was so effectually and so silently laying its thick blanket on house and garden and stables, and on the downs enclosing them, ensured his isolation, made his new freedom even more impregnable. That awful London! Heavens, he was glad to be away from the place! The devilish traffic, the crowds, the harassed faces, the lewd advertisements, the imbecile wicked newspapers, the unlovable buildings, the unwelcoming streets—he would be happy never to see them again!

The falling snow had hushed all sounds from without. He listened, and could hear only distant household noises. The sound of the raking out of the furnace echoed along the hot pipes to the study, with its comforting message of warmth and of smooth organisation below stairs. (God bless darling Helen!) Then there was the far-off sound of Rosie at the piano. Then, also far off, the telephone went—a tradesman, no doubt, ringing up from the village to say that the snow was too thick on the road for him to deliver his things. Good, good, good. Sir Alison was enjoying the slowing down of his life enormously.

He looked around his library. Up to now he had been spending a large part of the days unpacking his books and arranging them on the shelves. Everything was now in place. He could begin to read. What should he start with? Taking down the first volume of Gibbon, he settled himself in an armchair in front of the fire, put his feet on the chimneypiece and opened the book.

His eye rested on the bookplate, designed by his father, the dean, some fifty years ago. It represented a cathedral seen through an open window, the very view that his father enjoyed when he looked up from his writing table at the deanery. Beneath, on a scroll, was the Whitehead motto, *Doubte not*. What an inappropriate motto, reflected Sir Alison, if you heard it as the battle-cry of a bruising extrovert. Yet how suitable if it was the whispered warning of a friend 'This, you Whiteheads, this is your weak point! You think too much! If you will only believe enough in what you are doing, you will have no difficulty in getting to the top of the tree.' Alison Whitehead had heeded the warning. Life is long. It has to be lived. With that moral decisiveness which all who knew him learned to respect, he put away, at an early age, the fascinating, undermining, thoughts.

He had had a full life. He had met all sorts and conditions of men. His work, and his holidays, had taken him to many parts of the world. He had fought in a war. He had experienced the ups and downs of passionate romantic love, for better and for worse, in sickness and in health. He had had four children, only the youngest of whom, Rosie, was still at home. His elder daughter and his elder son had already made him three times a grandfather. Various people, of whom he was very fond indeed, had died. On the whole he had had his share of the joys and sorrows of life.

And what had they taught him? Certain rules. If he had his life over again, he might in certain of the circumstances behave in rather a different way. But—and with a delightful feeling of relaxation he permitted the family motto, in his case, to have spent itself—what had he learned of a general or philosophic nature about existence? What is the purpose of it all? What, if anything, happens to you when you die? Life did not seem at all long to him when such absorbing inquiries were allowed to make themselves heard. Confoundedly short, in fact.

Once these questions were admitted nothing else seemed worth a thought. The problems of existence were immeasurably more important than those of life. As to their answers, he felt that he knew no more than when he was a boy reading Greats. The process of living told you nothing about what happened on the other side of the great wall of death. It was rather at the subdued moments, at the moments when life was least lively, that you seemed nearest to penetrating the mystery. At such a moment as the present, for instance, when the midwinter hush lay on everything outside, and the fire had momentarily ceased crackling, and his mind was empty and his heart lay open to any manifestation . . . 'No, sir. Sir Alison is no longer in conference. He is free now. He is expecting you, sir.' But it was always the same. As you approached the looking-glass to pass through, you merely knocked your face into its own familiar image. Perhaps, he said to himself, I am quite on the wrong lines.

There was a discreet affectionate tap on the door.

'Come in.'

Lady Whitehead was still a very pretty woman. She came over to his chair and sat on the arm.

'Are you having a nice time?'

''Mm. Wonderful.'

'What are you reading?'

'Gibbon. As a matter of fact I hadn't got further than the bookplate. What did you want, my precious?'

'A Father Donnelly telephoned for you just now.'

Father Donnelly? I don't know any Fathers!'

'He was ringing up, he said, on behalf of Terence Pullen who is very ill indeed and wants to see you. He is probably dying.'

'Terry Pullen dying!'

'I thought you wouldn't want to talk to the man, so I said you were out, but I took the address and telephone number. Was that right?'

'Absolutely, my dear. Ah, Sussex Avenue—that's his brother's.'

Terry Pullen dying! Sir Alison got up, went to the window and stood looking out at the snow. His memory was taken back four decades to a summer day in the French Alps. The chalet-full of undergraduates had divided itself into two parties which were to climb a mountain from different sides. The don had come in the same party as Alison. He was getting middle-aged and stopped from time to time to take breath. At length Alison broke away from the party and hurried on by himself. As he came up on to the grassy table at the top of the mountain the Honourable Terence Pullen appeared from the other side.

'Terry!'

'Alis!'

'Surely this, sir, is a mountain?'

'Nay, sir, 'tis but a considerable protuberance.'

Dr Johnson at the moment was all the rage among the intelligentsia.

'Old Trigger goes so slowly, I've left my lot far behind,' said Alison.

'Mine were talking about God,' said Terence. 'Look at them!'

Far below his party could be seen toiling up a rocky path.

'I say, it's pretty wonderful up here!'

They gazed around in exhilaration.

'Have a swig?'

Terence took a flask of brandy out of the hip-pocket of his shorts. A pronounced taste for liquor had already shown itself in the young man.

'I don't mind if I do,' said Alison.

They each had a fiery gulp.

'Sir, there must be only one pleasure greater than that of being at the top of a mountain.'

'What is that, sir?'

'Drinking brandy at the top of a mountain.'

'But have you ever been at the top of a mountain, sir?'

'I was once up Boxhill. Vertiginous, sir, vertiginous!'

They roared with laughter. Terence put his arm in Alison's.

'I say, Alis, I've got an idea. I'd been meaning to ask you. What do you say to our sharing a flat when we live in London? Wouldn't it be rather fun?'

Alison was surprised and not a little flattered.

'Why of course, Terry! It would be grand!'

'You really mean it? How splendid! Let's have another pull for luck!'

Sir Alison turned away from the window. Oh Lord, a London shirt, a London suit, a train, streets—the day lost! Why couldn't they leave him in peace?

'I could take the eleven-twenty,' he said.

'You're not thinking of going are you, to-day?'

'Yes.'

'But—it's madness!'

'Well—'

'You don't even like him at all, do you? I thought you hated him?'

'Well—I think I ought to go.'

Helen Whitehead knew that when her husband said 'I think I ought,' there was no arguing.

'I could probably catch the four-twenty back from Paddington. I'll be home for dinner.'

'In that case we'll have the duck this evening. I suppose you'll be having your lunch on the train? There's a restaurant car on that train from Swindon.'

'Yes. I wonder whether Rosie will drive me to the station? We ought to allow at least half an hour on a day like this.'

'Of course she will. I'll go and tell her. But I think you're quite mad, you know.'

She went to find Rosie and he went upstairs to change his clothes. Rosie, in the middle of her Chopin, received the news that she was to drive her father to the station with annoyance. These hysterical adults! Always on the move! Why can't they leave one in peace? In the car, as they ploughed their slow way through the snow, she said:

'Who is this dying man?'

'He's called Terence Pullen.'

'Do you like him very much?'

'Er—no.'

'You hate him?'

'No, not exactly.'

'In fact, you're completely indifferent to him?'

'Well—perhaps.'

'Yet you choose a day like to-day to go up to London to see him, because you think you ought to! You know, papa, there are days when I think you're quite bats!'

'Yes, my dear.'

'You're always doing things you don't want to do! You're the slave of duty!'

'Yes, my dear.'

'You're always telling me to sit up straight. You and your generation have wasted your lives sitting up straight.'

'There is much in what you say, my love.'

'It's time you began to learn to sit down crooked, see?'

'I had hoped I was just about to start to learn.'

After half an hour on the branch line and twenty minutes' wait on Swindon station, he found a seat in the London train. Though he had the *Oxford Book of Latin Verse* on his knee, his thoughts wandered away from it and he looked out at the falling snow. Presently he went along to the restaurant car where he remained till the end of the journey. There is the duck for dinner he reminded himself as he paid the bill. The snow was falling less thickly when they approached the suburbs. In London it had turned to rain. The streets were dirty with melting slush. Sir Alison took a taxi from Paddington.

As the butler let him in, Lord Westbrook happened to be in the hall. Sir Alison had not set eyes on Terence's elder brother for many years. He was a distinguished figure, what Terence might have, ought to have, looked like. They shook hands.

'It's awfully good of you to come,' said Lord Westbrook. 'Terry seems to want to see you very much about something or other. Should we go up? You're going to find him very much changed, you know.'

This was true. The face which Sir Alison saw on the pillow was hardly recognisable. The bloated cheeks had shrunk away in loose folds, the nose, no longer bulbous, already had a sharp appearance. But what Sir Alison noticed more than anything was the new look in the eyes. The dying man was frightened; which, to do him justice, Sir Alison had never known him to be in life. Lord Westbrook left them together.

The man in the bed, normally so large, looked so diminished and so low, Sir Alison by an odd impulse knelt down beside him.

'Alis!' The voice was weak.

'Terry!'

'It's awfully decent of you to come. I'm dying, Alis.'

'Oh no, you aren't. You look as if you'd last a long time yet.'

'No, no. I know I'm dying. Alis—, Alis—'

'Yes, Terry. What is it?'

'Will you forgive me?'

'Forgive you? What for?'

'You know.'

'Why, Terry, I have nothing to forgive you for.'

Terry looked disappointed.

'Yes, you have,' he said miserably.

At this moment Sir Alison became aware that he was not alone in the room with the dying man. There was another kneeling figure on the other side of the bed.

'All right, Terry,' he said kindly. 'I'll say I forgive you, if that's what you want.'

A look of relief came into the anxious face.

'You forgive me?'

'Of course, Terry. With all my heart.'

'Thank you. Thank God.' He sighed. 'Now I can sleep a bit.'

He shut his eyes. There was now no sound in the room but the whisperings of the praying figure on the other side of the bed. Sir Alison, still on his knees, fell to wondering when he himself had last been in this unusual posture. For it had been his practice for many years, on the occasions on which he found himself in a church, to make a decent forward inclination rather than kneel completely. There was some particular occasion, not so very long ago, that he was trying to remember. Why, of course! 'Rise, Sir Alison!'

Terence seemed to be fast asleep now. Sir Alison rose. He had no wish to prolong the scene. He was uncomfortable. This was not his world at all. He wanted only to get away. Father Donnelly also got up from his knees and came with him to the bedroom door.

'Thank you so much for coming,' he said in a pretty Irish voice. 'It has meant so much to him. He wanted so desperately to see you, only you. I say, I had the devil of a time tracking your telephone number!'

There were a great many people out on the landing and on the stairs. Sir Alison had the impression of a gathering of the clans. He shook several hands, and was asked many times to stay and have a cup of tea. But he pressed his way to the front door and out into the street where he took to his heels. Thank God that's over, he said to himself. He was unlucky in finding a taxi and reached the station on foot, rather wet. Still, he found an empty corner seat and settled himself with satisfaction in the train which was going, this time, in the right direction. Thank God that's over, he said again to himself.

But something told him that that was not over. He was aware of certain itching interrogations at the back of his mind, certain *doubtes.* Now if there was one thing about which Sir Alison had always been particularly firm with himself, that was tidiness of the spirit. He strongly disapproved of a moral litter. He set himself to clear things up as quick as he could. At the moment he was aware that if he raised his eyes they would alight on objects that needed clearing up. Therefore he kept his eyes on his book, as the train moved out of London and the dirty afternoon became hidden in darkness.

He did his best to concentrate on the page. Then he read:

Multis ille bonis flebilis occidit
Nulli flebilior quam tibi

The apt inappositeness of the words was too much for him. He shut the *Oxford Book of Latin Verse* and gave himself over to his thoughts.

Something had been wrong about that scene at which he had just assisted. Not that he doubted the genuineness of Terence's fear and sense of guilt. The latter's part had been, in its way, an honest one. So of course had that of the priest. It was his own performance about which Sir Alison felt uneasy. Things must be thought out. He must go back to the beginning, to the mountain top.

At the moment of excitement, when Terence had suggested they should set up house together, he had accepted impulsively. It certainly would be great fun living with Terence. Life would not be dull with him for he always seemed to collect the best and most interesting people around him. He had such good ideas. He was always just off somewhere or just back from somewhere fascinating. He was rich. There would be lots of drink and parties. One could not, in a sense, want anybody better than Terence to launch one into London life. Alison was certainly flattered at being asked.

Yet, from the first, he had forebodings. The very attractions of the project held so many dangers. The money, the drink, the fun—he wondered whether Terence and himself had the same ideas about the laws of diminishing returns. The very disparity of their incomes might lead to all sorts of awkwardnesses. Terence had at times a carefree way with money that made Alison a little nervous. And the odd thing was, it was Terence who was doing the asking. Alison had no doubt about this. It was himself, Alison, who was to contribute the larger share of capital to the felicity of the *ménage*. The moral outlay, he feared, would all be his.

The household lasted for rather more than two years. Looking back through the haze of time Sir Alison could still see many details of that life but the episodes merged into one another and he could not always be certain of their order. Moreover, he found he could remember very little of the early, happier time, except that there had been such a time. Yes, things had not gone badly at first. He remembered how much, in the whirl of gaiety into which they had quickly been caught—surely in those days they had enjoyed themselves much more than the modern young?—He remembered how much he had enjoyed the moments of repose, the domestic moments when he, say, was in the bath and Terence was in the next room dressing for dinner and they were talking through the open doors. Or there would be a rapturous five minutes as they met by the fire adjusting their white ties and buttonholes and, over a quick drink, made a few unanimous brilliant judgments on their friends before going out their several ways. White ties! Did people wear such things nowadays?

Then, in the early hours of one morning Alison had been awoken by the door-bell. Going down in his dressing-gown he had found a taxi man at the door.

'Does that belong here?' the man asked, pointing to the open door of the cab. Inside Alison saw Terence lying dead drunk on the floor in a mess of sick. They heaved him out of the taxi and up to his bedroom and then Alison helped the man to clean his taxi. When they had finished he said:

'Have a drink?'

'I never touch the stuff,' said the man, with an expression as cold as the dawn that was appearing over the roofs. He did not however refuse the handsome tip Alison gave him as he paid the fare.

Alison stood a few moments at the door, watching the taxi go away up the street and savouring the harsh morning reality, then went in to undress Terence and put him to bed. He smelled horribly.

He was unconscious when Alison went to work that morning. Terence did not work and Alison found him still in bed in the evening, reading the newspaper, sulky.

'Hullo, Terry! How are you? Have you come round?'

'No!'

Alison waited. Then he said:

'You were quite out.'

'Yes.'

'You were damned heavy!'

'I don't remember a thing.'

Again Alison waited. Then:

'I settled with the taxi man.'

‘ ’Mm.’ Terence was looking at the newspaper.

‘His cab was in rather a mess. I made it worth his while.’

‘You were right, I am sure.’

Alison left the room. Pretty cool! I am not going to stand that sort of thing very often, he said to himself.

This ugly episode confirmed certain unfavourable opinions that Alison had been forming, as he saw him at close quarters, about his companion: first that he was a dipsomaniac, secondly that he had no scruples about money, and thirdly that he was an insolent overweening type who would rather lose a friend than say ‘I am sorry.’ As to the dipsomania, Terence’s intemperance was not like that of most of Alison’s friends, an affair of occasional excesses which, now that they had left Oxford and were learning the alcoholic rules, became more and more rare. With Terence an opposite process was taking place. Drink for him had an atavistic glamour. The Pullens in their time had drunk deep. Each generation produced, not a connoisseur of wine—it was not that kind of drinking, though of course wine went down with the rest—but simply a drunkard. Terence had an uncle who had had to be shut up. In the new generation it was Terence who had inherited the ancestral thirst for fiery waters. He found it increasingly unbearable to be sober. Alison discovered that he now began the day, not it is true very early, with gin.

As to money matters Alison came to the conclusion that very few of his friend’s actions could be assessed as merely thoughtless. Terence, it is true, liked to live in an extravagant manner, as though money were not a consideration. Actually he was a good deal interested in money. It amused him to score off people in a small way, to travel without a railway ticket, to exchange his umbrella at the club for a better one, to diddle tradesmen. He used to think these things out. He had devised a way of telephoning from a call-box without inserting pennies. A person perhaps needs some noble blood to be as ingeniously, as frankly, ignoble as Terry. There was that business of the new dinner jacket, when the tailors had to decide between Terry’s word and the word of their carman. They chose the word of the Honourable Terence Pullen and made him another dinner jacket free. So he got two, for all the while he had the first one in his cupboard, delivered correctly, as the man had said. And the man? Did he get the sack? Sir Alison still sometimes thought about that man and regretted that he had never done anything for him. The episode had taken place while he was away on holiday, but when he heard of it he ought to have done something or tried harder to make Terry do something about it.

When, therefore, Terry would look the other way while his friend tipped the porter or paid the taxi, Alison did not suppose him to be suddenly seized by a genuine oblivion. Terry knew perfectly well what was happening. He was simply seeing if he could get away with it, partly for the fun of the thing and partly because, for all his prosperity, he generally seemed to be short of ready money. Alison would try to make him come to some agreement about the division of the expenditure of petty cash, but Terence would wave aside any such idea in a lordly manner, complain that Alison was mean and give him a bottle of whisky to show that there was no ill feeling—which he would then proceed to drink himself. Alison no longer cared much for his friend.

Money matters would have brought the association to an end had there been nothing else. Terence was so aggressively inconsiderate. Their arrangement was to halve the gas and electricity charges. The bills that came in were enormous for the reason that Terence would seldom take the trouble to turn off a light or a gas fire. He paid no attention to anything Alison might say and twitted him in company for his meanness. One Monday morning, coming home from a long week-end, Alison found his gramophone rumbling round in a great heat. It must have been revolving since Saturday afternoon when Terence too had gone away, leaving it on. Does he simply do it to exasperate? Alison asked himself.

Alison hated rows, but that night after some guests had gone away they had a row. He told Terry some home truths; to which Terry would only answer 'You're so mean! Mean and prim!'

'Then I'm off!'

'What do you mean?'

'I mean I'm going! You can find somebody else to live with!'

Terence knew that Alison generally meant what he said.

'Oh, but you can't go, Alis!'

A look of real concern had come into Terry's face.

'Can't I? I shall.'

'Oh, but Alis, I so need someone like you.'

'Then find someone like me!'

'I mean you, I need you, Alis. You're such a tower of strength. Don't go. Here, have another drink. I'll do better in future, I promise.'

They sat up drinking and talking late and Terence made many concessions and promises.

'Then you'll stay, Alis?'

'All right.'

'Now I shall sleep.'

Next evening, when he came in, Alison found a present of a dozen bottles of champagne by his bed; and for some time Terence did indeed make a certain effort to be more pleasant. But Alison felt that their establishment was doomed. For one thing he had certain wild plans of his own. He was head over ears in love with Mrs Walters. Why should not Mrs Walters become Mrs Whitehead, now, at once?

Gazing out of the train window into the darkness Sir Alison had a most clear vision in his mind of Daphne Walters, her great innocent eyes, her lovely forehead, her slow movements. He even believed that he could remember her smell. He had loved her furiously. Whatever people might say about her he was not going to be deflected. And many unfavourable things were said. Her record was certainly not satisfactory. Though she was barely twenty-three the names of quite a long list of young men would come to mind when her name was mentioned. Nobody thought it appropriate to suggest that Tom Walters had been ungentlemanly in not feigning to be the guilty party in their divorce. Alison's family did not like her at all. Still, his impetuousness was not to be denied. He meant to take her over, if she would have him, for life.

His dream came to an abrupt end. Returning home one evening when he was not expected, he found Daphne Walters in bed with Terry. That, as far as he was concerned, was the end of both of them. He moved out of the flat at once. Daphne moved in. She had hopes of marrying Terry for, as her later life was to show, she had a great relish for getting married. But his religion would not allow it. She had to be content to live with him as his mistress.

Arrived at this point in his recollections, Sir Alison found himself unable to recapture any memory of that jab of pain he must have felt at the discovery of his betrayal. He could still see quite clearly those two heads on the pillow—*his* pillow by the way, for with a characteristic piece of bravado Terry had made use of his bed. 'Just for the fun of the thing,' he had probably said. But the vivid scene was so overlaid with wisdom after the event that Sir Alison could now feel no rancour towards those two heads. They were simply two dying heads on a pillow. The bitterness he must at first have felt towards his late friend was soon turned to a feeling of gratitude. What a benefactor Terry had been, to save him from that awful woman!

In the decades which passed between that fateful night and the next occasion on which he saw his head on a pillow, Alison from time to time set eyes on Terence Pullen. They had even in recent years found themselves on speaking terms. Terence was simply not worth not speaking to. No one indeed wanted to be long in his society for he had become a prize bore. He would stand by the hour at the bar of a club to which Alison also belonged, telling interminable boastful stories about the black market, forged passports, contraband in the diplomatic bag. His company was generally regarded as 'crashing'; yet kind people could often be found to help him home. Sir Alison himself, though Pullen was quite unaware of the fact, had performed this thankless service only a year or two ago.

Terence Pullen's life, so far as one could judge, had been wholly unproductive. He had done nothing except to spend money on the gratification of sterile desires. He had become good at nothing, interesting about nothing. He was a perfect nuisance to his family with his debts, his drunkeness, his untidy love-affairs, his various squalid adventures which from time to time found their way into the papers. In his middle thirties they managed to ship him off for some years to Central Africa. Then, there he was, back again, against the bar, holding forth, unamusing, unhumble, irrepressible. So passed thirty-seven years in which he might have asked Alison to forgive him.

And now what? Here at the eleventh hour, at the seven hundred and nineteenth minute, Terence, having been on the wrong side all his life, was coming over, just in time, to the right side. Sir Alison presumed to form no opinions about Terence's faith; though quite recently he had heard him declaiming in a manner of such irreverent and boastful disloyalty as would, one might suppose, preclude any chance of reconciliation on this side of the grave. Perhaps, Sir Alison argued with himself, something is happening which I do not understand. The argument appealed to him for he saw in it an exemption from the grievous decision that he was otherwise going to have to make. But he could not deceive himself for long with such an alibi. There might be things he did not understand; still, that was no excuse for giving up thinking. He must act according to his understanding, so far as it went. Things, as he saw them, were thus.

At long last, pushed up by subterranean warmth—by hell-fire, in fact—a tiny shoot of conscience had shown itself in the stony waste of Terry's spirit. For the first time in his life, or at least for many decades, Terry was experiencing moral anxiety. And what had he, Alison, done? He had said, Don't worry, Go to sleep. He had put his foot on the little crocus shoot and trodden it back into the ground. Was that right?

But Terence's soul, he told himself, was none of his business. Why bother? That argument, again, would not do. Terence's soul *was* his business, because he had been called in. But why, he asked himself, oh why did he call in me? Were there not scores of people whom he had more deeply wronged? Daphne herself, for instance, and the child, were generally thought to have been fairly badly treated. Perhaps as Terence looked back through his misdeeds, it was not till he came to the Alison period that he could remember feeling any sort of contrition at the time. His earliest sins therefore remained to him the most vivid. Whatever the cause, Alison had been called in. He was involved whether he liked it or not. And the more he thought, the more clear did his duty become. Terence having at last shown himself capable of moral anxiety, he ought to make sure that Terence died anxious.

There was one more argument by which Sir Alison sought to make his escape. You are quite sure, he said to himself, that you are not really being prompted by venom, by revengefulness? He examined himself carefully. No, frankly, he bore Terry no malice whatever. He had utterly forgiven him years ago. It was for that very reason that he was now able and bound, to unforgive him. Sir Alison would lend his shoulder to no last minute scramble into heaven. The mere fact of a scramble made him doubtful whether it was heaven into which Terry was being heaved. Virtue, in his opinion, should be 'well tried through many a varying year.'

Sir Alison searched himself in vain for any feelings of triumph over the prostrate Terry. His sentiments, on the contrary, were almost tender. For he had been touched by the summons and by the sight of the dying man. In order to make absolutely sure of his duty, he now went over all his thoughts again—and came to the same hard conclusion. There was no way out. If not as a friend, he owed it to Terry as a human being not to be gentle with him. Oh Lord, what a beastly day this was! Looking at his watch he found that they were only a quarter of an hour away from Swindon.

His decision made, he allowed his thoughts to wander. He fell to imagining his own death-bed. How different from the anxious scene he had witnessed that afternoon! There at last would be relaxation! Retirement indeed! All responsibilities would then at last drop away. Nothing could then possibly be his fault. With his feet out, at full length, a spectator at last, he would lie watching for the curtain to go up—or was it down?

He got out at Swindon into a cold starlit night. The snow had stopped falling but there was a bitter wind on the platform. The train for his home was waiting on another platform. He went to a telephone box.

'Hullo! Is that you, Rosie?'

'Yes, papa.'

'Look, I'm afraid I shan't be able to get back to-night.'

'Oh, dear! What a pity! The duck's already cooking. It smells scrumptious. I was just about to get ready to come and meet you. Are you still in London?'

'Yes. I'm afraid this business has been more complicated than I expected. Tell your mother I'm very sorry about it, and sorry I couldn't ring up earlier.'

'All right.'

'Have you had a nice day, my dear? What have you been doing?'

'I can't remember. Oh yes, this afternoon I had a bath and washed my hair. It was lovely. And then I've been sitting in front of your fire looking at *Vogues* and *Country Lifes*. It was lovely.'

'Bless you! Good night, Rosie.'

'Good night, papa, and don't forget to hold yourself up straight.'

Really, thought Sir Alison, lying to one's own daughter like that—it's too silly! But explaining the whole business over the telephone would have been so involved. He walked out on to the platform again and asked a porter when the next train was for London. He found he had nearly three-quarters of an hour to wait. What a day! After walking two or three times up and down the station he decided to go and have a drink in a hotel in the town. The decision was an unfortunate one, for it occasioned an unfortunate meeting. As he left the hotel, coming out in the bright light of the doorway, a man passing in the street touched his cap to him.

'Good evening, sir!'

It was Fletcher, a handyman who came and worked at his place in the mornings.

'Good evening, Fletcher.'

It was too silly. Fletcher would be there tomorrow morning telling the cook that he had seen him in Swindon and Helen and Rosie would be certain to hear of it. They would be bewildered. Here he was, playing cat and mouse with his own wife and daughter! When he gave them the full and truthful account of his movements, Rosie would say that he was bats. She was probably right. God, what a day, he muttered, as he strode up and down the station trying to keep warm. *Hodie diem perdidi!*

The train he got into was cold, his feet were wet and cold. When and where, he wondered, would he get any dinner? But his principal uneasiness came from the thought of that disagreeable and difficult interview for which he was returning to London. How sickening if he were to be too late! Sir Alison was feeling thoroughly out of sorts when at last he arrived again at Sussex Avenue. As he was shown in, Father Donnelly was about to go out of the house. He laid a friendly hand on Sir Alison's shoulder.

'Why, so you're back and all? Well now, he had a good friend in you indeed, God bless you. He passed away about an hour since. The Lord took him quietly at last, God rest his poor soul. He never woke again after you had gone.'

Sir Alison said nothing. The priest looked at him with concern.

'You're feeling bad then?'

'Yes.'

'Come and sit down for sure.' He took his arm.

'Where's the—?'

'Why, of course. Along here. That door on the left.'

In the lavatory Sir Alison, for the second time that day, fell on his knees. Leaning over the seat, he was very sick indeed.

Friends

The attendant held apart the heavy canvas curtains and a fat man walked through into the bath. He looked about him. This was evidently his first visit. He had the place to himself. Not only were there no other bathers but there were no signs of there having been any other bathers, no wet marks on the tiles, no displacement of the canvas seats around the bath. He must be the first arrival that day, perhaps for many days, for the place had a most unused air about it. The atmosphere, which had a disagreeably acrid smell, was hot and heavy. It did not seem that anything could ever have stirred the thick and torpid vapour that lay over the water. You could not suppose that the glass dome held any echoes of screaming and laughter and youthful splashings. There were no diving boards or shoots to this bath. It was not that kind of bath.

In contrast with the stagnant air the water was alive. It flowed from the far end and overflowed with a gurgle in the corner where the fat man was standing. Its movement was apparent from the sediment it carried. The fat man stooped and lifted out one of the little streaks of grey matter that were drifting towards the overflow pipe. As he crumbled it in his fingers he came to the conclusion that it was a mineral not a vegetable substance. Then he walked along the side of the bath looking at the water. It was greenish and slightly clouded, like Pernod as the water is being poured in. Sunlight coming through the semi-opaque glass dome played in the moving stream, finding clear places where the Pernod was not yet diluted. Many people, thought the fat man, would be put off by the colour and smell, and by the sediment. He was not put off. He had felt the water and it was as warm as the air. That was the chief thing. He was curious to see where it came from.

At the other end of the bath his curiosity was satisfied. The greater part of the wall of the bath at this end consisted not of smooth concrete but of the jagged and irregular surface of natural rock. Here was the very side of the mountain. From a crevice in the middle of this wall the water gushed powerfully, the force of the hot flow being shown by the copious stream of scum that was projected some yards into the bath, until, as the stream slackened, the several particles of sediment, each like a little piece of string with a knot in it, began to detach themselves, their helpless gyrations became less frantic, they were borne along ever more slowly, some, at the sides of the stream, to be caught in backward eddies that would return them towards the source, others to reach to perhaps three-quarters of the length of the bath, where their motion became so feeble that they were almost stationary when they began to be sucked into the stream that led to the overflow.

The fat man, clad only about his loins in a linen triangle, over which his belly oozed like ripe Camembert, stood gazing at the wall of rock. From what dark and seething caverns, he wondered, and at what depth within the entrails of the earth, was the milky fluid shot up into the light? He was fascinated with watching the jet of water and did not notice that another bather had come in through the curtains. The newcomer did not gaze about him as though this was his first visit. He was evidently an *habitué*. His eye alighted at once on the fat man and a look of disappointment came into his face. He was not alone.

Like the other he was in early middle age, but in appearance he could not have been more different. He was scraggy and long-legged and, in contrast with the glabrous whiteness of the fat man, his legs and chest were covered with thick black hair. From the top of his head, however, the hair had vanished, leaving a thin greyish half-circle from temple to temple. The fat man still had quite a good covering on his head of brown hair streaked with grey.

The thin man looked resentfully at the back of the fat man, then began to walk slowly towards him. Was it, could it be—? Why surely—? At that moment the fat man turned round.

'Philip!' said the thin man.

'Why! Roger!'

'Fancy meeting you here! I'm awfully glad to see you.'

'And I you! Well, I never!'

'Have you been here long?'

'We only arrived last night. We're staying three weeks. What about you?'

'I'm afraid this is my last day,' said the thin man. 'What a pity!'

'Oh, what a shame!' said the other.

And both of them, in their hearts, thought, what a good thing! For they were very old friends. They knew each other very well indeed. They knew that they could not bear to see each other for long. Each was to the other like a very good book, which was read at a receptive age and made an enormous impression. There it is, up on our shelves. We do not want to go on reading it. We know it too well. It is a part of ourselves. And if we do take it down and skim through a few pages, we notice only certain tiresome little tricks, little pedantries of style that we had forgotten about. So it stays up there on the shelf. From time to time our eye fixes on its title, we feel loyal, and look away. It is always possible that if we were to read the book through now we should no longer find it as good as we had thought.

In the same way Roger and Philip hardly ever met nowadays. A year might easily go past without their setting eyes on each other. Their social circles, it is true, revolved not far apart. At times they cut deep into one another, but seldom as far as the centres. London is a large place.

Meanwhile, they stood looking each other up and down. It was the first time for many years that Roger had seen Philip's stomach in the nude. Thank God, Philip was saying to himself, I still have my hair and my front teeth. Pundits, each thought, should not be seen without their clothes.

'There don't seem to be many people who use this bath,' said Philip.

'There aren't,' said Roger. 'There is never anyone here. The attendant explained the position to me. Those who have come for the cure almost all pay a supplement and have a private bath. The halt and the maimed apparently are shy about showing themselves in public. So the really ill never come to this place. And of course the well go and bathe in the lake.'

'My family have gone to the lake.'

'So have mine. They go there every day. They say that bathing in snow water is most invigorating.'

The two paterfamiliases gazed down at the water below them.

'What is this like?' said Philip.

'It's lovely,' said Roger. 'You mustn't mind the sediment. It's quite harmless. And you mustn't mind the smell of sulphur or whatever it is. You get used to it. In fact you get rather to like it. Should we go in?'

Philip, standing on the edge, seemed to be preparing to jump, if not to dive in.

'I generally go in like this,' said Roger, and slithered in feet first. Philip went in the same way.

They had entered the bath about in the middle, where the water was at its deepest. It came up to Philip's chin, his topmost chin, but did not cover Roger's shoulders. The fat man felt its buoyancy at once. Up went his feet and he swam across to the other side. Roger kept beside him, swimming with his hands, but with his feet on the bottom. At the other side they rested. A broad ledge ran round the bath for this purpose, on which the bather could sit comfortably with his head and shoulders, or, in the case of Philip, his head, out of the water.

'It's lovely!' said Philip, ecstatically.

'Isn't it? You must try under water, and keep your eyes open. It doesn't do them any harm. There's a wonderful greenish golden light.'

They fell forwards head first and came to the surface in the middle of the bath.

'Try swimming through my legs,' said Roger, and stood with his legs apart.

So Philip swam between Roger's legs, then Roger swam between Philip's legs. Then they made for the other side and rested on the ledge.

'I'm going to enjoy this place,' said Philip. 'But what a pity you're not staying!'

'I know. Isn't it a shame!'

Presently, with a sudden energy, Philip plunged forward splashing with his arms.

'Ha!' he shouted, and his voice echoed in the dome. 'Ha! Ha!'

'Ha!' shouted Roger, splashing alongside him. 'Ha! Ha! Ha!'

The attendant peeped through the curtains to see if they wanted anything, and withdrew.

The energy quickly spent itself. The bodies became inert, floating on their backs. Roger's eyes were shut. Philip was gazing up at the bright dome which was not so opaque but that he could distinguish the whiteness of a cloud floating across the blue. A line of poetry came into his head.

'*Et O ces voix d'enfants*—' he began.

'——*chantant dans la coupole*,' Roger finished.

Fancy remembering that, they thought. That takes one back. That helps to date us.

At length Roger opened his eyes.

'It's rather fun,' he said, 'to go and stand against the hot spring at the end there and let it take you along. Come and try.'

They ambled through the water to the end of the bath. Philip sat on the ledge at the side and watched Roger who made his way across the rocky end until he came to the spring. Here, by holding on to an iron ring in the rock, he was able to place his body over the dark fissure and receive the full force of the stream without being washed away. He held his stomach against it and then his back. He was battered this way and that by the hot jet. Then he let go and lurched untidily into the bath, a tangle of arms and legs that lengthened itself out into a piece of floating weed, or rather, thought Philip, a dead daddy-long-legs. The straggling object was carried nearly half the length of the bath.

'Now you have a go,' said Roger, standing up in the water and moving to the side to watch.

He watched Philip's body caught in the current. It revolved like a log in a stream, at length reaching immobility lying on its front, the arms stretched forward, the legs dangling helplessly. It looked, thought Roger, like a basking frog, becalmed in a pond. Or was it dead? Should he throw something at it? As the thought crossed his mind, it gave a jerk with its legs, and then was still again, the nose just above the water, the eyes shut, a beatific expression on the face as the mind, no doubt, was lost in some batrachian dream of loud and social frolics.

'Delicious,' Philip said presently, opening his eyes and wading slowly, pushing one leg at a time, frog-like, to the side.

'Let's do that again!'

So they did it again. And again and again. They swam on the water and under the water. They waded, wallowed and floated. They turned leisurely somersaults. It is possible that as they gambolled they remembered other and brisker bathes of long ago. It is certain that the thought came to both of them that of all the holiday resorts in the world they had, unknown to each other, both chosen this town, and that of all the people in this town and in the whole world, they, and they alone, had, separately, found their way this day to this bath. It seemed that they were probably both drifting towards life's overflow at about the same pace, side by side. It would be at about the same time—and any moment now—that they would begin to feel the suction from the front. Friendship never ends.

They were sitting again on the ledge.

'I say, Philip, I am uncommonly glad to see you. I mean it.'

'And I you, Roger. It's splendid. Couldn't we have a drink?'

'I was just going to suggest it. There is a speciality of the establishment.'

Roger clapped his hands. The attendant appeared.

'*Deux verres de champagne nature, s'il vous plaît—grands verres!*'

'*Oui, monsieur.*'

The Concert

'Are the others coming?' said Miss Grainger, looking over her shoulder.

'Yes, they're coming,' said Joyce Wainewright, putting her arm into that of the mistress as they were borne along with the crowd out of the Albert Hall.

'A wizard concert, Graingy.'

'Did you enjoy it? I'm so glad.'

Out in the road the girls gathered round Miss Grainger. 'Are we all here?' she said, peering. Miss Grainger was shortsighted. She had reddish untidy hair and a white skin and was plump and good-natured and young. She was never known to be in a bad temper. The girls loved her.

'Joyce, Ruth, Emma, Betty, Jennifer, Yvonne, Maud—Where's Jane? Anyone seen Jane?'

They looked around. The crowd was flowing past them but there was no Jane. They waited.

'It'll be very tiresome of her if she makes us miss the bus,' said Miss Grainger. 'We've just got nice time. Let's see,' she blinked at her watch, 'yes, we've just five minutes. If we miss that one we'll have to wait three-quarters of an hour for the next.'

They waited and the crowd began to be thinner.

'What can have happened to her?'

'Perhaps she went to the lav.'

'Not again. She went in the interval.'

'She's always going! She went twice in Current Affairs yesterday!'

'She went at the beginning of gym. the other day and didn't come back till it was practically over.'

'She doesn't really want to, I'm sure. It's only to get away.'

'I believe,' said Joyce, 'that she practically spends her life in the Dames, Damen, Donne, Toilette, Ritirata or Ladies' Convenience.'

'Oh, there's the bus,' Miss Grainger broke in. 'Oh dear! What had we better do? Now you, some of you, run and get on the bus and the rest of us will stay and find Jane!'

'No, Graingy,' said Joyce, 'it's much better that we all stay together. Anyhow, look! We're too late now to get the bus!'

'Oh dear,' said Miss Grainger. 'Miss Edgeworth will be so annoyed.'

'Don't worry, Graingy. We'll see that you get all your little girls home safely. Don't bother about Maria.'

The group moved back slowly towards the hall.

'Hadn't we better send out a search party?' said Joyce.

'Perhaps we had,' said Miss Grainger. 'But there had better be two parties. She may have gone out of some other exit. You, Joyce and Maud, go round that way, and you, Rosie and Yvonne, go round that way and see if you can find her. We'll be waiting here. And don't get lost, you!'

'O.K. Graingy.'

The adventure was being enjoyed by all the girls. Dusk was coming on. It would be quite dark before the next bus came and after eleven by the time they got back to school. The last stragglers were now coming away from the hall.

'She's funny, isn't she, Miss Grainger?' said Emma, a girl who looked as old-fashioned as her name. With her hair drawn back tight from her forehead, she looked like Alice in Wonderland.

'Who?'

'Jane, Jane Martin. But I like her, don't you?'

'Of course I like her. I like you all. But I wish she wouldn't be quite so odd sometimes.'

'It's because she's had a lonely upbringing in the depths of the country, Miss Grainger. Joyce is always ragging her, but I like her,' Emma insisted.

After several minutes the search parties came back leading their captive. They had found her on the other side of the building.

'How on earth did you get round there?' said Miss Grainger. 'You must have seen the way we went out.'

'I'm sorry, I'm awfully sorry. I lost you. And then people seemed to be going out all sorts of ways and I got lost.'

'Well, it can't be helped now. We've missed the bus. I hope Miss Edgeworth won't be angry.'

'Why do you keep saying that, Graingy?' said Joyce. 'Are you afraid of Maria?'

'Yes, of course.'

'Coo, I'm not! Are you, Maud?'

'No!'

'And you, Ruth?'

'No, of course not!'

'And you? And you? And you? And you? And you?'

'A little bit,' 'Not on your life,' 'No,' came the answers and 'Yes' from Rosie and Emma.

'And you, Jane?'

'And me what?'

'Isn't that like her not to be listening?' Joyce looked round for confirmation, raised long-suffering eyes to heaven and sighed theatrically. 'Jane, I was asking you whether you're afraid of Marpots?'

Miss Grainger winced at the vulgar form of the headmistress's nickname. The nickname itself, current even among the staff, was admissible. It was sanctioned by the highest usage and had recently appeared in print. An old girl, Evelyn Coutts-Calderon, had had a book of poetry published. It was dedicated 'To Maria: In homage.' But the name had some unattractive variants.

'Please, Joyce! Please!' said Miss Grainger, at the horrid word.

'Sorry, Graingy, it just slipped out.'

'Now!' said Miss Grainger, shepherding the party across the road. 'Cross now!'

They walked along the pavement on the other side of Kensington 'Jane, are you afraid of Miss Edgeworth?'

Jane thought.

'Look at her!' said Joyce. 'How like her! She's thinking before she speaks! No, honestly Jane, I'm not trying to be nasty but you really are rather awful. Why can't you just say something and take forty bites before every mouthful afterwards?'

'I shouldn't answer, Jane, if you don't want to,' said Miss Grainger kindly.

'No, I'll answer. The answer is, I don't know.'

'Hearken, all ye!' said Joyce. 'Isn't that Jane all over? Jane, I despair of you. It wouldn't be so bad if you were just keen. You're not that exactly. You're worse. You're so sincere!'

'I thought it was a very good answer,' said Miss Grainger.

'Let's play "Touch-you-last",' said Joyce. Suddenly the girls scattered, darting among the trees, laughing and screaming. Miss Grainger strolled slowly onwards, remaining the nucleus of the group. She had meant what she said about Jane's answer. The fact was, you did not really know about Miss Edgeworth. You not only did not know whether she was going to be angry but, when confronted with her, you often could not tell whether she *was* angry or not. Her manner was at all times so shy and strained, it seemed that the words she uttered conveyed only a fraction of what she meant. When she *did* utter—for there were those famous silences. The hands not only of girls and mistresses but of lecturers and visiting preachers, the parental hands of stockbrokers, generals and strapping hunting ladies, grew damp and fingered the chintz of Miss Edgeworth's sofa as their owners sat there trying to think of something to say. Everyone would agree that Miss Edgeworth's company was not easy. Where opinions differed was over the question of what lay behind her awkward exterior. There were those who thought her hard and unsympathetic. There were certain older members of the staff who held that, though no doubt she would have made an excellent University don, she ought never to have had anything to do with girls. Girls need to know where they stand with a mistress, and with Miss Edgeworth they never did know. Many parents, who had thought of sending their children to the school, decided, after their embarrassing half-hour on the sofa, that they could not entrust their daughters to the hands of that cold, difficult little woman. And those who decided to send them often did so with misgiving. 'I can't see what's supposed to be so wonderful about her,' said Jane's mother. 'She looks to me half-baked, as though she hadn't finished growing up herself yet.'

'Not necessarily a bad thing, my dear,' said Mr Martin, 'in one who is bringing up the young. I think she's magnificent. She's like Queen Victoria.'

'She's certainly very short.'

Jane's father after one interview had voiced the contrary opinion about Miss Edgeworth, the opinion at which most girls, before they left, arrived. For the headmistress certainly had her adherents. Those girls particularly who, in their last year, had the good fortune to belong to her small and select English class generally became ardent admirers. Her teaching of English literature was apparently most inspiring. It was as though in her classroom she suddenly felt safe. She could let herself go. Girls for whom she had been merely a prim tight little figure making an announcement after hall or reading a prayer in chapel, were astonished at the torrent of enthusiasm which she released within those four walls. 'It's not just literature, it's life too. She knows so much about life,' Evelyn had said, already at seventeen a poetess, already able to look back on a vivid and various emotional career. 'I am sure she has had at least one shattering love affair.'

Jane had not yet reached the English class. To her Miss Edgeworth was still a distant and enigmatic figure. But she held two secrets about the headmistress which disposed her favourably towards her. Only if, as seemed most unlikely, Miss Edgeworth were to turn out a positive dragon would Jane give away the two occasions on which she had caught her off her guard. One of these occasions was in the matter of the cherry stones. A notice had appeared on the board signed, it is true, by Miss Edgeworth, but in the handwriting of Miss Russell, the second mistress, saying that all the cherry stones about the place looked disgracefully untidy and were a nuisance. In future no cherries were to be eaten either out of doors or in the passages. Anybody caught making a litter with cherry stones would have a detention.

'Oh but Graingy,' said Maud, turning away disconsolately from the notice-board, 'it's such fun treading them out!'

'Well, you must think of some other kind of fun now. Miss Russell is very angry about the cherry stones.'

'Miss Russell,' Maud muttered under her breath, 'is a *cochon!*'

The same afternoon Jane happened to look out of the window of the end closet in Upper Lavatories. This window commanded a view down a paved passage between walls that led away to the back regions. Coming along the passage towards her, her eyes on the ground, was Miss Edgeworth. Suddenly the headmistress stopped and looked over her shoulder. The passage was deserted. She stepped back a pace and to the side, and put her foot out and pressed. There was a pop as the cherry stone broke. Then Miss Edgeworth remembered to look up.

I hope she didn't see me, thought Jane, bobbing back out of sight as quickly as she could, but not so quickly as to have failed to observe on Miss Edgeworth's face a broad grin.

The other secret had been acquired during the same summer term. Jane had been sent with a message to the headmistress in her study. She had found the door ajar, but heard Miss Edgeworth's voice within. She had peeped inside. There was Miss Edgeworth, sitting in an armchair, her feet on a footstool, reading aloud to herself from a French book. Miss Edgeworth's English may have been perfect, but even Jane knew enough French to be aware that her pronunciation of French could be much improved. Thus, whenever she had a moment to spare, the headmistress by reading to herself aloud would seek to remedy a weakness in her education. The words that Jane heard that afternoon were:—'*Son père, Monsieur Charles-Denis-Bartholomé Bovary, ancien aide-chirurgien-major, compromis, vers* eighteen twelve, *dans des affaires de conscription, et forcé*——' Miss Edgeworth stopped, took her feet off the footstool, sat more upright, and began again:—'*Son père, Monsieur Charles-Denis-Bartholomé Bovary, ancien aide-chirurgien-major, compromis, vers mil—mil huit cent douze, dans des affaires de conscription et forcé . . .*' As Jane looked and listened, she felt, even more than she had felt at the lavatory window, how vulnerable Miss Edgeworth was. It seemed to her that she held the headmistress like a precious and terribly fragile little china jug, in her hand. How terribly easy to shatter her! Withdrawing her head and retreating on tiptoe some way along the passage, she approached the study again, at a noisy run, so that Miss Edgeworth heard her coming.

'Now girls!' called Miss Grainger, 'it's time we began wending back.'

Presently the group was standing on the pavement under the light of a lamp-post, waiting for the bus.

'You haven't yet told me properly what you thought of the concert,' said Miss Grainger.

'It was lovely, Graingy.'

'It was wizard.'

'Awfully good!'

'Wonderful!'

'Wasn't Molkov adorable?' Molkov was the pianist.

'Adorable!'

'Oh, wasn't he sweet?'

'He simply is my favourite man!'

'I adored those little curls that came over his ears!'

'Oh, and that sort of sad look in his eyes!'

'And the way he shut his eyes and sort of looked as if he was praying or something just before he started!'

'He was all kind of bunjy and nice, wasn't he?'

'Didn't you think he was a perfect poppet, Graingy?'

Molkov had been too far away for Miss Grainger, with her short sight, to have an opinion on anything about him except his playing, and on this, not being in the least musical, she had no opinion. She had in fact only come with this party out of good nature, as Miss Erps had had a headache. She mentioned what seemed to her remarkable about the concert.

'I can't imagine,' she said, 'how he can keep all that music in his head.'

'Talking of heads,' said Joyce, 'did you see that scab on the back of the head of the man in front of me?'

'Did I not!' said Yvonne with enthusiasm. 'Wasn't it a whopper?'

'Yes, I saw it too,' said Jennifer. 'My word!'

'I was simply longing to scratch it off all the time, weren't you?'

'Simply longing!'

'I adore scratching scabs! It's the best thing I know!'

'Except . . .' And Rosie whispered the best thing she knew. There were screams and giggles. Conspiratorial heads came together and heard the best thing that Jennifer knew, that Betty and Ruth and Maud knew. Uproarious common laughter greeted each revelation.

'Girls! Girls!' said Miss Grainger. 'I'm ashamed of you!'

'You're not listening, are you, darling Graingy?' said Joyce. 'It'll spoil everything if you do!' And Joyce amid the giggles began to tell the best thing she knew, which was of course going to be far better than any of the other bests.

'Here comes the bus!' said Miss Grainger.

The girls climbed in. Two of them had to stand for the first quarter of an hour. Then people began to get out. At length, after Virginia Water, except for two people in the front, they had the bus to themselves. They were tired and hungry and thirsty, but at the prospect of soon being back they began to revive and chatter. Yvonne started to sing.

'Here we are now!' said Miss Grainger.

They got off the bus, walked a short way along the main road, then along a side road and in at the school gate and up the drive through the familiar smell of azaleas and rhododendrons and hot fir trees. It was a dark, still night. Only a light or two was on in the school building.

'Don't make such a noise! Hush Yvonne! You'll wake everybody up.'

They found some milk and bread and jam and biscuits waiting for them in the hall. Miss Grainger went at once to Miss Edgeworth's study to report the return of the party. When she came back she said:

'It's all right. Miss Edgeworth doesn't seem to be angry. She wants you all to go in and say good night.'

'I hope there won't be a *questionnaire*,' said Betty. 'I can never think of anything to say.'

'She's bound to ask us which bits we liked best and why, etcetera, etcetera,' said Joyce. 'Here, let's have a look at the programme so that I can mug it up in case it's me.'

Presently they had finished eating and trooped along to the study.

'Feigns go in first!'

'Feigns!'

'Feigns!'

'Go on, Joyce, you go first!'

Joyce was quite willing to lead the party. She had just thought of something interesting to say to Miss Edgeworth. It should impress her. They found the headmistress standing in the middle of her sparsely furnished room, and formed themselves into a half-circle in front of her, Miss Grainger behind them.

'Well,' said Miss Edgeworth, 'so you've had a good outing?'

'Yes, thank you, Miss Edgeworth.'

'Yes, lovely.'

'Lovely, thank you.'

'Wonderful.'

'And the concert—did you enjoy it?'

'Yes thank you, it was wonderful.'

'It was grand.'

'Lovely.'

'Awfully nice.'

'I loved it.'

'And Molkov—you have no fault to find with him?'

'No, Miss Edgeworth, absolutely none.'

'He was wonderful.'

'He was awfully good.'

Now, thought Joyce, now's my chance.

'I thought he played a bit too fast,' she said, 'He was sort of——'

'He was "sort of" nothing, Joyce.'

'I mean,' and Joyce wished she had not embarked on these statements. 'I mean it was like someone talking French very fast and you can't keep up.'

A look of interest had come into the headmistress's face. Quick, Joyce, withdraw! Get out of it while you can! She'll begin asking you, Where? When? In which bits do you mean?

'I mean just in general,' said Joyce, 'not particularly. Just sort of here and there, not all the time of course.' Joyce gave an awkward, apologetic laugh.

'Oh,' said Miss Edgeworth, and the interested look disappeared from her face.

There was silence in the room for some moments.

'And you, Jane,' said Miss Edgeworth, 'the lost sheep—you don't seem to have spoken. Did you enjoy it?'

'Yes, very much, thank you.'

There was silence again.

'It——' Jane began but did not go on.

'Yes?' said Miss Edgeworth encouragingly.

'Well, it's the first time I've ever been to a concert, I mean a proper one like that. I didn't know it would be like that. It was awfully exciting.'

'Yes?'

'It wasn't really till the last piece, the Beethoven. I wasn't listening particularly and then suddenly there was a bit that had just passed and I so hoped it would come again and then suddenly there it was, but I knew just before it came.'

There was a titter from the girls.

'Yes, Jane?' said Miss Edgeworth.

'Well then, of course, I waited for it again, because I was almost sure it would come once more and then it did. It was sort of—sort of——'

The girls listened for a rebuke, but none came. Miss Edgeworth's face was an expressionless royal mask.

'Yes?' she said.

'It was like mountains at the beginning of the bit, or clouds, going away behind each other into the distance very, very far and then it changed and you seemed to be on a line going down sideways like this——' Jane moved her hand in a vague way '——and then along straight for a little, and then down again in the same direction as the time before, and then suddenly there was something else and it was all over.'

Miss Edgeworth's expression, or lack of expression, kept the titters, if there were any, this time inaudible.

'And then,' Jane went on, 'I thought it couldn't come again and everything was finished, but then suddenly there it was again. Oh, Miss Edgeworth, it was so exciting! I think it's easily the best thing I've ever known. Just after that the piece was over and that was the end of the concert and everything was ordinary again and there were all the girls just the same as ever, and Miss Grainger, and I felt I had to stay away from them and so I got lost.'

There was an intaking of breath among the girls at Jane's outrageous words. Miss Grainger blushed crimson. There was a silence. Jane, now that her secret was out, was near the end of her power of control. As she realised the enormity of what she had just said, she would probably, had the silence lasted a moment longer, have burst into tears. But Miss Edgeworth spoke:

'You certainly seem to have had some interesting experiences, Jane. The rest of you can go to bed. Good night. You, Jane, stay.'

'Good night, Miss Edgeworth.'

'Good night, Miss Edgeworth.' Miss Grainger took herself, gladly, as being included in the dismissal.

Jane was left alone with the headmistress. She felt sick with fear. What on earth was going to happen to her? Presently Miss Edgeworth spoke:

'What you just said about the music, Jane, was very good.'

The headmistress's voice was so far from being angry that Jane risked looking her in the face. Instead of that look which seemed to be concentrated on nothing in particular she found Miss Edgeworth's eyes fixed intently upon her. Her own eyes dropped at once to a point on the fender to which they clung. In the heart-to-heart 'jaw' which she felt impending she must have something to cling to.

'Art is like that,' Miss Edgeworth went on. 'It lifts you up, then sets you down.'

There was a pause.

'And leaves you down.'

'Yes,' Jane murmured faintly.

There was another pause.

How long had this jaw been going on for? Jane had the feeling that it had already lasted an age. Her eyes were becoming quite sore with clinging to the fender. Surely one would soon be coming to the climax?

'Life too is like that,' the headmistress went on.

The words were platitudinous but Jane felt them to come directly from the heart, to be weighted with an experience.

'Heaven suddenly seems to open——'

Jane, clinging on desperately, felt herself quite unworthy to receive all this confession. It was infinitely flattering, of course, to be spoken to as a woman, but the responsibility of hearing all these secrets was very great.

'——then it's not there any more. But you are. And you've got to go on.'

The little china jug in Jane's hand was becoming unbearably precious. Surely the headmistress would realise that she had said enough?

'Things seem very difficult then, and it is then that you must make a particular effort to be—polite.'

'Yes,' Jane murmured, feeling that the climax was now passing.

After a moment Miss Edgeworth said in a different voice: 'You were very rude to Miss Grainger and to the other girls and you were very silly to get lost like that. You will be in detention for the rest of the term.'

The punishment was an extremely severe one. It meant that on every half-holiday for the rest of the term while the other girls were out, Jane would have to stay at her desk in her classroom engaged on 'some serious employment.' There were two half-holidays a week and six weeks more of term. But Jane was so happy she could have laughed. Her eyes at last left the fender and met Miss Edgeworth's.

'Oh, thank you,' she said. 'Thank you, thank you!'

'Now run along and apologise to Miss Grainger.'

Miss Edgeworth put out her hand. Jane, not knowing what she was meant to do with it, took it in both of hers and made a kind of curtsey.

'Good night, Miss Edgeworth,' she said, and bounded out of the study and along the passage and burst into Miss Grainger's room.

'Darling Graingy,' she said, throwing her arms round the mistress. 'I love you, I love you! I didn't mean what I said! I didn't know what I was saying! Forgive me! Forgive me!'

'Don't be so silly!' said Miss Grainger, kissing the girl and blinking and laughing. 'There's nothing to forgive. Here, have one of these marshmallows. Now run along to bed. You ought to have been asleep hours ago.'

Jane shared a bedroom with Joyce, Maud and Yvonne. She found the other girls already in bed.

'Well, what did you get?' they asked.

'Detention for the rest of the term.'

'Phew!' said Joyce. 'Oh, I must say! Though of course you did sort of ask for it, Jane. But, I must say, that is a bit much! Bad luck, Jane! Bad luck really! Gosh, she's frightening! Gosh, she's a hag!'

'She isn't,' said Jane. 'She's magnificent! Magnificent!'

The other girls looked at her in astonishment.

Afternoon Out

Humphrey Smithers swallowed a yawn.

'Have another piece of cake, Michael?'

'No thank you.'

'Another ice?'

'No, thank you.'

Humphrey was not sorry that the afternoon was coming to an end. It had dragged. Visiting his son at his public school, and taking him out had not been as enjoyable an experience as he had expected. Perhaps if the boy's mother had been there things would have gone with more of a swing. Unfortunately she had had to go to bed with influenza the day before, and Humphrey had come alone.

They sat in silence in the teashop. Other boys and their parents were sitting at other tables. They were all talking at the tops of their voices and seemed to Humphrey to be enjoying themselves enormously, and once again, as often that afternoon, he strove to think of something to say.

'How's the French going?' he said.

'Oh, not bad,' said Michael.

'Let me see, who is it teaches you?'

'Monsieur Fortelle.'

It seemed that this subject too would fall flat. But Michael also was making his conversational effort.

'Do you know what he said the other day?'

'No,' said Humphrey, with a show of eager curiosity but an inner apprehension.

'He said "You boys cannot say *souris*, but I can say *mouze*."'

'Oh no!' said Humphrey, laughing immoderately, 'I say, that's awfully good. Say it again.'

Michael said it again. His father laughed again. Something told me it was going to be that old one, thought Humphrey. They used to tell it of De Larson in my time.

Silence settled on them once more. But Humphrey, though bored, was not unhappy about his boy. He knew that at thirteen and a half Michael was about due to enter upon a series of 'difficult' phases. For the next five or ten years the boy might be wellnigh intolerable. And

Humphrey was determined to be infinitely tolerant. Remembering himself and his friends in their teens, he was prepared for a succession of assaults on his forbearance, phase after phase. He was prepared for loudness, clumsy awkwardness, showing-off and untidiness; for premature refinement, philistinism, a tendency to air embarrassing opinions, an obnoxious dandyism, a world weariness; for patronising omniscience, for ingratitude, for dishonesty, whether frank, furtive or unconscious, for unfunniness, for unholiness and for holiness. He was prepared for everything but what he had found—a nervous politeness. What a change had been wrought in the boy in six weeks!

He had noticed the difference at once as they walked away from the station where Michael had met his train. All the gusto seemed to have gone out of his son. He seemed embarrassed with his father. They might had been two people unknown to each other, meeting for the first time. Question and answer followed one another in a dead sort of way, like tennis balls hit into the net. Well, thought Humphrey, so be it; and adjusted himself good-humouredly to this unexpected and depressing phase.

'And who is the captain of your dormitory?'

'Daniels.'

'Do you like him?'

'I hate him!'

'Hate him? Why?'

'Oh, he's a beast!'

'Why?'

Michael did not answer. Humphrey looked at him, but Michael was looking the other way, into the window of a sweet shop. Humphrey suggested they should go in, so they went in and bought some sweets.

'Daniels—' said Humphrey ruminatively, as they were once more strolling along the High Street, 'have you seen his father?'

'Yes. He came down last Monday.'

'What does he look like?'

'Oh, I don't know. I say, father, what are we going to do this afternoon?'

'Anything you like, my boy. But tell me first—Mr Daniels, is he a person with eyes very close together and black eyebrows meeting over his nose?'

''Mm.'

'Then I know him.'

'Yes,' said Michael. 'That came out.'

Jack Daniels—a poisonous fellow. In the early part of the war he and Humphrey had been at the same fire station in London. They had watched together through many long uneventful nights; in watery exercises they had put out many imaginary fires together; then, when the raids started, they had worked the trailer pump side by side against real flames. And looking back on those strange times, the sleeplessness, the boring darts, the yellow warnings, the beer, the wet cold recalcitrant hose, the danger, the sweat, the dirt, the crackling, the bodies, Humphrey found that the only memory which was wholly unpleasant was that of the companionship of Jack Daniels. The fellow was a real bounder, a thief, a cheat, a cadge, a coward, a shirker, a mischief maker with a facetious manner and a serpent's tongue. There was nobody on the station who would not have corroborated this description of him. Altogether a most unpleasant type.

A distressing incident came to his mind. One of the first nights of the raids the squad had just fallen in, preparatory to action. Diagonally across the noise of the barrage there came a whizzing sound.

'O Lord God Omnipotent,' Humphrey murmured his temperate prayer, 'I promise not to forget any consideration You may care to show.'

The bomb crashed not far off. At that moment Humphrey suddenly felt his legs turn to water. It was as though they were not there. He clutched his neighbour, who happened to be Daniels, to stop himself from falling. His legs seemed to dangle. They might have been string. Clinging to Daniels, he tried to stand. But it was no good, his feet would not press the ground. Daniels led him over to a chair where he had the humiliation of watching the party leave the station without him. His disability only lasted about ten minutes. The strength came back into his legs as suddenly as it had left them and he ran out after the others. He was never again attacked in this way, though once or twice he felt the weakness might come on. The next day that they were on duty Daniels greeted him with 'Hullo, Wobbly!' Humphrey decided not to hear; but when later he overheard Daniels say to one of the others 'Ask Wobbly,' he walked over and said to Daniels.

'I advise you not to use that word again.'

Daniels did not use it again.

Ugh! A most unpleasant fellow. Humphrey was about to expatiate to Michael on the unpleasantness of father Daniels, but refrained. It would not be fair on the Daniels boy, even if he was a beast, to tell tales about his father to another boy.

'Well, Michael,' he said, 'what are you going to do with me this afternoon?'

As they approached the school buildings, their steps had for some reason become slower and slower. Michael now stopped on the pavement. Humphrey had expected a strenuous afternoon's sight-seeing.

First of all he would go and see Mr Bashford. Michael's housemaster, and have a quarter of an hour's talk with him. Then he would be taken to see Michael's classroom, and his seat in chapel and his peg in the changing room and his dormitory. They would see how his name was getting on over his bed. There was a tradition that the new boys should carve their names on the ancient panelled wall behind the bed they slept in their first term. For several generations people had said, 'The names will soon have reached the ceiling and what will happen then?' But there always seemed to be plenty of room. Michael wrote home that he was carving his name in a rather special way and it would probably take him most of the term to do, as there was not much spare time, also it was tiring to work at it standing on the bed and stretching up to the empty space he had chosen. His letters always mentioned the progress of his handiwork, which he was longing to show to his parents. After seeing and admiring this, Humphrey and Michael would then go and look at the name above a neighbouring bed, which Humphrey himself had carved just thirty-three years ago.

Then they would go and see where Michael sat in the hall, then they would look into the Junior Library. If the boys had not already gone out to games, there would be several of them in there. When Humphrey came in, they would stop talking and stand up. Michael would introduce him awkwardly to some of his particular friends and ask them to come out to tea in the town. With a few happy jests Humphrey would put them all at their ease. The boys would laugh loudly and say 'Thanks awfully, sir,' 'Rather!' and 'I say!' Then Humphrey and Michael would stroll out to the football fields. This Saturday afternoon the house was playing a match. In his letter of last Sunday Michael had said they simply must watch this match. It was going to be so exciting.

When, therefore, Michael said 'Let's go for a walk by the river,' Humphrey was astonished.

'But the school? Shan't we go and see the school now, and the match?'

Michael looked at his feet.

'The match has been put off,' he said at length.

'Oh what a pity! But I want to see your name, and chapel and everything.'

'Let's look at them later. Let's go for a walk first.'

Very well, then. The day was Michael's day out. But Humphrey was much surprised. In the first place, who ever heard of a boy wanting to go for a walk, simply for the sake of going for a walk? And then, this sheering away from the school was the last thing one would have expected from Michael's letters. His last Sunday's letter had been bubbling with excitement at the prospect of his parents' visit; of showing them how and where he slept and worked and ate and played and prayed, of pointing out everything to them and everybody. And now his only wish seemed to be to go for a walk by the river. Well, so be it. But Humphrey was disappointed, as he had been looking forward to strolling around the old place.

They turned into an alley that led off the High Street. Then Humphrey remembered.

'But old Bashford—I must see him. I've got an appointment. Come on, we'd better go now.'

Humphrey took charge and they turned back. Soon they were among the school buildings and a throng of boys in coloured caps. The boys in their path moved aside politely and took off their caps. Very good manners, thought Humphrey. A very pleasant atmosphere. What a pleasant change from London. They went under an arch into a quadrangle in the far corner of which was Mr Bashford's front door. Humphrey looked around him giving names to the windows—That's the Senior Library, and that's the Upper Dormitory, and that used to be Mr So-and-so's classroom, and that used to be called the Little Boot Room. Is it still so called? A long low window on the left was the Junior Library. As they passed it, a boy's face appeared and looked at them. Suddenly six or seven faces bobbed up and had a look then disappeared. Humphrey smiled pleasantly at the faces. 'Who were they all?' he asked. 'Tell me their names.'

But Michael had not noticed them. He had been looking the other way.

They came to Mr Bashford's door and rang the bell. While his father interviewed the housemaster, Michael waited in the hall. Mr Bashford was a somewhat stolid and slow-moving person. He gave his report in deliberate, pondered, words. It appeared that Michael was making satisfactory progress. If only he could get a little more power behind his kick, he should make a first-rate back. The same was true of his fives, it was only power that was needed, but that would come as he grew up and filled out. His work was decently average, and the music master reported well of his progress.

'A subject,' Mr Bashford smiled, 'on which I cannot pretend to have an opinion.'

'Well, thank you, Bashford,' said Humphrey. 'I think you have told me all I wanted to hear. So I can tell his mother that he's getting along nicely?'

'You can. I believe the boy is popular. I think you can safely tell his mother that Michael can stand on his own legs. Yes, he has definitely found his feet.'

'Thank you. I am glad to hear it. Well, I won't keep you any longer.' Humphrey got up.

'Good-bye,' said Mr Bashford. 'No doubt we shall meet again this afternoon watching the match.'

'Match?'

'Yes, hasn't Michael told you yet? He must have. We are playing Squirrel's. It should be a good match.'

'Yes, of course. Then I shall see you later. Good-bye.'

'Good-bye.'

Humphrey chuckled to himself. So he had caught Michael out in a lie. How should he bring it home to him? But why should Michael want to lie? What could his reasons be for wanting to avoid the football match? Perhaps they would come out during the afternoon. Perhaps not. A direct question, Humphrey felt, would be likely to make them only harder to extricate. They must be left to come out of their own accord, and, if they did not come out, it did not matter. Determined to be the best of fathers, he felt that all that did matter in this connection was that the boy must learn to lie better. As to the football match, if Michael was so keen to keep away from it, well, of course, they would go for a walk by the river.

They left the quadrangle by a passage that led out between high walls and was presently covered in by ancient building. Humphrey, before passing under the latter, looked up at the old brick face of a house, warm and ripe and rosy in the afternoon sun, a stone mullioned window, a window box with some yellow chrysanthemums, behind the flowers a boy's face. Charming, he thought. What a delightful place it is! No wonder foreigners are impressed.

The passage narrowed as they passed into the darkness and they could no longer walk abreast. Humphrey went in front. As he came out at the far end two boys pounced upon him with a cry.

'Oh, I beg your pardon, sir,' said one of them. 'I am awfully sorry, sir. We thought it was going to be a boy.'

The apology, thought Humphrey, was a little too ready. Indeed, it must fairly often not be a boy! And did he detect a slightly cheeky expression in the youngster's face, as though he was quite pleased it had not been a boy? But, of course, the episode was one to be taken in good part. Humphrey laughed.

'Why, you quite made me jump! You must be careful or you will be giving some old gentleman a heart attack.'

'I'm awfully sorry, sir.'

Humphrey laughed again and moved on.

'I'm awfully sorry, Smithers,' the boy said to Michael and

disappeared with his companion down the passage.

'A friend of yours?' said Humphrey. 'What's his name?'

'That's Daniels.'

Ah, Humphrey refrained from saying aloud, that accounts for the dishonest expression.

They walked past the end of the five courts and across the empty parade ground and into the fields, and soon were on the tow path following the river away from town and school. The November afternoon was warm and sunny. The trees, resplendent in their autumn colouring and unruffled by any breath of wind, had a look of timeless fixity and grandeur. The beeches of the famous avenue, the magisterial elms that stood about on the playing fields, supervising the little victims with a scholarly detachment, the willows that wept by the water's edge, all, on this still afternoon, were indeed worthy of whatever beauty might find its way into the Latin odes, written this term by the sixth form in their honour. It was very pleasant walking by the river. Humphrey began to be glad they had come. And all the while he kept the talk going, though this was not easy. He laughed and chatted and told reminiscences of his own schooldays. He dropped questions in an offhand way, he tried to pump his boy. But Michael had drawn into himself with a vengeance. Humphrey could extract only the most perfunctory information about his feelings. Did he enjoy school? Yes, of course, was the simple answer, as though Humphrey had asked a silly question. The father remembered that boys do not care to express their feelings and did not again touch directly upon the question of Michael's happiness.

This walk that he was being taken along the river bank—was its purpose a purely negative one, to avoid the school? Was Michael perhaps afraid that he might be ashamed of the appearance of his parent? No, surely that could not be the case. For Humphrey, with such a possibility in mind, had given particular thought to his looks that day. He had dressed in the most carefully non-committal manner. His clothes could not have been described either as smart or slovenly, loud or quiet, towny or countrified, rich or poor. His hair was neither too short nor too long. His hat gave away nothing. You could not possibly have said what his profession was. A more unemphatic exterior could hardly have been achieved. Yet—and here Humphrey flattered himself that there was a touch of genius—he somehow contrived not to look prim and mousy. On the contrary, there was an unmistakable air of quiet and effortless distinction such as one might expect to find in dukes and persons of supreme eminence. Surely it could not be any feeling of shame for his father that caused Michael to lead him away from the sight of the other boys? No, there must be some other reason which might or might not find its way out through the intricacies of the boy's mind. Curious, twisted, unenviable creatures, boys!

'Should we go to the Knoll?' said Michael with sudden enthusiasm.

'All right. Then we'd better step out.'

The Knoll was a grassy mound near the river, the favourite terminus of a Sunday afternoon's walk from the school. So far as Humphrey remembered, it was quite a long way to the Knoll if you followed the curves of the river. They strode forward, passing a master's wife with a perambulator. A fisherman was baiting his line. The heads of a few other solitary fishermen could be seen in the flat fields in front of them. A man on a bicycle was approaching along the towpath, with a dog running beside him. Far ahead a wooden bridge stood up over the river on one side of a red house; on the other could be distinguished the arms of lock gates, and beyond them a low green hump which was the Knoll. Across the fields, in a clump of trees, was the squat spire of Woodridge church. Could it be, Humphrey wondered as Michael led him forward with a perceptible lightening of spirit, could it be that this walk had no evasive purpose but signified an incipient love of solitude, of nature? Was this perhaps an early Shelley phase? He gently probed; but there was no response. Of course, of course—he was losing touch—the boy was only thirteen, years too young even for Shelley.

'Poor Shelley, he went to school at Eton,' Humphrey continued, and told the familiar anecdotes. 'There was a lot of bullying there in those days. When the boys could think of nothing better to do, they had what they called "Shelley hunts."' But Humphrey was not able to awake Michael's interest even in Shelley's schooldays.

How young the boy was now became apparent. He began to behave like a dog that is being taken for a walk. For a while he would remain at his father's side, then he would break away and go down to the water's edge and throw in a stone or a clod of earth, or run into the middle of a field where he thought he saw a mushroom. He pursued a ditch some way out from the river, confident that he had seen an otter disappear into it. He got left far behind. He ran on far in front. At length, as they approached the lock he rejoined his father and suddenly became entirely himself. Suddenly there was a joke, the simplest of jokes. He began to walk in step with Humphrey, but Humphrey would not have it and moved out of step. Each time that Michael got in step, Humphrey jumped out again. Then Humphrey allowed it to seem that he was no longer playing and walked along in step unconcernedly only to slip out again on the sly. Michael enjoyed the game enormously and laughed and shouted. Then, as they were walking along in step,

Humphrey stopped abruptly, balancing himself on one leg. Michael, on the alert, was just able to stop himself too and balance without falling.

'You're wobbling!' said Humphrey.

Michael, without a word, made no further effort to balance on one leg, but began to walk on in a normal manner. The game, Humphrey realised, was over as suddenly as it had begun. Just like a dog, the boy!

'I think I'll run on,' said Michael, who had presently crossed over the lock and the island and was to be seen on the bridge above the weir. Here Humphrey joined him and they gazed for a while at the rushing water.

'Now let's go up the Knoll.'

This strange hummock of earth, that rose almost from the river bank to a height of some fifty or sixty feet, was obviously not a natural feature. The purpose and date of its elevation were matters that divided archaeologists into many camps, the extremists on one side ascribing it to palaeolithic man and those on the other to the period of the Napoleonic Wars, in which it was to have been a defence against French invasion. Whatever its origin, it now served no purpose except as a resting place, with a view over the flat fields, for those who cared to walk so far. A path led in a gentle spiral to the top, where an enlightened county council had placed a wooden bench.

When Humphrey reached the top by the path, Michael, who had clambered straight up the steep side of the mound, had also run straight down again and was crouching on the bank of the lock gazing into the water. Humphrey sat on the bench and looked around him. A woman was standing at the door of the lock-keeper's house on the island talking to a child in the garden. There was no one else about. His eye followed the river through the fields back to the red roofs of the town. A train was puffing out from the station across the iron bridge over the river, its rumble still reaching Humphrey some time after it had crossed the bridge. At the other end of the little town, there were glimpses, through and above the golden trees, of the venerable brick buildings of the school that seemed to lean against the stone perpendicular tower of the chapel. Under the trees there were tiny figures moving on the football fields. From the distance confused and muffled sounds came to Humphrey, among which he distinguished a sudden noise of cheering. Someone must have shot a goal.

Thank God, he said to himself, thank God I am not a boy! For he was not one of those people who are sentimental about their schooldays. He never for a moment wished he might live through them again. Not that he had been unhappy. He had been as happy as a boy can be. But happiness, he held, consists mainly in the sensation of growth, in climbing up out of one state into the next. The reverse process is unhappiness. Yet how many people seem to wish for vanished youth! A pathetic state of mind, in Humphrey's opinion. You climb up out of the teens into the twenties, the thirties, the forties, then still climbing no doubt, the fifties, sixties, seventies, and at last you climb right up and out of the whole business. How well life is arranged!

Michael was now lying on the bridge over the weir looking down at the water through the crack between two boards. Poor boy! But at least, for all the moodiness which the father had this afternoon observed to be overtaking his son, the boy could have no realisation what a capricious, a spasmodic thing is the happiness of boyhood. An affair of spasms. In the twenties too, what is it but a matter of spasms? And the thirties? What a lot indeed has to happen before there is a steady vibration, a continuous and unmuffled note. Humphrey looked at the body of his boy with love and compassion, but without a trace of envy.

What then is the rôle of a father? Simply to be there, in full view, an enormously stable object, an example of solid growth, like a great tree, increasing each year in height and majesty, adding each year a circle to its girth, to those circles which no younger growth can possibly overtake. He must always be a full thirty-three years older than his son. In this arboreal rôle Humphrey believed himself to be doing well. In fact, as he sat on the Knoll, surveying his life and life in general, his reflections were as serene and sage as the tranquil autumn afternoon. He enjoyed some moments of exquisite complacency. Then he looked at his watch. If they were to see anything of the school before tea, it was time they started back. He came down from the Knoll.

But Michael could not easily be persuaded to leave the weir, and when at last Humphrey had him on the path homeward, he dawdled and dragged. The talk, too, dragged. The moment of exuberance had passed. When they were back, it was almost dark, and too late for sight-seeing, so they went straight to one of the two teashops in the town. As their tea came to an end, Humphrey was quite ready for the afternoon out also to come to an end. The company of the young suddenly becomes more boring than one can bear. There is something relentless about their very presence. Perhaps those enormous school fees are not a thing to grumble about after all.

They walked back to the school, where, at the entrance to the quadrangle, Humphrey said good-bye.

'Good-bye, pops, it's been lovely having you!' said Michael with a sudden warmth, and disappeared. It was as though Michael were suddenly the grown-up, who had looked down out of his adult abstraction and pressed half-a-crown into the hand of Humphrey, the boy. The latter was touched. These last words told him, in effect, that the afternoon out had been an unqualified success. He strolled away, feeling that he could give a perfectly happy report about Michael to the boy's mother. He would not perhaps tell her of his access of boredom in the teashop.

Now that he was alone something made him unwilling to walk straight to the station. He felt a desire to linger and turned back into the quadrangle. It was quite dark now. There were lights in some of the windows, but the chapel was a black mass. Humphrey stood still a while in the darkness. The atmosphere of the old place had an agreeable poignancy for him, though he could not have said that it carried many precise recollections. Like the air on the first day of spring or of autumn, it was laden with memories that seemed to have merged simply into imageless memory. Yet in this very imprecision there was freedom and life. The generous past gave you of its essence, then let you go.

There was a chink of light in the curtains in Junior Library. Michael would now be doing his prep in there. Humphrey went over and peeped in. He was not able to see much, but there were two boys immediately in front of him, sitting at a table. He recognised one of the boys as Daniels. They seemed to be shouting or singing something in rhythm. Humphrey caught the words.

'Smithers' father's wobbly! Smithers' father's a bomb-funk! Smithers' father's a wobbly bomb-funk!'

Suddenly the boys ducked. A missile passed over them. Then they looked up, and the chant continued.

'Smithers' father's a wobbly bomb-funk! Smithers' father's a . . .'

As Humphrey watched and listened, he experienced a sensation in his legs that he had not known since 1940. Indeed, if he had not held on to the window frame, he might have fallen.

Heads or Tails?

The Rev. James Bellairs was not good at making up his mind, but there was one subject about which he was quite certain—those pilasters. 'The place might be a hospital,' he said. And Candle church was worthy of better treatment. Architecturally it was indeed something out of the ordinary. Was there another classical church in the diocese? When Candle hall had been rebuilt in the middle of the eighteenth century and the brick wall of the huge kitchen garden had been extended to the edge of the churchyard, it had seemed to Sir George Gascoigne that the job would not be finished until his private chapel and the mausoleum of his family, otherwise Candle parish church, was also rebuilt in a style worthy of the age. Hence the roundheaded windows, the cornice, the stone swags, and, on each side of the chancel arch, a pilaster with a Corinthian capital. Mr Bellairs' predecessor, Mr Dewhurst, had had these pilasters painted a laurel green in shiny enamel paint.

The Dewhursts—and Mrs Dewhurst had been the moving spirit in these matters—had been people of taste; in Mr Bellairs' opinion, execrable taste. They had felt it bad luck, when there were so many fine churches around them in which you breathed the genuine intimate religious atmosphere of the Middle Ages, that they should have been landed with this chilly secular monstrosity. They, Mrs Dewhurst that is, had set about making it more tolerable. A liberal coating of the green paint on any surface that would take it was a great improvement and already gave a feeling of warmth. But there were some features that would not take paint. What was to be done with those two ghastly marble tombs in the sanctuary? There they lay, recumbent on their elbows like Romans at a feast, the father and the uncle of Sir George Gascoigne, with their bursting stomachs and their full-bottomed wigs, gross, complacent and carnal, on either side of the altar. The virtues of Sir Eustace Gascoigne and Frederick Gascoigne, esquire, J.P., were catalogued beneath them on wavy scrolls unfolded by podgy cherubs. Surely nobody had ever appeared at heaven's gate with such decisive credentials? 'Keep the change,' one can hear them saying as St Peter looks incredulously at the absurdly excessive entrance fee they have put into his hand. From the east window a kindly but unimpressive God the Father looked down over a cloud. He also was evidently a Gascoigne, but not an important one, a younger brother no doubt who had gone into the church. He had had a drink with his dinner, but thereafter the decanter only passed between the elder brothers. So small was the church that you felt their fingers would touch as they stretched over towards each other across the altar.

'I can almost feel them breathing on me when I am officiating,' Mr Dewhurst had said.

The only thing to do with these atrocities, in Mrs Dewhurst's opinion, was to hide them from view. (Luckily there were no living Gascoignes to bother about. They had left the place years ago and the hall had been pulled down.) It was found that a brass curtain rail could be clamped across the top of each of the monuments. Mrs Dewhurst herself made the curtains. They were of a fluffy woollen material, coloured magenta, on which she had embroidered the 'lilies of the field' in various bright wools. The herbaceous border in the vicarage garden had been the model for this gay frieze. Along the top, with the heads of delphiniums and hollyhocks coming up between the letters, were written, in angular Gothic characters, on one curtain 'They toil not,' and on the other 'Neither do they spin.'

Embroidery was not the only craft which Mrs Dewhurst practised. She worked artistically in brass, leather and cork. Also she was a painter. She had converted the Gascoigne box pew into a children's corner and on the wall above hung two of her canvases depicting, with a wealth of sentiment, imaginary episodes in the childhood of Our Lord.

Both Mrs Dewhurst's curtains and her pictures were popular with the parishioners. But the new vicar, though he expressed no criticism of the works themselves, had an irresistible desire to see what the church would look like without them. He had the curtains taken down and 'sent away to be cleaned.' There they stayed. The two Falstaffs were exposed from behind the arras, breathing heavily. The mottoes, thought Mr Bellairs, might have remained. They toil not . . .

As to the pictures, he pointed out to the churchwardens and the schoolmistress that the children would actually see more of them if they were moved into the school. How about trying it for a while as an experiment? Mr Bellairs then turned his attention to the green paint. He decided to do the repainting himself. Why not? He liked painting. But meeting a parishioner one morning, who looked surprised to see his vicar carrying a ladder and a tin of paint along the churchyard path, he felt that some explanation was needed. 'Six days shalt thou labour,' he said with a cheerful smile. Was that what he had meant to say, he asked himself as he passed the man. The toiling rustic already knew the force of the precept, whereas it was he, Mr Bellairs, who awoke six days a week in this little village and said to himself 'Now what shall I do to-day?' Well, no matter.

So there he was, half-way up the ladder painting a pilaster. He was painting it cream and intended to pick out the foliage of the capital with gold. Being alone in the church, or rather, alone with his Maker in the church—for, as he had said in his sermon last Sunday, there is no such thing as being alone—he was able to whistle at his work without causing any offence. For he did not have to stand on ceremony with his Maker. They were on the best of terms.

Suddenly one of those thoughts came into his head which make us feel surrounded by supernatural beings trying to attract our attention as they have something interesting to tell us. One of these beings caught Mr Bellairs' eye and said 'Go and look in the question box.' The 'question box' was a little oak receptacle which Mr Bellairs had had fitted next to the offertory box near the west door. In it he had asked that his parishioners should drop on a slip of paper any questions of a religious nature that might perplex them and he would try to answer them in a sermon. The idea was entirely his own. Being himself of a disputatious turn of mind, he had looked forward to the exchange of a lively bombardment between himself and his parishioners. The results had been disappointing. He had been at Candle now nearly two years and there had been only two questions. They had both, in Mr Bellairs' opinion, been uninteresting, if thorny. One was 'Are we the Lost Tribes?' the other 'Who were the parents of Cain's wife?' These tiresome questions had come in the first week. There had been no others. He had given up looking in the box. It had of course been a mistake to hope for much of a response from his simple rustic flock. 'Because you had a double first, you must not expect us all to be brainy,' his bishop had once said to him, charmingly associating himself with the brainless. That was dear old Horrocks, by the way, not this new man . . .

Coming down the ladder Mr Bellairs went to the question box. There, sure enough, was an untidy bit of paper on which was written in the hand of one evidently not accustomed to the use of a pen, 'Who was the better man, Jacob or Esau?' A good one? The vicar's first feeling was that this again was an uninteresting question. They were just trying to catch him out. Well, the first thing to do was to refresh his memory. He went to the lectern and opened the Bible in the middle of Genesis. Potiphar's wife, Tamar deceiveth Judah, Onan, Dinah ravished by Shechem—he was too far and turned back, too far back—circumcision instituted, Sodom and Gomorrah, Lot's incest,

Abraham denieth his wife—really, one forgets what an unsuitable book the Bible is to be left where all may read, nearly as unsuitable as that other book which is confidently put into the hands of the young, the *Works of Shakespeare*.

Here we are—Isaac prayeth for Rebekah being barren, the children strive in her womb, birth of Esau and Jacob. 'And Jacob sod pottage: and Esau came from the field, and he was faint.' Mr Bellairs read the two stories, how Esau sold his birthright for a pottage of lentils, and how Jacob stole their father's blessing, and how Esau forgave his younger brother both these ugly tricks. 'And Esau ran to meet him, and embraced him, and fell on his neck and kissed him: and they wept.' There is something grand and magnanimous about Esau. In his indifference to his own welfare, his unsuspiciousness, his sportsmanship, he stands out among these Levantines. If it were not for the emotional quality of that reconciliation, you might almost suppose him one of us, almost English.

Jacob or Esau? Esau, every time, cries the heart. Which, of course, is wrong, Mr Bellairs heard himself telling his congregation. Esau may appear the more charming character, but just to be charming is not enough. The important thing is to be on the right side. It is not even enough to love God. The important thing is that God should love you. For he does not love all equally. He does not distribute his blessing on all. 'Hast thou but one blessing, my father?' Yes. 'Bless me, even me also, O my father.' No. If you are too late, you are too late. You have been outwitted. You should trust no one, not even your brother. Hold tight on to what you have. To him that hath shall be given. If you start letting go, you will lose everything. Nothing succeeds like success. At least, it seems so. But the argument stuck in Mr Bellairs' throat. For he was not a success, and he knew it. And all because he could not make up his mind.

The defect dated from his birth. He simply was not born either a little Liberal or else a little Conservative. He was born with an open mind. He kept an open house for ideas and opinions. None had the least difficulty in entering—or in slipping out again. Which had served him very well at school and the university. The teachers had never had such a responsive pupil or one who played up to them with such delightful bravado. 'It does not matter which side you take in your essays,' old Fletcher, the history tutor, had said. 'The examiner does not mind in the least whether you are a Cavalier or a Roundhead. What he does mind is that you should present your case clearly and as though you believed in it.' What fun they used to have, Bellairs and his friends, the other bright boys! The things they could appear to believe in! They knew all about making the worse appear the better cause and the ablest of them all, abler even than Reeves or Buckley, was Bellairs. It amused him sometimes to keep not only the master but himself guessing what side he was taking. For with skill one could refrain from showing one's hand till an essay was at least half-way through. He played this game in the Economic History paper in his finals. Not until almost the last paragraph did he come down with a sudden, unexpected, decisive, swoop on the side of Free Trade. The examiner was fascinated and a word he did not often use came to his lips. 'Beautiful!' he murmured, giving the essay full marks, 'beautiful!'

The educational period over, the boys stood together looking at the battle of life. At what exact moment his friends left his side Mr Bellairs could not have said, but there presently he saw their heads bobbing up in the mêlée. They had been quick to show that they could take sides, assume responsibilities, champion causes, lead their fellow-men, and make careers for themselves which would bring them, while they were still on the right side of forty-five, to positions of distinction, Barker to be an Under-Secretary, Buckley an Archdeacon, Reeves a knight. How did they manage it? How did they make the decisions? How, Mr Bellairs asked himself, did they know that their decisions were going to be the right ones? For, of course, the decisions now had to be the right ones. It was no longer a case of 'It does not matter which side you take.' For the actual well-being of living people was now involved. They did not surely toss a coin in the old manner, and enter the fray for the fun of the thing? Sir Roderick Reeves for the fun of the thing? It could not be.

When your contemporaries begin to receive knighthoods, it is time to take stock of your own achievements, and Mr Bellairs, that brilliant all-rounder, at forty-four was the vicar of tiny far-off Candle. James Bellairs, you are a disappointment. So, every now and then, when he could remember, he would remind himself that he was a failure. So one says to a child 'You may be feeling perfectly well, but remember, you *have* got German measles.' For he did not feel ill. His malady was neither painful, nor was it new. For he had not changed. It was they who had changed. They had become public while he remained private, utterly, incorrigibly, blissfully, private. (Was Christ public or private? A good question.)

He was back on the ladder painting. How good the paint smelled. I wonder, he asked himself, do middle-aged men leaning against the chimneypiece in London clubs say 'Of course that was Bellairs' year. Bellairs was stroke that year' or 'Do you remember that night Jimmy Bellairs climbed into *Jesus?*'

Jacob or Esau, now which was it to be? The question was certainly not one with an easy ready-made answer. Even a less flexible mind than his own would have to give it some thought. Flexible, flexible—inflexible—how did the words go, on that Gascoigne monument? 'Inflexible to himself——' What was after that? He came down the ladder and went up into the chancel to read the scroll beneath Frederick Gascoigne, esquire, J.P. About half-way down—yes—'Merciful to others, inflexible only towards himself, amiable to his equals, indulgent to his inferiors——' from there he had it pat. Presumably it was George Gascoigne who had composed these decent eulogies to his father and uncle. I wonder, thought Mr Bellairs, what sort of a scroll Bob will write for me, when my time comes? He chuckled at the thought. It was strange how little anxiety that incredible moment caused him as it came steadily nearer. Perhaps, he sometimes told himself, reprehensibly little, for one in his position.

He returned to the ladder. Esau or Jacob? The more one thought of it, the more there was to it. In fact, it was a rattling good question. Who could have asked it? The writing was the writing of Esau, but the wording was the wording of Jacob. There was something about that expression 'the better man' which did not seem quite to belong to the child or the unlettered countryman who seemed to have penned the question. But who could it be?

'Hullo, Bob!'

His son had come silently into the church and was standing at the foot of the ladder.

'It's tea-time, father. We are having it on the lawn.'

Bob was just seventeen.

'Tea already! I've hardly done anything this afternoon.'

Mr Bellairs came down the ladder.

'Look at that.'

He took the paper with the question out of his pocket and showed it to Bob, who looked at it as for the first time.

'A good question,' said the boy.

'Yes. Which side would you take?'

'Jacob,' said Bob, to Mr Bellairs', and, it must be admitted, to Bob's own, surprise.

Mr Bellairs answered with a defence of Esau. They strolled out of the church and back along the churchyard path arguing, and throughout tea Bob made the best case he could for the 'Jacob type' against the 'Esau type,' though he felt that he would have been even more fluent on the other side. Mrs Bellairs watched and listened. He will be just like his father, she said to herself with love and pride.

The Voices

The noise of the voices on the lawn seemed to come from some pounding piece of machinery, a noise that, though fixed to one place, was all movement within itself, powerful, continuous, relentless. It was a familiar noise to the servants and the children, for it was there every Saturday and Sunday radiating from the chairs under the beech tree. They were aware of it all the time, whether their duties and their games took them to attic or cellar or to the far end of the kitchen garden. They kept as far away as they could from the monster, but if they had to come near they felt they were approaching an enormous revolving wheel.

The noise for the most part was an even one, but occasionally there would be some shrill or deep explosion. The machine would rattle or gurgle for a few moments, then resume its steady metallic whirr. One thing the machine never did. It never stopped. From the moment of their arrival until they rose to dress for dinner on Sunday evening, the guests, except at meal- and bed-times, would be in continuous session there on the lawn. During luncheon a footman would come out and set the chairs straight and pat the cushions and empty the ash trays, while the children, when they had finished their dinner in the nursery, would come running down to take possession of the site. They would sit in the chairs and pretend to be grown up. They would imitate Mr Winthrop's laugh. Tits would appear in the tree and blackbirds on the lawn. A moorhen, emboldened by the hush, would venture up from the lake on to the grass. But the machine had not stopped. It had merely been moved indoors. The vibrant sounds which came from the open windows of the dining-room were an indication of the clatter which the monster must be making in confinement.

Presently the interval of peace on the lawn would be over. The party—it generally consisted of twelve or fifteen people—would stroll out again, replete and vinous, to drink its coffee under the beech tree and there it would stay for the rest of the day. There was never any suggestion of a walk, so long at least as it was warm enough to go on sitting. The apparatus of croquet was laid out in a corner of the lawn but, like a bottle of Vichy water on a well-stocked tray of drinks, it served only as a reminder that there are people who have a use for such things, and was left politely untouched.

Rather a dull programme for the week-end? No, anything but dull. The Sunday afternoon conversation on Lady Swanley's lawn was probably more brilliant than that on any lawn in the country. Her company was as good as could be found. Politics and public life, literature, the arts, the stage, the law, the universities—even for a short period Lady Swanley had trawled in ecclesiastical waters. She trawled assiduously and with a wide net; but its mesh was large. It was intended to hold only the bigger fish and rarely indeed did Lady Swanley lift unworthiness to the surface. Jack Wilson was one of her few mistakes.

On just such a Sunday afternoon the vibration of the voices was striking the tall garden front of the house. It spent itself against the solid Queen Anne brickwork, but penetrated through open door and window. It came into Jack Wilson's bedroom, whither he had fled for some moments' respite, and reverberated round the walls. He was sitting uncomfortably in the middle of the room in an upright armchair. It was a rotten sort of chair in his opinion, but it was the best there was. It was covered in gold silk and, like all the furniture in the room, in fact in the whole house, it made you feel guilty if you even touched it. That elegant four-poster bed—he would have liked to lie on that for a little but how could one dream of disturbing such a lovely counterpane? He would never be able to get it straight again; and a servant might come in and find him lying on it, which would be terrible. They were always coming in, or lurking in the passage observing you; another of the discomforts of this supremely uneasy week-end.

He was not a man of taste but he believed the furniture and decoration of the room to be Regency. He hated it. There was no relaxation about it. There was nowhere to put your feet up. And what he particularly disliked was that it was all of a piece. It was all, obviously, perfect of its kind. Lady Swanley must have said 'Let there be Regency. Money is no object.' How different this from the kind of room in which Jack Wilson felt at ease, a room, that is to say, which was designed for masculine comfort and had acquired its welcoming character through having been lived in, a room of deep leather armchairs and sofas with some stuffing showing at the seams, of tables that would carry weights and had the kind of surface on which things can be put down with a good conscience, a room with a large Turkey carpet reassuringly frayed in front of the fire and at places where castors had come off. There would be lots of things lying about and the sides of the fireplace would show bootmarks. But here, where everything was just so—the fact was the house was a woman's house from top to bottom. Sir Eric had certainly given her her head over the house. Indeed, over most things it seemed; yet there could be no doubt, when you saw them together, that he was the one who held the reins. At this point Jack Wilson felt his reflections to be approaching a subject which they generally reached sooner or later, his own wretched marriage. Giving his lame leg a heave, he took a new position in the chair.

He was well aware of the philistinism of his ideas about interior decoration. He must take these ideas in hand. And the first thing was to learn about the subject. There must be some little illustrated book about furniture from which he could catch up. The trouble was there were so many things to catch up with. During the last twenty-four hours there had been a score of subjects about which he had planned to buy a little book. For he would have given anything to be able to hold his own among those voices out there.

Why had Lady Swanley ever asked him to stay? Well, he knew why. His was a kind of excellence she had probably never had under her beech tree and she had determined to give it a try. How could she have made such a mistake? And how could he have made the mistake of accepting? They had only met each other twice. The first time had been at a Garden Party. Another uncomfortable affair that had been, in those awkward togs from Moss Bros, under that scorching sun on the lawns among all those unknown faces. Then he had run into Bobbie Fisher and they had had a good chat about old times.

'Home James?' said Jack Wilson at length.

'Yes rather, I'm ready. One doesn't say good-bye here, does one?'

'No, I don't think so.'

'Well, you ought to know. You're an *habitué*.'

Jack limped along beside Bobbie Fisher through the crowd towards the Palace.

'Just a minute,' said Bobbie, greeting a man who was standing on the edge of a group of people paying court to—was it the Queen?—no, some other royalty perhaps—anyhow a *petite* figure with a large sky-blue hat.

'Wait,' said Bobbie, 'I'll join you in a minute,' and he went to have a word with his friend.

Jack Wilson limped on a few paces and waited. Presently he looked over his shoulder and saw that the group Bobbie had joined had turned to look at him. Evidently they were talking about him. As he looked, they moved towards him and suddenly he was alone with the pretty lady in the blue hat. Her hair was white, perhaps prematurely, her eyes as blue as her hat and dancing with humour and intelligence. She looked up at him with all her attention, taking him in. He did not remember afterwards what they had talked about but he simply had the impression that she had come very near; not just physically but with her whole being. It was her way thus to focus on people and the larger the crowd the more could she make you feel alone with her. Then, if it could be done, she would pluck out the heart of your mystery; an operation which most people found painless, for Beryl Swanley was indeed an enchanting person. Jack Wilson, who was used to curiosity, had never before felt himself caught in so many bright beams of scrutiny. Apparently he did not make so bad an impression, for as they parted she said: 'I hope we may meet again.'

They met again at a theatre about a week later, at *Othello*. By an odd chance Jack Wilson knew this play almost by heart. An eccentric headmaster at his public school had introduced the learning, and writing out, of pieces of Shakespeare as the regular form of school punishment, so many lines according to the offence. The idea may have been an enlightened one but it was unimaginatively applied. There was no selection of passages to be learned. The boy simply took a play and worked his way through it. If the particular number of lines he had to learn—fifty say, for smoking in the fives courts—ended in the middle of a phrase, the offender was allowed to break rudely away from the hated company of the bard without hearing him to the end of his sentence. And there was no discrimination in the choice of plays. Thus Jack Wilson in his early teens had worked his way through the unsuitable *Othello*. He had hated it at the time; but he sometimes felt now that those buoyant fragments of Shakespeare which still floated in large numbers on the surface of his mind were the only parts of his education that had not gone to the bottom. He now loved *Othello* and would not miss going, probably alone, to any production of it there might be. Thus he met Lady Swanley in the *foyer*.

She was prettier than ever in evening dress, so pink and white and blue. Again he was in doubt whether she was a young old person or an old young person. Again she seemed to come very near. Within a minute they were talking about the profundities of human nature. He admitted to finding Othello a most sympathetic character.

'Yes?' she said encouragingly, taking him in. 'Yes?'

He then took his courage in both hands and quoted Othello's *cri de coeur*.

Oh now, for ever
Farewell the tranquil mind, farewell content,
Farewell the plumed troop and the big wars!

Evidently Lady Swanley was immensely impressed. As they parted, she said, 'I hope you will come down for a week-end some time.' A few days later an invitation came. So here he was. And would to God he had never come!

The first twenty minutes had been enough to convince him of his mistake. He could not possibly keep up with these people, kind though they might be. For he was painfully aware that they were giving him every chance. He had no sort of complaint against them for being snooty. They went out of their way to draw him into the party, or to head the conversation in his direction. At least, they did so for a while. But as Saturday afternoon wore on such efforts became fewer and fewer. It had become apparent to all that he had nothing to contribute. The voices passed in front of him or through him. Bright eyes, which had met his with intelligent interest, now met other bright eyes across him. It was as though he was not there. He might have been nothing. He certainly felt himself to be nothing.

What was the source of their brilliance, he asked himself as he watched and listened in awkward fascination? It was not just that they were clever or grand or rich. The knowledge (which they appeared to have) of all literature and of all the best people, and the ability to afford to do interesting things, no doubt helped. But the origin of their sparkle was simpler than that. They just were intensely alive. Their talk came gushing up from their daily lives. That story of Winthrop's about the curate's suitcase which he had opened by a mistake in the train coming down, was clearly only one of a dozen such stories that came to the surface every day of Winthrop's life. How fresh it had been and how immaculately told! Literature and life seemed to become one in Denzil Winthrop. If, Jack Wilson reflected, I had had that experience with the suitcase I would probably never even have thought of making a story out of it. For in the city circles which were his, stories were not expected to be fresh. They generally began 'Do you know that one about the man who . . .?'

After dinner, over the port, Jack Wilson had found himself next to Denzil Winthrop. Turning his back on an interesting conversation that was getting up at the end of the table, the man of letters politely faced about towards Wilson and gave him all his attention. He pumped him upon his own subject and for three or four minutes listened with interest. The laughter and the voices at the end of the table meanwhile were becoming louder and louder. Winthrop's body began to move round towards the table again and his glance to wander, and Wilson read the verdict in his eye 'Not even interesting on his own stuff!' Winthrop let himself be caught in the general conversation.

'Apropos of your suitcase, Denzil,' somebody said on the other side of the table, 'may I tell them, Eric, now that there are no ladies present, about that footman the last time I stayed here?'

No ladies present—ah, thought Jack Wilson, perhaps this is where I come in at last. He felt now a desperate desire to assert himself. Already a little drunk, he took a gulp of brandy.

'That reminds me,' he said as soon as the anecdote was finished, and as he spoke he was conscious of making a most embarrassing blunder, 'do you know the one about the two clerks of Lahore?'

'Er, no,' said his host after a moment.

As Jack Wilson told his little rhyme, it seemed that the flushed alcoholic faces had suddenly turned to marble. The expectant smile, the contained laughter, the appreciative grunt were no longer there to help him to his climax. His vulgar words boomed out in an unnatural hush. A perfunctory titter greeted his performance. That evening he did not risk further speech.

On Sunday morning his sense of loneliness and humiliation was such that he hardly dared to go down and face the company. Think of it, a whole day more of this suffering! At length he pulled himself together and went down, and there they all were, ready to make the best of him, to give him another chance, for Beryl's sake no doubt. Not that his hostess any longer believed in him. He was sure of that. Hers had been the first pair of eyes to give up meeting his.

Denzil Winthrop, of course, had had an adventure during the night.

'I had a bat in my room!'

'Oh, so did I!' said Jack Wilson, suddenly remembering.

'*My* bat,' said Winthrop, 'positively had genius.' And he set out upon an elaborate and infinitely diverting story of his tussle with the bat. By the slightest gestures of his podgy hands he was able to indicate the absurd postures of his absurd great body as he had chased the bat over the chairs, behind the curtains, under the bed—'antics which'—and he looked down sadly at his *bon viveur's* paunch—'do not suit a—a—if you will forgive a joke in the worst possible taste——' and he looked across at Jack Wilson—'a *mutilé de la paix*.' His happy, infectious laugh alone was security for the good taste of anything Denzil Winthrop might say. With irresistible gaiety he then described how the bat had gone over to the offensive. It had pursued him round the room. It had dived down at him. It had lain in ambush and sprung out upon him. At length he had learned cunning, as one does, from the foe. Borrowing vespertilian tactics he had gone and hidden in the cupboard. With his hands Winthrop managed to convey that he had hung himself up, like a bat, in the cupboard, an exquisitely ludicrous picture. Coming out presently he had found his enemy apparently asleep, on the curtain. Emptying the water from his jug, he had caught the bat in it and put a book over the top to keep it in while he pondered its fate. He decided to leave it there till the morning and in the morning he had felt, like Uncle Toby with the fly, 'This world is surely wide enough to hold both thee and me,' and he had dropped the bat out into the honeysuckle.

'And now, *your* bat,' he turned to Jack Wilson as the laughter subsided, 'I'm simply longing to hear about *your* bat!'

Oh, if only I'd kept my mouth shut, thought Wilson.

'Well, I put the light out and opened the window and it went out.'

'Ah! it went out?'

'Yes, almost at once.'

'Ah!'

There was a silence. Jack Wilson had achieved the impossible. He had stopped the machine. But only for a moment. It started up again and gathered speed until its revolutions made a shrill whirr, which was maintained throughout the day and was now tormenting Jack Wilson in his bedroom. I'm only a simple soul, he said to himself. But the words gave him no comfort. For one thing they were not true. It was those people out there who were the simple souls. They had the lucidity of thought and word. By the pressure of their intelligence and character they had achieved simplicity. He was the complicated one, with the confused ambitions, the muddled ideas, the halting speech.

It was time for him to rejoin the party. Come on, Jack! But he did not move. He had shut his eyes and in the blackness the cruel voices had become the friendly sound of bombers. The night sky was full of them. He had been up there himself a few minutes ago, then he had baled out and now he was staggering across a French field towards the sand dunes with Alastair on his back. He had just stumbled into the latter, his rear-gunner, who appeared to have broken his leg landing. It did not seem to Wilson that they stood a chance. There was certain death among the dunes, or, failing that, on the mined beach, or, failing that, in the sea. Death was trebly certain—and never before had he experienced such calm exhilaration. The peace and freedom of it! A thing in a book he had studied at school, Ovid or Virgil or somebody, came to his mind. It had said how the people in Hades leave no footprints. As he came through the dunes and out on to the sands he felt, for all the weight of Alastair, an extraordinary lightness in his tread. He was ready for the moment after the moment which would blow them to smithereens.

The tide was low. Through the darkness he could not see the sea until a searchlight, suddenly sweeping the shore from a point on the dunes some way to the left, showed it to him a long way out. He lay down before the beam reached him. Surely he would be seen? The light passed and went out and he continued his way which was soon obstructed by barbed wire, stakes and various metal obstacles. The air was alive with the noise of the bombers. He seemed to be in a great humming bowl. After a long time he was walking in mud—there was at last no doubt about the solidity of his tread—and presently in water. The sea could hardly have been calmer, but even so what he was about to do now was surely as foolhardy as anything he had ever done. What earthly chance was there of being able to paddle himself and Alastair all the way back to England on one rubber dinghy (Alastair's having got lost)? As soon as it could be floated he blew it up and put Alastair on it and pushed it. His companion was now unconscious. He was quite alone in this adventure, pushing out into the sea towards certain death. So it would be death by drowning after all! Reported to be rather an enjoyable form of the experience . . .

At length he was almost out of his depth. Managing to heave himself up partly on to the dinghy, he began to use the hand paddles and so they set out on their voyage of—was it about a hundred miles across here? That should not take more than a fortnight if they were lucky with the weather. The bombers were no longer going over. For about an hour he paddled in silence. Then they began to come back. Presently as there was the first hint of greyness in the sky he saw a small boat quite near and he was being hailed in English and Alastair was being helped up into the motor-torpedo-boat and he was given a gulp of rum and then was speeding back towards England and safety and his ordinary and uninteresting personality and his wretched marriage.

Another time. He was in a fighter bomber, returning from an offensive patrol. He still carried his bombs. There was not a cloud between himself and the blue sea, twenty-two thousand feet below. Then he noticed his oil gauge.

'Red three to Red Leader. Red three to Red Leader. Oil pressure falling. Going to throttle back and take it easy.'

'Red Leader to Red three. O.K. Good luck to you. Good luck to you.'

He fell behind the wing and began to lose height. It was not far home; he would get home probably, but it might be wiser to jettison his bombs. Then he saw the submarine, lying, a little grey strip, on the surface. He was not in doubt for a moment. Falling all the time he made a great sweep so as to have the sun behind him, and dived. They blazed away at him. He could see it coming up, and again he felt that ecstatic tranquillity of mind as he plunged to certain death. Quite certain this time. No more Jack Wilson. Freedom. Peace.

Bump. Bump. He felt the shock of being hit rather than any pain. But his right hand no longer gripping, he took the stick with his left.

As he let go his bombs he saw the Germans scramble away from the guns and jump into the sea. And then, miracle of miracles, he was pulling out of his dive and levelling off. He could feel his feet wet with blood. To his great surprise he found he was maintaining height. He put the machine into a gentle climb and looking back saw that he had done a good job. Already perhaps three miles behind him, he saw a pool of oil forming on the water where the submarine had been, with tiny figures floating in it. And so home and back to his—Jack Wilson opened his eyes and got up from the chair. Now, Jack, go and face the music!

He went out on to the landing and limped, one step at a time, down the stairs. In the hall he loitered, looking at the pictures. I can't face it, he said to himself, I can't face it. A footman appeared from the back regions with a large silver tray with bread and butter and cakes on it and passed across the hall and out of the front door on his way to the lawn. Though he did not do more than give one expressionless glance at Jack Wilson, the latter felt guilty at being found loitering in the hall and approached his eye to one of the pictures as though he were giving it a most purposeful scrutiny. Below the picture was a table with a telephone on it and beside the telephone was a piece of cardboard on to which had been pasted a list of local telephone numbers. The list was headed by the word TAXI.

Jack Wilson waited for the footman to come back from the lawn through the hall, then he took up the telephone and dialled.

'Is that the taxi place?'

'Yes, sir.'

'I am telephoning from Lady Swanley's. Could you come round and take me to the station?'

'What train do you want to catch, sir?'

'The train to London. Come at once, will you?'

'There isn't no train to London before the 6.40 on Sunday, sir . . .'

'Well, come at once all the same, will you? How long will you be?'

'Very good, sir. I'll be round in five minutes.'

Jack Wilson went up the stairs a great deal faster than he had just come down. In his room he crammed his things into his suitcase and then he was limping downstairs again carrying it. The footman at this moment appeared in the hall with the teapot and hot water on a tray. Seeing Wilson on his way down the stairs with the suitcase he was visibly perturbed by a conflict of duties. After a moment's indecision he set down the tray and came to Wilson's help.

'Thanks, thanks,' said Jack Wilson. 'Just put it down there, please. I'm—er—just going. A taxi's coming. I say,' and he gave the man a pound, 'don't bother to tell her ladyship I'm going, by the way. She knows, by the way.'

Lady Swanley, meanwhile, was surprised to see a taxi drive up to the house. She was equally surprised to see the taxi drive away empty, but with a suitcase on the back. The front door not being visible from the beech tree, she could not tell what was happening.

The taxi, as a matter of fact, was not empty. Lying on the floor, so that he should not be seen by the party on the lawn, was Jack Wilson, rubber merchant, formerly Wing Commander Wilson, V.C., D.S.O., D.F.C. His hands, which were gripping a rug, were quite wet.

Men of Letters

The library was empty save for an elderly member dozing in an armchair. The door opened and a rather less elderly figure walked into the room; in fact, as they go in clubs, not elderly at all, a mere fifty-five or so. When the latter passed the armchair, the dozing member opened one sleepy eye. Having noticed that it was only Alan, the eye shut again. Though the club was a literary one, the library was never much used. Most members came to the place to get away from books. They came to talk and to listen and to drink. In so far as it was used at all, the library, a silence room, was generally used for sleep.

'Only Alan'—such was the normal phrase by which people would register in their minds the approach, the presence, of Alan Simmonds. There was nothing in the least hostile about the words. Quite the reverse. Alan was probably the most popular man in the club. For he was not only exceedingly amiable but a person from whom nobody had anything to fear. He was a failure. A first in Greats had got him nowhere, for he had not an ounce of creative ability. To those moving up or down a ladder of literary success, or obstinately stuck on some middle rung, it was often agreeable, instead of watching the movements of other figures on other ladders, to contemplate one that had never left the ground. Alan's company, therefore, was generally welcome. Moreover, he was such a pleasant fellow. For, unlike some failures, he was not in the least sour. There had, it is true, been some bad years. Then he had had the character to look facts squarely in the face. Why pretend to talents with which he had not been endowed? Climb down. Capitulate. Fail. Be plain Alan. Be just pleasant.

So he had given up the struggle in good time. Preferring still, however, rather to be a doorkeeper in the house of his God than to dwell in the tents of ungodliness, he had made his living doing menial jobs in the purlieus of literature. In this club he picked up ten guineas a year by acting as librarian. He used to write cards for the index and paste book-plates into new books and put labels on their backs. At the end of the library he had a desk to himself, and there he now sat and took a sheet of foolscap paper out of a top drawer.

He had rather a difficult job before him—Dick Rawson. *Who's Who* was open in front of him and he skimmed through the entry again.

Richard Rawson, author, it said, had been born in 1898. He had been to a public school and a university and had served as a gunner in the first World War. He had written some dozen books, the titles of which were given. He was a member of this club and of the Savile. He had married first Diana Greaves in 1924 (who obtained a divorce in 1931) and secondly Natalie Semnovich in 1934. Such were the bare bones which Alan had to clothe with flesh. It was a curious job, this, of writing obituary notices of people who were still alive, particularly when they were people he knew. In its performance he might find himself called upon to be any one of a variety of characters, from Pericles of the Funeral Oration to the gravedigger or the common hangman. For he spoke out. It was for the truthfulness, always of course within the bounds of good manners, with which, in a neat sentence or two, he could sum up a man's life work, that he had got, and kept, the job. And now before him lay the living corpse of his oldest friend, for the successful interment of which the paper would pay him the usual three guineas.

Well now, Dick, the truth! The library door opened and Emmitt, the publisher, came in, a young man with him. They stood by the door and looked at the room, Emmitt whispering. Evidently the young man was being shown round the place. Catching Alan's eye, the publisher advanced with his companion. 'Alan,' he whispered, 'I want to introduce you to Stanley Hill, the author of——'—'You don't need to tell me,' said Alan. 'We are all talking about it. I am very pleased to meet you and I heartily congratulate you on the book.'

A blunt hand gripped his powerfully. A miner's son, Stanley Hill had been hailed by more than one reviewer as a new D. H. Lawrence. His appearance seemed to substantiate the character. The eyes, intensely alive, had a defensive, if not a defiant look. The ill-fitting Sunday suit was but one indication of a man who was far from having come to terms with the whole of life. Stanley Hill's presence was uncomfortable. Emmitt was obviously exceedingly proud of his man of genius.

'I'm just showing him round this place,' he said. 'Perhaps we'll be able to persuade him to become a member, at least a country member.'

'I hope so indeed,' said Alan.

'I tell him that this club is a sure path to literary success. You can make all sorts of contacts with people who count. Well, Alan, I see you're working, we won't disturb you. Perhaps you'll have a drink with us after dinner? Good. Come on now,' he whispered to his companion, 'let's go and have a glass of sherry.'

They moved away, Emmitt pointing at the bookshelves—

'Biography here, you see, History there, Fiction there, Works of Reference there——' Looking suspiciously at the books, Stanley Hill followed him to the door.

For a moment or two Alan allowed his mind to wander, then, with an effort, he faced Dick Rawson. This was not going to be an easy or a pleasant notice to write. From *Who's Who* he copied out the preliminary biographical details. Then he came to the books. *Moping Owl* was third in date, after two volumes of what might be called juvenilia. And afterwards? Mighty little. The reputation would hardly have been less if he had remained a one-book man. How far the later novels were from fulfilling that early promise! And in recent years the source itself seemed to have been drying up. The last four titles consisted of a travelogue, the history of a firm of wine merchants, and two anthologies. Dick Rawson, it was as clear as daylight, had shot his bolt.

For some minutes Alan tapped his teeth with the end of his penholder. Then he wrote: 'Rawson's reputation will rest almost entirely on *Moping Owl*. A remarkable novel for a man of twenty-nine, it was the book of a generation. There must indeed have been few of his reading contemporaries who did not find therein a brilliant statement of their problems, of what we should perhaps now call their predicament. Yet, for all the maturity of its irony and humour and compassion, the book remained essentially a young man's book. It was a half-way house rather than a destination and its successors were eagerly awaited. It has to be admitted that Rawson's later work did not fulfil his early promise.'

Alan tapped his teeth. Just that? He thought a few moments. Yes, just that. The dead can take it; and the writer of the obituary notice, in Alan's view, is not present, as one might be at a funeral, in order to give pleasure to the relations. His words are directed at the ears of the dead man and they, if they can hear anything, can hear everything. Or so it seemed to Alan. The departed, he felt, are still able to be warmed by a kindly intention but are no longer capable of enjoying flattery.

Then, the private life. That too had been a downhill story. Of course, if he were really to start telling the truth, he would say that Dick Rawson had never been much good since he parted from the most beautiful woman in the world. How on earth could he have ever been such a fool? Poor, poor fellow!

And still the most beautiful! Alan had run into her in the street yesterday. It had given him quite a turn. He had felt at once that he might lose his head all over again, just as before. They had stood talking about Dick for five minutes and then she had asked him to go round and see her this evening in her flat. In fact, in about two hours from now he would be with her . . .

Alan looked at his paper and entered thereon the matrimonial details as they appeared in *Who's Who*. Then he read through the piece. It was certainly not very pretty, but there it was. Anyhow it was not final. It was only a draft for the newspaper's files. There were still twenty years in which Dick might do things that would demand a drastic rewriting. Putting his papers in the drawer of his desk, the librarian's desk, and locking the same, Alan went downstairs where he would probably have a glimpse of his victim.

The bar, and the smoking-room that led off it, were crowded. The party was in full swing. On all sides were animated faces, some of them of great eminence, laughing, recounting, persuading, arguing, holding forth or about to chip in. Between those leaning against the bar, in the standing groups, among the twos and threes sitting at tables, imperishable things were being said. Voices that were known in a million homes swelled the happy din as glasses were raised to lips. Over there by the wall a bearded traveller was in earnest colloquy with a B.B.C. official. Waiters moved about the room with trays of drinks. It was a boast of the club that, even in these days of hardship, it had not sunk to waitresses.

Alan surveyed the room a moment from the door, then walked across towards the bar, greeting and being greeted to left and right. He loved the place. It was home to him, the centre of the world. 'Hullo, Roger!' 'Hullo, Alan! Get yourself a drink and come and join us.' Alan moved onwards. Then he spotted Dick Rawson, sitting in a corner with Pendridge, and stopped a moment to contemplate him through the smoke. Yes—the bottle, of course, there had been that too—yes—yes—it was sad, for he was perhaps fonder of Dick than of any man he knew, but there it was—*stet*—what he had written, he had written. Pendridge too might be said to have shot his bolt.

As Alan was ordering his drink at the bar, a gong sounded above the voices. Certain of the oldest members at once began to move towards the dining-room, to make sure of their usual positions at the end of the long table. Others soon followed them and the smoking-room gradually discharged its occupants until, for about ten minutes, before the returning stream began, it was quite empty of members. In this interval two waiters moved about, clearing ashtrays and setting chairs and tables straight.

'I can't stick that Pendridge!'

'Thinks a lot of himself, doesn't he?'

'Not like Alan Simmonds. I like 'im.'

'So do I. Speaks kind of nice, doesn't he?'

'Is 'e a cissy?'

'No! At least, you can never be sure, can you?'

'No, not these days, you can't!'

Meanwhile, in the dining-room there was a roar and a clatter. The long central table was filled, as were most of the side tables, which were occupied by members with guests or those few misanthropic individuals who wished to dine alone. There, at a table for two, was Emmitt pointing out to his guest the celebrities at the long table. Alan was seated at the latter.

'I love club life,' said Alan's neighbour. 'It's wonderful not having to like the person you're sitting next to.'

'Quite,' Alan agreed. 'Absolutely.'

'It's so different from life in the home. What I mean is, the other day we had an American couple staying with us and my wife thought we ought to give a dinner party for these people, and there we were scratching our heads trying to remember whom we liked. It's an infernal bore.'

'Quite.'

'I mean, I find one doesn't care for one's friends all that. And then they will stay on and on. They don't want to, of course, but they think it's not polite to leave before half-past eleven. Just two hours too long!'

'Yes, quite.'

'Whereas here you just get up and go when the other chap is in the middle of a sentence and there's no offence. And there's none of that awful repayment of hospitality business that poisons social life. If I ask you to come and see me today you'll have to ask me to go and see you tomorrow. Those terrible guest-host complications!'

'Absolutely. Have a glass of port with me?'

'Thanks. I'd love to.'

Cigars were being lit. Flushed faces beamed expansively. Each man knew himself a wit. The atmosphere was extremely cosy, one in which it was not hard for the second to believe themselves first rate, the third second. Emmitt on his way out tapped Alan on the shoulder.

'Don't forget you're joining us. Do you think you could get Dick Rawson to come too? Stanley ought to meet him. He's a *Moping Owl* fan.'

'I'll try.'

In ones and twos people were getting up and going to the desk to pay their bills. They then went out into the hall, some bound for the billiard-table, some for the smoking-room and some, upstairs, for the cardroom. Alan stood by the desk next to Dick, fingering money.

'Emmitt wants you to meet a young man of genius. Will you come and sit with us?'

'Why me?'

'Well, as a matter of fact, it's the young man who wants to meet you. He's a fan of your writings.'

Dick gave Alan a dark look.

'All right.'

Presently the four of them were seated in deep leather chairs around a table on which were four glasses of brandy.

'So you live in the country?' Dick was saying.

Stanley nodded.

'Stay there. Yes, stay there. May I know how you make a living?'

'Schoolmaster.'

'Excellent! A schoolmaster in the country! Shakespeare himself! Excellent! Stay there! Don't change.'

Emmitt gave Stanley an explanatory smile as though to say, This one of our great men is a bit of a wag.

'But Shakespeare didn't stay there,' Emmitt said.

'So much the worse for his work.'

'I hadn't noticed it had suffered.'

'Full of dead wood! Full of dead wood! Read Plutarch, Hall and Holinshed and you'll see how much.'

Emmitt laughed loud, entranced by the culture, the wit.

'May an old buffer give a word of advice to a promising young writer?' Dick went on. 'I'm only of course talking to the imaginative writer. Avoid literary circles. Take a look at them now and again, if you like, then go whizzing back where you belong. Have a job which has nothing to do with literature. Literary people have two ways, at least two ways, of getting you down. One is to eat into your self-confidence by exposing it too much to the acid air of criticism. You hear X and Y over at the bar there, handling the latest book of poor A or B. Then you go home and read what you have written that morning and tear it up. You try again, next day, and, in your anxiety to do better, do worse. And each day you do rather less. And at length they get you in their other way. You find their company is perfectly delightful. It is far more fun to be with them, and talking, than to be alone and writing. And you come to see that it is for them that the whole literary game is being put on. A and B, the makers of the books, are the ball-boys or the men who put up the skittles. It is the literary people, it is you, who are playing the game. You have become X or Y.'

He sipped his brandy.

'It's much pleasanter in every way to be X or Y. For one thing, you get brandy and cigars, the legitimate companions of the talker, who doesn't have to bother about waking up with a clear head in the morning. Am I being a bore?'

'You're doing splendidly,' said Alan, who was indeed agreeably surprised at the way Dick was talking. The young man's bright eyes also showed no sign of boredom. The smile, however, had left Emmitt's face.

'I repeat,' Dick went on, 'that I'm only referring to those who have an angel to wrestle with, not to the hewers of criticism, biography, and travel—those who start, and go on, with their feet always firmly on the ground. I'm only talking about the senior service, those of us who commit ourselves to the waves. Well, then—the angel. You give up wrestling a bit and take to reviewing and giving well-paid talks about English cheeses or smoke abatement. You say to yourself, this does me no harm, one can perform at different levels. Which is like making love at different levels. You presently find one level becomes much the same as another, and pretty low.'

'Good, Dick, good.' Alan was looking at his friend with interest. Emmitt was restive. His eyes were wandering. Dick Rawson took another sip.

'Then what I say is, don't be afraid of being local if you want to be universal. Wait for them to flock round you instead of you flocking round them. I liked your book very much. I particularly liked what that asinine reviewer called "the provincial taint". In Shakespeare's beginning is our end. Except in small doses, avoid this club——'

'Hullo, Pendridge,' said Emmitt, 'I want you to meet Stanley Hill. Bring that chair.'

The young man turned, reluctantly it seemed, away from Dick Rawson towards the newcomer.

'I've never heard you talk in this vein before,' Alan said to Dick. 'It was rather inspiring.'

He looked at the clock. In five minutes he would be going.

'Did you mean anything special when you said "our end" just now?'

'I did, as a matter of fact. I had hoped to get away without speaking to you, but I see I shan't.'

'Get away?'

'Yes, this is my last night in the old home.'

'What on earth do you mean?'

'I'm off tomorrow morning. Seat booked.'

'Where to?'

'I'm not telling anybody, particularly not you.'

'I see. I'll take that as a compliment. Are you going for long?'

'Yes. Perhaps for always.'

'Dick, what on earth has come over you? I am absolutely astonished.'

There was a silence.

'Any address?' said Alan.

'No. Letters to this club will be forwarded to my bank which will forward them.'

'Ah. I say, Dick, what's all this about? Won't you open up?'

There was a moment's hesitation, then Dick Rawson raised his eyes to Alan's, determined, exasperated eyes.

'Very well. I'm just making an effort to pull myself together, that's all. You see, contrary to your opinion, your probable opinion, I think there is still hope for me.'

'Yes—I mean——'

'If I get right away.'

'What is it you particularly want to get away from?'

'Well, what I've just been saying—all this'—he waved his hand around—'and—and you, particularly you. I cannot bear continually to see someone who knows me as well as you do.'

'Perhaps,' said Alan slowly, 'perhaps again not absolutely an insult. Dick, I can't at once take all this in, but my first reaction is that it's rather wonderful.'

'You didn't know I had it in me, did you? Perhaps I haven't.' He looked sombrely at the other. 'As we're talking, Alan, I must say a thing. I wish to God Diana was coming with me!'

'Diana! But——'

'It's all I want.'

'I hadn't the least idea you ever saw each other nowadays.'

'We don't. She'd look the other way, anyhow.'

'I mean, I didn't know you ever gave her a thought.'

'Well, I do, most of the time. Though you might not guess it, she's always been the only person for me. With her—ah, that *would* be a new start! I suppose you never see her?'

'No,' said Alan, fumbling with a match in his agitation.

'How she must loathe and despise me,' the other went on, 'if she ever thinks about me at all!'

Shall I, shan't I? thought Alan. And he decided not to tell Dick that, after her divorce, he himself had made a proposal of marriage to Diana. Who was the person who proposed to Sarah, Duchess of Marlborough when she was a widow, and what was it she said? Whatever the words were, Diana's to Alan were something in that style. It was a snub from which he had been smarting for twenty years.

For a few moments the two men looked thoughtfully into their brandy glasses. Then Alan spoke.

'It was not true just now when I said I never saw her. Having not set eyes on her all this time, I happened to meet her in the street only yesterday. She lives just round the corner from here, at 10 Davies Court

Mews. As a matter of fact, I had half arranged to go round and see her this evening, now. My suggestion is that you go instead of me.'

After looking at the other for a moment, wide-eyed, Dick carefully set down his glass on the table. Then he sat back, panting.

'Alan,' he said, 'you have taken my breath away. What? Me go round and get a slap in the face?'

'Nothing of the kind. I got the impression from five minutes' conversation with her that a visit from you would be the thing she would most like in the world.'

'Good God! What did she say?'

'Much what you've just been saying to me about her.'

'Did she indeed?' He sat holding the arms of the chair.

'How does she look?' he said presently.

'Just the same. Wonderful, Dick, if I may say so.'

'You may, you may.'

'If you're going, I think you ought to go now.'

Dick lifted his glass, but put it down without drinking and stood up.

'Aren't you finishing your brandy?' said Alan.

'No,' said Dick. 'Another resolution. Bless me if this isn't being a *vita nuova* with a vengeance!'

They walked together out of the room.

'Good luck!' said Alan in the hall and went up to the library where he sat at his desk retouching the piece of writing he had done before dinner. When he came down again to the hall he was aware that something was wrong. People were standing about in twos and threes and talking in hushed voices.

'What's happened?' said Alan.

'Dick Rawson, knocked down by a car, just a few minutes ago. He stepped off the pavement there without looking. They've taken him into the billiard-room. Apparently he's pretty bad.'

Alan went across the hall and looked in through the open door of the billiard-room. Three or four people were in there, standing by Dick Rawson, who was lying on a long seat by the wall. One of the members, a doctor, who had been stooping over him, raised himself and turned to the others. He spoke slowly.

'I'm sorry to say, it's killed him. Poor fellow!'

Alan glanced at the dead face, then turned and went through to the bar.

'A large whisky, please.'

He took his drink to a seat, had a gulp and shut his eyes. When he opened them, he was aware of somebody standing over him. It was Stanley Hill.

'I'm sorry,' said Stanley. 'I'm sorry about him. I took to him. I daresay I owe that man a good deal. I'm truly sorry. Glad to have met you. I must be off now. Goodnight.'

'Goodnight.'

Alan glanced at the clock. Five minutes to ten. Not too late. Better finish the job. He put down his empty glass, then went up into the library, took out his papers from the drawer and sat over them for a few minutes. Then he took what he had written down across the hall, where now amongst others there were a policeman and some ambulance men, and went into one of the telephone boxes in the passage beyond. He dialled. It occurred to him that this was probably the first night for many years that Dick Rawson had left the club more or less sober.

'Hullo? Mr Cummings, please. Is that you, Cummings? This is Simmonds. I've got a little bit of a scoop you might care to have for tomorrow morning's paper. Richard Rawson has just been killed, run down by a car—yes, just outside this club. I thought you'd perhaps like his obituary. As a matter of fact I was writing it only this afternoon. All right—are you ready?'

And then he began to read.

'"Rawson's reputation,"' he said, after reading for a minute or two, '"rests mainly on *Moping Owl*. A remarkable novel for a man of twenty-nine, it was the book of a generation. There must indeed have been few of his reading contemporaries, who did not find therein a brilliant statement of their problems, of what we should perhaps now call their predicament. Nor, for all its contemporaneity, can it be said to have dated. Its irony, humour and broad human compassion are as fresh after a quarter of a century as they ever were. None of Rawson's subsequent novels attained the significance of *Moping Owl* and there were some who thought that he had spent himself. Those who knew him well, however, were far from despairing of his genius, and it may well be that his early death has deprived our literature of other masterpieces."'

'"——other masterpieces." Simmonds,' said Cummings, 'you surprise me. I must observe that you surprise me.'

'I'm right.'

'O.K. I hardly knew him at all. It's just what one heard. I had always supposed he was finished. Yes?'

'"He will also be remembered with gratitude for the advice and encouragement he so generously gave to young authors."'

'"——to young authors." Yes. Is that the end?'

'Yes, except for his marriage. "He married Diana Greaves. There were no children of the marriage."'

'Is that all?'

'Yes.'

'But, I say, weren't there divorces and things?'

'No.'

'I could have sworn—wasn't there a Russian or something?'

'You must be thinking of someone else.'

'O.K. But I could have sworn. Anyhow, this is entirely your column, Simmonds. Of course, I didn't really know him at all. Well, thanks for the scoop. Jolly good! Goodnight.'

Alan put down the receiver. Now for Diana. She would be waiting for him, and she was going to get him, only him, only Alan.

The Restaurant

The *Madame Bovary* had not been open many months when Catherine went to work there. It was kept by two young men, Pat and Steve, helped in the kitchen by two other young men, Freddie and Bertie. Besides Catherine there was a second waitress, Lesley. There were only ten tables to be served, for the restaurant was small and intimate. Its atmosphere was more that of a night club than of an ordinary restaurant and it was indeed only open for dinners and suppers. A mural at the end of the room depicted a four-wheeler, with the blinds down, perambulating the streets of Rouen.

The food was exceedingly good and not expensive. An important actor had discovered the place and talked about it to his friends. Suddenly the *Madame Bovary* had become the rage. Those who did not book a table stood little chance of finding room. The restaurant was patronized not only by actors, intellectuals and upper Bohemia, but by the smart and the grand. It was in the company of some of the latter that Catherine had been taken there. At the end of the dinner she had spoken to the waitress who was clearing the table and laying the coffee-cups.

'Jolly good dinner! Will you tell the chef how much we've enjoyed it?'

'Certainly, Madame, thank you.'

'Yes,' said Stacy Ferminjoy, 'it's been excellent. We'll be seeing you again.'

'Not me, sir. I'm leaving in a few days.'

'Oh, I'm sorry. You'll be hard to replace.'

'Thank you, sir.'

'As a matter of fact,' asked Catherine, 'do you know if they have got anyone to take your place?'

'I don't believe anything's actually settled yet.'

'Which of those two—' Catherine looked at Pat and Steve, who were busy behind a counter, 'which is the boss?'

'Both. They're equal.'

'They look it,' murmured Stacy.

Catherine got up and walked over to them, watched by her companions. The conversation that took place across the counter appeared to be extremely gay. The teeth of the young men in their bronze, sailor-boys' faces glistened as they laughed.

'Ever seen anyone exercising her charm?' muttered the Hon. Derek Harbottle.

Now Catherine was writing something on a pad. Presently she walked back, beaming, to her table.

'I've got the job!' she said. 'They're bliss! I'm mad about them!'

'The job!' said the other girl at the table. 'Honestly, Cathy, you don't mean it really, do you? Are you mad?'

'Perhaps I'm mad. I mean it, anyhow.'

'What's the idea?' said Stacy.

'I want a change. One can't just go on being a deb.'

'But—why, you'll never be able to come out again in the evenings! Honestly, Cathy, what's the idea?'

'I want to see life.'

'This! Life! Aren't we life?'

Catherine looked at last year's President of Pop, at the heir to the Harbottle millions and at the daughter of the Lord Privy Seal.

'Perhaps not absolutely the whole of life,' she said slowly.

There was a silence at the table.

'I'm sorry,' she said, 'that was frightfully rude. I didn't mean to be unpleasant. Promise, you'll come and dine here often, won't you? And I have one night a week off. Oh, I forgot, I wonder what my parents will have to say!'

The fact that she had forgotten to wonder what her parents would have to say was evidence not of any indifference to their opinion but rather of the trust that existed between them and herself.

'Cathy's head is screwed on the right way,' said Lord Westfield to his wife, 'I'm sure she'd never do anything irrevocably foolish.'

'So am I, absolutely. It's just sometimes her taste that I'm a teeny weeny bit doubtful about in the present phase she's going through. Those jeans she's now wearing—they are so terribly tight!'

'It would be insincere of me to say I disapproved of them. Do you know, when I was her age, *I* used to be thought rather loud. It's hard to believe, isn't it?' It was indeed.

The job in the restaurant, after some moments of surprise, received full parental sanction, tempered only with regret that they would now be seeing so little of her in the evenings.

'Not that we can say we've seen much of her in the evenings lately!'

'True enough! How long will you be doing it for do you suppose, Cathy?'

'At least until I've saved up enough to buy a portable radiogram.'

The idea of getting a job had been establishing itself in Catherine's mind some weeks before that evening at the restaurant. Partly, she wanted the gramophone and was not going to ask her father for it after all he had lately coughed up on her behalf. Then, she did indeed want a change. She was sick of the Dereks and Stacys. She had seen enough of them during this crowded summer, in which, though she had taken a prominent part in all the fun which is offered to a lovely and exuberant girl of her position, she had not once felt her heart go pit-a-pat. She had refused five proposals without a second thought. It was a little boring that her affections should have remained so completely unmoved through these months of exposure in the Marriage Market, though she told herself that she was in no hurry whatever to meet her fate. She had not been six weeks in the *Madame Bovary* when she met it.

The hour was about nine o'clock. Things were in full swing in the restaurant. There was a babble of voices. Catherine, by the counter, drawing a cork, glanced towards the door.

'Look, Lesley, look what's just coming in! Isn't that rather bliss?'

Two men had just entered the restaurant and were taking off their coats, one of them elderly and prosperous-looking, the other still perhaps in his thirties, thin, pale, with an interesting face, or so Catherine at once thought it.

'That's a Mr Rutherford,' said Lesley. 'He comes fairly often.'

Catherine moved towards them. Steve, too, advanced.

'Good evening, Mr Rutherford,' he said, 'this is your table.'

'Thank you, Steve,' said the fat man, taking his seat and motioning his guest to the place in front.

'A new young lady I see.'

'Yes,' said Steve, 'this is Cathy.'

Catherine smiled entrancingly.

'Now what do you recommend this evening, Steve?' said Mr Rutherford, taking up the menu.

'The *Bœuf Stroganov* is very good.'

After some discussion *Œufs Bovary* were ordered, followed by *Bœuf Stroganov*, and a bottle of Burgundy. Cathy wrote down the order, then hurried away to attend to it.

'Isn't he bliss?' she said to Lesley, busy at the counter.

'Him? Isn't he rather fat?'

'Not the old one, silly.'

'I hadn't noticed the other.' She looked over her shoulder. 'A bit washed out, isn't he?'

'He has suffered, you see. I am sure there is much to reclaim. Those sensitive eyes—he keeps lowering them. Bertie,' she called into the kitchen, 'are those eggs ready, yet?'

The restaurant, as always, was full. For the next hour the

waitresses were continuously on the move. There was no chance for what Catherine described as 'hovering'. She learned little about the new client to whom she had taken such a fancy. The elderly man was doing all the talking, mostly about books, it seemed.

'Cathy,' he said, as she put a Stilton cheese on the table, 'will you please get us another bottle of this excellent Burgundy. And, Cathy, do I yet know you well enough to ask where Steve gets his waitresses?'

Cathy glanced at the other man to see if he shared Mr Rutherford's curiosity on this point. He looked down.

'I mean,' Mr Rutherford went on, 'where does he find such remarkably pretty young ladies?'

'The highways and hedges,' said Catherine, with a smile of glittering gaiety, as she turned on her heel. In the mirror towards which she walked she noticed that they were both, yes both, looking after her.

As Mr Rutherford plied his guest with wine the latter became more animated. Catherine removed the cheese, cleared the table and brought them cups of coffee.

'They're getting fundamental,' she said to Lesley. This was another of Cathy's words, descriptive of the talk generated in some clients by a good dinner. Lesley giggled. She found Catherine extremely funny. Indeed, she admired and adored her without reserve. What Catherine could find so wonderful in that young, or not so young, man was, however, beyond her.

'I'm going to hover,' said Cathy.

The conversation of the two men, much of which she was able to overhear, had indeed become rather fundamental.

'The consolations of religion,' the younger man was saying, 'what are they? The promise of eternal life. What does that mean? The survival of my ego for ever and ever. Do I want that? Absolutely not. Just the opposite. I want to be relieved of the thing. It simply isn't interesting enough. I don't exactly hate or despise it. I just don't love it, in the way that one can love things.'

'Or people?'

'No doubt. All I am saying is that when the magic ends and one returns to the common light of day, there again is the inevitable companion, whom one had forgotten about for a full hour perhaps, that old fellow the self, quite a nice fellow in his way, sometimes rather amusing, but not very gifted or very interesting, and, oh dear, *connu*. And you are offered this eternal companionship as a prize! People who make such an offer must be quite ignorant of rapture. Is a death-wish the sin against the Holy Ghost?'

'Cathy,' said Mr Rutherford, 'would you get us two brandies?' He looked at his companion. The time had come to broach a matter of business.

'Let's get back to Charles Braid,' he said.

'One always gets back to Charles Braid.'

'Why do you say that?'

'Because on almost every subject you can think of he said something decisive.'

'True enough. You do honestly hold a very high opinion of him?'

'Of course. He is balm. He was unquestionably the dominant writer of our time.'

'You adored him?'

'Of course, on this side—no, on the other side idolatry. Why do you ask such obvious questions?'

'I just wanted to be absolutely sure before making my proposition. You see, I am, as you know, his literary executor. Will you write his life?'

'Me? Charles Braid's life? My hat!'

'You look surprised. Before we go any further, let me say that you were his choice for the job.'

'You don't say! Good heavens! But why me?'

'He had a high opinion of you. It was only about a fortnight before the end that I got him to talk about this matter of his biography. He wasn't, as you know, terribly keen on thinking about his own death. Perhaps he had an inkling how dreary the place was going to seem after his departure. Anyhow, that day he was quite willing to talk. He admitted that he would prefer that the life was not written by just anyone. We are talking about the official life. There will, no doubt, be various other lives by various admirers or by those of his less-successful rivals or imitators who have scores to pay off and those who want to put themselves right with posterity. I know of one or two such already brewing. And there will of course be a spate of effusive female books. What I am talking about is the life that will be written with access to the three suitcases of papers I have at home. Well, there we were talking over luncheon in that restaurant on the terrace that he was so fond of. You know the place, of course. There is a trellis of vines over the tables. It was May and the vines were in flower—one of the sweetest and headiest of Mediterranean smells, almost as good as that of a hot fig-tree. We were going through the names of possible biographers. He was keen on it not being anyone of his own generation or near it. "I can't stick anyone over forty," he said. "They're so busy trying to make names for themselves." Then he insisted that the person should be a gentleman. Also it would be desirable that he should show some evidence of being able to write. So, at length, we came to your name. "By God," he said, after only a moment's thought, "the very man." He looked out to sea, picking his teeth. "I like him," he said, "I like him very much. My heart goes out to the unambitious. What a feeling of civilization it gives one to see fine talents being put to no use whatever! Yes, he's our man. He'd do it excellently, I believe. But look here, it mustn't be forced on him. He has far better things to do. I'd hate to interfere with his young life."'

Rutherford paused.

'He said all that, did he? How beautiful! How lovely! I'm overwhelmed.' The young man did indeed look much moved.

'You needn't decide at once,' said Rutherford. 'I'll give you, say, a fortnight, to think it over. You realize of course that there will be a good deal of research to be done. There are various veils one ought to lift, if only to prevent anybody else lifting them. The Oxford period, for instance. He once told me that the three letters he wrote to the Master of his college at the time of his being sent down were the best things he ever wrote. I don't imagine they were quite the kind of letter the recipient would want to keep. Still, what a scoop if they did happen to survive! Anyhow, the whole incident needs a good deal of clearing up. Then there are various memories that should be tapped while they are still with us, both here and out there. Old Mirella, for instance. Cathy, may I have the bill, please?'

'Pat,' said Cathy at the counter, 'the bill for number four, please. Lesley, you're quite wrong about him being washed out. He's on fire, behind those lids. Have you ever thought of a honeymoon, Lesley, an interesting man opposite you in a restaurant-car, pouring out ideas, and it is all yours? I love him to distraction. Thank you, Pat.'

She took the bill to her clients, whom she found writing in their engagement books. They were meeting again for dinner at the *Madame Bovary* that day fortnight.

Catherine's passion survived a night's rest. Indeed, next morning she realized, somewhat to her astonishment, that her whole life had suddenly become dedicated to a single end. It was simply a question of waiting—weeks, months, years?—until he should come to a similar realisation. What hope? There had been hardly an indication of any hope, had there? The fourteen empty days ahead of her seemed unbearably long. Still, she was not a person to waste her time.

'Papa.'

'Yes, my love.'

'Have we got any of Charles Braid's books in the house?'

'I've got *Lotus Land* in the study, and one or two others, and that collection of apophthegms from his works that somebody made. Why do you ask?'

'I was reading him in a friend's house the other day. He's balm.'

'I shouldn't have thought he was terribly suitable for a maiden of tender years.'

'Still, can you lend me one? I need it to be *au fait* with the people I meet at my work.'

'Do you indeed?'

'Be an angel and let me have the apo-whatnots?'

Then there came one of her nights off and she went with a friend to a concert and there, as they were moving across the *foyer* at the end of the interval, she had seen him. He had passed quite close, coming towards her, and had he or hadn't he recognised her and faintly smiled? It was exasperating not to know. She turned to look after him. He, too, had turned to look. An indication—surely this was an indication?

'Papa,' she said next day, 'don't you think that Charles Braid is the dominant writer of our time?'

'I advise you not to pay too much attention to him, my treasure.'

'He says, "Those who give advice generally have nothing else to give."'

'Does he? Does he indeed!'

'Papa.'

'Yes, my love.'

'Would you say it's tartish to take a bull by the horns?'

'No, I wouldn't say so, not necessarily by any means. Though it was never your mother's technique. She—no.'

'Oh, come on. She what?'

'No.'

'Oh yes, come on. You began. That's not fair.'

'Very well, then. Perhaps you've reached years of discretion. Well, when I popped the question, what do you think she said?'

'I can't wait.'

'It was by the Serpentine. She was looking at a duck. She simply said "What?"'

Catherine screamed.

'"What"! "What"! By the Serpentine! Oh, my aunt! Looking at a duck!' She shrieked convulsively and ran along the passage to her mother's room to laugh at, and with, her. For some minutes her ecstatic screams pealed through the house as she reconstructed the scene of her parents' engagement.

At length the fortnight passed. The evening had arrived. Catherine as usual was at the restaurant at about six o'clock. For half an hour she and Lesley were busy laying the tables. Then, when all was set, and before any clients had arrived, Steve, as usual, poured out a glass of Burgundy for each member of the staff.

'Hear me, Lesley,' said Catherine. '"It is a function of art to draw off the melancholy from life.' 'Hope yes, Faith yes——' No! As you were, try again. "Hope yes, Charity yes—but what has a scholar to do with Faith?"'

'Cathy, what on earth are you talking about?'

Catherine explained.

'It's just a question of what openings they give me. Oh, Lesley, don't you think he's balm?'

'What's that?'

'I'm not absolutely sure, but I think it's the same sort of thing as bliss, only more so.'

Customers began to come in and dinners to be served. At length, after more than an hour and a half Catherine was taking the money at the table that was reserved, at half-past eight, for Mr Rutherford. And then—there they were.

'Good evening, Cathy.'

'Good evening, Cathy.'

'Good evening.'

'Well now,' said Mr Rutherford, looking down the menu, 'what shall it be this evening? What do you feel like? *Homard Homais?* How's that done, Cathy?'

'Cooked in butter, with prawns and *Calvados*.'

'Sounds all right. Should we try that?'

'I'd like just what I had the other time.'

'The eggs, yes,' said Catherine, 'but *Bœuf Stroganov* is not on tonight, though of course I can get it if you specially want it.'

'So you remembered,' he said, looking up at her for the merest fraction of a second. 'Yes,' he went on, 'I'd like it to be just like the first time.'

'And I'll have the *Homard* and after that a *Tournedos*,' said Mr Rutherford.

'And the *Burgundy* as before?' said Catherine.

Mr Rutherford glanced at his companion, who nodded, and Catherine left them.

'Freddie, precious,' she called into the kitchen, 'could you manage a *Strog*? Yes, I know it's not on the list, but this is a matter of the heart, *vous savez*. Oh, that's angelic of you, I'll never forget it.'

'Well?' said Lesley, at her shoulder.

'An I mistake not, there may be indications, just the faintest indications. If only I could hold his eyes for four seconds I believe that'd do the trick.'

Meanwhile a gay young party of six was coming into the restaurant, friends of Catherine. She and Steve moved two small tables together to accommodate them. Derek Harbottle was among them. Before sitting down he pinned an orchid on to the front of Catherine's dress.

'Be making up your minds what you're going to eat,' she said, 'and I'll be back in a minute.'

She moved swiftly, ravishingly.

'*Homard Homais*,' she said as she put the hot plates in front of her two male customers, 'and *Œufs Bovary*.'

'I like the orchid,' said Mr Rutherford. 'Lucky Cathy!'

'Luck? "It is a principle of mine (my only one) to regard whatever good fortune may come my way as deserved."'

The two men looked at her in astonishment as she moved away to take the orders of the large table.

'My God,' said the younger of them suddenly, 'that's Charles Braid! Those are the opening words of *Lotus Land*!'

'Are they indeed? I'd forgotten. I say, what an extraordinary young lady she is, our Cathy! And, by the way, that brings us to business. How do you feel about it? Will you do the job?'

'Of course I will. Try, that is.'

'I'm delighted.' And Mr Rutherford plunged into certain financial matters. Presently Catherine was setting the next course before them.

'Cathy, you brilliant girl,' said Mr Rutherford, 'I gather you're a Braid fan. Do you know his works by heart?'

'Nearly.'

'I believe he is not generally thought a very suitable author for a young lady.'

'My father keeps pressing him on me.'

'You must have a most enlightened father.'

'He's all right.' She gave a rippling laugh.

'Well, you're among friends. This gentleman,' he indicated his companion, 'is no less than Charles Braid's biographer-to-be.'

Well, look up properly, for heaven's sake! That's not the way to be won by a fair lady!

'Cathy! Lady Catherine!' Her friends called.

'Excuse me,' she said, moving away to attend to them. It was a busy night for her. There was no time for hovering. She was rushed off her feet, and when Mr Rutherford and his friend had left, she found herself in possession of little new information about the latter. She did not even know his name and she knew of no assignation to look forward to. Perhaps they would never come to the restaurant again. Perhaps this was the end, the whole episode was finished. Yet, surely, surely she had made some impression?

The days passed and nothing happened. On her evening out she went again with a friend to the concert hall, the only place she knew where hope might flower. Blank. Another blank week then followed. On the next evening out she went again to the concert, this time alone. Again blank. She was getting angry.

Returning home that night, she found a note on the hall table in her mother's hand to the effect that the restaurant had telephoned. It was nothing important. No message left. Unusual, thought Catherine. What could that be about? She learned the next evening from Lesley. *He* had been to the restaurant, himself, alone, to dine.

'I thought you'd like to know he was here, so I telephoned.'

'Lesley, you angel, how blissful of you! Tell me everything. Did you talk to him? What did he say?'

'He didn't say a lot. He seemed very disappointed that you weren't here.'

'Oh, did he? More.'

'He asked questions about you, who you were, etcetera. I hope I got it right.'

'More.'

'Well, there wasn't any more really. He's going away to the country for some days, then he booked a table for himself and fatty for Tuesday week. He seemed all sort of worked up.'

''Hm. I see. Yes. What's happened you see, Lesley, is that he doesn't know whether he's coming or going. It's proving too strong for him and he's struggling against it and he feels he's slipping. He's absolutely *déconcertato*.'

She pirouetted among the empty tables, then stopped before the wall painting and, with an operatic gesture, stretched her arms towards Rouen cathedral. 'I know that my,' she yelled with a full-throated and vulgarly tremulous gust of song, 'I know that my Redeemer liveth.'

Bertie's face appeared at the kitchen door.

'Has she laid an egg or something?'

'Here,' said Steve, passing her a glass of Burgundy,' I expect that's made you thirsty.'

With a fixed date ahead the days passed to some purpose. There was something restful, too, about the knowledge that he was out of London. It ruled out the daily hope and disappointment that lay in the possibility of meeting. On three mornings a week now she was having Italian lessons.

'All her own idea, these lessons. Paid for by herself too. The child has some gumption,' said Lord Westfield proudly to Catherine's godfather. More gumption perhaps than he supposed. Might not she assist at those confabulations with old Mirella. . . .?

Then, there they were again one evening at the usual table.

'Defence, Lesley,' said Catherine. 'You watch. That's the order for tonight. Defence in depth. Each position to be defended to the last cartridge!'

The young man had much to say this evening. He was describing his visit to Oxford and his efforts, at Braid's college, to run to earth some priceless Braidiana. He had obtained interviews with the Master, the Dean and various of the fellows. He had the impression that they were ready for him, that he was not by any means the first of such inquirers. They were uniformly polite. Suavely, smilingly, they met him with an unequivocal *non possumus.* They knew of nothing that the college could tell him about Charles Braid.

'But, good heavens!' he said at length to the youngest of the fellows. 'Isn't the college proud of having harboured, even if only for a year, the greatest prose writer of our time? Univ. has a monument to Shelley.'

'I know. Personally I admire him very much.'

'Well, then. All I am asking is this. The letters that Braid wrote to the Master, Weatherall—he once told a friend of mine that they were the best things he ever wrote. It occurs to me that as the great Weatherall had such a feeling for literature and as he is known to have been such a humorous and large-minded man, there is just a chance that he kept those letters.'

The other hesitated.

'Yes,' he said. 'I may as well tell you. There is in the college archives a little packet of papers about Braid and his expulsion. It includes the letters.'

'Ah! And you have seen the letters?'

'Yes.'

'What are they like?'

'Superb.'

Catherine stood by the table uncorking a second bottle of Burgundy.

'So they survive,' said Mr Rutherford. 'How fascinating! But why won't they let us see them?'

'Apparently the fellows have decided that at least another generation should pass before they are released. Silly old dodderers!'

'Who looks after them?'

'The Dean acts as college archivist.'

'Is there no way round him? Is he——?'

'No, apparently quite the reverse. I became rather chummy with one of the porters, who told me a lot of scandal about the Dean and undergraduettes.'

'Cathy,' said Mr Rutherford, 'do you think you could find us some of that French mustard?'

Catherine's policy of defence showed itself sadly ineffective during the evening. Though she could not doubt that the enemy was fully mobilised, nothing in the nature of an attack took place. And the evening was slipping away, and already they were having their coffee, and, oh dear, they would go away leaving her nothing to look forward to but just that terrible blank, and already she was making out the bill and—damn defence!

'Would you like a table reserved for another night?' she said.

'Should we?' said Mr Rutherford. 'Or are you sick of this place?'

The younger man looked up at Catherine for nearly two continuous seconds. 'I couldn't bear to go anywhere else,' he said, but did not follow up the attack, and, two minutes later, they were gone.

'Papa,' said Catherine a few mornings afterwards.

'Yes, my treasure.'

'Should one strike while the iron is hot?'

'Of course, every time.'

'And if it's cold?'

'Strike all the same. What's the suitcase for?'

'I'm going away for the night. It's my night off. I'm going to Oxford.'

'Don't get into mischief.'

'How singular that you should say that, when it's precisely for that purpose that I am going.'

The days were getting noticeably longer. It was light now as Catherine walked to her work through the square off which the *Madame Bovary* was situated. A blackbird each evening was singing in a plane tree. Catherine, too, was singing as, some days later, she passed under the tree.

'Steve,' she said, taking off her coat, 'your teeth are flawless pearls. It is conceivable that I might like to leave a little early tonight. Could I, just this once?'

'Of course.'

'*Grazie infinitissime!*'

The evening proved a particularly strenuous one, at least in the early part. It was difficult to know quite why, for almost all the seats were occupied all the time every night. There just were some customers some nights who had the knack of running the waitresses off their feet. Catherine had little opportunity of hearing the conversation of her adored one, though she was conscious of his eyes continually upon her. Anyhow, what did she care about their conversation? She was swift, indifferent, remote, this evening, immortal, the archer goddess. Now she was taking their money.

'Cathy,' he began, in a new sort of voice. A declaration? Far too late, my fine fellow!

'Excuse me,' she said turning away.

She brought the change and, as she put it on the table, put also in front of him a paper packet tied in string. He undid the string and looked at the little file of papers in the packet. Taking out a letter, he unfolded it. It was headed 'The Bullingdon Club. 3 November 1891.' 'My dear Master,' it began. He read a few lines, then looked up, pushing the packet towards Mr Rutherford.

'My God!' he said.

Catherine at that moment, in coat and hat, was leaving the restaurant. He got up and hurried after her. 'Cathy,' he called in the street. 'Cathy!' She did not look round. He began to run. She, too, began to run. 'Cathy, stop! I adore you. I absolutely worship you. You are my life. Cathy, don't you see? I love you! I love you!' She turned into the square, dark and empty at this time of night, and ran along beside the railings. 'Cathy, stop! Don't you see, I love you! I adore you! I've known it from the first moment!'

She stopped suddenly.

'You've known it from the first moment,' she panted. 'Then why in heaven's name? All these weeks! Oh, it makes me wild!' She stamped with fury, then began to run again. She ran as fast as she could. But he could run faster.

Nice Things

'I'm just an Aunt Sally!' the director muttered to himself as he wearily slit open the envelope of the fourth letter in the pile. The first letter had been anonymous, from someone who signed himself 'formerly a frequent visitor to the gallery'. The writer complained that he now hardly derived any pleasure from his increasingly rare visits. For one thing, the pictures were always being moved around. You could never find your old friends in the places where they had always been. And then the crowds! You could hardly see your picture even if you were lucky enough to find it. What on earth was behind this policy of trying to make art popular? Just part of the general national degradation, he (or she?) supposed. The fatuous comments you heard on all sides were enough to make you sick. How different things had been in Sir George Kingston's time! (Sir George Kingston was the last director.)

The second letter was from an address in Cambridge. 'Dear Sir Frederick Mayne,' it began, 'Art is surely one?' It went on to say that the arrangement of the pictures by schools was a great mistake. It lulled the intelligence to sleep. Why not boldly juxtapose Giotto and Gainsborough, Hals and Rossetti, until people began to realise that art is, in fact, one? How pleased with himself (or herself) was Julian Allen, of Trumpington Road, to have been visited in the middle of a foggy night by this brilliant idea! The director wondered whether the silly ass had ever been to his gallery. If so, he (or she) cannot have got as far as the north alcove where was now to be seen a series, changing monthly, of juxtapositions of pictures which the director and his colleagues, after much thought, believed to be interesting to the art historian; pictures in which artists of different schools and periods approached a similar problem in a different way, or a different problem in a similar way. The choice was made with great discretion, and the experiment had, in the director's opinion, been a success. It aroused each month the critics' contempt, condemnation, derision and unflagging interest.

The third letter was from one of the trustees of the gallery. Would the director oblige him, Lord Kenroul asked, by standing some day at about one o'clock in the middle of the Poussin room, as he, Lord Kenroul, had stood there yesterday at that hour? Would he then take a deep breath through the nose? If he was not practically asphyxiated by the smell of food (bad food, from all accounts), Lord Kenroul would be very much surprised. The director would remember that Lord Kenroul had strongly opposed the introduction of a restaurant in the basement. To his various other objections to the unfortunate project, all of which experience was proving valid, could now be added this new one of the smell, which he had not foreseen. If the director thought this was the kind of atmosphere in which to enjoy Poussin, he, Lord Kenroul, could not agree with him.

'I'm just an Aunt Sally!' muttered Sir Frederick. The fourth letter was from the headmistress of a girls' school. She thought the director ought to know what an unsatisfactory day she had had last Wednesday, when, as usual towards the end of term, she had brought up the art class to look at the originals of the pictures they had been studying from reproductions. They had been doing Flemish art this term. Imagine her dismay when she found that three or four of the most important pictures, including 'The Crowning of Priapus', had been taken away to be cleaned. Surely, if the most important Rubens in the gallery was going to be removed, the public should be warned? Could not there be an announcement in *The Times* or on the wireless? Then this so-called air-conditioning—you came in from the fresh air outside and perhaps felt all right for about half an hour, then there you were going through room after room breathing this synthetic stuff—well, it might be all very well for the pictures but she was not at all surprised when one of the girls fell in a dead faint on one of those slippery (surely needlessly slippery?) floors! Of course she had at once asked one of the attendants for the first-aid room. Imagine her astonishment to be told that there was no such thing! Well, they managed to half-carry, half-drag the poor girl till they got her outside onto the steps, where a kind person appeared with a thermos of coffee which brought the child round. Surely this episode did not reflect much credit on the gallery? And one last point. Could not that disagreeable snappy woman at the picture-postcard counter be replaced? She had practically reduced one of the girls to tears. She, the headmistress, believed she would be voicing the opinion of many people in complaining of that woman.

Sir Frederick could well believe this last episode. Miss Papworth was indeed a formidable personality. She dated from well before Kingston's time. For a quarter of a century she had presided at that counter in the entrance hall. And time had not mellowed her. She became only more offhand and snappy with her clients. Again and again the director had had to ask her whether she could not try to be more polite. The moment when she could be decently threatened with dismissal, if she did not mend her ways, had long passed. She was now an institution; one, moreover, that no member of the gallery staff would have welcomed the end of. 'Between ourselves,' said Sir George Kingston as he was handing over to his successor, 'if you're ever in doubt about anything, ask Miss Papworth. She knows the gallery backwards. I think if you were to cut a square inch out of any picture here, and show it to her upside down, she'd be able to tell you where it came from.' The new director had found that she lived up to the character given her. He soon learned to respect, and almost to like, her, and never passed the counter without trying to get a smile out of her. Still, she could be an awful nuisance. He would have to speak to her again.

The fifth letter—ah, he knew that hand—an old enemy—that one could wait to the end. The sixth letter—there was a knock on the door.

'Come in. Oh, hullo, Collins. Good morning.'

'Good morning.'

Collins was one of the younger assistant Keepers.

'I've brought the cuttings.'

'Anything nice?'

'Much as usual. And here's a photograph of the Rubens since it's been cleaned.'

'Phew!'

They gazed at the photograph.

'I expect Miss Papworth knew it was there all the time,' said Collins.

'No doubt she did. I'm sorry to say she's been getting us into trouble again. She seems to have bitten the head off a schoolgirl.'

'Good old Pappy!'

'I dare say "Good old Pappy!" But it's a nuisance. We can't have her behaving like that.'

'Do you know, Miss Heston, the new typist, told me this morning that she had actually gone to tea with Miss Papworth at her home last Sunday. I dare say no one on the staff has ever done that before. Can you guess what she found? The walls of her room are entirely covered with postcards of pictures. Also the bathroom.'

'Indeed? It is rather touching; in fact, moving. Well, come on. Let's look at the cuttings.'

Sir Frederick supposed it to be part of his duty to keep in touch with the public opinion of his administration of the gallery as shown in the Press. At first he had taken each small blow as it came. He now preferred to let them accumulate and to receive one mighty knock once a month. He began to read, paragraphs of art critics, articles of 'Our Museums Correspondent', and letters from all and sundry, noblemen, dilettanti, artists, professors, the knowledgeable and the knowing, the ignorant and the silly, letters indignant, defiant, scornful, aggrieved, pleading, suffering. One condemned the cleaning of old masters altogether, another complained that if they were going to be cleaned at all the job ought to be done thoroughly. Moreover, it was a great mistake to hang cleaned and uncleaned pictures side by side. A great opportunity, said another, was being missed in not hanging cleaned, half-cleaned and uncleaned pictures side by side so that the public could form its own opinions on this matter of cleaning. Again, the institution of a restaurant in the basement had been an excellent idea, but why, in heaven's name, if they were going to make a restaurant, did they not make it large enough? After you had been trailing round the gallery for an hour or two you hardly felt like standing in a queue for your lunch. As to the quality of the food, it was asked why the opportunity had not been taken of making this into one of the better restaurants in town? A large part of its clientèle was foreign, and what must foreigners think? Again, it was asked, why you should be expected to have a sit-down meal. A snack was all that most people wanted on these occasions.

Then, the lectures. Why could not more of these be arranged for the lunch interval, which was the only time many people had for visiting the gallery? Those lectures! another complained. You were forced to tiptoe your way into a room and there, in front of the very picture you had come to see, you would find some spectacled official loudly delivering himself of vapid imbecilities to a circle of schoolgirls. If the officials must parade their ignorance somewhere, let them do it in front of the pseudo-Duccios on which they threw away the country's money and leave in peace the treasures we have known and loved for years! And worse almost than the lectures were the students who seemed to delight in blocking one's view of a Rembrandt with their miserable daubs. How on earth could one be expected to remember which was students' day? To judge from the efforts of these young persons one supposed that reproductions would be perfectly good enough for them to work from. A letter from a group of students, however, complained of the obstructive officialdom which only allowed them one day a week. Why not give them the run of the gallery all the week? After all, art was their bread and butter, and among their number presumably were the Constables and Turners of today. Did their voice count for nothing? 'Dear Sir,' began another letter, 'the blind officials who occupy——' Sir Frederick pushed the pile of cuttings from him.

'Collins,' he said, 'why does nobody ever say nice things?'

'Oh, but they do.'

'Not to me.'

'People are like that perhaps. They think that all the other people are saying the nice things all the time.'

'Well, they aren't.'

'No, but they think they are. So they take them as said, and just say the few things they feel ought to be said on the other side. I'm sure that adverse criticism means that the show is fundamentally going very well. All they have to do is to pick a little hole here and there.'

'A little hole here and there! My dear chap, have you read this stuff? No, Collins. I wish I could think there was something in what you say. Leave me, please. I've had enough for today.'

At the door Collins paused.

'What do you think we shall be doing with the Rubens? We presumably can't hang it.'

'Oh, can't we! Hang it in the front hall! Next to—no—over the Duccio! Oh, Collins, to hell with the gallery! To hell with art!'

Alone, the director took out of the drawer of his desk a book he had been reading in the train that morning. It had nothing whatever to do with his work. He became absorbed at once, forgetting all his worries. When he looked at his watch he was surprised to find the time was ten to one.

Experience had made the director of the gallery somewhat thick-skinned. On Luke Fines, who happened at that moment to be walking under the director's window on his way to his club, experience had had the opposite effect. With each book that he published he became more sensitive to public opinion. Not that his books had been ill received. On the contrary, he had been far more successful than he had dared to hope. His two novels and a book of essays had been highly commended by the best critics. He had quickly become an established figure, a success, one of the literary names to be reckoned with. And now he had written a third novel, which had been out about a month. He knew it to be an improvement on the others, in fact, first-rate through and through. Several reviewers had already greeted it as such and he had had some charming letters. And as he approached his club—this was the first time he had ventured there since the book's publication—his stomach was quite weak with nervousness.

It was not the praise any longer that one was interested in, at least not once they had started talking. They were not likely to think of anything nice to say that one had not thought of oneself. It was the silences for which one listened. No doubt a comedian in his triumph is scanning the stalls for one glum face, and, if he finds it, his evening is spoiled. Luke's club was a literary one. Everyone there would know that his book had come out; a good many would by now certainly have read it. Those who had read and enjoyed it would surely come towards him and say so? We are not a demonstrative race, but it was surely hardly possible that a person who found himself face to face with the author of a book he had just read with delight should not say something in gratitude and praise. Experience had taught him that there would be a certain number of people who had not read it, but had enjoyed it. Even if one discounted these, Luke could reasonably hope for a surging towards him of genuinely appreciative faces. Then there would be those who held back, the silent ones. Some of these of course would be of those who had not read it. (Yet how easy to say, 'I *am* looking forward to reading your book!') Some would be those who had read it and thought it bad. Some would be those who had not read it and thought it bad. Surely these last, when identified, could be looked defiantly in the eyes?

It was a humiliation to Luke to find how much he cared about the opinions of others. Fundamentally, of course, he did not care in the least. There were only a very few of them that might be of any interest to him. He believed himself to be far and away his own best critic; and anyhow, the only thing that really interested him now was his next book, already well under way. He was making something and so was as happy as the day is long. Still, on the level on which people impinged, the social level, the level of manners, he was increasingly sensitive. And would he, after every book, become more and more tender-skinned? He remembered with what complacence he had watched the pile of praise going up after his first novel, with hardly a thought then of the loads that might have been, but were not being, emptied on to that pile.

Meanwhile a group of literary connoisseurs, their sherry glasses in their hands, was standing around the fireplace of the club, discussing Luke's book.

'My word, it's good! It's such a treat to find somebody who has a story to tell.'

'And can write subtly. All those poetical echoes. That bit about the corn, and then the Corn Flakes at the end.'

'Yes, and the way Mrs Hargreaves laid her umbrella down on the bank where the tramp had been lying. That was most moving.'

'Brilliant! Brilliant! The book's far better, or rather, even better, than *Jealous God*.'

'He must be feeling fine. To my mind this puts him right at the top of the tree. I mean, who else is there?'

'There isn't anybody else of his class. As a matter of fact, I've just corrected the proofs of a review in which I say just that. There was only one tiny fault I could find with the book. It seemed to me slightly exaggerated to leave Mrs Hargreaves sleeping in the railway carriage. What do you think?'

'I quite agree. That did seem rather pointless.'

'Psst! Look out! Here he comes.'

Luke joined the group. There was a silence.

'Is it still cold out?'

'Fairly,' said Luke. 'Not as cold as it was.'

'No, I thought it would get better. It generally does about this time.'

'Yes.'

'There was quite a frost at my place this morning.'

'Yes.'

In the silence that followed the writer of the review tossed back his sherry and kicked the fire.

'Should we go and eat?' he said.

As they trooped into the dining-room, one of them said to Luke,

'I expect you're feeling fine?'

Why? Why? Why should I be feeling fine? Tell me. If you insist, I'll stay here the whole afternoon while you tell me why I should be feeling fine. Speak!

'Oh, I don't know,' said Luke demurely, as though he saw the talk might take a dangerous turn. The other seemed glad to take the hint and said no more.

They sat at a round table in a bay window looking out on to a courtyard, the end wall of which was fitted with a wooden trellis in the shape of an arch up which creepers grew in summer. On a column in front of the trellis was the bronze bust of a Roman emperor. Waiters came to the table and took orders. A conversation started.

'Seen the Duccio?'

'Indeed I have! Isn't it a beauty?'

'Well, I think so. I don't myself see how anyone could possibly have any doubts about it. And what a bargain!'

'Indeed, yes! You know, I was thinking only yesterday when I was in there how Freddy has absolutely transformed that place in four years. One is apt to forget how awful it used to be in Kingston's time. Do you remember the feeling of dilapidation there used to be, as though nobody took the least interest? And certainly the public never did take the least interest. Do you remember how depressing those empty galleries used to be? A regular museum! And cold! It's properly heated now.'

'Yes, he's certainly brought the place to life. It's difficult now to imagine what one could have seen in some of those pictures before they were cleaned. And as to making art popular, it's obviously quite extraordinary what he's achieved. Heaven knows—heaven knows—' allowing the waiter to move away—'heaven knows I don't care about the people, but as a liberal one has got to welcome that sort of thing and art, one hopes, will help them, as soon as anything can, to cease to be people.'

'Quite. Have you ever tried the restaurant there? I went one day last week. It's really very good indeed, and cheap. As a matter of fact, I didn't know about it till I got into conversation with a student who was copying the Leonardo. I adore it when the students are around, don't you? It gives the impression of a workshop, a studio. Of course, you don't want them there all the time. But then, they're not there all the time.'

'Then there's the north alcove show. In my opinion that's a brilliant idea.'

'I quite agree. Mind you, it has to be very carefully handled. But then, he has the most perfect judgment, in my opinion. Have you seen this month's?'

'Yes, I have. I saw it this morning. I was lucky enough to coincide with one of those lecturers. His voice was a bit quiet, but, my word, he knew what he was talking about.'

'I'm afraid I am a bit of a Philistine,' said one who had not yet spoken. 'I haven't been into the gallery for years. I associate it with getting a headache from stale air.'

'Well, my dear Miles, you can't make that your excuse any longer for being a Philistine. The air is now conditioned. It's purer than any air you are likely to find outside.'

'Then, I must try again. As a matter of fact, I made Mayne's acquaintance the other day. He is the first of these picture chaps I've ever met who was capable of talking about something else.'

'Yes, indeed. He's a person of the widest interests, and great sensibility. I'd put his opinion on a book above anybody's—present company, of course, always excepted.'

There was a pause.

'You know him, I gather,' said Luke, speaking for the first time and addressing a face on the opposite side of the table.

'Yes, I know him.'

'Have you ever told him?'

'Told him what?'

'What's just been said. That he's making a very good show as director of the gallery.'

'Er, have I? I don't think I ever have, not to his face. Why should I?'

'He might like it.'

'Oh, I hardly think so, from me. I am not so vain as to think that my opinion on such matters would count with him at all. Besides, there must be hundreds of people, who do count, who are telling him that sort of thing all the time.'

'I wonder,' said Luke. 'You can't say nice things too often.'

There was another pause.

'Seen the new *Cornhill*?' said somebody, and the talk was off again in a new direction. For a while it remained general to the table, then it disintegrated into separate conversations between neighbours, rallying itself again from time to time into a general encounter, only to disintegrate again. During one of the latter periods Luke's neighbour said to him in a low voice, 'Do you mind if I say something to you—your book——'

'No, of course I don't mind.'

'You're sure? Some people are so sensitive.'

'Of course, I couldn't mind.' And Luke's bored, faintly amused, laugh surely conveyed the impression that until his neighbour mentioned the fact, he had quite forgotten that he had written a book.

'Go ahead, I can take it,' he said, his laugh ending in a good-natured yawn.

'I think it was a mistake to leave Mrs Hargreaves asleep in the railway carriage. It seemed rather pointless. That's all.'

Ah. And that's all? And what of the rest of the book? Was it a mistake, too? Was it all pointless? These questions remained unanswered. Luke's neighbour had apparently said his say on the subject and was now talking about something else. There was a hand on Luke's shoulder.

'I say, I'm so looking forward to reading your book. They all say it's wonderful.'

'Do they? Thank you, Jackie. See you afterwards in the billiard-room.'

No one quite knew how Jackie had ever become a member of the club. Mere alcoholic amiability was not usually thought a sufficient qualification. Perhaps every village must have its idiot. He was reputed to be unable to read.

After luncheon Luke went up to the library and sat in an armchair glancing through the pages of *The Field* and *Country Life*. How wonderful to be a farmer and drive in to Wisbech or Chipping Damerel on market-day and lunch at the Farmers' Union Club and chat about combines and silos and ticks on the backs of cows! His eyes wandered above the papers to the fireplace, in front of which a well-known cartoonist was standing, staring sadly into vacancy, and above him to an old master in a majestic frame. It was still just possible to perceive, through the grime, that the picture was a landscape. A few more years and the coating of soot would have become opaque. Then Luke had an idea. After he had had the idea, he sat on a few moments taking courage, then, with an air of resolution, went downstairs, put on his hat and coat and strode out of the club. His steps were directed towards the gallery, which was only ten minutes' walk away.

'I may as well begin here,' he said to himself, stopping to admire the work of a pavement artist by the wall of the gallery.

'I say, that's jolly good. And that one, that seascape. I like that particularly. Where on earth did you learn to draw so well?'

'The Slade School.'

'Ah. Oh. Well, jolly good. Better than most of the stuff inside there. I hope I'll see more of your work sometime. Go it.' He shook hands with the bearded tramp.

'Thank you, sir.'

Behind the beard there was something familiar in the face. As Luke went up the steps of the gallery he tried to remember. Then suddenly—why, Burtenshaw, of course! Yes, it was quite likely. Burtenshaw had been expelled for his artistic habits that term they had taken the School Certificate together. Luke decided to speak to him again on his way out.

He pushed through the swing doors and went to the counter of the cloakroom.

'Thank you. A hat, a coat and a stick. I won't say, don't get them muddled, because you never do get them muddled here. I've been leaving my hat and coat here for twenty years and there's never been a muddle. A smart set of men you are here.'

'Thank you, sir. Thank you very much.'

Luke walked through into the entrance hall and stood for some minutes in front of the Duccio. Then he moved to the postcard counter.

'Good afternoon,' he smiled.

He looked about among the postcards.

'What a beautiful Duccio that is!'

He went on picking out cards.

'What a beautiful Duccio!'

'Pardon?'

'I said, what a beautiful Duccio!'

'Don't finger the postcards there!' the lady snapped across Luke at two foreign students.

'You don't know me,' Luke went on, undeterred, 'but I know you well. I've been coming to this counter for twenty years. I've always found you rather formidable.'

'Pardon?'

'I say, I've always found you rather formidable. But then you have the right to be. You know such a lot. Yes, I've been buying postcards here for twenty years. I think some of the happiest times of my life have been spent buying postcards here. You have such excellent reproductions, and they are so cheap. And you always have what one wants. In the Louvre they never have a picture of what one wants. I'll have this little lot, please. Oh, and the Duccio, of course. What an excellent reproduction. You know, I simply adore picture postcards. I like putting them all round the walls of my sitting-room. And the bathroom.'

With the flicker that rewards a kneeling gentleman who has for some minutes been holding a newspaper outstretched in front of a grate, a smile unquestionably flickered on the face of Miss Papworth; and, as is the way with such flickers, it went out at once. Having paid for his cards, Luke walked into the main gallery.

'Good afternoon,' he said to an attendant. 'Could I see the director?'

'Have you an appointment, sir?'

'No.'

'Then I'm afraid you can't. Would you mind putting your complaint in writing, please?'

'But, I haven't a complaint. I think everything's grand. I simply want to tell him so.'

The attendant was nonplussed.

'You're not a foreigner, are you, sir?'

'No. Might that make it easier?'

'Well, one expects them to be more unusual somehow, if you know what I mean, sir.'

'Quite, quite. You don't think there's much chance of me being able to get through, then?'

'Not without an appointment, I don't. But look, sir, you go along to the end gallery there and ask the head attendant. Perhaps he'll be able to fix you up, perhaps with one of the assistant Keepers. I'm sorry I can't do more, sir, but our instructions are to tell people to put their complaints in writing and not to bother any of the officers with people who haven't got an appointment.'

'I quite see. You're doing your job properly. By the way, I've always found you chaps in here particularly obliging and well informed.'

'Thank you, sir. Thank you very much.'

Luke walked on. An idea had come to him. He had a certain gift of mimicry. He could make himself into a tolerably convincing American. In the end gallery he went up to the attendant.

'Say, can I see the director?'

'Have you an appointment, sir?'

'No.'

'Well, I'm afraid it's not possible. Would you mind putting your complaint in writing?'

'My complaint? Gee, I haven't any complaint! I think it's a swell gallery! The pictures are swell, the restaurant's swell, everything's swell! I just wanted to tell him so. What a grand smell of coffee in here!'

The attendant looked at him in perplexity.

'Perhaps Mr Wagstaffe or Mr Collins—excuse me, sir, I'll just find if there is anybody who could see you.'

While waiting, Luke gazed at the picture in front of which he found himself standing, a large landscape by Poussin. Rather dull, it seemed at first, yet, as he looked, it became alive with echoes and subtle overtones, as the eye wandered from a temple on the right by a path that wound through a thicket and over a bridge and up the side of a hillock to that other temple and then back with the low sunshine that came transversely from behind a crag striking the face of that running man, the stone of the bridge, the prow of a boat and finally that distant tower. And surely he could hear the cry of the boatman, coming over the water in the evening air, binding one side of the picture to the other? Nothing scamped, everything observed, and yet all the detail subordinate to a whole that could be taken in at a glance. Moreover, as he got inside the picture, he had the feeling that that landscape and that moment of that evening had been there for ever and ever. Such is classic art. Ah! if one could write like that!

'Is there anything I can do for you?' said a voice at his shoulder.

'Good afternoon. I am Jakes, Solon Jakes, of Wilmington, Delaware. To whom have I the pleasure of talking?'

'My name is Collins. I am one of the assistant Keepers.'

'Pleased to meet you, Mr Collins. Can I see your director?'

'Well, he is very busy this afternoon. Is it anything I can do for you? If you had any com——'

'No, I haven't any complaint. I just wanted to see your boss and tell him this is a swell gallery.'

'Just that?'

'Just that.'

Collins shook a lock of hair back from his forehead and gazed at Mr Jakes.

'I think perhaps he might be able to see you,' he said. 'Will you follow me?'

'Thank you, Mr Collins. I appreciate your kindness.'

In two minutes Mr Solon Jakes was closeted with Sir Frederick, delivering himself of a panegyric on the gallery. There would perhaps be many people, Americans and others, from whom such a eulogy would have given no particular satisfaction to the director. It became clear, however, from the first that Mr Jakes, of Wilmington, Delaware, was by no means a greenhorn in the matters about which he was talking. He was a travelled man and spoke familiarly of Brera, Accademia and Prado. He was evidently a knowledgeable and intelligent amateur of the arts. Moreover, he had learned, no doubt through bitter experience, to set at rest an Englishman's first fear, that ignoble dread of being bored, of not being able to get away, perhaps of becoming socially involved. Mr Jakes let it be known from the first that his speech would be short and that as soon as it was over he would rise from his seat and return at once to Wilmington.

It would be tedious to rehearse the things he said. Sufficient to say that he commended the arrangement of the pictures, the judicious cleaning, the admirable way in which the place was being popularised, the first-rate lectures, the interesting experiment in the north alcove, the excellent restaurant, the ventilation, the civility of the attendants, the facilities given to students, the beautiful new acquisitions. Sir Frederick beamed upon him as he spoke. From time to time he interjected a few words expressing his gratification. At length Mr Jakes seemed to have finished.

'Well, I must say,' the director said, 'I've never had so many nice things said to me in my life, never!'

'Oh, and there's just one other thing I wanted to mention, Sir Frederick Mayne, or rather person, that charming young lady who sells postcards.'

'Charming——? Young——?'

'Well, Sir Frederick Mayne, she's maybe not a chicken. I can only say she gives one a most welcoming smile.'

'Does she? You know Mr Jakes, I can almost believe that she would to such a person as yourself.'

'Well now, Sir Frederick Mayne, I guess I'll be getting along.'

'Oh, don't go! Please don't go! Sit down again. Have a glass of port.'

The director reached to a cupboard and brought out a decanter and two glasses.

'Cigar?' he said.

'Thank you.'

The director passed across a cigar-cutter.

'You know, what you've said to me has done me no end of good. I was feeling suicidal this morning. You've about saved my life—you and a book I've been reading.'

A book, thought Luke?

'What book?' said Mr Jakes.

Sir Frederick took the book out of his drawer.

'I dare say you don't read novels much. You've probably never heard of this chap.' He held the book up.

'I don't believe I have,' said Mr Jakes. 'Tell me about him.'

'Well, you're going to hear a lot about him from now on. I have no hesitation in saying that this book is a classic. I am going to insist on your promising to buy it.'

'Sure, Sir Frederick Mayne.'

'I won't spoil it for you by telling you the story. But what I will say, if I may, is that you must keep your wits about you reading it. It's so full of subtleties and echoes. It's what I'd call a classical classic.'

Classical classic, Luke murmured to himself shutting Mr Jakes' eyes, classical classic.

'By which I mean that it doesn't sprawl about like so much modern writing. It gives you the feeling of being a really finished work, tightly knit, all the parts related, most beautifully related—I hope I'm not boring you about this book but it has really made a very strong impression on me—most beautifully related to the rounded finality of the whole, with the—the discreet but vibrant inner harmony you get in some old masters, I'm thinking of the sort of thing you get in, say, Poussin.'

Get in, say, Poussin, Luke murmured, get in, say, Poussin.

'There's one point, by the way, I'll ask you to look out for. Watch for a cat asleep on a shelf. And then, at the end, there's an old woman asleep in a carriage. It's one of the most beautiful touches. I nearly missed it. Then there's a wonderful bit where——'

'Listen,' said Luke, 'I shall swoon if you say much more.'

Sir Frederick looked at him in astonishment.

'May I have the honour of autographing your copy,' Luke went on, 'and then let's forget the bally thing.'

The Lodger

Miles Enderby went for his usual walk in Kensington Gardens. This walk was not a leisurely bird-watching affair. He hurried along, with his eyes, for most of the time, on the ground. When he raised them to the view, or to meet a human face, they did not focus upon the object with conscious intelligence. His thoughts were far away. His was a preoccupied, working walk.

A writer of fiction, and one who was not far from making a living out of that alone, he had learnt to divide his craft into two activities, thinking and writing. Many year's experience had taught him a positive fear of the pen. No sooner did you take the thing in your hand than it began to vibrate with the potency of a road drill. Unless you held on tight, it went skating all over the place, and if you held on too long at a time, it shook you into a state of silliness. He had learnt, therefore, the importance of deciding, before he started to write, precisely what area he was about to break up. Some days he was almost word-perfect before he dipped the pen in the ink. This preparatory process, the main part of his creative activity, took place during the morning walk. The writing was done in the afternoon.

Many of his colleagues used to deride his laborious method of work; but there were few of them who did not readily admit that it was justified by the results. For himself, he was never happier than during the periods of composition. He much resented any intrusion upon his slow and steadfast routine.

Today, though he took the usual walk, he did so rather to get out of the house than with any hope of being able to grapple with his imagination. For his thoughts were entirely occupied with the lodger. In the early hours of that morning Richard Graves had given them all a nasty jolt.

For many years the Enderbys had let a bed-sitting-room at the top of their house. In the case of male lodgers they would undertake the cleaning of the room and the making of the bed. Females had to do these tasks for themselves. No other service was provided. A gas-ring allowed of a modest amount of cooking, and there was a basin with hot and cold water. The use of the Enderbys' bath was permitted, with half a day's notice and not more than twice a week, at a shilling a time. The use of the upstairs w.c. was free. Nor was any charge made for sun-bathing on the leads which were reached through a trapdoor in the ceiling of the lodger's room. The yearly rent was worth three or four short stories to Miles.

They had on the whole been lucky in their lodgers. Catering, as they did, for people of humble means, they had found them as a rule from the class of students or girl secretaries or lonely foreign refugees. They had once had a Chinaman for a few months. None of these were people who stayed for long. The Enderby children, when they began to go to school, lost count of the lodgers. One lodger would often recommend his successor, and thus at length arrived Richard Graves. His character sounded as though it were that of the ideal lodger. The young man was reported to have no rowdy friends, indeed few friends at all, to have no extravagant or untidy habits, to be quiet, continent, a tee-totaller and a non-smoker. A glance at his face confirmed the character that had preceded him. The Enderbys took him in gladly.

He had been with them about six months when Miles woke up suddenly one night with a feeling that something was wrong. His heart was beating fast. After he had been awake a few seconds, there was a thud on the floor above.

'Did you hear that?'

'Yes,' said his wife, who had wakened at the same moment, aroused by the same instinct. So immediate was the sympathy between these two, not only in larger matters of taste and judgment but in their minutest physical reactions, so uncanny was it at times, that they were almost persuaded to believe in the theory that love creates a third and compound personality, 'that abler soul which thence doth flow', as Donne calls it.

'I'm sure something's wrong,' he said. 'I'm going up to look.' He found the light on in the lodger's room, and there on the floor lay Richard Graves with his throat cut. The bread-knife he had used lay beside him. The blood was still pumping out of the wound and had spread off the dark carpet on to the white skirting-board where it showed a brilliant red. Miles, who hated the sight of blood anyhow and would cross the road to avoid passing a butcher's shop, was much shaken by what he saw. Ugh! What ought he to do now? Too late for the last words, he looked about for an explanatory note. There did not seem to be such a thing. Then he went downstairs to telephone for the police. Oh damn! Damn for a thousand reasons—that it should happen at all, that it should happen in the holidays when all the children were at home, that it should happen just at the moment that Miles was reaching the nervous crisis of his book, far the best book he had yet written! And not the least damnable part about it was an uncomfortable feeling at the back of his mind that by just a little more effort on his part the whole thing might have been avoided.

As he strode over the grass, Miles made no attempt to direct his mind towards his work. He knew he was much too much put out for profitable cogitation. Instead, on this enforced holiday, he allowed his thoughts to wander in a direction he normally avoided, towards first causes and eternal verities. It was the Lord's doing if his morning was wasted.

Miles, it must be admitted, was a person of limited piety. He was not one of those people who have a family feeling about the universe; who, though they may have much to criticise within the family circle, are unswerving in their loyalty to the organisation. He did not believe, or at least he did not want to believe, in an almighty God. For if God is almighty, he is responsible for everything that happens. Nothing that happens is not part of his plan. While thus being the friend—and in that capacity one is apt to forget his existence—he is also the enemy, that familiar person who, seeing a promising shoot of happiness somewhere on the surface of the globe, says, 'This must be nipped in the bud!' He it is who devised each horrible thing. He invented asthma, cancer and insanity. He made animals prey upon one another for food and for pleasure. He sent flies to torment horses on summer afternoons and had the pretty idea of teaching hawks to settle on the horns of gazelles and peck out their eyes. He invented bombs and forced high-minded young men to drop them, for the highest motives, unwillingly, on foreign children. He invented lonely lodgers and arranged that they should commit suicide. Look, almighty God, look at him lying there in his blood! You did it! You are wholly responsible. The full credit is yours. *Inv. del. et sculp.* It is entirely your handiwork. Ugh! A most bloody affair, an act of God if ever there was one!

When one contemplates the management of creation, he thought, one must surely hope that there is no single directing hand? Better no meaning to things than that meaning. Belief in human sin, even in original human sin, hardly helps. What do our little, hesitant offences amount to? With the best will in the world, we cannot, in reason, hope to take enough of the blame to permit the existence of an omnipotent friend.

Towards the enemy, the bomber, the pecker, Miles could feel no filial loyalty. Gratitude for all things bright and beautiful did not diminish, indeed it increased, resentment at all the unattractive things. Thankful for large mercies, less thankful for small mercies, he was not thankful at all for those many frustrations which are sent to prevent one getting on with one's estimable work.

The suicide of Richard Graves had come as a most violent interruption to Miles' work. It would be two or three days at least before he could get back to business. Curse the fool! Why had he gone and done it? The investigations of the morning had uncovered no particular motive. There was no evidence of any love affair. The people at his office had no ideas. A dim sister was unearthed from somewhere but could throw no light on things. And Miles felt confident that, in fact, no particular story would unfold itself. Mrs Fletcher, the charwoman, had, he was sure, said all that there was to say. 'He always seemed a very lonely kind of gentleman.'

Richard Graves had not been long with the Enderbys before they had remarked on his loneliness. He used to sit up there in his room night after night by himself. No one ever came to see him and he never brought anyone in with him. His life seemed to be centred entirely on his books and on a gramophone which he played with commendable quietness. His office, one gathered, was just a dreary place where he earned his daily bread. Miles never learned exactly what Richard's work was. As for his social life, it took place, so far as there was any, under other roofs. 'Going out somewhere?' Miles would say, meeting him in the hall.

'Yes, I'm going to the club.'

What 'the club' was Miles never discovered. Richard was a cagey fellow. The way he answered questions did not encourage one to ask more. Not being in the least curious about him, Miles was perfectly content to leave it at that. One could not want more in a lodger than reclusive self-sufficiency. Richard seemed at first to be the ideal lodger.

Yet, one day, Mrs Enderby said:

'That new lodger gives me the pip!'

'I know,' said Miles. 'Me too.'

For all its caginess, there was something obtrusive about the presence of Richard Graves, a kind of concentration or inward pressure that was not at all restful to have about the place. Beyond a timid smile in the hall, and perhaps, in the case of girls, a discreet fragrance on the stairs when they have passed, one wants to be able to forget the existence of lodgers. It was not possible to forget Richard Graves. His presence, up there in his room, could be felt all over the house.

'When I pass him,' she went on, 'I feel as I used to about passing an engine in a station when I was a child. I always used to think it was going to explode. I cannot bear to meet his eyes.'

'I know, I know. Someone ought to take him in hand. In fact, he ought to take himself in hand. He must be thirty. Do you think we ought to start being kind to him?'

'No, not really. Besides, it would probably be kinder to leave him alone. If you were to succeed in winkling him out of his shell, what would you do with him then?'

'Just so. And, anyhow, we are not saints. We value our time too much. Something tells me that if we started being kind to him, there would be no end to it. Besides, I have enough on my hands at the moment with Cyril.'

Cyril was their first-born, a youth of immense charm and promise but not yet of much stability. Still, the Enderbys did make certain friendly gestures towards the lodger. One day coming back from the country, Mrs Enderby found that she had brought more flowers than she had vases for.

'Cynthia.'

'Yes, Mummy?' Cynthia was fourteen years old.

'Would you like to take these flowers up to the lodger?'

'No.'

'But will you, please?'

'Must I?'

'Yes, please. It would be kind.'

'All right, if I must. I hate Graveyard.'

The errand did not take long.

'Well, was he pleased?'

'I suppose so.'

'Did he say thank you?'

'Er—I don't remember. Yes, I suppose so. Oh, Mummy, he's so awful!'

'How?'

'Oh, I don't know, just sort of awful!—He laughs so loud.' Richard Graves, when he laughed, did indeed laugh much too loud. Fortunately he did not laugh often.

Miles made considerable efforts to get on terms of easy, if non-committal, cordiality with his lodger. Effort was certainly needed. The fellow was so fiercely on the defensive.

'Ah, Graves,' said Miles in the hall one day, with a pleasant smile, 'been getting some new records?'

He bent to look at the top record in Richard's hand.

'Schubert,' he said. 'Nice.'

'Oh that tosh! That's just the odd side,' said the lodger, clasping his records to him while his eyes blazed scorn and defiance. For Richard Graves was prodigiously highbrow. The books and records that littered his room showed that, with the aid of the most advanced literary weekly, he aimed only at the highest in literature and music. From time to time, *à propos* of some volume Richard was carrying, Miles would have short conversations about books with his lodger on the stairs, on the landing. Names were mentioned, many of them foreign, that were only names to Miles. The conversations generally ended with Richard giving Miles to understand that until he had read So-and-so, his cultural life could hardly have been said to have begun. As to the culture of his lodger, one thing Miles noticed was that Richard Graves read foreign works only in translation. His ignorance of foreign languages extended even to the pronunciation of the names of some of the foreign authors. Clearly he could never have heard these authors named.

It was important—and Miles thought he made this quite obvious—that these literary colloquies should be short and should take place, as it were, *en passant*. One evening there was a step coming down the stairs and a knock on the Enderbys' door.

'Come in.'

It was the lodger.

'I've brought that book I promised to lend you.'

Richard Graves was advancing into their room. The Enderbys exchanged a meaning glance. This sort of thing must be nipped in the bud. Miles rose to meet the lodger and within a minute had him out of the room and had shut the door after him. In his hand Miles held a translation of the prose work of Leopardi. Leeoppady, Richard called him.

Another evening Miles had gone into the hall to turn the light off before going to bed, when the lodger came in at the front door.

'Hullo, Graves! Been to the club?'

'No. At least, yes.'

He seemed embarrassed.

'Good night,' he said, hurrying past Miles, but as he passed, he fumbled with a book in his hand and dropped it, scattering some photographs over the hall floor. Miles helped him pick them up. They were photographs of naked girls; nothing sensational of their kind, but there was no doubt about the kind. When they were all picked up, Miles put a friendly hand on Richard's shoulder.

'My dear chap,' he said. The words were intended to convey, Don't be embarrassed; relax, I like you better than ever. But Richard winced away from the touch. His eyes were blazing. Miles' heart went out to him.

'Come in and have a drink,' he said recklessly, 'before going to bed.

I'm alone.'

'No. No thanks. Good night.'

The lodger disappeared up the stairs. Miles did not insist. He allowed him to disappear, though he was saying to himself: Now, if you ever mean to do anything about him, now's the time to strike. The fact was, he did not mean to do anything about Richard, at least, not anything big. A limited courtesy, in the passage, was all he intended. Frankly he had not time for more. After all, is one one's lodger's keeper? He, Miles, was a breadwinner, a paterfamilias, a valued clubman, and, not least, an artist. The days simply were not long enough for him to do his duty by his family, his friends and his art, without bringing half-baked lodgers into the picture.

Moreover, he believed it would in the end be kinder not to go any further with Richard Graves. He fancied he could see well what would happen if he began to take the young man in hand. 'Richard,' he would say, putting a friendly arm in his and disregarding the wince, 'Richard—by the way, you don't mind if I call you Richard?—we like to be on Christian names with our lodgers—I'm Miles, by the way—Richard, I was wondering whether, if you happen to be free, you'd care to come in and have a drink with me . . . Oh, that doesn't matter, you can watch me drink—I want to pick your brains. You know such a lot; it isn't often we have such an interesting chap about the house. I'm determined to take advantage of you, in spite of that Olympian manner of yours—are you, by the way, as Olympian as you appear?'

There would follow an hour of excruciating boredom as Richard delivered himself of pretentious opinions upon things of the mind. At length Miles would say, '. . . now, Richard, I expect you're busy. I won't keep you any longer. But I must say I've enjoyed our talk enormously. Let's do it again. In fact, I'm going to pin you down. What about tomorrow, or Friday? Tomorrow? Splendid! Thanks. By the way, I don't believe a glass of sherry has done you any harm, has it? In fact, come on, just another half-glass for the road. That's it! We'll make a drunkard of you yet, Richard!'

Oh, nauseous!

A certain confidence established, things, the next time, would become more personal. After an hour of it, '. . . no, no, Dick, of course I haven't been bored. I have been simply fascinated to hear about your family and childhood. I hope that next time you will carry on the story and bring us up to date.' And so next time, and the time after, the uninteresting tale would be continued. Having never had anyone to listen to him like this before, Richard Graves would be enjoying himself enormously. You would get the impression that he thought the universe a pretty badly organised place in which the authorities had a particular down on Richard Graves. The time had come for the serious taking-in-hand.

'Listen, Dick, what's wrong with you. . . . I dare say, I dare say, but I repeat, what's wrong with you is that you take yourself too seriously. . . . Oh yes, it *is* possible. If only you'd relax. . . . Oh no, you don't, you're much too pleased with yourself . . . well, as a matter of fact, I think you're the most conceited person I've ever met. . . .'

After this conversation there would be a short period of coolness. But the new intimacy in Richard's life would have gone too far for him now to be able to get on without it. He would feel those arrogant defences, which he had erected between himself and the world, falling around him like the walls of Jericho. The snail had been unshelled. His regeneration had begun. A humble Richard would come back a few days later for more.

'Relax, Dick, that's what I say to you. Don't fancy you're a great man. Frankly, you're not. Relax on the intellectual stuff. Go slow on Goethe—yes, Gurter, G-U-R-T-E-R. Give Kierkegaard and Rilke a rest. Drink, smoke. Learn to mix with people. I know it's difficult in London to find any people. There must be no area of the same size on the face of the earth in which it is so hard to find a friendly face. All the fun, I know, seems to be happening on the other side of doors and walls and railings, in other people's lighted rooms. It is "members only" and people in passing cars who are having the fun. I know all that, because I used to feel lonely in London myself once. What did I do? I pulled myself together and got married. What you need, Dick, is a woman, a real live woman!'

'You're awfully good to me, Miles.'

Then would come the unsatisfactory moment, the moment Miles so clearly foresaw. To have brought Richard to this point would have already cost his mentor many valuable hours. If, now that he had put Richard on the right road, he could have withdrawn, those tedious hours would perhaps have seemed well spent. But would Richard, gaily shouldering his pack, now bid Miles a grateful farewell and stride off out of his life? No such luck! The trusting dog-like eyes would look up to him for further direction. Organise me, they would say; take me in hand, don't leave me now. Miles would find that he had taken on much more than he had, in conscience, time for. There would have to be a break sooner or later. He would have either to say, or to convey, to Richard the following: Look, let's face facts. I can only stand a very little of your company, and I do not mean to impose you on my friends. You are not interesting. You are singularly lacking in charm. Your looks are utterly undistinguished. I've given you what I believe to be a few good ideas. It's now time for you to stand on your own feet. I'm busy.

When the lodger found himself thus abandoned, what would he do? His last state would be worse than his first. He would probably commit suicide. For these reasons Miles abstained from allowing his relationship with Richard Graves to grow into more than the occasional friendly exchange in the passage. He told his wife about the photographs.

'I'm not surprised,' she said. 'How pathetic! Should we get rid of him?'

'Well, what do you think?'

'I don't care. You decide.'

'Well, what I think is, that if we give him the sack now, it would look as if it was directly because of the photographs, whereas I don't mind in the least about them, do you?'

'Not in the least. Provided he doesn't scatter them about the place, it's much better from the point of view of an example to the children that he should have them rather than the real thing. Now that Cyril is reaching an impressionable age, it's lucky for instance that we haven't got someone like Ferruccio up there.' Ferruccio was a former lodger who had in the Enderbys' opinion abused the hospitality of their house.

'Quite,' said Miles. 'From that point of view, and indeed from many others, Graveyard might be a good deal worse. One thing, he's exceedingly punctual with his rent. So we'll let him stay now, and if after a while we simply can't stand him any longer, then we'll give him notice.'

'All right. But in the meantime I'm not going to send Cynthia up with messages to him again.'

So anxious was Miles to make Richard feel no embarrassment in the matter of the photographs that he planned a rather particular and personal gesture of kindness towards him the next evening. Meeting him casually on the stairs—and, by the way, to meet him casually on the stairs had involved listening a long time for Richard's step and then an undignified leap to the door and swift and furtive movements on the landing—let all this expenditure of time and attention please be remembered by whoever tots things up—meeting Richard then casually on the stairs, he had said, 'I was wondering whether perhaps you'd care for a copy of this little affair. It's my last novel.'

'Oh,' Richard took the book.

'I expect you'll think it terribly middle-brow stuff. I don't expect you to read it, by the way.'

Richard said nothing. Miles began to feel embarrassed.

'I'll just write your name in it, shall I?'

'Oh, don't bother.'

'It's no bother. Have you a pen on you, by the way?'

'No.'

'Just a minute, I'll get mine.'

'Oh, don't bother.'

Miles decided not to bother.

'Well, good night.'

'Good night.'

Really, being kind to this lodger was not an encouraging business! Still, within the limits they allowed themselves, the Enderbys did their best. At length Christmas came round. The family was discussing Christmas presents.

'I suppose you'll be wanting to give a present to Graveyard?' said Cynthia.

'Yes,' said her mother. 'We must not leave him out. Anyone got any ideas?'

'A book token.'

'No,' said Miles. 'He has more books than are good for him already.'

'What about an engagement book?'

'Don't be unkind, Cyril.'

'All right. Some spats then.'

'Some anti-spot syrup,' said Nigel.

'Yes, or a salad bowl,' said Anne. 'I'm sure he doesn't eat enough green food.'

'*I* know,' said Mrs Enderby. 'The poor man only has a blunt stainless steel knife for cutting his bread. Let's give him a bread knife.'

So they gave him a bread knife for Christmas. But their little kindnesses were not enough to ward off the catastrophe.

Moral Tale

Sir Hanson Wainwright, in dinner-jacket, followed his wife down the gangway of the concert hall. He was aware how easily, and with what justification, his Christian name gave itself to a play on words. Sir Handsome knew himself to look most distinguished. He also knew that looks are a gift of the gods, and, as inherited capital rather than earned income, add no credit to the character of their owner. In totting up the virtues that had led to his success in life, a thing he did rather often, he was in the habit, therefore, of passing them over. Still, there they were. They were not to be despised on such occasions as walking into a concert hall, stepping across the feet of other people on the way to one's seat, and, having found one's seat, not at once sitting in it, but standing there, nodding to an important acquaintance or two, seeing and being seen.

Who could deny that Sir Hanson had made a success of life? The facts spoke for themselves. He was head of a Government department, trustee of this, governor of that, vice-president of the other. Established socially, matrimonially, parentally, he had lately had his virtues rewarded by becoming a grandparent. Yet, withal, a modest, human, Christian man, with a sense of humour. His long entry in *Who's Who* ended on a note of impeccable simplicity: Recreation, walking on the downs. As the First Commissioner of Tunnage and Poundage at length lowered himself into his seat, he did indeed feel that he deserved this place in the third row of the stalls.

Not that concerts were things he enjoyed. They bored him exceedingly. He could make nothing of music. Still, every now and then, for social or professional reasons, it had to be endured. This evening was one of the occasions on which he deemed that not only his patronage as the buyer of two tickets, but his presence, was required. For the sake of this important charity he must face the two hours of nothingness. Charity—yes, of course, he was forgetting that. His was perhaps the only head in the hall that evening which was visited by thoughts of the welfare conferred by his generous outlay on the widows of lifeboatmen.

The music had not been going on for long when he noticed, in the row in front on the other side of the gangway, Leslie Hammond. In spite of the passage of years, of the receding and greying hair, he recognised him at once; and, as he looked, he found himself becoming possessed by a feeling of indignation. The little bounder! Why was he cropping up again? For Sir Hanson was aware that the next day he would have to make a certain important decision with regard to Leslie Hammond and Leslie Hammond was an individual he would have been happy to continue not to think about, as, for a quarter of a century, he had not thought about him.

Not that he still bore him any rancour for the old days. He could honestly say to himself that he had the greatness of soul not to harbour any such feelings. Pity, surely, was more what one felt in the long run for such a cad. It was the only feeling that a gentleman *could* have for an outsider. To say therefore, that he had forgiven Hammond for those old offences would hardly be true. Forgiveness, in Wainwright's view, can only take place between those who are more or less equal. The only thing to do then, the thing that he had done, was to expunge Hammond from his mind and resolve, if he should ever turn up there again, to thin contempt with a little benevolence into pity. He had thus got on very well for many years without a thought of Hammond. The man anyhow was a nobody, a mere writer.

The offences referred to were two. In the first place, when Hanson was passionately in love, and his suit was prospering and everything was practically fixed up, that little twerp had stepped in and walked off with the young lady right under his nose. All is said to be fair in love and war and Hanson was, of course, not the man to take an ungenerous view in these matters, even where his own feelings were concerned, but—well, he could honestly claim that it had not been a very pretty performance. Of course, as time had proved, he was well quit of it. Things had shown that Desirée was not cut out to be a wife, and though he had never experienced anything like the feelings for her that he had had for the other, he had clearly done much better with Joan.

The other offence concerned money. During the same short period that his and Hammond's paths had been crossing, there had been an occasion when Hanson had bought some theatre tickets. The plan was that he and Hammond should go halves over the tickets. He had told Hammond the price and the latter had said he would give him the twenty-five shillings he owed him when he had some change. That money was never paid. The sum was trifling, it is true, but, in Hanson's opinion, dishonesty was dishonesty, whatever the sum. He found this conduct unpardonable. Exceedingly correct himself in all money matters, Hanson had already formed a most unfavourable view of Leslie Hammond's character before ever he committed the other, and, in Hanson's view, hardly greater, offence.

All this was long ago and, though not forgotten (Hanson had the memory of an elephant), could be remembered dispassionately. Why then the indignation tonight? There was something else. As he looked across at his enemy—no, no, not enemy, that pathetic little bounder should not be dignified with the name of enemy—as he watched him sitting there listening to the music, he was exasperated to realise that Hammond, as once before, had something that he himself had not got. It was the music. The man was rapt, his hand gripping his chin, his eyes far away, his body taut.

Hanson had from time to time had it brought to his notice how responsive some people were to the arts. A blissful world seemed to open to them, something immeasurably more rich, more important, than the world of everyday. Well, one must accept the fact that some people were rewarded with these delights and others not. But reward for what? That was the question. For it was often the least estimable people who were so endowed. Here, for example was the morally despicable Hammond evidently in a state of bliss. It was not fair. Not on the short view. Here was where Christianity came in. This was one of the things that an after life would rectify. Heaven then would be for those who had earned it, for those who, without thought of reward, had here made their stand for moral rectitude. The others—well, one must not gloat.

In the interval Sir Hanson had the satisfaction of cutting Leslie Hammond. Meanwhile he had made up his mind on the attitude he would take about him the next day. Hammond's name had been proposed for election to a certain distinguished club in which Sir Hanson sat on the election committee. As he thought about the morrow's meeting, it had seemed to Sir Hanson that he heard the clear call of duty.

There, then, the following evening, he was sitting with a dozen other members of the committee at a long mahogany table in an upper room of the club. Outside the window, in a gap between the foliage of two massive planes, his eyes rested upon a portion of the creamy pediment of the building over the way, which became every moment yellower as the summer evening declined. The names of the candidates were submitted, one by one, by the chairman, who read out in each case the letters sent in by his supporters, then asked if the company had any opinions to express. 'I know him,' one would say, 'a decent fellow.' 'Yes, an amusing chap. He'd definitely be an asset.' So after a few observations, the ballot box would be handed round. Two blackballs would exclude, but their use was rare. It was rare for a doubtful name ever to find its way into the proposal book.

'We come now to Hammond, Leslie Hammond,' said the chairman, taking a draught of whisky and soda. He then read three letters he had received about this candidate, commending his distinction as a writer and his charm as a man, and affirming that he would make a most suitable member of the club.

'Well,' said the chairman, 'I don't know him personally, but he sounds all right. What does anybody say?'

One or two members spoke up for Hammond, confirming what had been said by the letter writers.

'Then,' said the chairman, looking round the committee, 'shall we proceed to the ballot?'

Sir Hanson cleared his throat.

'Haven't we enough scribblers in this club?' he said.

'Scribblers,' said the chairman. 'I say, Wainwright, I think it's a bit unfair on Hammond to call him a scribbler. I mean to say, by general consent, he seems to be looked upon as one of the established writers.'

'Of course, of course,' said Sir Hanson, with a knowing little laugh. 'I was only hoping to by-pass what I have to say.'

He cleared his throat again, straightened his back and lengthened his face into an expression of extreme seriousness.

'It is an exceedingly disagreeable duty I have to perform,' he said, 'but I should be letting down the club if I did not do it. It is my unwelcome duty to have to say that Hammond is not an honest man.'

'Not honest?' said the chairman. 'In what way not honest, Wainwright?'

'Money.'

There was a movement round the table.

'I never found that,' said one.

'I never heard that,' said another.

'I hate to have to say it,' Sir Hanson continued, 'but I speak from personal experience. Money.'

His gaze moved slowly round the faces at the table. Embarrassed eyes were lowered as it met them. Two, at least, of the faces owed their presence in the club, and at this committee, to Sir Hanson's recommendation.

'Yes,' he repeated, 'money.'

There was a silence. The chairman was looking down at the table, frowning.

'Thank you, Wainwright,' he said at length. 'You have, of course, done quite right to tell us this. We mustn't elect pick-pockets to the club. Can anybody else corroborate, from his own experience, what Wainwright has told us?'

'It's complete news to me,' said one.

'I've always found him recklessly indifferent to his own interests in money matters,' said another.

There was silence again. The chairman looked around to see if anyone else wanted to speak. There was silence.

'Let us then proceed to the ballot,' he said.

The box was passed round amid an unwonted hush. The ballot was generally an occasion for facetiousness and laughter and irrelevant conversation. Ping, went the balls, as they were dropped into the box, which at length reached the chairman again. He took out the drawer on the left-hand side of the box.

'Three blackballs,' he said. 'Hammond is not elected.'

Some twenty minutes later Sir Hanson Wainwright stepped out of the club. It had been disagreeable, but he had done his duty. He had, of course, not been actuated in any way by personal considerations. Indifferent to his own popularity, he had simply done, as he always tried to do, the right thing. He felt he was entitled to hope that that was the last he would hear of Leslie Hammond in this life.

But no. It never rains but it pours. He had not been outside the club two minutes when he saw Hammond on the other side of Pall Mall. Then an extraordinary thing happened. Driven by some unwonted force, far stronger than his own will, he crossed the street and stood in Hammond's way.

'You have not been elected to the club,' he said. 'I saw that you got blackballed.' He paused. The other moved to pass him. 'I want you to know,' Sir Hanson went on, 'that I did it out of envy.'

The two men looked at one another for a moment in amazement, then Sir Hanson walked on. He did not know what had happened to himself. He knew only that he was dragging along behind him the moral wreckage of Sir Hanson Wainwright. The curious thing was that the said wreckage was so light. It weighed nothing at all. Indeed, his step on the pavement felt as springy as that of a schoolboy, in gym shoes, running on grass.

The Master

'Rather an odd story this, about the Master of St Michael's,' said the Solicitor-General.

'What about him?' said Alastair McColl. 'I was talking to him in this club only two or three weeks ago. A nice old boy. I remember our talk well.'

'Look at that,' said the other, passing over the newspaper he had been reading. But we must go back to the conversation between the Master of St Michael's and Alastair McColl.

The Master of St Michael's did not often come to London. Only business would take him there. He did not care for the place. It made him feel out of things. Today he had come up to see his lawyer and his dentist, and, if there were time, his niece and great-nephews and great-nieces, who were somewhat on his conscience. He had had to have luncheon somewhere and so, taking his courage in both hands, had come to this club—this intimidating club, that was so unlike the high table at St Michael's. You did not know whom you might not find yourself next to, judges, distinguished men of letters, Members of Parliament, people with the gift of the gab, of darting minds and quick responses. The Master of St Michael's, on his rare visits here, found that he was left far behind in the talk and used to think of those agonizing weeks he had once spent in a French family, working out, from time to time, a telling contribution to the conversation of five minutes ago. He knew, of course, that he never ought to have been elected, a shy, parochial, academic type like himself. Nor would he ever have been elected had not his predecessor in office, at the moment of his retirement, pushed him into it. 'Nonsense,' he had said, 'of course the Master of St Michael's needs to have a London club. You'll love the place. It'll take your mind off the college.' The new Master was grateful and flattered, but none the less conscious that no Amurath had ever been less like the preceding Amurath than he was like the retiring Master. Besides, he did not want to have his mind taken off the college.

Sir Lennox had come to St Michael's from the outside world, a public and social man, a man of speeches, committees, commissions and boards, who quickly became Vice-Chancellor of the university. He would frequently go up to London on important affairs and persons of great eminence would come down to stay with him at the lodge. The new Master, on the other hand, was a professional don. He had spent all his life at St Michael's, in loyal and single-hearted service, until one day he had found himself the favourite candidate for the Mastership which was about to become vacant. After the somewhat flamboyant reign of Sir Lennox, it was felt that the college would benefit by a more quiet and anchored, if less distinguished, ruler, and he had been chosen. The only possible rival had been Coleridge, the Dean. But then Coleridge, though a worthy fellow, was five years his junior; and, of course, if he himself did not hang on too long, the younger man might always succeed him in the place. The Master, now in his sixty-sixth year, had, indeed, begun to fancy from time to time that he could detect a something in Coleridge's eye.

Not much given to regrets or self-questionings, he was, however, aware that his life might be regarded by some people as unenterprising. As he left his anchorage, in the train to London that morning, the thought had struck him forcibly. He had been reading a book about the Charge of the Light Brigade. Looking up from the fascinating pages, to right and to left, at the suburban houses through which he was charging so triumphantly, and with so little danger, he had said to himself, 'I have never in my life done anything brave.' 'Oh come!' he had argued, 'it was pretty good at your age going up that ladder yesterday to look at the ivy. Then, if you go to the club today, that will be brave. Then——' He reflected. It was clear to him that the most memorable occasions of valour that he could instance from his whole life were unspeakably tame.

As he took his seat for luncheon at the club in the next vacant place at a table already half filled, a young man sat down on the further side of him.

'Good morning,' said the young man briskly. 'My name's McColl.'

By 'young' in this context the Master would have understood something between thirty and fifty. He found it increasingly difficult to place with any exactitude those of middle years.

'Good morning.' And the Master introduced himself.

'Ah,' said the young man, 'that sounded rather an interesting suicide at your university the other day.'

'Interesting? It was a bad show.'

'Would you say suicide is always a bad thing?'

As usual that plunging *in medias res*, which the Master was wont to find so disconcerting at this club.

'Er—yes—I suppose so. I have never given the matter much

thought.'

'What I mean is, it's not always an unhappy affair, is it? There's such a thing as positive or constructive suicide, isn't there?'

'There was always Cleombrotus of Ambracia.'

'Who was he?'

'An ancient Greek philosopher. One day, having read about Plato's Elysium, he leapt into the sea in order to enjoy it as soon as possible.'

'Splendid! I like that. Thank you. A truly classical performance. Head first into the blue Mediterranean! They say that drowning is most enjoyable. I think that's the way I'd choose to do it, wouldn't you?'

'Er—I don't know. Perhaps. I've never thought.'

'But—my question. Is suicide necessarily wrong?'

'I suppose so. You're not supposed to take your own life.'

'But aren't you, ever? Let us agree that to do so out of cowardice or laziness, to avoid pain or shirk responsibilities or get yourself out of a tangle, is despicable and probably, if there is another life, most unwise. But your Greek philosopher was better than that. He was positive. He was trying to grasp something not to let it go. Yet his action presumably is open to the charge of egotism. One can imagine, can one not, noble or altruistic suicide, that is wholly commendable?'

'I'd always imagined it couldn't be right ever.' After his momentary advantage with Cleombrotus of Ambracia, the Master felt himself again to be hopelessly on the run. He really had no ideas on the subject of the conversation and could not be sure, from the twinkle in the young man's eye, whether he was serious or not.

'But consider, is not almost all heroism more or less suicidal? When it comes to a crisis, a war, we do not speak disparagingly of those who allow their lives to be terminated unnecessarily early by doing something brave. But is not all life a crisis?'

Emphatically not, the Master was disposed to answer. He had always fancied that the one inevitable crisis would be quite enough. It gave a tragedy and violence to the quietest of lives; though, if pressed, he would probably have allowed that he did not anticipate too great a violence even from that crisis. He supposed that you went either to heaven or to hell. With regard to the latter place his ideas were curiously precise. Being extremely sound in body, he had had little experience of physical suffering. At an age when most people have not much left to bite with, he was for the first time in his life finding that his teeth required stopping. The possibilities of the electric drill much impressed him. Suppose, when your groans informed him that he had found the intolerable spot, the Great Dentist were to press there for ever and ever and ever, and you could not die because you were already dead. Such would be the Master's bodily hell. His soul meanwhile would be handed over to Sir George Parkins. This individual had been his chief in a ministry in which he had worked during a war. Perish the memory of him! An overweening bully and know-all, he would wear down the staunchest with the merciless insistence of his voice. Delighting in minutiae, pompous, cunning, restless, he made it his business, by fair means or foul, to break the will of each person within his command, from the lowest to the highest. That affair of the conveyor belt. . . ! A man without humour, without music, without peace—a detestable man. The mild soul of the Master had been much shocked to find itself becoming possessed by some of the more disagreeable symptoms of hatred. His own peace was going. What on earth would have happened to his character had that war not come to an end? Oh, forget those wretched days! With the passage of the years he had learned to keep them from his mind. Yet the memory, when he thought of them, was as fresh as ever. He knew quite well that there could be nothing worse in store for him, not even the electric drill, than to be handed over again to the power, the voice, of Sir George Parkins. The combination of the drill *and* Parkins was unthinkably horrible. It was so bad that he did not imagine he could possibly be destined for that. He had not earned it. Indeed, the weight of guilt lay extremely lightly upon him. Searching his memories for something bad had the same result as looking there for something brave. Hell was not for him. Heaven, then. On this subject his ideas were quite unformulated. He vaguely supposed that his mansion would be much like St Michael's. He would take his oboe there with him, and there would certainly be a towpath and the company, continuously renewed, of fine and well-bred young men. . . . But his interlocutor was waiting for an answer.

'Suicide is always wrong,' said the Master. 'It is unchristian.'

'Unchristian? Are you sure? Listen. If killing yourself is a great vice, keeping yourself alive must be a great virtue. According to such a view of things, any action tending to reduce the number of your days is wrong. If the maintenance of breath is the ideal, you would avoid all such suicidal activities as smoking, drinking coffee, eating meat and working, anything in fact that is in any way wearing or tiring to the system, such as love, indignation and patient forbearance. Is that the Christian ideal? Why, nobody, surely, courted—yes, courted—death, like the supreme example of conduct?'

'Er—yes. I suppose you could say so.'

'I can imagine,' said McColl, with a wistful air, 'I can imagine a perfectly beautiful suicide, a Christian suicide, something done without either bitterness or self-seeking, out of pure love. Someone, we can suppose, who feels that he has done his work in this world, yet realizes that he may live many years more on the money that is so desperately needed at this moment by his prospective legatees, someone, it must be, who is happy and in good health and unafraid of disease and decrepitude, who yet realizes that by his withdrawal the sum of life would be enhanced and—but I see that I am boring you. I'm sorry. It's perhaps time that we talked a bit to our other neighbours. But I must thank you again for Cleombrotus of Ambracia. One's heart goes out to him, does it not, to the civilisation, the privacy, the lovely seriousness of the man?'

With that he turned to his other side. The Master did likewise and found a face of the same sort of age as his own.

'Excuse me,' he said in an undertone, 'who is it I've been talking to on the other side?'

'McColl, he's called. He's in the government, an undersecretary, the Ministry of Health, I believe.'

'Rather the man for the job, I should say.'

'I always find his talk a bit exaggerated. Means no harm, I dare say. He has a V.C. by the way. To whom have I the honour of speaking? I'm ——shire.'

The Master introduced himself.

'Ah,' said the other, 'I have a nephew at your college.'

From that moment the Master was perfectly at his ease. He was able to talk shop till the end of the meal, making discreet propaganda on behalf of many purposes connected with the institution over which he presided, that were thwarted by lack of funds. He felt that it would be surprising if Lord ——shire did not, in the next few days, let him have a cheque. In considerably better heart than he had entered it, the Master left the club, directing his steps towards Lincoln's Inn. He would be able to walk there comfortably in time for his appointment with his lawyer.

He had brought away from the club a sense of high purpose that could not be entirely explained by his second conversation there. Indeed, his experience of the kind of cheque just mentioned, was that it did not often exceed ten pounds, and whatever good was that to St Michael's? The college had always been a poor one. Thirty or forty years ago the fellows had been subjected by one of their number, Bond, an economist, to a bombardment of proposals for bettering their state. His science at that time was a somewhat new one and his colleagues listened to him with respectful, if nervous, incomprehension. He was plausible and insistent. The upshot was that they had entrusted the college finances entirely to his care. Let him do what he liked, provided he put them firmly on their feet. The result had been disastrous. Within a few years the college, far from being able to pay its way, let alone expand, had had to tighten its belt more than ever. Only by drastic economies had it managed to remain solvent. One of the most regretted of these economies had been a reduction in the already meagre scholarships it offered. When Sir Lennox, a man of means, had succeeded to the Mastership, he had restored the value of the scholarships by putting back into the pool half the Master's stipend. This last, even before it was divided by two, had never been a generous sum, and it was always supposed that with a new occupant of the post the scholarships would again be cut. Sir Lennox's successor, however, had £6,000 of his own, derived partly from the lifetime's savings of a bachelor of inexpensive tastes and partly from a legacy of the parent of a pupil who had been killed in a war. In spite of the protests of his colleagues at his generosity, the new Master insisted on continuing his predecessor's practice. (If he was content with an excuse not to be shaken out of his modest habits of life, whose business was that?) The scholarships were maintained. The fabric of the college, however, became each year more dilapidated. As the Master walked past St Martin's-in-the-Fields and observed the bright stone refacing, he thought painfully of the first court at St Michael's, and it seemed to him that as he crossed the court he was suddenly face to face with Coleridge——

Now, Coleridge, the excellent Coleridge, had married a woman with money, and they were without children. The man's heart, as indeed that of his wife, was given entirely to the welfare of the college. It could be presumed that if he were to succeed to the Mastership, he would occupy the place on the same terms in the matter of the scholarships as his two predecessors. And occupy it, of course, very well indeed, and with an asset to which the present Master could make no claim. The latter was not given to eavesdropping but college architecture—buttresses, sudden turnings into cloisters, rows of open ground-floor windows, the wells of staircases—lends itself to the overhearing of words intended for the ears of others. He had been much impressed by the words of one of the bed-makers which he had heard the other day—' 'E's all right, but it 'ud be nice to 'ave a lady at the Lodge again, if yer know what I mean.' The Master knew what she meant and suspected that her opinion was held by many persons of higher rank than herself on the staff of the college. Well then, let him now make way for Coleridge. For, if it was to be done at all it must be done soon. Then what would he himself live on? He could scrape along in retirement on his own money. Yes, but—by the way, what an extraordinary conversation that had been with the young man, McColl, a most unusual conversation!

The Master walked on through Covent Garden, carrying the Coleridges in the palm of his hand. After Coleridge, there was no one among the fellows with any private means. Coleridge in the saddle, the scholarships should be safe for another ten or fifteen years. If he himself hung on until Coleridge was too old for the job, the next man obviously would be Skipworth (unless, of course, there was an outsider, and the Master hoped there would not be another outsider for some time). Skipworth would make an excellent Master in many ways, but, with his large family and his convivial habits, he was known to have the greatest difficulty in making both ends meet. He would be hardly the man to help things out. Money, money, money, that was what the college needed, and at once!

The ivy, for instance, in the first court—there was a problem that needed an immediate solution. Where was the money to come from? You could not go on every year issuing appeals to the old members of the college. There had been a fair response a couple of years ago in respect of the boat-house. It had simply not been possible for the college to carry on for another season with that disgraceful tumbled-down shed. The new building was indeed something to be proud of, the best thing of its kind in the university and worthy of the fine tradition of the college oarsmen. It was something to have solved that problem. The ivy in the first court was another and more serious affair.

Of course, it never should have been allowed to grow there at all. It dated, no doubt, from romantic ideas of the last, or even the eighteenth, century about ivy-mantled towers. It had grown so thick that, thwarted of further external space on which to fasten, it had now for many years been writhing its way through cracked brickwork, rotting timbers, crooked window-frames, right into the rooms of the first court. It bored, like a gimlet, through mediaeval mortar and would be found, in rooms that were re-opened after the long vacation, creeping along floors and hanging in pallid, funereal tendrils down the walls. The chaplain asserted that it had hidden his toothbrush.

Why not cut it down then? The point was, according to the architect, that it had worked such havoc upon the walls that, when it was removed, an immense amount of renewal of brick- and stone-work would at once have to be done. Though, in a few generations, the ivy, if left, would certainly drag the first court down in ruins to the ground, at present it might be said to be holding the first court up. It should not be taken down until the plans were ready for covering the nakedness that would be exposed. And what would be the cost of the re-facing? Difficult to say. Perhaps ten or twelve thousand pounds, to make a good job of it, with the stone quoins and swags and things renewed to their original state. And cutting out all such frills as carved stone-work, and scrapping the cornice on the south side and, generally speaking, doing the thing on the cheap? Perhaps half the sum quoted. And the absolute minimum, simply to point the walls and stop up the cracks, simply to make the place stand up safely and keep the water out? Perhaps two thousand pounds, that is, if the work was undertaken at once. Every year that passed made things so much worse.

Now, two thousand pounds, a third of his fortune, happened to be precisely the sum that the Master was proposing to leave to the college. He was on his way at this moment to his lawyer's to draw up his Will. He ought not to leave the thing any longer. He believed himself to have a good life. Both doctor and dentist declared him to be remarkably young for his age. Still, you never knew. As he entered the venerable square of Lincoln's Inn, that was so like the quadrangle of a college, yet so unlike the first court at St Michael's, he could not but notice the newly-painted window-frames and well-pointed brickwork. It was now, at once, that St Michael's needed that two thousand pounds, not in ten, fifteen, twenty years.

Mr Tippett was expecting him. The business did not take long, not as long as the Master had hoped. He had rather hoped that he might have been able to telephone with a good conscience to his niece at about five, saying that he had been kept at the lawyer's and would not have time to come and see her before his train. So he would be saved from trailing out to Battersea. Neither his ingenuity, nor Mr Tippett's, however, nor the drinking of two cups of tea, could extend the proceedings much beyond an hour. The provisions of the will were exceedingly simple. The Master left a third of his wealth to the college to spend as it liked, and the other two-thirds, four thousand pounds, to his niece Alice. And the remainder of this little sum, upon her demise? asked Mr Tippett. Was she married, had she children? Yes, she was married, she had children. The remainder then, if she predeceased him, to her husband? No, said the Master, not to him, to her children. How many children had she, asked the lawyer, and what were their names? Here the Master found himself at a loss. He could answer neither part of the question. Moreover, it occurred to him that the matter was irrelevant, for she would surely have spent all the money on their education. He must find out what the plans were in that respect. Promising to send further information in a day or two, he said goodbye to Mr Tippett and presently was sitting on the top of a bus bound reluctantly for the south side of the river.

It must not be supposed that he did not like his niece. She had a firm place in his heart, almost that of a daughter, though he had seen little of her in recent years. The scoundrel who had married his sister had lived in the north of England and, when he had run away from her, their daughter was still at school. Mother and daughter had remained in those parts, living, the Master supposed, in pretty modest circumstances. From time to time he sent them a cheque to help things out and he had paid for a course of typing and shorthand for Alice, as a result of which she had obtained, locally, quite a good job. About ten years ago, soon after he became Master, they had come to stay with him for a few days at the Lodge, and shortly after that his sister had died, and after that Alice had got married and almost at once had begun to have children. The Master had gone to the wedding and the young couple had once come to stay with him. Then, though there was correspondence at Christmas and birthdays, he had not set eyes on them, until a few months ago, when Alice had written to say that they had moved to London. Could they come down for the day on a Sunday? They had found a kind neighbour who was prepared to look after the children for them, so they would only be bringing the baby. They could not of course come for longer as it was impossible to leave the family for the night.

So they had arrived one Sunday for luncheon, bearing a portable cot between them. The Master found his niece, as he might have expected, a good deal changed. The slim, retiring maiden had become a broad and capable, if harassed, woman. It was clear to him after a few moments that it was she who wore the trousers. Leonard certainly had not much vitality. His face perpetually wore a docile, almost a deferential, smile. He was exaggeratedly agreeing. The Master, though he tried hard, failed to find any subject in which his nephew seemed to have much interest, except, of course, the children. The children were the staple talk of his visitors. The infant stage was immediately before his eyes that Sunday, the stage of nappy and potty, of Karri-Kot and Treekle-Teet. Later stages of childhood were made vivid for him, as they talked. The world was practically unknown to him and, as he listened, he began to feel himself very much on the periphery of our civilisation, of our famous English home life, with its children's hours and television, its playpens, chocolate cigarettes and tricycles, and its subordination of all adult endeavour to the health, welfare and entertainment of the kids. After luncheon they walked around the college buildings. Leonard observed how much he wished he had been to a university. The Master could not help reflecting that if Leonard had appeared in the queue of would-be entrants to St Michael's he would not have been among those accepted.

Alice talked a great deal at first, perhaps feeling shy with the uncle whom she had not seen for so long. It seemed to him that she was become a little bossy. Later on, she was quieter. A few of their old jokes came up out of the past. At one moment, when Leonard was out of the room seeing if the baby wanted turning over in its cot, she sat at the piano where he remembered her once sitting and playing Chopin so prettily. She struck a note or two, then turned round on the stool towards him with a helpless look.

'Oh, Uncle James,' she said, 'I can't. I've forgotten everything. You might as well ask me to fly. All that sort of thing is over for me!'

'Only for the while,' he said. 'It'll come back. You haven't time for everything at once, my dear. You're doing very well.'

He gave her five pounds before she left and stood them a taxi to the station. She waved at him from the window. He waved back. Good luck to her. She was doing bravely. She was at least producing something, whereas he himself, with all his family sense, was allowing the family name to perish with him.

Genealogy had for many years been a hobby of the Master. The attraction of it was quite free, in his case, from snobbery. For him the spell consisted simply in pressing backwards, step by step into the past. He followed, in their astonishing expansion, all lines, male or female, that at length converged upon himself. He calculated that in 1800 forty-seven people were alive from whom he was directly descended. The forty-seventh was baptized in St George's, Hanover Square, in May of that year. Many of the lines he followed a great deal further back than that date, three or four, at least, well into the Middle Ages. Then something happened which cooled his zest, for it seemed to bring him suddenly to an end. He found an indenture witnessed by one of the forty-seven—yes, no older than that—from which it was apparent that his direct, and so recent, forebear could not write his name. There it was—'George Cartwright, husbandman, his mark'. The oafish scrawl seemed to take him back, all in one moment, over an immense span of human history, practically back to Adam. The thrill it gave him seemed to preclude further genealogical thrills. The genealogical tunnel was now sealed at both ends. Yet, of course, at this end, by the tiniest deviation from himself to his sister, there was a way out. It was while he stood waving to Alice in the taxi that he decided he really must do something about his will.

He had not expected to enjoy his visit to Battersea, nor did he enjoy it. Leonard was away at his work, but all the children were there, Stephen aged nine, Alec aged eight, Belinda aged four and Heather, the baby. After a moment or two of silence, during which they were taking him in, they all simultaneously found their voices. The clamour was very great, aggravated by the voice of Alice trying to shout them down. The urchins certainly seemed to have plenty of spirit; but that poky ground-floor flat would have been far too small comfortably to house one of them, let alone four. While Alice got the tea ready, they pressed upon him with their books and toys, each one screaming to obtain his individual attention. His eye lit upon various objects that were familiar to him from his old home, that elegant walnut writing-table, now supporting an unsightly wireless, that embroidered stool, that obsidian paper-weight with which Stephen was now playing catch to the great danger of everyone in the room. This last had used to lie on his father's study desk and the Master suddenly had a vivid childhood memory of the view from that study window of a dewy lawn stretching on either side of a copper beech to a ha-ha fringed with pinks, and beyond that a field with black-and-white cows. His eyes went to the window of his niece's flat to take in the analogous view that would be treasured by his great-nephews as the comfort and inspiration of a lifetime. He looked out at the street. A bus had that moment drawn up at the stopping-place immediately opposite the window. With a grinding of gears it moved on, exposing a view of the houses on the other side of the street. 'Hm. How hard it is for the poor to enter into the Kingdom of heaven. Certainly, the best things in life, the serene and spacious things, are only to be had with money, unless, perhaps, by husbandmen. His reverie was broken by a word used by Stephen, that made him wince. Never mind what the word was. Let it suffice to say that it was evidence that the genealogical graph which had risen, socially, so steeply from George Cartwright, was now, no less steeply, descending. Well then, back to husbandmen, if such people still exist. Why not? Why not indeed, if they could go straight back! It was the intermediate stages that the Master did not care to contemplate. Moreover, it was in his power to arrest the descent. The two boys, he found, went to a school just up the street. If Alice had the money now, she could pay for a decent education for both of them. But she must have it now. It was already time for both of them to be away at a private school. In fifteen, ten, even five years the money would be of no avail whatever for educational purposes. She must have it now. And so the—the sum of life would be enhanced. 'Oh, for heaven's sake, Stephen,' Alice shouted, 'throw that beastly stone in the dustbin! I'm sick of it!'

The Master was deep in thought as he left the flat, so deep that he changed into a wrong bus and missed the train he had intended to take. For more than an hour he had to hang about the station. Much of this time he spent gazing in at the window of a travel agency which he found just outside the portal of the terminus. Here was stretched out a large and excellent map of the Mediterranean. Wondering where the place was and what the modern equivalent of the name might be, he let his eye wander around the coasts of Greece and Asia Minor. He did not find it and moved across the blue Ionian Sea to Magna Graecia and Sicily. He was looking for Ambracia.

'Read that.'

Alastair McColl took the paper and read about the extraordinary disappearance of the Master of St Michael's. He had been a passenger on the night boat from Naples to Palermo. He had had dinner on the boat. The waiter distinctly remembered serving three brandies one after the other—a rather unusual order—to the white-haired Englishman. His bunk, however, was not slept in and he was nowhere to be found in the morning on arrival at Palermo. The shipping company pointed out that it would be exceedingly difficult to fall accidentally overboard from one of the company's ships, particularly on such a tranquil night as that. Enquiries at St Michael's only deepened the mystery. Most of the fellows were away during the vacation, but the reporter found the Dean, who seemed stunned by the story. He had had no idea that the Master was going abroad. It had been many years since he had taken holidays abroad. The Master was not known to have anything on his mind, any worries. His health was exceptionally robust. Indeed, he was a peculiarly sane and happy man. The purpose and destination of his journey, and how and why he disappeared, remained quite unaccounted for. There was an oboe with his luggage.

McColl put down the paper.

'My hat!' he said. 'My hat!'

The End of all Things

That was Mackenzie minor, there could be no doubt about it. Silvester Mullins was quick to recognise his old pupils. A quarter of a century had added its weight to the face, but the eager, intelligent eyes were just those that had looked up at him from the sixth form benches. He became a barrister, I believe, Mr Mullins said to himself. Their eyes had met for a second and a look of recognition had come into those of the younger man, but the old schoolmaster, as his manner was, had returned the look with one of such determined blankness and had then so abruptly looked away, that the other was discouraged and they passed one another without a greeting. Ten yards further on Mackenzie turned round and looked back along the sea-front at the erect figure that was hurrying away from him. I swear that was Mully, he said to himself.

Silvester Mullins never recognised people if he could help it. Not that he genuinely hated his kind. He would have probably much enjoyed a few minutes' conversation with the middle-aged barrister to whom he had once taught Latin Grammar. Simply, he was exceedingly shy. In a lifetime he had not learned to overcome a natural shrinking from adult human contacts. He was without a friend in the world. He had never had such a thing. He could get along well enough with boys. But then, boys take you at your own valuation.

Today he had also a special reason for not wishing to be interrupted in his walk. An interruption might turn his will from the grim purpose he had in hand. For he had set out that afternoon with the determination to do no less than bring his unhappiness to an end, once for all. His sense of failure, upon which the leisure of retirement had given him all day to brood, had at length driven him to this violent decision. And no one would have the least idea why he had done it! They would suppose, in so far as they thought about it at all, that there had been an accident. An old man had slipped, that was all. A few perhaps, suspecting something more, might fancy that the old sage, in that hard-boiled way of his, had decided for no particular reason that he was ready for the end of all things, had made a good meal and walked off happily to his doom. Hard-boiled indeed! How wrong they would be! They would never guess what tender dreams of greatness, what delicate lifelong hopes had perished with that old man. They would never suppose what a longing for fame had been there. They would never imagine for one moment that he was a martyr to literary ambition. They would think—in so far as they thought about it at all! For the fact was that the extinction of Silvester Mullins would be almost unnoticed. It would make as much noise as a body falling into the roaring waves.

The front at Eastmouth is nearly two miles long and is absolutely straight. At one end the high white façade of buildings disintegrates into brick bungalows and at length into shacks and caravans which lose themselves in the sand dunes. At the other end the frontage, while still compact and stuccoed, is abruptly terminated by the steep rise of a line of cliffs, which rear themselves, at the highest point, to some four hundred feet above the sea. The modest residential hotel Silvester Mullins had chosen in which to end his days was almost the last Victorian building towards the flat end of the town. He had therefore to walk along the greater part of the front to reach the cliffs. It was his daily walk. He seldom turned inland. He liked walking along that straight line of front, on the edge of that grey sea, buffeted by those merciless east winds. For his pleasures, such as they were, were of a stern and Spartan nature. Life-long habits of temperance in all things had kept him, at three-score years and ten, in the best of training. His athletic figure would stride along the front and up the cliff path with that hurried and purposeful step which is so often a sign of fundamental lack of purpose.

On this particular day in April, as he climbed up on to the grassy ridge, the sun was shining brightly, the sea was positively blue, and gay with white horses. The town extended to the left, an arm of it stretching along a dip parallel with the sea and culminating in St Luke's cemetery, an enclosure of many hundreds of white gravestones around a red brick chapel. Silvester Mullins walked briskly onwards along the crest of the cliffs. Unlike his usual self, he was panting a good deal and his forehead was covered with beads of sweat. As he approached the highest place, where the cliff face became most precipitous, he read the notice:

PEDESTRIANS APPROACH THE
CLIFF EDGE ENTIRELY AT
THEIR OWN RISK

The place was known as 'Dead Man's Drop'. At low tide the bodies of suicides were sometimes found, a mangled mess, on the rocks at the base of the cliff. At high tide the sea would receive them at once, keep them for a day or two, then deposit them near the main pier against the centre of the town. Today the tide was high.

Silvester Mullins walked slowly towards the edge. A failure, an utter failure! His was indeed a sorry life to look back on. It was nothing! Just seventy, no fifty, years of killing time. As a boy he had been some good. He at least had hopes. He had been going to be a great man. At the age of thirteen, like most other boys of that age, he had no precise idea what form this greatness would take. There were all kinds of trees at the top of which he could imagine himself. By the time he reached the university, however, their number was much reduced. It was clear to the timid undergraduate that his manifest inability to command his fellowmen or to make a public speech ruled out such forms of distinction as being a great statesman, administrator or general. It was evident also that he would not be a great musician, sculptor, scientist, or—for his early promise had hardly been fulfilled—a great scholar. His ambition narrowed itself into a channel where he believed that one does not have to be born with an instinctive mastery of some technique, and that his social shyness, far from being a disadvantage, might positively be an asset. He would write. He would be Goethe, Shelley, Hugo. This vague and naïf ambition became only more intense from being undeclared. For he had no friend with whom to share the inmost longings of his soul. Friendly, relaxing laughter never penetrated into those recesses.

When the time came for him to earn his own living he reluctantly faced the fact that literature would not, at any rate for the present, supply his bread and butter. His literary efforts so far had brought in nothing at all. There were several poems in his drawer that had been rejected by literary periodicals and a novel that had been rejected by three literary agents. Like many a greater man, he became, temporarily and for want of anything better to do, a schoolmaster. The job was only a stop-gap. He would hold it at most for two or three years, until something better turned up. Meanwhile it was a job in which the long holidays would give plenty of time for writing.

He had been a schoolmaster, at the same school, for the rest of his life. Yet, though he had been an exceedingly good schoolmaster, he never regarded his work as anything but temporary, a disagreeable necessity from which, at any moment, he would liberate himself. For many years, during those holidays, he used to write, poems, novels, stories, but never had the least success with them. They were, as he half suspected, woolly, out of touch with life, romantic in a dead mode. Yet with the sentimentality of the lonely man, he clung to his dream. 'It's because I really haven't the leisure,' he told himself at length. 'When I am retired and have all of every day before me, then, in the full wisdom of old age, I shall write something that will live.' The implication in this promise to himself, that he was growing wiser as he grew older, was, as he knew perfectly well, a false one. His mental age was absolutely stationary and had been so for as long as he could remember. If there was ever a case of arrested development, it was that of Silvester Mullins. For nothing had really ever happened to him since his 'teens, since that first flowering of his spirit when he had read Greek and Latin and felt himself to be a poet and a philosopher.

Nor was the prospect, to which he professed to himself he was looking forward, of having every day empty before him for the rest of his life one on which he cared to dwell. Frankly, it frightened him. With no daily work, with no next term to bring the emptiness of the holidays to an end, how would he get through the time? Writing, of course. Surely he was not going to funk it at the last? The moment came, he took the plunge and retired. Need it be said that during the two or three years he had been at Eastmouth he had not put pen to paper? And now, here he was, stepping slowly, with heart beating, towards the cliff's edge.

'Sir! Sir!'

He stopped, but did not look back. The boy came up with him.

'I say, you've got awfully near the edge, sir. Come away a bit, it makes me giddy.'

He led the old man backwards.

'I'm going to sit down a bit and get my breath,' said Silvester Mullins. So they sat down together, at a safe distance from the cliff, looking out to sea.

'I can't think how I missed you,' said the boy. 'I was at the usual place at the usual time. Then you didn't come and I thought I must have missed you, so I came running on up here. My last day too!' he went on ruefully. 'I wish I wasn't going back to school tomorrow. It's such a waste. I'm sure I don't learn half as much there as I do from you!'

A casual acquaintance on the sea-front, the thirteen-year-old boy had quickly become a disciple. During the last three weeks the old schoolmaster had in fact, quite informally, been cramming him for the examination he was to take next term.

'Well then, Martin, let's get down to business. Where had we got to? The Gender Rhymes. "Third-nouns feminine——"'

The boy recited:

'Third-nouns feminine we class ending *is, x, aus* and *as, s* to consonant appended, *es* in flexion unextended.'

'And just what do those last two lines mean?'

'Sir, you said the other day that Coleridge said that poetry was most appreciated when it was only imperfectly understood!'

'Ha! Good!' chuckled the old man. 'Clever of you to remember that!' Here was a pupil after his heart, one who both listened to what you said and had some cheek. If he had been having charge of his tuition for a few months he might have given the boy a proper start.

The qualities which made Silvester Mullins no good at anything else made him first-rate as a schoolmaster. There are different kinds of good schoolmaster. Most parents are happy if they find that their son's form-master is a person of easy manners, with whom conversation flows easily as between men of the world, a married man with children, a thoroughly normal man who can be trusted to inculcate in their child only what is sane and reasonable. Such, of course, are admirable in their way. But perhaps the greatest educationists have been of a quite different type, odd and lonely people, of partial but concentrated development, 'characters', people of strong and unsatisfied imaginations, original, independent, queer. Such types have been the great sowers of mustard seeds in the minds of the young. The trouble with them is that, from Socrates downwards, they have not always known where to stop. From being the educators, they have sometimes become the corrupters of youth.

Silvester Mullins, though belonging to the latter class, had always known where to stop; and never had there been a more inspiring teacher of boys on the threshold of their 'teens. His own personality having crystallised at an age very little in advance of their own, he stood before them with a character, in all its enthusiasms and attitudes, that they could be quickly led to make their own. The elder boys in a sense *became* Mr Mullins before they left Homefields. Yet they were boys and he was a man! No wonder that in after-life they looked back on their association with him as the beginning of their adult existence.

The character which he presented to them was twofold. It was partly that of some ancient stoical philosopher. He was full of bracing pessimistic maxims from classical authors. Death, he was fond of saying, is the end of all things. *Debemur morti nos nostraque.* Life is a grim business at best, and you will be beaten in the end. Learn to grin and bear it. *Victrix causa deis placuit sed victa Catoni.* Get your head into the wind and learn to stand on your own feet. Be self-sufficient. Above everything, avoid all kinds of conversion. Whatever is catching must be diseased. Health is not catching.

It was with a sense of exhilaration that the young, following Mr Mullins into the wind, learned to grin and bear their delightful lives and found that they too might, all of a sudden, become philosophers. They did not at the time notice how easy it was.

Such was one Mr Mullins, stern, enclosed, defensive. There was another, who looked out from his battlements upon the world with a wistful curiosity. What a lot of things he would like to know! Ancient and modern literature, history, geography and all the -ologies opened in avenues around him. It is true that, through timidity and the lack of a companion, he had never ventured far along any of these avenues. Yet the idea of doing so remained in his mind as fresh as on the day it had entered there. His spirit was fixed, as it were, in a state of permanent incipience. He was just about to set off in a hundred directions. Catching his excitement, the young prepared to set out after him. They had sometimes left him behind almost before they had left Homefields. Yet there were few of them who did not remember the beginnings of their enthusiasms and think of Mr Mullins with piety. The editor of the Oxford Chaucer dated his lifelong passion from a chance remark of Mully's. An Astronomer Royal used to say: 'I first looked intelligently at the sky when I was twelve years old. One June night a master at my private school said, "That's not a star. It's a planet. It's Venus."'

Sometimes Mr Mullins, who had never been abroad, would forget the lesson for a moment and gaze longingly at the map of the ancient world which hung on the wall of his classroom. 'Sagunto,' he would say, 'What fun to go there! And Segesta and Sunium and Palmyra and Petra . . .' Years afterwards, travellers, threading their way among the disks of broken columns, treading upon Roman pavements, or feeling in the hot sand for classical coins, would remember Mully and murmur

> '*s* to consonant appended
> *es* in flexion unextended.'

The private school, Homefields, at which he taught, was one of those institutions at which the children of the well-to-do are prepared for the public schools. It was one of the best of such establishments in the country. It had always been so from a social point of view; from the moment that young Mr Mullins came to teach there, it became so also from the point of view of the instruction. He had a perfect genius, not only for giving a lasting stimulus to the young minds, but also for getting the boys through their examinations. Three or four scholarships would be won every year at Eton, Winchester or one of the greater schools. Infinitely patient, he would go over the learnt lesson again and again until it had got into the very bones of the pupil. For learning from him was not at all a slack or easy matter. It was also sharpened by fear. He knew with an unerring sense when he was not receiving a boy's best and would pull the short hairs of the boy's temple until he obtained his due. Boys would do their utmost not to lapse into tears in his presence, for he showed the greatest contempt for tears. They evoked the cruellest sarcasms from him. Were they not womanly? And of the opposite sex it seemed that he had the lowest opinion.

Brilliant though he was as a teacher, his success meant little to him. He never allowed himself to look on his work as more than just a job. He professed to despise it and to regard it as an unwelcome burden imposed upon him by economic necessity. Perhaps he had not the least idea how great his influence had been on many generations of Homefieldians. For he was not a person to whom it was easy to make a heart-felt declaration. Nor did his old pupils keep up with him. Some of them used to try; but the Mully they met when they went down to the old place was not the Mully they had known, of the sixth-form classroom. They found an awkward person, nervous and unresponsive, with whom polite conversation was exceedingly hard work. Could this be the great man they had known? They were disappointed and did not try again.

'Talpa!' said Mr Mullins.

'Oh, yes, of course,' said Martin.

> '*Bos, damma, talpa, serpens, sus,*
> *Camelis, canis, tigris, perdix, grus.*'

'Right,' said the old man, getting up. 'Come on, it's getting chilly sitting here, let's walk on a bit.'

Some ten days later Mackenzie minor, otherwise Sir Maurice Mackenzie, K.C., had occasion once more to go down to Eastmouth for the day in connection with a case he had on hand. Returning by train to London in the evening, he spent the first quarter of an hour of the journey writing in a notebook. What a case! The things people can take pleasure in doing! He had thought he knew all about human depravity by now. Shutting the book and dismissing the case from his mind, he opened the copy of the *Eastmouth Gazette* which he had bought on the station. One of the first things to catch his eye was an obituary notice: 'Silvester Mullins, of 133 Grove Road. Funeral, Saturday 2.30 at St Luke's cemetery.' Then it *had* been Mully. Good Lord, Mully dead! Here was a piece of information that could not simply be registered with surprise or regret, then dismissed from the mind. It had dealt Sir Maurice a powerful blow. It had killed something inside him, or brought it to life again, he was not quite sure which. There was a commotion in his inmost being. He shut his eyes and gave himself over to the kind of stocktaking reflections for which a busy man does not often find time.

Arrived in London, he took a taxi to his club where he went at once to the telephone-box.

'—hullo? Is that *The Times*? Can I speak to the editor, please? What? No, *the* editor. This is Sir Maurice Mackenzie speaking—hullo, is that you, Jack? This is Maurice. Have you heard about Mully?'

'No, what?'

'He's dead!'

'Good God! Mully dead!'

'Does your paper know about it?'

'I've heard nothing. I'll see at once. When did it happen? Hadn't he retired to some seaside place?'

Mackenzie explained how he had heard the news.

'Then we must have it in tomorrow morning,' said the editor. 'Today's only Wednesday. But aren't there various people we ought to telephone to? Oughtn't we to ring up Homefields and get a list of people and make sure that as many know as possible? And then there are people abroad—Reggie Manwaring at Lisbon, for instance, and——'

For a few moments they discussed telephones, cables, air-mail editions.

'It's an odd thing,' said the editor at length. 'I was thinking of Mully only last week-end. *A propos* of a crossword, people began talking about the parts of speech. Do you know, hardly anyone knew them properly. The Lord Chancellor was there. He had the vaguest ideas. There was only one other person besides myself who got them quite right. It turned out that he too was a Mully pupil, a boy called Younghusband, Willie's boy in fact. By the way, Willie, that's another one we must ring.'

'Yes, I believe I know the boy. He's just become a member of this club.'

'Maurice, do you know, I can't get used to this idea of Mully being dead. I feel either much older or much younger, I can't quite tell which!'

'That's exactly how I feel.'

Putting down the receiver, Sir Maurice went into the sitting-room. A new member was standing a little self-consciously by the fire.

'Younghusband?'

'Yes, sir?'

The new member had not expected to be addressed by anyone so eminent.

'You're a Homefieldian, I believe?'

'I am.'

'Have you heard about Mully?'

'What about him?'

'He's dead!'

'Good God!'

The young man sank into a chair. 'Good God, Mully dead!' The new member seemed dazed. Sir Maurice too sat down.

'Press that bell, will you, please,' he said, 'and we'll have a drink. What's that you say?'

The young man was mumbling something.

'Well, as a matter of fact,' said Younghusband, 'I was saying *Bos, damma, talpa, serpens, sus——*'

Silvester Mullins learned of the death of his namesake, not from the papers, but by calling at the shop to replenish his tobacco-pouch. Yes, it was the incredible fact that one day, in a small street in Eastmouth, he had seen his own name above a little old-fashioned, rounded, shop-window. From that day he had always gone to this grubby little place for his tobacco, though he had never given away to the proprietor the reason that brought him there. He learned from the daughter, Connie, that her father's internal pains, from which he had suffered off and on for years, had come on him suddenly very badly. He had groaned and struggled for some hours, then fallen asleep from exhaustion and had passed away peacefully in his sleep. The funeral was on Saturday afternoon.

Mr Mullins had half a mind to go to that funeral and set out as usual after luncheon on Saturday along the front. When he was at the most crowded part, he saw a man just in front of him on the pavement hail a taxi, and heard him say to the driver, 'St Luke's Cemetery, please, wherever that may be.'

That was Babington major, said Mr Mullins to himself, dodging away so as not to be seen. Why could Babington major be going to St Luke's Cemetery? Mr Mullins walked on thoughtfully. He decided not to attend the funeral.

He went on as usual and up the path to the cliffs. As he walked along the crest he could look down into St Luke's Cemetery. In that part of the enclosure that was not filled with gravestones a funeral was certainly going on. There were a great many black figures on the grass, a great many top-hats. But there was something about the large gathering, a movement, a breaking up into groups, which suggested that things had gone wrong. Mr Mullins turned his eyes away from the scene and strode onwards at greater speed. He walked much further than usual that afternoon, right along to where there is a gap in the cliffs, then down to the beach and far along the wet sands before he turned for home. The sun was already low when, on his return, at length he took the way inland toward the cemetery.

The place was deserted. He threaded his way along the paths to where the gravestones ended. He did not have to look long for the place of today's funeral. On the new grave there were four or five modest wreaths. 'To the best of Dads from Connie,' he read. 'For Fred, in deepest sympathy, from Albert and Jessie.'

Some yards away, on the grass, belonging nowhere, there were other wreaths, grander wreaths, scores of them. The florists of London and Eastmouth had done their best. There were lilies and orchids and roses and gardenias and white waxy jasmine. Mr Mullins approached the bed of flowers and began to read the cards: 'In sorrow and sympathy, from the Earl of Wiltshire'; 'To Mully, in homage, Sir Reginald Manwaring, the British Embassy, Lisbon'; 'In deepest sorrow, from the Mully Club, Newcastle'; 'To my old tutor and the friend of my boyhood years, from Prince Kamalished'; 'In gratitude to Silvester Mullins, a great teacher, P Winton: Ep:'; 'For dear Mr Mullins, from Martin'; 'In homage to Mully, from all at——' But Mr Mullins could not tell where the latter came from, for, to his consternation, a liquid haze had come over his eyes and he was no longer able to read.

The Lecture

The two men sitting opposite one another in the railway carriage had been eyeing each other's faces for some time. At length the younger man spoke.

'Excuse me, you are Mr Barton, aren't you, who used to teach me history?'

'I am. And you are Peveril, H. E. Peveril, exhibitioner at King's in —' and he named the year precisely.

Hugh Peveril laughed. It came back to him, that blunt, no-nonsense manner, the prodigious memory that knew *Wisden's Almanac* backwards.

'You always were good at dates,' he said. 'Yes, you've got it right. That's me.'

'But that's where I stop,' said the other. 'What has happened since? What do you do? Didn't you write a book?'

'Yes, I do a bit of writing. Art history, you know.'

'Oh yes. Not my line, I'm afraid. You don't often visit us. You're on your way down to stay?'

'Only for the evening. As a matter of fact I've been asked to lecture to the art society. And you, sir, you still teach history?'

'Yes, and French, of course, with the extras. We're doing the nineteenth century this term. Rotten chaps!'

'Oh? Isn't there much talent now?'

Mr Barton leaned forward.

'I'm not talking about the boys. They're all right. I mean these French chaps. The way they love their mothers! It makes me sick. We're always brought up to think of them as the embodiment of sophistication and civilization and worldly wisdom and what not. And what do we find? A set of mothers' darlings! Great, grown men hanging on to their mothers' apron strings! Take Flaubert. As a young man he goes travelling with a friend in the near east. They get to a place, I forget where, somewhere in Turkey or Syria, and gaze out eastwards. What fun to go on further! 'Come on,' says the friend, 'let's go on, to Persia, Afghanistan, India . . .' Flaubert wants to very much. What does he say? 'Oh no,' he says, 'I had a letter from my mammy this morning. She's missing me badly. I think I'd better turn back.' It gives me a pain! Baudelaire, Verlaine, it's the same story. Mammy's apron strings!'

Having said his say, Mr Barton sat back and looked out of the window.

'Ye-es,' said Hugh doubtfully. The subject upon which Mr Barton had pronounced so violently was not one that Hugh much cared to follow, for he felt himself to be, or rather to have been, of the company of those French chaps. He had loved his mother very much indeed and been bewildered by her death some eight years ago. Only gradually had a thing come into his life that had somewhat restored the balance of his soul.

It had all begun in his infancy. Perhaps, if he had had brothers and sisters, things would have been different. As it was, he had to play a good deal by himself. And whatever the game, an essential part of it was that his mother should be watching. He did not expect her to play with him. Indeed, he was extremely inventive at amusing himself and much preferred to play alone. All he demanded was that his mother's eye should be upon him and that she should say from time to time, 'What fun you're having, darling! I'm watching you.' If, seeing him apparently absorbed in making himself a house in one of the apple trees or playing with mud at the edge of the pond, she were to steal out of sight, she would presently hear him calling, 'Mother! Mother! Where are you?' 'I'm watching you from here,' she would call, appearing at a bedroom window. 'But can you see properly?' he would shout. 'Yes. I can see everything. You're having a lovely time.' After a moment's hesitation, while he satisfied himself that she was not trying to deceive him, he would return to his blissful, solitary game. Of course, she spoiled him. No doubt, if his father had not died when he was only a few months old, all this nonsense would have been knocked out of him before he had left the nursery.

As it was, his mother's role became as indispensable to the grown man as it had been to the child. He still needed to be assured that he was happy. And certainly, he *was* happy, having been generously endowed with intelligence, curiosity and sensibility and, not least, with a respectable private income. He had never known what it was to be bored. How could one be bored with all art and literature lined up there in front of one? At first an aesthete, he became with time also something of a scholar and, at length, with the discovery of the Ridolfi frescoes at Barning Churton, an authority, a pundit. From then on, it was rash for any art historian to make a pronouncement upon Tudor mural painting that contradicted a published opinion of Hugh Peveril. At thirty-seven he had become a man with a subject, or, if you like, with an object. After putting Ridolfi so decisively on the map, he was now in full cry after John of Padua, Toto Nunziata and those shadowy figures, now hardly more than names, who came from Italy to decorate Nonesuch and other palaces long since demolished.

A familiar figure in art galleries and print rooms, Hugh Peveril became well known also in libraries, archive repositories and the muniment rooms of the nobility, where he searched indefatigably amongst inventories and wills, wardrobe books and household accounts. A man with a purpose – how should he not be happy? Though his means and his freedom, as yet, from matrimonial and parental ties allowed him to avoid almost any claims upon his time that were not of his own choosing, the days were too short for him by many hours. There was, however, the one tie. He constantly demanded, and constantly received, his mother's assurance that he was having a delightful life and missing nothing. For herself, she would have liked some grandchildren by now. But this she kept a secret; for which some people, no doubt, would say she was to blame.

At length he found himself entering his fifth decade. The fortieth birthday probably represents for most men a climacteric, an occasion for rather wistful stocktaking. It certainly did for Hugh. It coincided with various important victories of the forces of decay upon his body. For one thing he had to have a denture inserted into his upper jaw. For another, he had to have a second pair of spectacles for daily use, in addition to the pair he used for reading—an infernal bore. But much more than either the denture or the spectacles he minded what was happening on the top of his head. That circle of baldness on the crown, that had so recently been like a three-penny bit, was now like a great plate. There could be no longer any pretence of hiding it under the long hair brushed back from in front, as that hair itself became thinner and thinner. Having always gone about bare-headed, Hugh now reluctantly took to wearing a hat.

Then, the mental or spiritual condition, what of that? Well, he knew himself to be a success in his way. Moreover, the way was one that he respected and had chosen. He had made a certain name. He was proud to be himself. Yet, at this moment of stocktaking, he allowed himself to reflect upon a tendency he had noticed in himself of recent years. He had noticed it also in others and perhaps it simply went with growing up. None the less he could not help regretting it. How should it be described? No doubt, one should not hope to sustain the raptures of youth. The greatest art can only be seen for the first time once, and a man of means has presently seen most of the greatest art. Yet, what Hugh noticed was that the very words 'How beautiful!' came less and less to his lips. They had been replaced by 'How interesting!' The quest had become one for knowledge rather than for feeling. Playing for safety, you might say?

Then, one day, thick with dust on the roof of a cupboard, he found his palette and paint-brushes and remembered that he had once meant to be an artist. Why had he not pursued this happy ambition, for he had a certain talent and is not anything that is worth doing well, worth doing moderately well? Whatever the reason, the stamina had failed him. Perhaps he had been too intelligent to go on, perhaps too sensitive. Those terrible silences of one's friends before one's canvases! Hugh stood for some time in thought, fingering the dusty objects. 'What fun you might have had!' said a still small voice. Was it not a second, no, a twenty-second best occupation, this amassing of the dates of birth and death of minor Italian painters whose work does not survive, indeed, who may not have existed, to venturing oneself, however uncertainly, on the sea of artistic creation? That same day Hugh gave away his painting apparatus to a poor student.

Yet even the combined loss of hair, of teeth, of palette and of the raptures of youth would probably not have caused a serious dislocation of his spirit. It was accompanied, however, by a far more painful bereavement. Quite suddenly his mother died. If there had been an illness, he might have been able to prepare himself a little. As it was, the shock was very great. A change in him at once became apparent to his friends. His ease of manner left him overnight, while his face took on a strained and nervous look. He became touchy and morose or else rather too assertive, and always seemed tired. Indeed he *was* tired, for he had begun to sleep badly. A wretched complaint! There are pills you can take, of course, but it seemed to him that these only made his head heavy in a different way. Suppose he was to lose that priceless morning lucidity once for all! This was only one of the terrors that troubled his wakeful nights. Another came at him as with a pointing finger – it's your turn next! He had never given much thought to his own death. So long as the generation above him was still about, there seemed no urgency. Moreover, it was not his inclination to reflect upon the shortness of human life, except as an incentive to harder work. He had always been too busy for such profitless cogitations. Now he found he had plenty of time, in the early hours, to brood thereon. His confidence, his very identity, seemed to be slipping from him.

Then one night he had a vision of eternity. It was a most disagreeable experience. Whether or not he was asleep when it began, he was certainly wide awake before it faded. The ring of light that surrounded him was narrow and distant, such as would be visible from the inside centre of two enormous disks or cymbals that did not quite touch one another. He was at this central point, inside, alone, the upper disk pressing upon his head, hard enough to cause him continually to cry out with the pain but not hard enough to dull his thoughts. There he was, for good. The distant light informed him that something was going on outside. What it was he would never know. Some things, however, he did know. He knew that there would be no change for him ever again, because time, though it felt as if it was going on, had in fact stopped. There was no hope whatever of sleep now, or of death. Nor would he go mad—not quite.

He did not come to himself with the kind of amused relief that usually follows nightmares. He had not just been taking part in some ridiculous fairy story. On the contrary, he had had an experience of what might well be the real order of things and the horror of that unloved predicament was not a state he was going to forget. He would know what he was in for the moment that appalling lid began to come down. Hugh's mother had not been dead many months when it was clear to all his friends that he was on the way to a nervous breakdown.

Had he consulted doctors or psychiatrists, no doubt they would have made various suggestions. Would they, one wonders, have lit upon the thing that, more than any other, checked his despair and helped him to recover his self-confidence? That kind man, Hollis, deserves the credit.

'Hugh,' he said, meeting him in the street and putting a hand on his shoulder, 'Hugh, the very man! I say, you wouldn't come down and talk to our archaeological society, would you, the West Rutland Arc. Soc., that is? I'm the president, we have quite good meetings honestly, I'll put you up, of course, and all expenses paid. It'll be great fun. Say you will, won't you?'

'But—but it's not a thing I've ever done. I don't know anything about lecturing.'

'Nonsense. Of course, you do. You talk for about fifty minutes, with lantern slides if you like, and then we have about twenty minutes for questions and things afterwards. We sometimes get about fifty or sixty people, and some of them are really quite bright. Now, the question of dates—'

'But, I say, I say—I've never lectured in my life. I don't know anything about it.'

'Nonsense. You'll be a terrific catch. I'm jolly lucky to have met you. Now, it's either Thursday the twenty-first of next month—' Hollis was looking at his diary.

'But what am I to talk about?' said Hugh.

'The subject? Oh, anything you like. Picasso, if you like. But your approach, if possible, should be antiquarian.'

So Hugh gave his first lecture. The subject he chose was the Ridolfi frescoes. He felt on absolutely safe ground here. Moreover, the story of his discovery of them was an exciting one by any standards. Even those members of the audience who did not much care about art would hardly fail to respond at the butler's intervention. 'It *must* be hollow in there, my lord,' the man had said. 'If you place the eye at this crack, you can just see light.' The lecture was preceded by much hard work. Hugh had written out in full everything he proposed to say and knew the script practically by heart; for it was his hope, if possible, to speak rather than to read his lecture. For this latter purpose he had written on a single sheet of paper the main headings and sub-headings of the talk in case he forgot himself and lost his way. There were to be some slides, only about twenty, some of them depicting the frescoes themselves and others, in order that they should be seen in their European setting, analogous work of the time in Italy, France and Flanders. It did not seem as though anything much could go wrong with the lecture. Yet, as the time approached, the lecturer's stage-fright grew upon him and he slept worse than ever. It was a haggard and exhausted man who arrived in West Rutland on the day.

'Drink this,' said Hollis as soon as he saw him, pouring out a large whisky and soda.

The lecture was a great success. The audience proved most enthusiastic. Before he had come to the end of the introductory passage which preceded the first slide, Hugh realized that all was going to be well. His voice was not wavering. They had laughed heartily at the first mild witticism. Their faces were eager and expectant. He had dreaded having all the eyes fixed upon him and supposed it would be a great relief to withdraw into darkness during the showing of the slides. Actually, as the lecture progressed, he found that it was the periods of light, when he was the focal point of all those eager eyes, that he most enjoyed. Yes, enjoyed. For, as his nervousness left him, its place was taken by a great happiness. Never before, at least since he left school, had he done anything which instantly received approval from a congregation of people. How different this from the kind of appreciation your literary efforts receive! You write something and then you get it typed and you correct the typing and, as you do so, correct the thing itself, and then get it re-typed and correct the re-typing, and then send it to a publisher, and afterwards to another publisher, and then another, and at length find yourself correcting the proofs of passages you do not remember having written, and then, after a few more years, there it is, a piece of cold, stale fish, the book you have written, and you heartily agree with the reviewer who says that you are not as important in your day as, in theirs, were Aristotle, Diderot or Ruskin. How unlike the experience of the lecturer! There, in the heat, the rows of clapping hands and bright, attentive faces are telling you, in a way there is no denying, that you are interesting, intelligent and amusing. It was at length with positive reluctance that Hugh took leave of the bright faces and sat down amidst applause as loud as any that had been heard at a meeting of the West Rutland Arc. Soc.

'But, my dear fellow,' said Hollis, 'you're a born lecturer.' That night, in a large bed, in one of the Hollis's large Victorian spare bedrooms, Hugh Peveril slept for nine hours without a break.

The news of the success of the lecture was spread abroad by Hollis. Presently Hugh was asked to speak to another local society, to which he delivered the same lecture with equal success. He was then asked by the director of a London gallery to be one of the eight speakers in a winter course of lectures entitled 'Eight centuries of English sculpture'. Hugh's lecture, on the sixteenth century, was universally held to have been far the best of the series, and when, a week before the last lecture, the lecturer got appendicitis, Hugh was asked whether he could possibly take Professor Winckl's place. Thus, almost impromptu, he gave a discourse on nineteenth-century sculpture that was generally regarded as brilliant. He now began to be much sought after as a lecturer. To the learned he would talk about one of the subjects on which he was a specialist, to the more general audience he would talk about almost anything to do with the arts. He would lecture with slides or without, though, unlike almost every other lecturer, he preferred to be without. Of course, the more time he gave to lecturing the less time he had for research. In this he had a sense of loss, a feeling that he was living on capital. When you knew how to do it, was not holding forth the easier, lazier pursuit? It was certainly the more pleasant. For one thing it was restoring the word 'beautiful' to his vocabulary.

And as he discovered himself as a lecturer, so he receded from the edge of that abyss of loneliness into which he had looked. His confidence returned. If so many people believed in him to his face, how should he not believe in himself? He slept a great deal better and, should he find himself lying awake, now had a remedy much better than any pill. He would imagine himself rising from his chair on the dais amid the clapping and would start to say over his last, or his next, lecture. Two or three hundred pairs of fascinated eyes would sparkle to every modulation of tone, every surprising adjective and telling understatement, and every joke. During those careful hesitations for a word, you could hear a pin drop in the hall. As the charming, enthralling, immaculate performance was proceeding, Hugh would slip into the land of dreams to the honeysweet sound of his own voice.

So, at length, he was asked down to his old school. The invitation came from one Desmond Lestrange, secretary of the art society. It was written in an Italian humanist hand, embellished with almost too many flourishes, on a foolscap sheet of hand-made paper, as thick as canvas.

'Do you know a boy called Lestrange?' Hugh asked, breaking the silence that had fallen between himself and Mr Barton. The train was already slowing down for the school station. There, rising above the trees, was the brick tower of the chapel.

'Lestrange? I do. A boy with much to unlearn. Tell me, have I got it right? Didn't you get a hat trick against Lowry's when P. B. H. Pennyfeather made 108 not out?'

'Er—now you mention it, I seem to think that that is correct. What an extraordinary man you are, sir!'

Mr Barton took his stick and a parcel down from the rack.

'It's been nice to see you,' he said. 'Why don't you come down and play cricket some time?'

Hugh opened the carriage door and they stepped on to the platform.

'Now I'll hand you over to the aesthetes,' said Mr Barton, waving good-bye, and strode away past a dark-haired boy who was approaching. With long white fingers the boy lifted a curling lock on to the top of his head from which it fell at once back on to the white forehead.

'Mr Peveril?' he said. 'I am Lestrange. I wrote to you. It is very kind of you to have come.'

'How do you do?' said Hugh, taking that white hand. 'It was very kind of you to ask me.'

'We are so flattered and pleased that you accepted, sir. Quite apart from its intrinsic merits, of which we all have the happiest anticipations, a lecture from an old boy will be a great encouragement to our society which is somewhat frowned on in certain quarters.'

'Oh, how's that?'

Lestange held open a gate to the path which led, after five minutes' walk through a wood, to the school.

'There are people about who regard art as *malsain*. Him for instance.' The boy nodded towards Mr Barton's hurrying back.

Hugh laughed.

'He doesn't seem to have changed much with the years.'

'Grotesque, is he not? That such a man should be set to teach French! No doubt he knows the grammar perfectly, but his pronunciation—! And, of course, the *esprit* quite escapes him. Still, he is more harmless than some. A *faux monstre*, you might say.' The guttural sounding of the *r* and the prolongation of the mute *e* were, in

Lestrange's mouth, a little overdone.

'May I say, sir,' the boy went on, lifting his lock, 'how much I enjoyed your article in last month's *Burlington.*'

'Good heavens! You don't tell me you have read that?'

'Anything you write, sir—And, of course, any nail in Webster's coffin is a delight.'

Webster was an elderly pundit whom Hugh had already, on more than one occasion before this article, convicted of serious error. The boy spoke further on the subject, showing that he had indeed read and understood Hugh's abstruse little piece. By the time they reached the school the lecturer had realized that this evening would not be an occasion for 'talking down'. In fact, he was a trifle nervous as to whether he would show himself worthy of the deference of this paragon of enlightenment.

Lestrange took him to have an early dinner with Mr Lennox, the art master, a mild and affable young man, who believed, he said, in giving the boys their head, a policy that sometimes got him into trouble. Mr Lennox described the unfortunate reception given by certain of the parents and older masters to a recent exhibition of the boys' work. Hugh said he would like to see some of this work and promised to come down again for an exhibition that was going to be held at the end of the term and perhaps to mention it somewhere in print.

The lecture took place in the library. It was attended by about thirty boys and a few of the younger masters and their wives. Hugh was introduced, a shade fulsomely, by Lestrange. Then he rose to his feet to deliver his Ridolfi lecture. He was well aware of the importance of the first sentence or two in any discourse. Win the attention of your audience at once if you can. Either provoke them. 'Nobody who has never thought the prose of Walter Pater good is entitled to find it bad' was one of Hugh's openings. Or flatter them, take them into your confidence. The Ridolfi lecture generally began, 'It all goes back—but what doesn't?—to Vasari.' Today this lecture began with different words. Hugh had thought of them on the station path. 'It all starts,' he said, 'on one September afternoon at the great Elizabethan house of Barning Churton, or, as I heard it called by a young lady the other day, Churning Barton.'

There was hearty laughter from boys, masters and masters' wives. The lecturer was well away. His pleasant voice proceeded, smoothly, charmingly, as effortlessly as running water. He had learned with the years a certain use of gesture, that added to his sense of power over his hearers. He felt that he held them in the palm of his hand. He would draw them towards him or push them away or lift them from one place and set them down in another. He placed their eyes to the chink through which the butler had peered. He manipulated them as he wished. They had no will of their own. Never had Hugh had a happier evening. Lestrange, watching the expressive hands, saw himself as a lecturer one day.

'. . . which brings me back at last,' said Hugh in conclusion, 'to my starting place, to Churning Barton—I mean— well, I see it's high time I sat down!' The laughter and applause were followed by the questions, in which the secretary of the society led the attack with a fine show of erudition. Simpler questions followed, which were all answered by the lecturer with good-humoured urbanity and charm. Finally, at a nod from Mr Lennox, Lestrange proposed a vote of thanks. This he did in terms of warmest eulogy. Mr Peveril's performance was '*inoubliable*', his treatment of his subject had been 'supremely adequate', his personality was '*simpaticissimo*'.

After the clapping the audience came towards him and Hugh found himself at the centre of a group of appreciative faces.

'What a pity I have to go back to London tonight,' he said. 'But I much look forward to coming to the exhibition at the end of term.'

'Would you care to come and have a drink now before your train?' said Mr Lennox.

'Thank you very much,' said Hugh, 'I'd like to. But just a minute, my eye has been caught by something.'

He went to the library shelves and took down one of a series of leather-bound volumes that might have been old visitors' books. In gilt lettering on the spine of each was written 'Resolution Book' and below that the dates covered by the book. In these books it was the practice for boys when they left to express their hopes and ambitions for life.

'I had forgotten all about these books,' Hugh said. 'I wonder if I ever wrote anything. I have no memory of it.'

He turned over the pages of the book towards the date where, if he had written anything, his resolution would appear. Three or four heads bent over the book beside him. The entries varied very much in tone and in length. Some covered two or three pages and read almost like pieces of the *Dictionary of National Biography*, with full particulars of appointments, marriage, children and death, and the glowing verdict of posterity. Others consisted of a single line. Some were in the nature of moral precepts such as '*My country right or wrong*' or '*I hope I shall never let down a friend.*'

'That's a good one,' said Hugh, pointing. 'My word!' he read, '"*I shall be Foreign Secretary at forty.*' Not "*I mean to be*" or "*I hope to be*" but "*I shall be*"! And he's brought it off. That's pretty impressive, I must say!'

Many of the resolutions were quite lacking in such high purpose. A good many were jocose and vulgar.

'I like that one,' said Hugh, 'Ronnie MacDougall. "*I mean to be bishop of Sodor and Man.*' I know Ronnie Mac Dougall. His interests are divided between rather dubious picture-dealing and horse racing!'

He turned the page.

'Ah, here we are.' And he read out his own resolution. '"*If the sound of my own voice ever becomes like music in my ears, may I start slipping up over banana peel several times a day.*"'

Hugh led the laugh.

'I say, I say! That's a shrewd one! You know, I've completely forgotten writing that.'

Mr Lennox was looking at his watch.

'I think,' he said, 'if you mean to catch the five to ten *and* have a drink . . . I expect you need a drink.'

'Coming,' said Hugh.

He bade good-bye to Lestrange and the other boys and followed Mr Lennox to his study where he quickly drank a glass of beer. The art master thanked him warmly for his excellent lecture and expressed the hope that Hugh would visit the place more often. He then accompanied him along the path to the station. He spoke of various things as they walked, but his companion, who had been so gay, only answered in monosyllables. Hugh Peveril was deep in thought.

The Facts of Life

'Mother, what's a womb?' said Robin, as they walked away from church. A twittering and fluttering came to Barbara's rescue.

'Look,' she said, 'some long-tailed tits! They're over the hedge now.' And the boy ran to look. When he was back at her side he had forgotten his question. The occasion, however, had impressed itself upon her. It was not the first of such occasions. The Sunday before, at about the same place on the church path, he had asked 'What is meant by "the paps which Thou hast sucked"?' It was clear to her that her son had reached an age—he was eleven—when someone must talk to him. Whose job was that? A father's presumably. But then, Robin's father had died nearly two years ago and not been replaced. The job of an uncle then or the headmaster of his school. It was high time somebody took it on. She was exceedingly reluctant to do so herself, not knowing how she would begin or where to lay the emphasis, and dreading the curtain of embarrassment that would fall between them.

Her brother Micky was the obvious person. It was a pity he lived so far away. Something must be done soon, yet it was only about three weeks since Micky had been to stay, just before Robin's holidays, and he could hardly be summoned again so soon to this distant shire. He, on the other hand, was always pressing her to come up to London for a jaunt. Would it not be the best thing if she went and stayed with Micky for a few days this next week and talked to him about Robin and persuaded him to go down and see the boy at his school early next term and give him the necessary instruction? Yes, this was a good idea. There were certain bits of shopping that she wanted to do in London. Moreover, it was fun staying with Micky. There was always such a lot going on and though she felt out of her depth with his friends, they were never as intimidating as she feared and there were enough of them who did not seem to mind in the least how much out of touch she was with many of the things they talked about. Noticing what she was wearing, men she met with Micky would pay her delightful compliments on her appearance, such as she never got at home. Micky's world was full of mysteries to her, for she had married young and gone off to live in the wilds and her visits to her brother had been rare and fleeting. Since her widowhood, when their mother had come to live with her, it had been incumbent rather on Micky to visit her than her him. She had not now been to London for more than a year.

There was another reason for going to stay with Micky. Barbara was not one of those widows who think it would be a betrayal of a happy love to try to find similar happiness with a new man. To look for the same sort of thing again was, rather, a tribute to the former happiness. Barbara did not care at all for the single state. The wretched cold nights! Both for her own sake and for that of Robin she was anxious to be re-married, and candidates for her hand were not lacking in the neighbourhood, for she was a rose of beauty, with a gay and friendly giggle and eyes that laughed. She had that kind of innocent and radiant desirability that seems to extend from its possessors not only to what they are wearing but to everything they touch, to the prayer-book in their hands and along the pew in which they sit. One of the candidates was becoming insistent.

Though she had a vague wish to break new ground and not marry a farmer this time, she would probably have accepted him, had it not been for the memory of a certain encounter at a party of Micky's last year. It had been the shortest of meetings. She knew nothing about the man except that he was called Verney. Standing together with cocktail glasses in their hands for two or three minutes, they had said nothing significant to each other. She had just felt that if she were free—and at that time she had hardly yet realized that she was free—he might be the man. She remembered thinking afterwards how strange it was that he should have been almost the only one there who had not complimented her on the glass seahorse Micky had pinned in her hair before the party. Before making up her mind, therefore, about the other, she wanted, if possible, to see this Verney man again. Perhaps Micky and Gerald would give a party for her again and ask him. Gerald was the friend who shared his flat with Micky. When, by the way, was Micky going to get married? Hadn't he been a man about town for long enough?

'I suppose it isn't often,' said Robin, 'that one has the luck to see a whole lot of tits together at once?'

Yes, it was high time something was done. Barbara wrote to her brother that afternoon.

And so, a few days later, she put the finishing touches to her face in front of Micky's looking-glass and came out into the passage, where she met Gerald carrying a tray of glasses.

'Barbara,' he said, 'you look a dream.'

'Can I help at all?'

'No, no, thanks, everything's done now. Oh, Marco,' he called into the kitchen, 'have you got the ice? Now, come along, Barbara, and let's have a little preliminary stoke-up. I expect you need one after your journey, and anyhow I think it's rather hard on you to expect you to be social before you've been half an hour inside the house. At this point in a party I generally feel I'd give anything to call it off, don't you?'

In the room they found Micky placing a vase of jonquils on a bookcase.

'How does that look?' he said, standing back. He turned to Barbara. 'Darling,' he said, kissing her, 'you're perfectly lovely.'

Anyone could tell that they were brother and sister. He too had laughing eyes and teeth that gleamed.

'Come on,' he said, 'a drink.'

She sat upon an *empire* settee and was about to take the glass he offered when he withheld it.

'Just a minute,' he said. 'Put your feet up. So. And this arm like this, the hand loose—yes—and the other arm like this—just a moment, another cushion here—that's it. Oh, and you must take your shoes off. There! Now, look this way. That's it, that's perfect! Look, Gerald, isn't that Madame Récamier herself?'

'It's marvellous,' said Gerald.

They stood looking at her.

'*È bella la signora*,' murmured Marco in the background.

'Who is Madame Récamier?' said Barbara.

Damn! She must remember not to ask questions and just to look as though she knew what everything was about.

'Darling,' laughed Micky, 'it's a woman in a picture. Here's your drink. You may relax now. What are you having, Gerald?'

Barbara sipped. The drink seemed pretty strong. She took a gulp. Unless she was well primed, she would not possibly have the nerve to talk to Micky's friends. A second gulp went to her head. Quite suddenly she felt ready for anything.

'How's Robin?' Micky was saying.

This seemed a good moment to broach her business.

'I want to ask you something,' she said. 'Will you tell him the facts of life?' She giggled. Micky laughed loud.

'Poor little Robin!' said Gerald, with mock concern. 'Has he got to learn those wicked facts?'

'No, but will you?' she said.

Micky thought a moment.

'Which facts?' he said.

'Oh, I don't know. I thought you'd know. Well, I suppose, how babies are born.'

'I'm not much of an authority on that. You mean, don't you, how they get conceived?'

'Yes, I suppose I do. And I'd like him to know the meanings of words he picks up in church, without asking me, words like eunuch and womb and fornication and whore.'

'Eunuch, yes. Womb, as I say, I don't know much about. Fornication and whore I should say he was young to be told about.'

The last of these words was one that Micky could never say without a certain feeling of nausea from the memory of a single disgusting, decisive episode. Ugh, never again!

'Oh,' said Barbara. She had not realised that her request would involve such difficulties. There was a ring at the bell.

'Here they come,' said Gerald. Barbara drained her glass.

'The sword! The sword!' cried Micky. 'I was forgetting.' And from a drawer he took a little silver sword, about two inches long, and clasped it on to Barbara's bosom.

'Oh, Micky, you shouldn't! It's perfectly lovely.'

'Now you can keep them at bay. Hullo, Peter. You met my sister, I believe, once before?'

Yes, Barbara remembered this face.

'Tell her the facts of life, Peter. She's asking.'

Peter looked at her interrogatively. She laughed.

'Well, it's just that I've got a boy of eleven who ought to be told something, and it's a question of who should do it and what he should be told.'

'I see. I was told them by the headmaster of my private school. I think he did it very well. He was quite an old boy. He played it down very much. It was all very remote and off-hand. I remember he began with the words "You may have noticed below the base of your stomach"—'

'Barbara, you remember me?' Without a glance at her companion, a new arrival shook her hand and Peter moved aside. Yes, she remembered this man too, but not his name.

'I adore your sword,' he said. His eye already was wandering and suddenly he was gone. The room was quickly filling with people. What a din they made!

'Barbara,' said Micky, 'I want you to meet—' She did not catch the name, but from the face felt that this was a nice man.

'Don't leave my side,' she said to him as soon as they had been brought together.

'I can't think of any reason why I should want to.'

'Hold out your glass, Barbara,' said Gerald, passing with a shaker in his hand. 'Have you learned the facts of life yet?'

'What did he mean by that?' asked the man.

'It's just that we were talking before the party began about someone having to tell the facts of life to a boy of mine, and what he should be told. The boy's eleven. Have you any ideas?'

'Indeed I have.' The nice man had a thoughtful, rather pedantic manner of speaking. 'There should be three main occasions, each more important than the last.'

'Gosh!' said Barbara, taking a drink.

'At the age of your boy, he should be told something, a few things, not too solemnly; in fact, if he can pick them up from other boys only slightly older than himself, so much the better. Then comes the next stage, the stage when—may I speak frankly? If I can't, we'd better talk about something else.'

'Of course, of course,' laughed Barbara. 'That's what I'm here for.'

'Well then, the stage when the boy should lose his virginity. This often gets left much too late in England, with the result that they either become irredeemably queer or permanently immature, like Shaw. You wouldn't want that, would you?'

'Of course not,' said Barbara, hoping her expression looked intelligent.

'This age,' he went on, 'should, in my opinion, in England as it now is, be not later than nineteen. There should be a little preliminary instruction. Lastly, and far the most important, the stage when they think of getting married. At this occasion there should be a most solemn and comprehensive lecture, which should on no account be given by a man whose wife is under fifty. It should be of the utmost seriousness and pitiless realism.' He stopped. This must be the end of what he had to say.

'Thank you,' she said. 'I will remember what you have told me. You've certainly given me some ideas. Now, tell me who all these people are. Who's that little man with bright beady eyes?'

'That's Miles Fantock.'

'Oh, is it?' she said interestedly. This was a literary name that she, even she, knew a little about.

'And the grey-haired man behind him is his brother, Julius, the scientist, and that lovely girl with Julius is Elspeth Campbell and the man they're talking to is Bunny Campbell, her father by his first marriage. They're all rather tied up because Miles's wife, Rachel, was Bunny's second wife. His (Bunny's) third wife, Anna, is now in a nursing home having just had a baby and that woman with him is Anna's sister who is taking the opportunity to run away with him.'

'Goodness!'

'It's going a bit far, don't you think? They're quite open about it. Apparently they walked into the nursing home together and told Anna about it while she was feeding the baby. I must say it shocks me. So, just a little, does Julius and that girl. Quite apart from the incestuousness of her being his brother's wife's first husband's daughter, she has only just left school.'

A handsome man came in at the door and stood gazing around the room with an air of complacent authority.

'Who's that?' she asked.

'He's called Basil Wheeler.'

'He looks rather—' she was going to say 'wonderful', but changed to 'striking'.

'He does that certainly. He's a bit of a dog. *Cave canem*, I say. Beware that privy paw.'

'You two have been together long enough,' said Micky. 'I'm going to break you up. Here's someone to give you all the advice you want, Barbara. She's had experience. She's got a boy of her own.'

The woman's face certainly looked as though she had experienced a good deal. She was fitting a *Gauloise* cigarette into a holder, which she then lit from a lighter. After blowing out some smoke, she gave Barbara her attention.

'The principal thing,' she said, 'is to warn them about the queers.'

Again that word. Had it some special meaning?

'I suppose,' Barbara ventured, 'it's all right if they're not too queer?'

The woman shook her head.

'No. There's no such thing. I mean, if there's the least doubt, there's no doubt at all.'

'How can one tell?' asked Barbara, beginning to twig.

'Well, in the first place, anyone unmarried of thirty-five or over.'

So that was it! Micky was thirty-seven. To say that this revelation gave her a knock would be untrue. Her consciousness, being carried along, as it was, on the mid flood of the alcoholic stream, was hardly in a way to make impact with a solid object. Moreover, the revelation was perhaps no more than the confirming of a suspicion. Still, so far as she was able, she noted that something important had been said.

'Barbara,' said Gerald, 'I want to introduce you. Mr Fantock. Miles, this is Micky's sister, Barbara. Penelope, angel!' he went on, putting his arm round the waist of the woman with the *Gauloise*, 'I want to hear all about the Seychelles. Oh, Miles,' he said, looking back and laughing, 'Barbara wants to be told the facts of life.'

The bright, uneasy eyes in the long, large head opposite her played indecisively over her face for a moment or two. They were tiny craters down which you had a glimpse of the cauldron within. Then he looked away, saying in a dry voice:

'The subject is not one I know anything about. In fact, every day I seem to learn something new.' And with that he turned his back on her.

'Don't mind him,' said a tall man who had overheard. 'He's terribly touchy. You see, he thinks we're trying to get at him *à propos* of his wife.'

'Rachel?'

'That's it, his wife Rachel. Do you know about her?'

'Not much.'

'About her and Wanda?'

'No.'

'Well, of course, we've all known what Wanda is like for years. I think it's very odd he should have left them together. He presumably never imagined anything of the kind was possible with Rachel. Anyhow, he did leave her, to stay on a few days with Wanda in Paris. The few days have turned out to be several weeks. Apparently they've gone off to the Pyrenees and there's no news of any heads being turned for home or anything. Miles is understandably sour. He's particularly sour about the Pyrenees. I mean, that she should be getting all that extra trip abroad, while he has had to come back. He'd almost sooner it was happening right under his eyes.'

The tall man drank from his glass and talked on, as much to himself as to Barbara.

'Natural? Unnatural? What do the words mean? We seem to have got their meanings reversed. Natural is doing what you want to do. It is good behaviour, not vice, that is unnatural. What is called vice is surrendering to the promptings of nature, not resisting them. If, therefore—'

'You're Micky's sister, aren't you? My name's Basil Wheeler. I saw you from the other side of the room. There could be no doubt you are brother and sister. You're the image of each other. He's the most outstandingly good-looking man I know.'

Barbara's new companion gave her an irresistible smile. He stood very close to her and, between his sentences, he hummed. This musical accompaniment to his flirting gave it a kind of continuity, a liquid, flowing quality, as though it were moving effortlessly towards a known destination.

'You're well armed, I see,' looking at the sword—hum—hum—'pretty well armed myself'—hum—and again that irresistible smile, which an enemy might have described as a leer.

Unlike the other people who had talked to her, whose attention she had every moment feared to lose, this man's eyes never wandered from her person. She now felt that she preferred the former way.

'What's this'—hum—'Micky tells me about your wanting to be told the facts of life?'—hum—hum—'I should have thought you knew a thing or three'—hum—

'It's my boy who has to be told.'

'Ah, your boy'—hum—'I'll bet he's good looking'—hum—'and, therefore, the principal thing is to keep him away from the b—rs.'

Bump! A solid object. Suddenly Barbara was sobered. Nothing she had said—indeed she had hardly spoken—and no look of hers, had given this seducer the right to use that word without her permission.

'The nuisance is,' he was saying, and his knee was rubbing against hers, 'the nuisance is'—hum—'that I have got to leave now. I wonder whether you will lunch with me tomorrow?'

Barbara drew back.

'I'm b—d if I will!' she said and turned and moved to the window where she looked out at the April sun setting over the roofs in a gusty sky. She watched the hurrying clouds. Poor little Robin! Must he really learn the facts of life?

'Hullo,' said a voice at her shoulder. 'We met before. My name's Verney.'

Some two hundred and fifty miles away, Robin had been spending the afternoon, in the company of two boys from the village, digging out a badger's hole in a bank on the edge of a wood. They had not got down anywhere near as far as the badger, but the afternoon had not been wasted for Robin. The boys, who were older than he was, had told him certain things that had interested him very much indeed. He went to sleep that night thinking about them, and thought about them the next morning as soon as he awoke and, with hardly any intermission, throughout the day. The next day was a Sunday, and there, as soon as he awoke, these new things were with him again. As he sat in church with his grandmother behind Mr and Mrs Bateson, it seemed to him astonishing that a man and his wife should have the face to sit there together like that, as it were advertising their rude secret. This fact, and all the facts the boys had told him, seemed to him quite extraordinary and perfectly fascinating, and were to continue to seem so for many a year.

Honeymoon

The young man and young woman, who were walking out of the castle of the Sforzas, were evidently tourists. Their clothes, his particularly, betrayed the fact that their travelling wardrobe did not include attire for use in cities that was different from that in which they walked on the hillsides or slept in trains. Mary, the girl, who, like Kenneth, the boy, was making her first visit to Italy, became increasingly conscious, as the days followed one another in the best dressed country in the world, how alien they made themselves appear by their bohemian look. In London, of course, their appearance showed them to be adherents of the arts, members of the intelligentsia and believers in a sophisticated, uninhibited love life. There they contrasted most favourably with the stuffed shirts, the business men, the philistines. Here, however, it was being every day borne in upon her that it was Kenneth and herself who were the barbarians.

'Why,' she said, 'we look just like Germans!'

Kenneth was nettled by the remark.

'No, we don't,' he said. 'We don't just stand about gaping indiscriminately and saying "*wunderschön!*" We can criticize things intelligently. I'm sure our talk is better.'

'Honestly, Kenneth, what do you know about the talk of Germans? You don't know a word of their language, any more than you do of Italian.'

'You can see what they're saying.'

'Well, anyhow, I wasn't talking about talk. I was talking about our uncivilised appearance in Italy.'

'Good heavens! You surely don't care about what the macaronis think of your appearance?'

He gave a pitying laugh. Kenneth was an Italophobe. He was so before ever he had set foot in Italy. He had been confident that this country would not come up to Greece which he had visited with a friend the year before. At every turn he was being proved right. The tamed and pretty-pretty landscape, the simpering art, the babyish mother-worship, the scented dandies combing their hair in public places, the ubiquitous ices and orangeade—it was all exactly as he had foretold. Not a man's country!

It may be asked why he had brought his bride to Italy for their honeymoon.

'We are young,' he had said. This was certainly the case. He was just twenty-two and she was nineteen. 'We should tick off Italy before I take you to Greece.'

The observation, made one evening in a London coffee bar, had seemed to her profound. It had that quality of intellectual mastery that she found in so much of what Kenneth said and to which she submitted so gladly. The prospect of having her education so authoritatively taken in charge had not been the least of his attractions for her. He was certainly brilliant. His talk made play with all the great names in literature and the arts, and with many others that were new to her. She watched his friends, the others in their gang, listening to him with respect. How lucky she was to have caught him!

It was true that his genius had not yet had time to assert itself in any very material manner. He had got a job as an assistant master in a progressive private school in the north of London. He did not, of course, look on the job as anything but temporary, or indeed, though he had no further plans to divulge, as anything but the necessary prelude to a career of greatness. What great man, he said, has not started life as a schoolmaster?

Mary was the child of a broken marriage. Tossed from parent to parent and from school to school, she had not made much headway in conventional education. She had learned, however, to look after herself and when, two years ago, her father had died, leaving her a little money, she had taken a bed-sitting room in Chelsea and enrolled herself at an art school. Perhaps the most important date in her spiritual development up to the time of her marriage, had been the occasion when a white-headed man had said to her 'May I see some examples of your work?' The idea of regarding painting and drawing, the happiest occupations in the world, for which any child will hope for a wet afternoon, the idea of regarding this form of play as work seemed to make her suddenly adult. If they were prepared to take her as seriously as that, she would not fail them, and amongst the new friends she was making there was every encouragement to be serious. For whatever they might lack in collars and ties and a change of clothes, they did not lack the habit of conviction. There seemed to be no question under the sun on which she would not hear a confident, decisive and generally indignant, verdict. The intellectual excitement went to her head. When the brilliant Kenneth asked her to be his wife, she had no doubts about accepting him.

'I must of course tell uncle Oliver,' she had said. 'You will have to meet him. And I suppose you should meet my mother.'

The latter meeting was the occasion of a double introduction, for the young people were presented at it to the man whom the mother was about to marry as her fourth husband. The foolish creature made Kenneth drunk and pronounced him a darling.

'We needn't see them again,' said Mary.

The meeting with her uncle was a different matter. Uncle Oliver, her father's elder brother, was the only one of her family who meant anything to her now. 'He's like an old monk ploughing in my otherwise empty background,' she had said to Kenneth. 'He's always there.' Though he had no legal responsibility, he had assumed a kind of moral guardianship over his homeless niece, which she was glad to recognize. Himself childless, and recently a widower, he was happy to step into the role of father, which poor Andrew, sick, drunken, and demoralized by that wretched woman, had so inadequately filled. Moreover, his age had just forced him into retirement. With the plough taken from his hands, he had no strong attachment in life other than his Mary. He recognized, however, that at her age, and with her experience of the older generation, he could hardly expect her to do other than present him, for most of the time, with her back view.

The meeting with Kenneth had been a success. The boy had been on his best behaviour and uncle Oliver had taken no offence at the arrogance which showed itself only just below the surface. Meeting few young people, he had forgotten what it was to see the world in black and white. He found Kenneth full of promise. But when Mary divulged that they intended to get married in a few weeks, he was appalled.

'But you're still growing up so fast,' he said. 'You hardly know each other. Give it a year or six months, at least.'

His advice had not been taken and here they were, in the second week of their honeymoon, walking across the bridge over the dry moat that encircles the castle of the Sforzas. Beyond the bridge, they sat on a stone bench a few yards from the parapet of the moat, looking at the castle wall. Behind them there was the public park. From beyond the castle came the roar of the city of Milan. Against this muffled bass accompaniment, a shrill performance by the treble voices of several hundred swifts was being given just in front of them. As they shot and dived and glanced and swerved over the moat, the birds were shrieking with ecstasy. Occasionally one of them would stop to perch for a second in a crevice of the castle wall, occasionally one or two would soar away from the congregation of their fellows high up into the blue; but the multitude was entirely absorbed in its violent, rapturous interweaving, between the moat and the battlements, a few feet away from the brickwork of the castle.

The evening sun shining directly upon the wall threw the shadow of each swift streaking along the bricks. The result of this was that there appeared to be twice as many swifts as there actually were. Mary was about to comment on this phenomenon but withheld her observation. In her hand she had a picture postcard of the Michelangelo *pietà* which they had just been looking at in the museum of the castle. Kenneth was talking about Greek sculpture. He was describing the figures of Harmodius and Aristogiton. These were long names and Mary had never heard them before and knew nothing about Greek sculpture. Suddenly, to clinch the moral of his discourse, he pointed to her card.

'. . . whereas that yearns,' he said. *Q.E.D.*

She looked at the photograph.

'It doesn't yearn,' she said. 'Perhaps you could say, it droops, but then it's meant to.'

'All right—"droops". That's just as bad. But what can you expect from a pansy?'

How wrong he was, Mary thought. She looked at her card with love. This *pietà* seemed to her about the best of all the things they had yet seen. She decided to send it to uncle Oliver. Such an action would be breaking a compact made but ten days ago. 'Let's have no letters to families, no picture postcards to anybody!' Kenneth had said. 'It's just you and me!' 'Of course,' she had agreed enthusiastically, ten days ago.

The castle wall, like so many old walls in Italy, was punctured with untidy holes, as though the builders had had to leave before finishing their work. Kenneth was quite sure that these were the apertures where the scaffolding poles had been. The workmen had simply been too lazy to fill them in. 'How like these people!' he had said. Mary was not convinced. If that was the explanation, it seemed to her rather *un*like these people. However it might be, the holes had their uses. She had become aware that many of them were occupied by pigeons, watching, like dowagers, in staid detachment, the frantic revelling of the younger generation.

Kenneth was now talking about homosexuality, of the difference between the ancient and the modern varieties. 'Greek homosexuality was virile,' he said. 'The pansy came in at the Renaissance.'

The subject was one on which she had nothing to say. She listened suspiciously. Listening to Kenneth, now that she had him to herself all the twenty-four hours of the day and night, had become a most different experience from listening to him in London. How little, it seemed, they had been alone with each other before their honeymoon! How rarely they had looked at anything new together, to test their observation and their taste! Here, where all was new to them equally, and her opinion was as good as his, his talk had daily become for her less oracular. And it was not just in matters of taste that her confidence had been slipping away; his famous mastery of facts had been called in question too. The unwillingly acknowledged confusion of Mantegna and Montagna the other day had filled her with doubts on both scores. She had begun to ask herself whether, on the subjects about which she knew nothing, he was always right.

He was talking about Socrates and his pupils. '. . . whereas these people,' he was saying, and with a comprehensive gesture of the arm he included all Milan, all Italy, 'they don't begin to be moral adults. Of course their religion doesn't give them a chance. Permanent adolescents.'

A loving couple, sauntering hand in hand over the bridge from the castle, now passed between them and the parapet. It was possibly speech that was coming from the mouth of the girl. It sounded more like a cooing. The pair looked as though they knew all the rules of love. No bungling there. A little further on, there was another stone seat, unoccupied. The man, with his spare hand, brushed a place on it for the girl to sit upon. As he did so, he evidently observed that the stone was warm (the sun had indeed only just left it), for the girl, with her spare hand, felt it. She then sat down, lifting her skirt, with her spare hand, in order that her flesh might receive the warmth through one less layer, perhaps through no layer, of clothing. The act was performed with simple, ungiggling decorum. How at home in the world! thought Mary.

Kenneth was back at her postcard.

'It's all emotion and thought,' he said. 'He'd given up using his eyes by the time he did that.'

'Bosh!' she said. 'Absolute bosh! And as for using eyes, we've now been sitting here for twenty minutes and you haven't yet even noticed the swifts!'

She got up and went to the parapet. Lucky swifts, happily screaming all together! Presently she would scream, and it would be the unhappiest and loneliest scream in the whole world.

Two or three days later Sir Oliver Brock, K.C.B., walked into his club. The man at the desk received from him a large envelope and at the same time handed him his post, a letter and a postcard. He took them into the morning room, sat in an armchair and put on his spectacles. The postcard told him that his niece was having a marvellous time, that Italy was even more wonderful than she had expected and that the best thing they had yet seen was the piece of sculpture represented overleaf. He turned the card and contemplated the *pietà* for some moments. He hoped it was indeed true that the girl was having a marvellous time. A rough passage was what he had foretold for her.

The envelope in his hand bore no stamp and no address beyond his name, for the letter it contained was written on the writing paper of the club. It said: '"If Poggio was the Brunelleschi of Italic handwriting, Ascham was the Inigo Jones." Do you agree with this statement? Your answer should be amply illustrated. If you are not skilled in the use of a quill pen, special calligraphic pens can be bought at most stationers.'

Sir Oliver looked at the letter for some minutes. It was itself certainly a calligraphic performance. Leo prided himself on his writing, whereas Oliver, as Leo well knew, was an inept penman. The question was in fact simply designed to show up Oliver's incapacity. It was, no doubt, an interesting question, in the answering of which he, Oliver, would learn a lot. It remained, all the same, an unkind, low and ungentlemanly question.

Sir Oliver stared at the ceiling for a while, then went and sat at a writing-table in the window. On a single sheet he wrote: 'Trace the history of the word "gentleman". You are not expected to attempt a definition of your own.' He folded the sheet and put it in an envelope, on which he wrote 'Leopold Hayward, esq., C.B.E.' On his way out of the club a few minutes later, he handed the envelope to the man at the desk.

This strange correspondence between two members of the club had had its origin some months ago, soon after Oliver, unwillingly laid upon the shelf, had begun to find himself spending a good deal of his time in the place. Sitting down one day in the reading room next to Leo, he had observed that the latter was reading one of his (Leo's) own books.

'Good stuff that,' he had observed.

The other put the book down on his knee.

'Since you have said it,' he remarked, 'I cannot but agree. It's first rate. I'd forgotten how good it is.'

The thought did not seem to give the old man much satisfaction.

'You will appreciate that the fact that you find me reading this is not, for me, a jolly fact. My predicament is God's. "And God saw everything that He had made and behold it was very good." Once you have started looking back on what you've done, you're finished. Creation is over.'

'I don't know much about creation,' said the other, 'but I certainly am finding it hard to get used to the vacancy of retirement.'

'It's not much fun to get used to,' said the exwriter to the ex-administrator. 'I've been at it some years now. I'm older than you and I retired earlier. You find that the events of the day follow one another without a theme. Your mind, though not your memory, seems as good as ever. You are as alert as you always were for the stab of curiosity, the illuminating phrase, the sudden moral bracing—and they don't come any more. How different from what it used to be! The day was always full of significant moments. There would be a blackbird on a London chimney-pot, or a lady in an expensive shop smelling the skewer with which the shopman had just punctured a peach-fed ham, or a child scratching the ridges of corduroy, or oneself seeing off a Venezuelan on the boat train. And the air would be full of ideas to connect the moments, like fingers manipulating the cardboard letters in a word game, which would nearly, then quite, take shape and as they fell into place, I would have my story, my book.'

'I see the sort of thing you mean. It's certainly very different for me, this aimless passing of the day, from that allocating of priorities, that careful spacing of energies, to which I had become used.'

Oliver was aware, however, that he had one link with life that the other lacked, namely his niece. Leo, though he had many friends, seemed to have no strong emotional or family bond of any kind. He only had his mind. And, of course, thank God, there were meals. The two old men sat glumly for a few minutes, listening for the luncheon gong.

'One should, I suppose,' said Leo, 'try to love mankind. Boys' clubs, or something of the kind. Yet I wonder whether the youth of England would benefit much from my company.'

'I have an idea,' said Oliver.

His idea, which they quickly developed and at once put into execution, was that they should set each other examination papers. On the first of the month each would find at the porter's desk his new question. At the same time he would hand in his essay for the month before. Answers should consist of not less than five or more than ten thousand words. They would be handed back, criticised and marked, in the middle of the month. The game had now been going on for nearly a year and had given them both much happiness. Passing one another in the London Library as they toiled at their question papers, each would stare blankly at the other, as at an unknown face. One day, however, Leo had answered the other's empty stare with a smile. 'We are Bouvard and Pécuchet,' he had said, 'a couple of old sillies.'

Two or three weeks after receiving the postcard from Milan, Oliver was sitting in the club one evening. Leo sat down next to him.

'By the way,' said the latter, 'how's that niece of yours getting on? Is she back from her honeymoon yet?'

'As a matter of fact, she had lunch with me today.'

'How's it going?'

'Not too well, I'm afraid. After a certain amount of beating about the bush, she opened up. She said "Uncle, I wish I'd taken your advice. I find I've married a bore, an inaccurate bore. He notices nothing and he gets everything wrong."'

'What did you say?'

'What would you have said?'

'I don't know. I expect I would have advised her to get out as quick as she can. Did you?'

'I did nothing of the kind.'

The emphasis with which this was said surprised Leopold Hayward and caused him, as at a word of command, to sit up a little straighter in his chair.

'I said,' the other went on, '"he may be boring now, but he is still far too young to have taken on the definitive status of a bore. And it doesn't matter if he's wrong about things now. He'll get right. He's got the thing that matters at his age, impetus." I said, "Marriage, creative marriage, is not play, it's work. The rewards come at the end not at the beginning," I said. "It is for you to make him not a bore, to teach him to notice things. It is your life work. You have given yourself plenty of time. You should have a clear fifty years." I said—'

While Oliver was speaking, Leo imagined himself to be the niece listening. As the uncle struck and struck again, he experienced a kind of elation, for he felt himself being carried up into reality, almost into a book.

Full Circle

Rather a fascinating book this about the *jeunesse* of André Gide. It was not often nowadays, that is to say, at the age which Harry Rivington had now reached, that one looked at several hundred leaves of a book still to be read (and this book was in two volumes, each of two inches across) and said to oneself 'Good!' He had just been reading that extract from the diary of Pierre Louÿs: '*je suis jeune, j'ai dix-sept ans, je suis vierge et ça ne peut pas durer comme ça . . . je jure Dieu que le mois de mai ne se passera pas sans que . . . Oh! la première nuit et la première femme!*' Meanwhile Gide, the friend, was writing in his diary: '*je voudrais, à l'âge où la passion se déchaîne, la dompter par un labeur forcené et grisant. Je voudrais, tandis que les autres courent les plaisirs, les fêtes et les débauches faciles, goûter les voluptés farouches de la vie monastique. Seul, absolument seul . . .*' Harry's eyes wandered from the page. Ah, how it came back!

What came back? Something of the conflict that besets a youth in his teens, which those two young Frenchmen in about 1890 were planning to resolve in such different ways, something of the disturbance of realising that you are no longer simply one of the dramatis personae of a family or a school, contributing to the work and the play and the table-talk in a manner suitable to your age, but a radio-active nugget of great danger anywhere in the world.

He got up from his chair and strolled about the room, enjoying the loneliness. For they had all gone out for the afternoon. He had the house to himself. The experience was an unusual one, as, in addition to the major security, he had made several later investments against solitude, which had been blessed with happy increase. The second generation now out-numbered the first, there was no stopping them. And in the summer months they would come and fill the house. A young family would break like a wave into the hall and spread outwards with its litter over the ground floor, presently, before it had quite receded, to be overtaken by the litter of the next wave. Sometimes two waves, approaching from rather different directions, would converge upon the place, breaking one another's fall, yet, none the less, sending a double volume of surge to wash against the walls of the rooms. Harry's investments had certainly paid, for which he was abundantly grateful. Once in a way, however, he was no less grateful to have the house to himself.

It should be said that he did, of course, frequently have the experience of being by himself, in the wood-shed, in the orchard, in a field. The unusual thing about this afternoon's loneliness was that he was in an entirely empty house. The indoorness was the unusual thing. If he had gone to the end of the garden and looked over the fields, he would have had much more extensive evidence of the absence of human beings around him than could be given by looking through the open door of the drawing-room into the hall; still, just as you may walk from under the sky into a church and feel that your range of vision has been greatly expanded, so today the house seemed to him enormous. It was Versailles or Tsarskoe Syelo, with views that had no end through room after room after room. He began to saunter through his palace, silent but for the wasps and blue-bottles that buzzed against the window-panes in the drowsy August afternoon. Surely there had been such another afternoon, in another house, long ago? *Seul absolument seul . . .*

As he progressed, unhurried, unfollowed, unwatched, uncalled-for, unwaited-for, taking no message, setting no standard of godly life and making no outlay of love, goodwill, information, advice, praise or rebuke, the half-forgotten delight of solitude lit, like a flame, upon his head. To be, again, the only actor on your stage, the only pebble on your beach, to renew acquaintance (and find him as fascinating as ever) with that person whom the family man has got to drop, that old friend and enemy, the *ego*, to lift that mask of a character which circumstances and your own compromises have made of you and become again what you know you have never ceased to be, that immensely promising young fellow, to recover as it were your virginity of soul—from an upper window Harry Rivington saw attractive Mrs Weldon walking up the drive towards the house.

The sight of her took him back wholly to that other house and that other distant dreamy Tennysonian afternoon. Again, they had all gone out, this time leaving young Harry to struggle with Stubbs's *Charters*. Not many minutes passed, however, before the youth gave up the struggle, leaned back in his armchair and began to lotus-eat. Under the influence of his brilliant friend, Whitworth, he was passing at the moment through a Plato phase. It seemed to him that the room around him was full of Platonic ideas. The moted sunbeam that lay across the bookcase was the sunbeam of all time; the turning motes were performing their slow astronomical dance in eternity. The golden rows of books formed the world's general library. Even the blue-bottle that buzzed over the vase of pink poppies was no particular fly, but buzzed for all the summers there would ever be. The house was young Harry's moated grange, in which nothing would ever happen. Yet he was not a pining, melancholy tenant. Simply his life had been arrested by the stopping of time. He was gathered up, as one of them, into the general ideas. He was perfect man, Michelangelo's Adam, forever prolonging the farewell to his creator. The moment would never come for him to turn his head towards the world. Though all curious, he would never now take a book from that sunny shelf, nor, though his head was full of imperishable words, would he ever make a book of his own to put there, and, though he was now of an age, he would never, never kiss. The fall of a poppy petal set time going again.

What nonsense! Of course he was pining and melancholy and misunderstood and whatever else a young *ego* well can be. No one of his age could ever before have been so world-weary. His shy soul shunned the day. At least they should not get at that. Bat-like, it flitted away from them to an ever darker and more inward sanctum. Just who 'they' were, the pursuers, he could not well have said. He only knew they did not reach him in the inmost caverns that were sacred to the silence which answers desperate prayer.

'All that is just so much word-making!' would be the comment of Buckley, another strong brain to which he increasingly gave ear. For he was now more and more venturing up from his catacombs into the light, where he strode and sauntered and lounged with lordly nonchalance. How prodigiously at ease he felt! Surely he was the salt of the earth? What fascinating deeds were ahead of him! What manhood! 'A period of narcissism may be allowed,' Whitworth had said, 'provided it does not go on too long.'

Over and above these his subterranean and his daylight characters, there was yet a third young Harry. This person was reclining on the sunny side of a cloud, looking down with half-amused compassion on the human scene. The guardian of sanity, he knew, in his wisdom, that all mundane techniques are mere approximations; that things will be given long before they can be appreciated, while things longed for will be granted, in ironical abundance, when they are no longer wanted; that the most earnest lover will be torn, like Garrick, between the seriousness of his intention and the comedy of the deed. With this Olympian eye upon him, terrestrial Harry was, generally, able to prevent the pressures to which he was subjected from leading to violence or bad manners.

It will be seen that young Harry Rivington was a thoroughly conventional young man in his late teens.

Getting up from his chair he strolled along the room and out into the hall, questing, expectant, dangerous. Through the hall window he looked across the drive at a yew hedge and a high brick wall, behind which were loaded apple trees. The chimney of Peggy Rossiter's cottage showed above the branches. This horsy and alcoholic widow, who had lately come to live in the village, had been pronounced by Harry's parents 'a good sort'. 'An awful old tart, of course,' his father had added.

Suddenly self-conscious, or rather—for he was self-conscious already—suddenly embarrassed as by stage fright, young Harry began to go upstairs. It seemed to him that all the arc-lights were on him and him alone. Everybody was watching him, not just, as usual, God and the Devil, but far more real people, like Alcibiades and Eleanor of Aquitaine and Napoleon and Cleopatra. Indeed, what else had the dead to do? With which last thought his shyness left him as suddenly as it had come. Bounding up the steps, he found himself before the bookcase on the landing.

Do people who write books have the faintest idea of the trouble they can cause? How lightly they say things! Yet one of their asides, a mere half-dozen words, may turn a young mind crazy. There were two sayings Harry had lately encountered in books, which he could not forget. One of these was Wilde's, 'In a woman chastity is divine, in a man it is ridiculous.' The other was slipped into some conversation in a novel, 'The coming together of two virgins can be a fiasco.' Now, Harry had no wish either to be ridiculous or to be involved in a fiasco. So these *dicta* had lodged in his mind, like grit in the shoes, and chafed and chafed.

The second held an urgent challenge. There were, it seemed, technical matters to be learned, that could only be learned by experience. But how to come by that experience? The idea of buying it revolted him. That would be degrading and, yes, wicked. How then?

Looking out of the landing window he imagined the lavish figure of Peggy Rossiter appearing round the corner of the drive. Smoking a panatella and swaying in her walk, she would advance purposefully towards the house, happy, generous, blowsy, knowing, humming hoarsely to herself. There would be, as always, the uncertainty as to how long her too-tight clothes could hold what they had to hold. Set her beside the maidens with whom Harry played tennis—Peggy every time! Harry's breath was coming fast, his heart had begun to pound.

She would come up to the front door, open it without knocking and step inside. He would be half-way down the stairs.

'Hullo,' she would say in that husky voice.

'Hullo,' he would say. 'I'm afraid they're all out. I'm alone in the house.'

'I know,' she would say, shutting the door behind her.

He watched, panting, the corner of the yew hedge round which she would appear. Presently, growing calmer, he began to perambulate. He wandered through the sunny, sleepy, dusty, buzzing, bedrooms, keeping a look always out on to the drive. Wild, unmentionable things must have happened in these rooms. He began to imagine his father's lusts, and his grandfather's, but was not sorry, at a frown from the Great Headmaster, to stop thinking of these things. He sat at a window, one of the lattices of which was wide open. On a small pane in the other lattice, not six inches from the way out, a bee was buzzing furiously. The foolish thing, he helped it through into the garden. His gaze followed it vacantly. She cometh not, he said. The curious thing was that it seemed to be with the faculty of recollection that he knew she would not come.

Old Harry, whose excitement, such as it was, had quickly run itself out into these sands of memory, came down the stairs and opened the door to Mrs Weldon.

'Hullo,' he said.

'Is Mamie about?' she asked.

'No, she's out, I'm afraid. They've all gone out for the afternoon, to the sea. I'm alone in the house.'

'Oh, I never knew.'

You knew perfectly well, he said to himself, amused.

'Well then—' she lingered.

'Anything I can do?' he said, watching in himself for any symptoms of suffocation or speeding of the heart. There was not one such faintest symptom. The erotic wheel had done its full circle.

'Well then,' she said, turning away.

'I'll walk with you to the gate,' he said.

The Donkey

The Masons had the idea that it would be fun to hire a donkey for August, partly for the amusement of their grandchildren and partly to eat down the grass in the orchard. The third and strongest, but undeclared, reason was the amusement of Mr M., whose soul, in the course of a mainly urban life, had been starved of dependent four-footed animals. So they put an advertisement in the local paper in the early summer. There was one answer, from some people called Greene who lived in a village a few miles away and had a donkey they would be prepared to hire in August while they were on their holiday.

The Masons went over one week-end to see them and the donkey. The latter, Mrs Greene explained, could perfectly well remain in its, or rather her, field while they were away, but they were afraid she might get a bit lonely. She was so very affectionate. If a good home could be found for her, where she would get lots of love, she (Mrs Greene) and her family would go off happier. They had had her nearly a year. She was about five. And the rent? Oh, say ten shillings a week. It was not the money they were thinking of, but finding a good home for the donkey. Two bright-eyed schoolgirls were listening attentively to the negotiations.

'But you must come and see her.'

They walked across a lawn and through an orchard to the edge of a paddock. When the donkey saw them standing by the fence she came running towards them, braying loudly. She nuzzled her nose into Mrs Greene's hands and rubbed her eyes against her apron, then threw her head back and looked at the visitors, with one ear pointing forward and the other back. Mr Mason took hold of the ears and stroked them. They were hot and responsive, and for all the freedom with which she moved them, supremely dependent.

'She's lovely,' he said. 'I expect the flies are rather a bother to her.'

'They are rather,' said Mrs Greene, 'but she can go and stick her head into the tree there.'

'The trouble with us is that she will have to be pegged. We only have an orchard we could put her in and it hasn't got a fence on the garden side. Also she'd eat too many apples if loose. Do you think she'll mind being pegged?'

'I don't suppose she'll like it at first, but that can't be helped. I think she'd get bored if she was just left in one place for very long without seeing anyone. She likes a good deal of attention, don't you, Bessie? You'll be taking her out for rides, I suppose?'

'Yes, of course. I wanted to ask about that. Our little boys are only five and three. They're too young to go out by themselves. A grown-up will have to lead her.'

'Yes, but I'll let you have the reins and the saddle. She keeps this head-piece on all the time..The reins fasten on here. There isn't a bit.'

'I see. What fun it's going to be for the children! By the way, she'll need water, I suppose? She can have a bucket.'

'She drinks very little. In this sort of weather'—Mrs Greene looked up at the approaching storm—'she gets all the wet she needs out of the grass.'

'Well then,' said Mr Mason, 'is there anything more we ought to know? I'm just wondering, suppose for some reason she did not like being with us, after you had gone away?'

'You could simply bring her back and put her in this field.'

'I could? Good. Just in case. But I see no reason why she shouldn't be very happy with us. Well then, I will telephone at the beginning of August, when we come down here to stay—we're normally only week-enders—and fix a day to fetch her. Thank you very much.'

One Sunday in June Mr Mason scythed the grass in the orchard, with the satisfaction of knowing that he would not have to do so, as normally, a second time that year. He was slightly apprehensive as to whether there would be enough grass to feed the donkey for a whole month. He need have had no fears. That summer was the wettest for fifty years and the grass grew prodigiously. Day after day throughout July Mr Mason watched the rain come down in torrents on the London streets and he was glad in his heart, saying to himself, 'This means it will be fine in August.' The light green leaves of the hop growing in his London back-garden looked as though the sun was shining through them even on the darkest, wettest days. But the light that shone in Mr Mason's heart through that dank summer came chiefly from the prospect of the donkey's company during his holiday. Sitting at committee tables amongst insufferable self-important men, he thought, 'In August I shall have Bessie.'

The grandchildren, who lived not far away in London, were told by their mother of the treat in store for them.

'Grandfather is getting you a donkey.'

'Why?' said Michael, the younger.

'So that you can go for rides on its back.'

'Why on its back?'

'Because that's where people who ride ride.'

'"Ride ride",' John, the elder, pointed out, 'you said "ride ride".'

At length the holidays came. The family assembled in the country. In spite of the rain some of the corn looked almost ready to be cut. Much of it, however, had been dashed to the ground. Weeds were growing profusely in the wet earth. The nettles at the edge of the plantation were as high as a man. There were a thousand jobs to be done about the place, jobs that were not expected of Parker, whose function was limited to keeping the lawn mown and the kitchen garden dug. The hedges needed clipping and the paths weeding and the nettles scything, some of the young fruit trees had broken away from their supports and needed tying up again, that branch on the young bush tree needed staking or the weight of the apples would break it, that rusted nail holding the pear to the wall had come out and, of course, the wall badly needed re-pointing. Indeed, there were a thousand and one jobs that Mr Mason noticed as he walked around with his son-in-law on Saturday afternoon. One job, however—and they were looking at the grass in the orchard—would be done this year by someone else. Going into the house, Mr Mason telephoned to the Greenes and it was arranged that he should fetch the donkey on Wednesday.

On Sunday the children's parents left in a car for three weeks abroad. In order that there should be no tears, the boys' attention had been directed to their zoo at the moment of departure and the parents' absence was not noticed for some hours. The zoo was contained within the walls of a toy fort and already included a toad and a frog and many snails, slugs, worms and woodlice. For the first few days it absorbed a great deal of the children's time. Monday was Bank Holiday. On Tuesday at breakfast Mr Mason said, 'The shops will be open again today. Can I get you anything, my dear, if I go into Molton this morning? I must see about a chain and a collar for the donkey.'

Mr Mason had an old poker which he intended to use as a peg for the donkey's chain. He had tried hammering it into the ground in the orchard, using a log as hammer, and it went easily into the clay. Only the last two or three inches were hard going. It must have reached the chalk. Indeed, when he pulled the poker out, it was a little bent.

'Would you like to come, boys? I'll be going to the blacksmith. You remember, that dear old man we saw hammering the red-hot iron?'

They did remember their visit to the blacksmith nearly a year ago and were keen to accompany their grandfather into Molton. Immediately after breakfast, the piece of muslin, stained with mud and blood and slime, was accordingly laid again over the fort to hold in those inhabitants of the zoo who had not escaped during the night, and the stones were replaced to hold it down. Then the gentlemen of the party set off in the car, with a long shopping list, waving good-bye to the ladies, Mrs Mason, Luciana, the Italian girl, and the infant, Rachel.

The market town of Molton was some four miles away. In spite of the traffic that passed along the high street with such a flow that there had to be a policeman in summer time to stop it for people to cross between the Plough Inn and the post office, in spite of this modern martyrdom by which the little town was continuously being sawn in two, the many small-paned shop-windows (that only made the jazzy front of Cardew's stores a worse eyesore), the narrow streets and alleys that led off the market square, the public houses that seemed to occupy the site of at least every fourth capital messuage in the centre of the town, the plate glass window next the Crown against the lower half of which, on the inside, a dark screen was fixed of the kind of fine wire netting that encases a meat safe, on which screen was written in faded gold, in a sloping copy book script, 'Th. Wilkins, commissioner for oaths', words that looked as if they could hardly have been written later than 1860, so that one asked oneself about Mr Wilkins or the Wilkins dynasty and turned back to see if the 'Th.' had been written over later (no, it hadn't)—all these things, of old-fashioned aspect, made it easy to imagine Molton in Victorian times, when horses clattered in the cobbled square. A visit to the blacksmith confirmed how decisively that age had passed.

The old man, pottering amongst the scrap iron in his yard, said he never had a cart-horse to shoe nowadays. Tractors didn't have shoes. He was looking to see if he had a bit of chain for the donkey. He might have a bit but he didn't think he had. It would have to be about twenty feet long, Mr Mason said; any longer and the donkey would be able to get at the fruit trees.

'She's not going to like it, if she's not been pegged afore.'

The blacksmith, who was not given to looking on the bright side of things, was gloomily playing spillikins with the rusty piles of metal. At length he shook his head. Sorry, no chain. They would have to go to Andrews'.

'We didn't see any red-hot thing, which you said we would,' John said as they walked away. He was carrying the bent poker.

'We'll be going back,' said Mr Mason, 'to get him to put a ring on the chain, then you can see some hammering. Mind that poker, John. Now, hold my hands, both of you, while we cross the road.'

In the ironmonger's they bought a chain twenty-two feet long that cost a shilling and a halfpenny a foot and was far heavier to carry than it looked as if it should be. Then they went into the butcher's and the grocer's and the chemist's. The shopping bag became nearly full. Then they came to the leather shop.

'This shop smells nice,' said Michael.

Here they bought a collar for the donkey. The man persuaded Mr Mason to buy the strongest collar he had, a good two inches across, such as was put on cattle.

'If it's not used to being pegged,' he said, 'it's going to tug at it. You'd better be on the safe side.'

He punched some extra holes for the buckle, in case the collar was too large.

'How much?' said Mr Mason.

'Twenty-five shillings,' said the man, which did not seem excessive for what was indeed a splendid collar. John put it round his neck and they walked out of the shop and across the high street and back to the car in the market place. Mr Mason put the shopping bag into the dicky, then said, 'Now come along again to the blacksmith and watch him hammering.'

The boys were already in the back seat of the open car looking up at two aeroplanes that wheeled, their wings at right angles to the ground, screeching over the town.

'Javelins,' said John.

'Are you coming?' said Mr Mason, when the noise had passed.

'I want to stay here and watch aeroplanes,' said John.

'So do I,' said Michael.

'Very well,' said their grandfather, walking off with the chain and the bent poker. Let them do what they liked, but it was a pity they should not come to the blacksmith. For himself he had a most enjoyable quarter of an hour in the forge watching the fitting of a ring to the chain and the straightening of the poker. The blowing of the fire, the shaping of the metal under the hammer and its hissing and smoking in the water, were as fascinating as they ever had been, and he still looked, as he had fifty years ago, for Shadrach, Meshach and Abednego walking in the midst of the furnace. It was found that the poker was so slim it would go through a link of the chain up to its knob, so it was only necessary to put a ring on the other end of the chain, to hold the collar.

'It's not very strong, your poker,' the smith said, 'she'll bend it, maybe. You ought to have a proper peg.'

Still, Mr Mason, who had spent nearly fifty shillings on the donkey that morning, thought he would trust to his poker.

And so, the day's shopping done, they went home.

At breakfast the next morning Mr Mason said, 'Well, the great day has arrived. Today I'm going to fetch Bessie.'

'Who's Bessie?' said John.

'Why, Bessie, the donkey.'

'Oh, the donkey. I'd forgotten about the donkey.'

It was arranged that Mr Mason should be driven over at the end of the morning by Mrs M., who would bring back the saddle in the car while he led the donkey. He would take his lunch with him to have on the way.

The principal anxiety that he had had about the walk, namely that he would make a fool of himself in front of the Greenes by failing to persuade the donkey to set out with him, proved groundless. She started at a good pace without turning her head to acknowledge their good-byes. Not till she was out of sight of their gate and had reached the cross-roads at the edge of the village did she stop and appear to become aware that she had a new master.

'It's me,' he said reassuringly, 'it's only me. Now, this way, to the left, come along.'

But she would not follow his pull. Turning her head to right and to left and over her shoulder, she refused to budge. Her eyes were full of questions.

'It's only me,' he said, taking hold of one hot ear. She tweaked the ear away.

'You can't maken her go,' said a man leaning on his fork in a cottage garden. 'She'll not go afore she wants to.'

And so it was. Quite suddenly she decided to accompany Mr Mason to the left up the hill.

'We'll stop and have a bite when we get to the top,' he said. The route lay for most of its six miles along narrow lanes in which, at places, cars could not pass one another. The road accordingly was avoided by traffic. It belonged to Mr Mason and his donkey who strode up the hill through a tunnel of high banks and hedges. He put his hand affectionately on her back.

'Here we are, Bessie, you and I at last. It's come off. I'm happy.'

Much literature seemed to be walking with them.

'There was Balaam, Bessie—'

At that moment a jet fighter shrieked overhead. The donkey seemed more inured to the assault than the man. At least, she only cocked an ear, whereas the noise dispersed Mr Mason's literature and, with a decisive 'Here Endeth', closed his Bible. Consider. One does not, in the middle of the twentieth century, have to have a donkey, as Balaam did, to get about. One only plays at having a donkey, and the game can only be played by those who can afford it. Bourgeois fun, like Mr Mason's scything, digging, clipping, hammering, chopping, snipping, and splashing of mortar. For by thirty-five years' diligent work in an office he was now at last able to afford some grass and earth of his own to play with, and hedges, stakes, logs, dead heads of roses and a tumbled-down wall, together with the appropriate tools to apply to these things. He was now rich enough to pour with sweat and strain his back and blister his fingers and, during a three weeks' holiday, to get his hands as rough as any labourer's. And here he was at fifty-eight, unnecessarily toiling up hill, on a steamy hot day, with a donkey. Nothing biblical about it at all. Just an old man's tennis.

'Why don't you ride 'n?' said a man passing on a bicycle. The idea had not even occurred to Mr Mason.

'I'm much too big,' he said. 'Besides, besides, she's a lady.'

'I'd ride 'n up this steep bit,' said the man and zigzagged on up the hill.

What a monstrous suggestion! The donkey's elegant little front legs looked as fragile as the most delicate drawing-room furniture. Mr Mason frowned after the bicyclist.

'Silly ass,' he said, '—I mean, man!'

At the top of the hill he diverted Bessie on to a grassy patch by a gate into a cornfield. From here, though the sky was overcast, there was a broad view. It seemed to the man that the donkey's eyes were focused through the gate on to the distant hills. Then she brayed.

'I know,' he agreed, when the last agonized vibrations had spent themselves, 'I know. Life is like that, but we must try to forget it. Have this.'

And, taking his sandwiches from his pocket, he gave her one. The flies gathered around them as they stood there munching. He picked up an ash stick with some leaves on it and brushed away the torment from her. From time to time she rubbed her dripping eyes up and down against his thigh. At length he said 'Onward!' and led her out on to the road. She faced down the hill, the way they had come. 'No,' he said, 'this way.'

She did not agree. Very well, he would wait. After two or three minutes a baker's van passed them, the man grinning as though to say 'What's up? Won't she go? Like a lift?'

When he had gone by, Mr Mason spoke sharply to his charge and gently applied the stick to her hind quarters. With this action he found her to become entirely docile. She turned the right way and they strode off. He much enjoyed the walk, and making the friends, which in the donkey's company, he so quickly made. In the one village they went through children crowded round them and adult faces would relax and smile.

'Isn't it sweet!' said a woman. 'Looks kind of sad, doesn't it? What's its name?'

'Greene. Bessie Greene.'

'Run and fetch a carrot for it, Jackie.'

The donkey had had quite a feast by the time they were through the village, of carrots and apples and pieces of bread. Out in the country again, they were overtaken by a shining car that had strayed from the main roads. It stopped alongside them, windows were lowered and four towny faces leaned their way, murmuring endearments.

Send us walking around the world, thought Mr Mason, and there would be universal love and peace.

A little further on, with a great neighing and stamping of hooves, two magnificent hunters appeared, straining their heads over a hedge. The donkey stopped a moment to look at them, then walked on quietly, indifferent to the wild-eyed, yearning agitation, that moved along in the field beside her until another hedge brought to an end the attempts of the horses to gain her interest. It seemed to Mr Mason that the decent comportment of his humble charge compared most favourably with the itching hysteria of the upper classes.

'Good, Bessie, good. You are nature's gentlewoman. And you are no snob.'

Soon after this they came to the Golden Crown, where a main road had to be crossed. Four young people were sitting at a table drinking beer in the sunshine outside the public house.

'Oh look! Just look at that!' said one of the girls, who wore her hair in a horse tail. She got up and came forward to caress the donkey's ears.

'Isn't he a beauty!'

'She,' corrected Mr Mason.

'Beg her pardon. Would she like a potato crisp?'

The other girl had lifted a drawing pad on to her knee and was busy with a pencil.

'Can I get you a drink, sir?' said one of the bearded young men. This had not been part of Mr Mason's programme.

'I insist,' said the youth, and presently Mr Mason had a glass in one hand while with the other he held the donkey, which was showing a great taste for potato crisps.

'Can't she keep her ears still?' said the drawing girl, rubbing vigorously.

'I must get on,' Mr Mason said, 'or the children will be wondering what's happened to me.'

One of the young men stood out in the main road like a policeman and held up a lorry in front of him, while a low two-seater, with a squeaking of brakes, stopped behind him. The man and the donkey then proceeded across the road, the padding of her unshod little hooves on the concrete sounding so soft that he said, 'It's not too hard for you, barefoot, is it, Bessie?'

The landlord and some other customers had appeared outside the inn to watch the progress. All applauded, while the couple in the two-seater stood up and saluted and the driver of the lorry put his head out of his window and grinned. Safely across, Mr Mason turned and waved, then went on round a corner and was out of sight. All this pride, or rather humility, he thought—we must take care it does not lead to a fall.

And so at length, they came to Woggett's lane, a muddy track that led up between corn fields and past a hazel copse to Mr Mason's village. He had expected to see his wife and the children coming to meet him in the lane. Such had been the plan. There was no sign of them, however. He must have made better time than they had expected. Indeed, when he came into his own drive and up to the front door, there was nobody about.

'Hullo!' he shouted.

Luciana looked out from an upper window and came running down. '*Oh, l'asinuccia!*' she cried. '*Com'è carina!*'

She kissed the donkey on the nose and enveloped her with love.

'Where are the children?' said Mr Mason.

'They have gone to play with Ian.'

'Oh, I see. Then I'll go and tie her up.'

He walked down past the woodshed and the kitchen garden where he found his wife bent over the soil.

'There you are,' she said. 'I'm sorry we didn't come and meet you but they so wanted to go and play with Ian and he's going away tomorrow morning.'

'That's all right. I'll tie her up.'

'She's lovely,' said Mrs Mason, walking with him to the orchard. 'What fun they're going to have!'

He led the donkey through the long grass to a place equidistant from four young fruit trees, where he had fixed the poker, with chain and collar attached. The donkey stood perfectly still while the collar was buckled round her neck.

'I want you to understand,' said Mr Mason, 'that, like the stove, she's entirely my responsibility. I'll move her on and all that.'

'Still,' said Mrs M., collaborative as always, 'show me what I do, in case I have to.'

'You just give the top of the poker a bang or two from the sides with this log and then it'll come out easily, and you just move it to another place where she can't get at the trees and hammer it in. Come on, Bessie.'

He walked her round in a circle to see if the chain moved freely. It didn't, getting entangled in the long grass around the head of the poker, so that after two or three gyrations there was a knotted lump of chain and grass at the centre of the donkey's domain and the chain had become proportionately shorter. Mr and Mrs Mason freed the chain of grass and pulled up the longer grass about the poker and he also pulled the poker an inch or two more out of the ground. The chain then seemed to swivel satisfactorily. The donkey had begun eating.

'Let's leave her.'

From the kitchen garden they looked back.

'It's all we needed,' said Mrs Mason, 'to make this place complete.'

'And look!'

Something was happening which they had indeed anticipated; but as they looked at all the long grass that Bessie was going to eat, and excrete, during the next month, it seemed that the fertilisation of their poor garden soil would perhaps be the chief of the many services she would do them. They went indoors where Mr Mason sat down to the piano.

After playing for about twenty minutes, he got up to go and see how his donkey was getting on, taking an empty bucket with him from the kitchen which he filled from the tub at the corner of the wood shed. He found Luciana with the donkey. She was measuring with her fingers the length of the nose and the distance between the eyes. '*Poveraccia!*' she said. 'They are devils, the flies. I will make for her—how do you say?—a mask.'

Mr Mason put the bucket under the donkey's nose. She sniffed the water and turned away.

'Drink, *bestia*, drink!' screamed Luciana, cuffing her. '*Mal educata bestia!*'

'She's not thirsty,' he said, setting the bucket down out of her reach. He noticed with disappointment that she had dragged her chain through the manure, spreading it thinly across the grass. If one wanted to get the stuff in lumps, one would evidently have to stand with a spade and barrow, watching.

I, however, *am* thirsty after my walk,' he said. 'It must surely be getting near tea time.'

'I go to see and to prepare,' said Luciana, running off towards the house, with a burst of song.

The flies were tormenting the donkey who was shaking her head up and down. With a sudden toss she lurched a few yards, straining at her chain. Mr Mason observed that the few inches of the poker that stood out of the ground were beginning to be bent. If there was much more of a bend, the chain would no longer be able to swivel. Moreover the pull of the poker had already widened considerably the top of the hole in which it was embedded. The poker would soon be dangerously loose in the ground. Tomorrow he had better see about getting a proper peg.

Coming back into the house he found that the afternoon post had brought him a letter from which it was apparent that he would have to be in London on Monday and Monday night and most of Tuesday. Confound! Well, that settled the matter of the peg. He could not leave the donkey in charge of the women and children unless she was secure. He was also anxious to see how easy an operation it was going to be to lead the children out for a ride, whether, for instance, it was a thing that Luciana could be trusted to do. His wife was answering the telephone.

'That was Ian's mother,' she said, putting up the receiver. 'She was very anxious for the boys to stay to tea, so I said they could. Let's go and have a cup ourselves.'

After tea Mr Mason went down to see the donkey, accompanied by Luciana with the mask she had made, which consisted of a rectangular piece of linen with two eyeholes and strings at the corners. They found the donkey feverishly working her head up and down. She rubbed her dripping eyes against Mr Mason's legs.

'There's no shade in this orchard,' he said. 'We'll have to move her during the heat of the day to that patch by the woodshed under the big trees.'

'*Carina, carina*,' said Luciana, as she tied the mask in place. It seemed to fit and perhaps gave some relief to the tormented eyes.

'As soon as the children come back,' said Mr Mason, 'I'll take them for a little ride round the garden, which will give her a change.'

By half-past six, however, already past their bed-time, there was no sign of the children, so Mrs Mason went across the road to fetch them. It seemed that they had had an ecstatic afternoon with Ian, playing in the house he had built in a tree. They were both still bubbling with excitement as Mrs Mason led them upstairs to their bath.

'Say good-night to Grandpa,' she said, meeting Mr Mason on the landing.

'Wouldn't they,' ventured the latter, 'just like to see their donkey before going to bed?'

Their cries showed that they would of course welcome any deferring of the grim moment. The face of their grandmother, however, who was congratulating herself on having got them upstairs without a protest, showed the faintest hesitation. The Masons were sensitive to each other's faintest hesitations and quick to compromise. It was arranged that the children should be brought downstairs after their bath and Mr Mason would lead the donkey to the drawing-room window where they could say good-night to her.

So, a few minutes later, Mr Mason was undoing the donkey's collar and adjusting the mask which had slipped, so that it was covering her eyes. As soon as she realized that she was to be walking she plunged forward and all but escaped from his hold. Would his wife, he wondered, have been able to hold her? Moreover, the donkey, which had been for a good long walk that day, might be supposed to be fairly tired. With what force would she not plunge when she was fresh?

'Mind where you're going, Bessie,' he said, as he walked her through the garden. She did not seem to have much sense of keeping to a path. It would be a disaster if she were to trample on Mrs M.'s peonies.

The children were at the drawing-room window. Instructed by his grandmother, Michael held forward the flat of his hand with a lump of sugar on it, but as the donkey's muzzle approached, he withdrew it and the piece of sugar dropped. Mr Mason picked it up.

'Try again.'

'I don't want to.'

'Like this,' said Mrs Mason, giving it.

'Its teeth are brown,' said Michael. 'Why are its teeth brown?'

'Because it doesn't brush them. Now your bit, John.'

It was found that John had eaten his bit.

'Well then, good-night, donkey. Tomorrow grand-father will take you for a ride.'

'Tomorrow,' said John, 'Ian said we can play in his house after he's gone as much as we like.'

Mr Mason walked his charge two or three times round the lawn, then took her back to the orchard. The flies had disappeared with the cool of the evening, so he removed the mask and hung it on an apple tree. There seemed no point in moving her on yet, as there was still a great deal of grass in her present circle to be eaten. Also he was apprehensive about moving the poker at all, as any hammering now would only bend it more. First thing tomorrow he would go and get a peg from the blacksmith.

Mr and Mrs Mason took a stroll together in the garden before dinner. The sun was setting in an almost cloudless sky.

'Perhaps the summer is really going to begin after all,' said Mrs Mason, looking at the flowers which had been terribly dashed by the incessant rains. At length, they came to the orchard.

'Why, she's gone!'

'No, look, there she is.'

The donkey's ears showed above the long grass. They found her sitting with one leg stretched heraldically in front of her. She did not get up in alarm at their approach.

'She's beginning to know us,' said Mr Mason.

'She's a perfect pet,' said Mrs Mason, stroking the ears.

'But I recognise,' he said, 'that she's going to be something of a responsibility, and, as I said before, all mine.'

During the early hours of the following morning, just as it was getting light, Mr Mason awoke with a jangling noise in his ears. After a moment's thought he got out of bed and peeped through the curtains. It was as he had divined. The donkey had just dragged her chain across the brick path below the window, and was now browsing on the lawn. Putting on some clothes, he tiptoed to the door.

'What is it?' said Mrs Mason.

'I'm just going along the passage.'

Downstairs he put on his gumboots and mackintosh and, taking the drawing-room poker with him, went out to the donkey. 'Naughty,' he said, gathering up the chain and leading her back to the orchard. It was not difficult to follow the track she had made, which by a miracle had done no damage to the flowers. On the way they came upon the bent poker, which would have to be used again, as he had just found that the drawing-room poker, with its ornamental brass stem, was too fat to go through a link of the chain. The promise of yesterday evening's weather had not been fulfilled. A light rain was falling and must have been falling for some time. The grass in the orchard was wet and the ground soggy. With his hands he pushed the poker into the soil until it was invisible. He noticed meanwhile that the donkey had had a go at the young bush apple trees. Yes, she had had all the seven russets and the five Cox's Orange Pippins that he had been carefully watching.

'Naughty,' he said, 'though I recognise that it's entirely my own fault.'

'Are you all right?' said his wife, as he tiptoed back into the bedroom.

'Yes,' he said, 'it was nothing.' He had decided to keep the episode a secret.

He was up early and off to the blacksmith's before the children had come down to breakfast. Before leaving, he visited the orchard. The donkey was standing motionless in the drizzle, with an appearance of abject misery. Her chain was all knotted.

'Cheer up,' he said, 'at least the flies aren't so bad this morning. Presently I'll be back and we'll start a new life.'

It was not in fact till nearly eleven that he returned with the new peg, a splendid peg, four feet long, with a ring that swivelled attached to the top. It had cost a guinea. He had also bought a sledge-hammer for thirty-two and six to knock it in with. He was doing things properly this time.

Leaving the car by the front door, he hurried at once, with his weapons, down to the orchard. The sun was now shining. He would give the children a ride before luncheon. But where was the donkey? There was no sign of it among the fruit trees. Oh Lord! Dropping his iron with a clank in the long grass, he came up through the flower-beds, past the devastated peonies. Oh Lord! He found his wife standing by the donkey's head on the lawn, the chain trailing behind. It is at such moments that one digs deep into the capital accumulated by thirty years of sweet reasonableness. Luckily this amounted to a good big sum in their case.

'It wasn't your fault,' she said at once, 'it can't be helped.'

The children came running towards them evidently at a loose end. It seemed that playing in Ian's house without Ian was no fun at all.

'Are you going to ask grandfather to give you a ride?'

'Please, grandfather, will you give us a ride?'

'All right, if you'd like it. I'll get the saddle and reins.'

The boys showed an unusual courtesy towards each other as to which should have the first ride. At length John was in the saddle and they set forth out of the drive and along the road to do the round of the outskirts of the village, a walk of about a mile and a half.

'Don't get behind her, Michael,' Mr Mason said, 'or you'll get kicked. Come next to me. Whoa, whoa!'

'I want to get off,' said John.

'Whoa! Brave boy, John, you're all right! It's quite safe. I've got her. Hold on to me with this hand—Brave boy! Don't get just in front, Michael! Whoa, Bessie!'

The progress was uncomfortable, but presumably the donkey's exuberance would soon spend itself.

'When's Michael going to have a turn?' said John, whose face was taut.

'He can have a go when we get to that corner.'

Suddenly the donkey was disturbed by an iron gutter in the road and stopped with a jolt.

'I want to get off,' said John.

'All right, off you get,' said his grandfather, helping him down.

'Mind! Don't stand behind her! Whoa! Mind the car, Michael, stand in! Whoa! I say, confound you, Bessie, don't bite me! Now, Michael, come along! Mind out, John!'

He heaved the younger boy into the saddle, who proved a little more courageous than his brother. Indeed, after a few minutes, he consented to have the donkey trot, Mr Mason running alongside. The latter was glad that Ian's mother should have passed in her car just at that happy moment.

'Wait for me!' shouted John, as they turned the corner. At least, thought Mr Mason, we're now out of sight of home. Then there was another gutter. As the donkey was trotting, the jolt when, again, she suddenly stopped, was more violent than before, and Michael fell off.

'Bad luck,' said his grandfather cheerfully, 'up you get! No bones broken, just a little scratch on your cheek! Good boy!' Mr Mason was sure that the incident would have been quickly closed had not a tiresome woman come running from a cottage door.

'The poor little man!' she exclaimed. 'What a bump! Don't cry, dearie!' For in deference to her petting Michael had set up a lusty howl. 'He's bleeding,' said John, coming up with them. 'Does it hurt, Michael?'

'Ye—es,' sobbed the younger brother.

'There, there,' said the woman, 'would you like an apple?' And she fetched an apple each for the boys and one for the donkey while Mr Mason satisfied himself that Michael's damages only amounted to one tiny scratch. Presently they walked on, neither boy mounted.

'I want to go back,' said Michael.

'So do I,' said John.

'We *are* going back,' said Mr Mason.

'No, we aren't. Back's back that way.'

'It's this way too,' pointing ahead, 'because we're going in a circle. If you're going round, you're always going back. I'll tell you a story. Once upon a time there was a king who said, If there's anybody in my kingdom who can draw an absolutely round circle I'll give him—'

At length they were past the point at which home had become nearer to them in front than behind. Mr Mason judged that the boys' morale was sufficiently recovered for him to suggest that John might like to try another ride. Moreover he himself now wanted to get back as soon as possible, for an ominous black cloud had moved up over the village and they had come out without their coats. With a promise that there should be no trotting, John consented to mount. While Mr Mason was leaning over the donkey to fit the boy's foot in the further stirrup, there was a flash of lightning. The boys did not notice it but the donkey did and swung her head up in alarm, cracking Mr Mason on the chin. With a hideous skid and scrunch his lower teeth crashed into the upper row breaking to pieces the two expensive crowns in the middle. As he spat the rubble out into his hand he remembered the noise of broken glass being swept up from a pavement after a bomb. He must look terrible now with those two great gaps. Here was a pretty problem! He must have the crowns replaced by Monday, but what chance was there of anyone down here being able to do it? Would he have to go to London tomorrow?

'—!—!' said John, repeating the word which had unfortunately escaped his grandfather.

'Go on about that king,' said Michael.

At that moment there was a clap of thunder. Michael began to cry. Then the rain started, a violent, cold, perpendicular torrent on their uncovered heads and sleeveless vests.

'I want to get off,' John shouted.

'Yes, all right, off you get! Whoa! Go and get under that tree there! Run! Don't get just in front of her! Here! Mind! Don't get just in front of her, I said! In here, by the bank!'

'The rain hurts!' blubbered Michael.

'Oh!' John screamed, 'it's trodden on my foot! Oh! Oo!'

'*Che disastro!*' shouted Luciana, appearing on her bicycle, carrying coats for all.

'Indeed,' said Mr Mason, 'a perfect shambles. Come on, it's no good waiting here!' At length the party reached home, Mr Mason and the donkey first, the others some way behind, John, who could not walk with his trampled foot, on the saddle of the bicycle.

The rain stopped as suddenly as it had begun. By the time Mr Mason and the donkey had reached the orchard the sun was shining again. Flies had gathered round the donkey's nose.

'I'll move you up to that patch by the woodshed, Bessie, for a while, so that you can get more shade. And mind you don't slip on the bank there. I somehow don't think we'll be going for another ride today.'

Leaving the donkey, he came in to find his wife bathing John's foot.

'You seem to have been rather unlucky,' she said. 'Why, whatever's happened to your teeth?'

'What can Luciana be doing?' said Mrs Mason during luncheon. The Italian girl had gone to fetch the pudding and had been away an unduly long time. A noise then as of an exciting hockey match between two girls' schools came from the lawn. Mr Mason ran out.

'*Maledetta bestia!*' the girl was shrieking as she chased the donkey. Bessie's track across the flower-beds was all too evident. It appeared that Luciana had seen the animal from the kitchen window sauntering up to the back gate which was open. In another minute it would have been out on the road. So she had been chasing it. How on earth could it have got away this time? Mr Mason asked himself. He noticed to his astonishment that the donkey had not got her collar on.

'Mind the pram!' he shouted, as the chase all but overturned the baby.

At last, in the corner of the lawn, the donkey let him take her and lead her back to the peg, and there on the ground was that mighty collar broken. What a wrench it must have been given! It seemed to Mr Mason that even if the donkey had taken what run the chain allowed and leapt from the top of the bank, careless of whether she throttled herself or not, she would hardly have had the force to make such a break. Yet this was what she must have done. He stood a moment in thought, then led her up to the front door where his wife was standing.

'I'm going to take her straight back where she belongs,' he said.

'Oh but, are you sure? What a pity that would be!'

'There's nothing for it. There's nothing to hold her by, now. Then can you follow on in about a couple of hours, with the saddle, and fetch me home? Telephone to the Greenes who won't have left yet for their holiday.'

And he set out at once. And the man spake not to the ass, for his heart was hardened against her. And when they had passed the Golden Crown about half a mile, the ass stopped in the middle of the way and brayed. And behold, the sound of the braying was exceedingly grievous. And the man said, 'Bessie, oh, Bessie!' And he was reconciled with the ass.

They were at length coming down towards the corner that turned into the donkey's village, when Mrs Mason, with the boys, came up with them. She stopped the car about a hundred yards further on. Mr Mason allowed the donkey to break into a trot. The boys, standing in the back of the car, cheered as he came alongside. Then the donkey, spurred on by the downward gradient and perhaps recognising how near home she was, suddenly lunged forward.

'Look!' shouted John with delight, 'it's running!'

'Whoa!' panted Mr Mason, 'Bessie—Elizabeth—'

With an irresistible stampede the donkey broke away from him and soon disappeared round the corner homewards at full gallop.

About an hour later Mr Mason carried the scythe over his shoulder down to the orchard, nodding on the way to Parker who was digging in the kitchen garden. He snatched the donkey's mask from a branch of one of the trees as he passed, and stuffed it into his pocket, then went to the far corner of the orchard, where, after sharpening the blade, he began to jab furiously at the long grass. Parker watched him for a few moments, then walked across to him.

'Excuse me,' he said.

''Mm.' Mr Mason did not look up.

'Excuse me.'

'Well, what is it?'

'You'll not do no good to your scythe like that. Let me—' Parker took the scythe and showed how it should be used. 'You want to go at it evenly, like this—gently, gently.' He handed the tool back.

'Like this?' said Mr Mason.

'That's it. Gently. Gently does it, gently.'

Mrs Webster

'I rather think I'm feeling a bit better,' Mrs Webster said to herself. This was her third day in bed with a mild attack of bronchitis. Her arms folded beneath her head, she lay looking out at the clear wintry sky of which her window commanded a wide prospect. The view was given depth at the lower edge of the frame, for from her pillow she could see, a little above the window ledge, roofs and chimneys and aerials, the tower of St Luke's, the dome of the town hall, the far-off spire of St Mary's and the still more distant smoking chimneys of the power station. At this season the London air was thronged with gulls. In twos and threes they dived and swooped over the roofs, or singly followed some straight and leisurely course, or circled majestically at a great height. Occasionally one of them passing close to her window would catch her eye.

Mrs Webster loved her view. Where she commanded so much space without, the pokiness of her flat did not seem to matter. She need not, of course, have been a working woman living in a poky flat. She could have been the wife of various successful men who had laid their hearts at her feet during the fifteen years of her widowhood. None of the latter, however, had come anywhere near success with Mrs Webster, for the romantic reason that she had never felt disposed to share herself with anyone but the husband she had lost in the first year of the war. Childless marriages may end in bitterness and disaster. They may, on the other hand, remain a perpetual honeymoon, relaxed by no new affections and only more intensely held by the bond of a shared disappointment. Such had been Mrs Webster's marriage, which had also become in no way loosened by a posthumous condition.

I could write some of those letters, she thought. The letters she had in mind were such as many people think of writing but only the more vital or the leisured actually write. The most vital, of course, generally settle their accounts verbally on the spot. Mrs Webster was not one of these. Her reactions were slow, and she rarely lost her temper. It was, as a rule, not until long after the moment of crisis, that she could think of the words she would like to have said then.

Bus driver [she wrote],

You saw me, a tired woman, with a loaded shopping bag, hurrying towards you. You would have had to wait perhaps fifteen seconds to give me time to get on the bus. You pretended not to notice me and started your bus. You were aware, however, when I fell, that you were just going to miss me. Give me another chance and you shall go over. Perhaps, above the sound of the traffic, you will be able to hear the snap of the breaking thigh bone.

Mrs Webster folded her letter and took another sheet of paper. She wrote:

Dear Mr Bannister,

I have read a number of your notices of plays and thought they were well written. The other day, on your recommendation, I saved up and went to see *Waiting for nothing*. How can you be taken in by such witless trash? It is clear to me now that you have no judgement whatever. In future, if you say anything in an interesting way the fact will be noted, but I shall know that your opinion is worthless.

It must not be thought that Mrs Webster was in the habit of nursing grievances, still less of picking quarrels. The letters were never sent. They were written simply to satisfy that very slight need for self-assertion that remained with her, in the way that the writing of an outspoken diary, which is intended for no eyes but those of its author, may be the single violence of the mildest and sweetest tempered of people.

Dear Sir Aubrey [she wrote],

You believe yourself to have an excellent sense of humour. In this we none of us agree with you. The telling of ready-made stories for the *n*th time, and then leading the laugh, cannot very well be combined with a sense of humour. It is only because we are your subordinates that you get a titter.

The telephone rang. It was Peggy Thornton. She had rung up the office and been distressed to hear that Mrs Webster was ill. Could she come and see her? What about today? It was arranged that she should come to tea. What could she want? Had she heard about Barbara at last? Putting down the receiver, Mrs Webster opened the *Radio Times* and noted that there was a concert that afternoon she meant to listen to. After skimming through the pages of the paper to the end of the week, she got out of bed and had her luncheon off a boiled egg and some toast and marmalade.

Back on her pillow, she took up a book, but her eyes, as they were apt to, soon wandered from the page out of the window. At an immense height a tiny silver aeroplane, leaving a white trail behind it, was climbing steeply up the sky. Its ascent seemed nearly vertical. It must reach the top somewhere straight above her head. When it had passed out of sight, she turned again to her book, giving a nod of recognition to a little group of thoughts who were always loitering, smiling and inoffensive, on the roadside of her mind. I seem to spend all my spare time, they said, either watching things or listening. Am I almost too passive, too negative, too lazy? I sometimes wonder whether I have any character at all. Yet—why worry? Life is a waiting game, and when you have everything to wait for, why, indeed, worry? Suddenly she fell asleep.

She slept for about twenty minutes and awoke struggling to remember what she had just been dreaming about. Quick—before everything should come flooding in! As is the way, she clutched at a void, for the dream had gone utterly. She only knew that it had been good.

Presently, turning on the wireless and shutting her eyes, she was again in a dream world. From this world she returned to self-consciousness an hour or so later with several precise and blissful memories. An hour of bliss, of intense consciousness and no self at all. No expenditure of character whatever. Heaven should be like that . . . She lay again looking at the empty sky.

Then, all at once, out of the void, without expecting or asking for it, she felt herself about to grasp an experience she had had two or three times before, which is perhaps quite common, particularly among those who are not busy minded, but is not much talked about because difficult to describe. It is far from being a state of emotional abandon, of blissful transport; it is rather a clarity, a focusing. A child realises one day that his parents do not know everything. He believes, however, that the knowledge is still there, though spread now among all the old and wise. When, sooner or later, the question 'What does anybody know?' has received from him a dubious answer, he is ready for Mrs Webster's experience. He has reached the line beyond which no reference can be made to anybody. To be aware of crossing that line is the experience. Without the least effort this afternoon Mrs Webster felt herself stepping outside human knowledge and looking back. She made a great effort, however, to hold the vision—no, not vision, the word is loaded with religious over-tones—the moment of lucidity, which was hardly there before it seemed to be slipping away. Tick, tick, half a tick and it was gone, leaving behind only a ripple from that splash of astonishment at how particular the creation looks if you seem to be looking at it for the first time. When he could have made it any way, that he should have made it just this way, sky blue, people with heads but only one each, the moon round not square, water, hunger, hate and love! That everything should be just so, when it might have been quite different!

Another aeroplane was mounting the sky. Catching the last sunlight as it soared ahead of its white wash of vapour, this one was gold rather than silver, giving the dreamy and the bed-ridden a feeling of high endeavour and some high, golden attainment. Before it had passed from sight, with rude actuality the door-bell rang. Peggy already! Mrs Webster got up and opened the door.

'Elizabeth,' said her old friend, putting her arms round her, 'how are you? I'm terribly sorry about your being ill. You certainly do look washed out. And with no one to look after you—up here'—she looked round the little bed-sitting-room compassionately—'you poor darling!' She kissed Mrs Webster warmly.

'Well, let's make it cosy,' she said, taking charge and drawing the curtains. 'You get back to bed at once and I'll put the kettle on.'

Her eye lit upon a bunch of grapes in a bowl and a white hyacinth in a pot.

'I say, I haven't brought you anything! You see, I didn't know what you'd be feeling like, so I thought it better to find out when I got here. Also I've been rather occupied with Anthea today. Really, that girl! Do you mind if I talk about Anthea for a moment?'

Leaving the preparation of the tea things, she sat on the bed and took Mrs Webster's hand. The latter knew that this grasp meant, You poor darling, I know you haven't any daughters at all, please don't think it selfish of me if I talk about mine.

'Of course not,' said Mrs Webster, 'go ahead. Are there any developments?' She already knew something about the breach that was opening between Peggy Thornton and her daughter. It was not the art school as such that Peggy objected to. It was possible to go to an art school and still be normal; there was that Cazalet girl, for instance, and Jennifer Bland. But the people Anthea picked up there! They must be the absolute riff-raff of the place.

'It's really rather hard, when we're always offering to give dinner parties of eight or ten for her and her friends and send them dancing or to the theatre, and she simply turns up her nose! She can't say we're not generous. And who are her friends? Well, we don't have the honour of being introduced to them. But the ones who pass me on the stairs and come in cars to the door look practically like teddy boys. None of the nice ones ever seem to come to the house now. The other day I simply decided to burst into her room when she had a gang of them in there and she made a show of introducing me to them and it turned out she hardly knew any of their surnames. They were just Harry and Bob and so on. When I think that our parents would have expected not only to know them but who their parents were! I mean to say!'

Mrs Webster laughed.

'It may sound funny,' Peggy said, 'but don't you think one ought to do something?'

'What can you do? She *is* twenty-one.'

'I know. But it makes me so sad that she should drop all the nice ones.' Then there was a story about a letter from one of her friends that Anthea had left lying about in a public place. Private letters should not be left lying about. Peggy had put it in a drawer and given it back to Anthea later. And what thanks did she get? The girl had put on a great act of indignation, telling her to mind her own business and not touch things that didn't belong to her, etc.

'Did you read it?' said Mrs Webster.

'Yes. What would you have done?'

'I'd have read it, but left it in the public place.'

'What earthly good would that have done? Then there's the question of money. I've always been in favour of keeping it all as informal as possible. I mean she's only got to ask. We never refuse her anything. George gives her pocket money and anything bigger she just asks. Well, now she's wanting a regular dress allowance. It seems somehow so sort of untrusting and unfriendly, don't you think?'

'You shouldn't take it that way. I think it's only natural to want to have some independence. What does George think?'

'Well, he's on her side over that. As a matter of fact, George—' Peggy Thornton paused on her husband's name and her face expressed inner conflict from which, after a moment, she escaped with a compassionate smile.

'Enough of my family!' she said.

'No, do go on!'

'No, enough!' said Peggy with determination. 'Tell me, you're going to Beakie's presentation, of course, on the twenty-eighth?'

Miss Beckwith, who had been their headmistress some thirty years ago, was at last retiring. They talked for a while about Lorn House and their contemporaries there and the presentation.

'I need hardly say,' Peggy observed bitterly, 'that Anthea is not going. She simply said "That bitch!"'

'I expect we had the best of Beakie in our generation.'

'I dare say. Still, it's not very polite. One certainly doesn't get much thanks for sending the girl to the best school in England!'

She then told Mrs Webster about the incident of the new suitcase and the incident of the borrowed cat-basket and many other rankling incidents that showed the unpardonable selfishness and ingratitude of her daughter. Behind each of these sorry little anecdotes could be felt the presence of the second enemy, the daughter's ally. At one moment he again almost came into the open.

'George . . .' she began.

'Yes?'

Once more she sheered away from the subject, standing up.

'It's time I was off,' she said. 'Let me wash the tea things.' She took the cups into the kitchen and rinsed them.

'I hope I haven't tired you out,' she said. 'Don't get up.' But Mrs Webster had got up and followed her to the door.

'Let me know,' said Peggy, embracing her, 'if there's anything you want, you—'

'I'm *not* your poor darling!' said Mrs Webster.

The embrace relaxed. They stared at one another for a moment.

'Oh,' said Peggy and turned and walked out.

Mrs Webster turned slowly, drew back the curtains, switched off the light, got into bed and gazed at the starry night. A smile came over her face in the darkness. He had once said, 'Being with you is almost as good as being alone.' How could one not marry a man who said that?

Presently she put on the light and took her pen and a piece of writing paper.

Dear Peggy [she wrote],

That's not the way to visit the sick. Mean as ever, you brought me nothing. Except to say that I looked washed-out—the kind of thing one tries not to say to ill people—you showed no interest whatever in my illness or in any of my affairs. As a matter of fact, I thought you looked pretty rotten yourself. I should say you are near breaking point.

The time has come for a show-down, Peggy. Our schoolgirl friendship has continued for so long, admit it, mainly on your initiative. You are a chatterbox, and really good listeners, like myself, are not easy to come by. Then my childlessness and Christopher's death gave me a new attraction for you. You could be sorry for me. When, on top of that, I am ill, I can see that I must be irresistible to you in your present state.

Let's get this straight once for all. I am *not* an object of pity. Happy grief is a treasure you have no conception of. Being me is extremely happy and interesting.

Now for your affairs. I suppose you have at last heard that George is having an affair with Barbara Weatherall. I think you came to see me half hoping to talk about this. Had you done so, however, you would have lost the pity for me for having no George of my own, and you could not bring yourself to lose that. As to George, and Anthea too, if you want my opinion, it is you and you alone who make them behave as they do. It's because you won't let them alone. You will go on at them. You should on no account 'burst into' a girl's room. You're a busy, bossy, nosy parker and one of these days, if you don't take care, you're going to find yourself an entirely left woman. They'll both have gone. And to show you that I'm your old, old friend, Peggy, may I advise you to get rid of that red little wart thing on your neck. I'm sure it could be done quite easily.

with love from Elizabeth

As Mrs Webster put down her pen, there was a knock at the door.

'A parcel 'm,' said the man. 'I hope you're better.'

'Thank you, Roberts. Yes, I am.'

'That should do the trick,' he smiled, handing her the thing.

The parcel consisted of a bottle which, on being unwrapped, was found to be whisky. A card said, With love from Angus. Dear Angus! How delightful of him! Two minutes later there was a blessed tingling throughout the body of Mrs Webster as she sat in bed. She read through the letters she had written and slipped them into the drawer she kept for such things, the first, the second, the third, and Peggy's letter was going the same way. No, by God! That one should be sent! And she addressed and stamped an envelope. Then she took another gulp of whisky. 'I really think,' she said to herself, 'that I'm feeling a bit better.'

Autumn Fields

'. . . and it's no wonder,' Philip concluded, 'that we can't produce anything like that nowadays. They had faith. What have we got but our decadent deathwish?'

'Ye-es,' said Peter, feeling, as he had often felt during the last fortnight, that he was being stampeded into agreement. Philip had got everything so pat. As an art historian he was no doubt only doing his job in sorting out causes and effects. But is it not possible to be too good at this job? Time and again Philip had claimed to find order where Peter could only find a muddle, to see black and white where Peter could only see grey. How neatly his ideas slipped into place! How tidily that phrase, 'our decadent death-wish', would round off a paragraph in the next book! And what a confounded number of questions he begged!

Peter finished his cup of wine.

'I don't agree with you at all,' he said. 'I think you're quite wrong.'

There was no answer. Looking round, Peter saw that his companion was lying on his back with his hat over his eyes and appeared to have gone fast asleep. On his other side on the rug, amid the refuse of the picnic, the two wives also were sleeping. He looked again at the view. On the slope opposite, perhaps half a mile away, at about the same level as he was sitting, was the edge of a wood of Spanish chestnuts that stretched along the crest of the hill. Here and there among the golds and browns of the chestnuts were the reds of cherry trees, the colours glowing in the sun. The sides of the valley between him and the wood were covered partly with grass, partly with patches of vine, the leaves of the latter, some of them, almost as red as the cherry leaves. At the bottom of the valley there was a stream. A white cow was reclining there beside a poplar tree. Behind Peter was the road and behind that a railway embankment. There was not a house in sight. In the distance, to the front and to either side, France stretched away, as it so often does, to an unattainably remote horizon.

An old woman, with a sack on her back and a stick in her hand, was walking up the side of the stream. As she approached the cow, the beast heaved itself on to its legs. Suddenly she dropped her sack and made after it waving her stick and shouting. It lurched away. Her shrill imprecations cleft the noontide hush like the squawking of a jay. She did not come up with the cow and her fury seemed to spend itself as suddenly as it had arisen. Shouldering her sack, she continued her way and was disappearing behind the curve of the hillside when she stopped, turned and discharged some last vituperative shrieks down the valley. The cow watched her out of sight then came back and lay in its former position.

Peter looked among the picnic things. There was still most of the second bottle of wine undrunk. He filled his mug. And there was still a good deal of the *pâté* and garlic sausage left. He cut open a roll of bread, stuffed it and took a mouthful. A pity to leave anything. What does one come to France for? Not only for Romanesque tympanums, thank heaven! 'Decadent death-wish' my foot! The expression had got him on the raw.

The tympanum they had seen that morning had been the cruellest yet, the cruellest only because the largest. A particularly wide doorway had given the sculptors an unusually broad area in which to be horrible. The plan was the normal one. In the centre on a throne sat God the Father, blank and pitiless. On his right were the saved. One gave them a glance, then looked to his left. Here, amid the turgid convolutions of bodies, it was difficult at once to find any plan. Then it could be seen that many of the bodies were being driven by devils, armed with spikes and tridents, into the maw of a dragon. One of the spikes—look—had impaled a sinner through the backside and was sticking out through his stomach. Below him a female was being urged forward with the prong of a trident through each breast. Beside the dragon were two cauldrons into which busy fiends were tumbling the damned, head first. A gleeful imp with bellows was fanning the flames that kept this hellbrew on the boil. Beyond the cauldrons were various scenes of individual torment. Here was an old bearded man being clubbed on the head, there was a woman held up by her hair and assaulted with tongs and pincers, there was a writhing malefactor to whom no less than four devils were giving their attention. One held his head and one each leg. The fourth had torn open his stomach with the claws of one hand and was drawing out the entrails which dangled over the claws of the other hand as he lifted them to his mouth. A most adroit piece of carving, this last. Other such scenes led the eye at length to the soffit where it focused itself upon a figure on a much larger scale, facing inwards and curving with the arch, an apostle or saint, with his hands crossed over his breast, who gazed out over the seething butchery with blessed unconcern.

Philip too had seemed unaware of the horror. He had been in raptures as, standing back, he allowed his outstretched arms and fingers to move in sympathy with the rhythms of the sculpture. He said he was much reminded of the illuminations in the Winchester Bible. Never before or since, he said, had there been less of a time-lag in the visual arts between England and the continent.

So we had these ideas in England too? Ugh! Faith? Perhaps. Fear, certainly. Of course they had no death-wish in the age of Dante! They must have been terrified. And it is we who are the decadent ones? What nonsense! Another cup.

'I don't agree at all,' Peter said again, aloud.

There was no answer.

The slumber of his companions only aggravated a mood of sententiousness which the wine was bringing on. Surely we have moved forward a bit since detestable Dante? Gone the horror. Also holiness is not now the price of entry into heaven, or not the only price. Being good is all very well, but it is not an occupation. It is not a way of passing the time. It is a brake upon the machine, that has to be applied from time to time, it is not the machine itself. The price of entry into heaven is knowing about heaven. And how little they knew! What impoverishment, for instance, to have been born before modern orchestral music, not to have known Mozart or Beethoven! Practically non-starters, all of them. The later in time the better, obviously. Come—a walk across the valley to that chestnut wood while the stirred mud of the mind is settling. Perhaps, now all are asleep, some shy sylvan genius will share his secrets.

Peter stood up, swaying a little, blinking in the golden sunshine. A goods train was passing. The guard was looking out of the window of the last coach. He had an amusing face and grinned at Peter, who emptied the bottle into his cup and raised the cup in salutation. The guard waved and Peter drank. Now for the walk.

Happy autumn fields! Now might one cease upon the midday—just slip over into bliss—and as for there being anything disreputable about a death-wish what is it but reverence for the immutable state of things, finding them good instead of bad, and, after many curiosities satisfied and much love, being ready to exchange the good for the better—it's never quite real, the here and now, indeed it isn't, and sometimes positively unreal, *between* something and something, like the 'q' in Colquhoun—and as for it being escapism, which Philip evidently wished to imply, rubbish again, when you're thinking of it as 'into' and not as 'from', if it isn't positively brave or at least meeting things half-way as they ought to be met; not, that is to say, with any precise expectations, but just Hope, and of course Charity—Faith is so perplexing and so often at issue with the other two—if, for example, like some carefree sentence that plunges on into the wood with bacchic lurchings till who shall say which is the way out—if, I say, one is ready for the next thing a little ahead of time, what's the harm?

Walking down the edge of the vines, he stooped and picked up from the ground a black grape that had been left last week by the pickers. It was sugary to the taste, and already half dry like a raisin. He stood still for a moment, dizzy after stooping, while his eyes came back into focus on the sunny landscape. He felt on fire with well-being as the vapours of the wine and the flames of the garlic issued from his lips. The Kingdom of heaven is within you.

Down by the stream were two grey wagtails, flitting, strutting, trotting, scurrying, flitting, settling, poising. He watched them out of sight along the valley, the darlings. He liked watching birds. Philip did not watch birds; or rather, as he called it, bird-watch, thereby relegating the activity to a special subject. He was a great divider of human enjoyments into subjects. There was first of all the big division into those subjects that are admissible for a cultured man and those that are not. Then, amongst the former, there was the division into those that one has time for and those one has not time for; having time, in this context, meaning having time at least to master the essential jargon. Better to keep right off a subject than not to have at least the appearance of being a specialist. Bird-watching was one of the latter subjects. Even in his own subject, art-watching, there were the most rigid subdivisions. How many sunny *châteaux* and dreaming Gothic spires they had sped past, eyes front! Philip gave the most careful thought to the adjustment of his art-critical blinkers.

There is more kindness in bloody Homer than in Dante! Whoreson Dante! A pox on him! Easeful death. The thing is, being alive at all is a most exceptional state. Far the greatest numbers of people are either dead or not born yet. Is it unhealthy to want to get back to normal? Hullo, cow. Oh, don't move, please. Look, I am coming no nearer. I mean no harm. I am just cow-watching. Cusha, cusha. *Ne vous dérangez pas*, gentle creature. Oh, please, Madame, don't get up. See, I am going.

Peter jumped the stream and walked up to the trees. The ascent was steep and he was glad to lie down on some dry leaves at the edge of the wood. He shut his eyes. A gentle air was stirring the trees. From time to time bunches of chestnuts would fall with muted thud. Then suddenly, immediately over his head, there was an unexpected noise, a cawing of rooks. Opening his eyes, he saw two or three of them circling above him. An unexpected noise—somehow not a French noise at all. It was an English, indeed an Anglican, noise. Answering the sober dominical call, he shut his eyes again and allowed himself to be transported, in space, some six hundred miles to the north, and more than thirty years backwards in time, to the rectory lawn at Lackby-in-the-fen where he, a boy, was sitting on a wooden bench with Father Tyrrell, listening to the latter discoursing on the subject of Atonement. It was a bright April day. At the top of the high elms and beeches which encircled the garden, the nesting rooks held their clamorous palaver, a noise that was, as a matter of fact, far from sober, dissolving, as it did from time to time, into helpless liquid gurglings. Daffodils were growing in the long grass at the edge of the lawn. If you peeped outwards through the shrubbery you were aware that the rectory, within its circle of trees, was an island in the great bright sea of the fens.

Father Tyrrell was in his early forties. He was fat and dumpy and wore a skull-cap on his bald head. Strong spectacles magnified his bulging eyes. He had the kind of face that seems hardly able to contain its amusement. His podgy hands were clasped over the black silken curve of his stomach. There was good reason for mistaking him—and the mistake he knew was sometimes made—for a Roman Catholic priest. 'So near and yet so far,' he used to say. As he talked to the boy he took to pieces the word which was his subject. Atonement, at-one-ment, the process of becoming at one again. At length he stopped speaking and they sat a moment listening to the joyous din above them.

'Now, I expect there are some questions you would like to ask,' said Father Tyrrell.

Of course there were, thousands of them. Why did there have to be either good or evil? Why did Our Lord never laugh? Why was He not kinder to His mother? But Father Tyrrell had put a bar on questions that began with Why. There was, he said, no answer to such questions.

'What was the point of creating a world that had to be atoned for?'

'You are cheating, Peter. You know perfectly well that that question begins with Why.'

Peter thought again. The priest watched him with amused expectation. He enjoyed question time with Peter. It was very rarely indeed that he had a candidate for confirmation from whom he could strike half the number of sparks that flew of their own accord from this inquisitive boy.

'Isn't it possible,' said Peter, 'just to feel "at one"?'

'It is possible.'

'I think I feel it most of the time.'

'You are young. You will learn that that is not the whole story.'

'Don't you feel it sometimes?'

'Yes, sometimes.'

Peter hesitated.

'Often?' he ventured.

With a crescendo of screeching the rooks sustained their loud arguments, only to collapse in babbling ecstasies.

'Yes,' said Father Tyrrell slowly, 'even often.'

Thank you, Peter nearly said. It seemed to him, he did not quite know why, that Father Tyrrell had conceded much to him. For a while they said nothing.

'Is that all?' said Father Tyrrell at length.

'Yes,' said Peter.

'You've let me off lightly today, Peter! Well, should we go across to the church and say a prayer?'

They walked down the drive and out of the gate. There, a little way along the road, was the church with a few houses beside it, and beyond, and all around, was the ocean of ploughland. It was a rest to the ears to move away from the rooks. Not that there was silence out here. The air was alive with sound that seemed to come from nowhere in particular as the song of larks filled the whole firmament with its blissful palpitation. Peter and Father Tyrrell stopped in the middle of the empty road, listening. They were gazing into the distance. It seemed that if you walked for ten or twenty miles you must come to the edge of the world.

'Peter! Peter!'

Philip's voice came across the valley. Peter opened his eyes and saw Philip standing near the car, looking round for him. The wives were packing the picnic things. Peter got up and waved and started down the slope.

'Hullo!' he called. 'Hullo! Coming!'

He felt equal to the afternoon's tympanums. Come on, any number of them!

The Dull Man

Even now, three or four years later, when I hear that whirring above the noise of the traffic, I look up at the airliner whose nose is pointed towards London airport, and say to myself, 'That's where you belong, up there.' And I perhaps get something of the feel of those two exalted days and nights of mine. I should say that, having flown very little before my big flight, and not at all since, I am exceedingly naïve with regard to flying. It still seems to me quick, high and unsafe.

And then, perhaps, I remember that man. It is odd how these people fade from one's memory, people with whom one has lived for several hours in almost connubial intimacy, as companions in a cabin or a railway carriage. One reads in an old diary of the woman with blue hair and the man with a golden bracelet who got in at Sinigaglia with their bottle of marsala and doped mandrill (what on earth? Their baby perhaps?) and kept us all in fits of laughter throughout the night, all the way to Otranto, and one simply cannot remember their existence, let alone give them faces. Perhaps my aerial companion to the Far East will similarly fade from memory. Somehow I do not think he will.

I saw him first at London airport, a thick, military, little man, of perhaps forty, with a moustache, bald, going to fat, and extremely embarrassed by the scene in which he was taking part. He was doing his best not to appear to belong to the hysterical woman who was saying good-bye to him. Was this just a good-bye or a quarrel as well? None of my business, it may be said. Moreover, though my own good-byes had taken place an hour ago at the air-terminal, I was in no mood dispassionately to watch a farewell scene, and so, like the other passengers, averted my eyes. There was, I think, general relief when the travellers on flight 248—Frankfort—Istanbul—Basra—Karachi—Calcutta—Rangoon—Kuala Lumpur and Singapore—were led away through a barrier and along a passage to a further waiting-room. We had crossed our Rubicon, England was already behind us.

There were fifteen or twenty passengers, including three Indians and five or six Malays or Burmese or Chinese—I was not yet much of an adept at distinguishing Far-Easterners one from another. There was a young English mother, with a baby in her arms, an English couple and their children with whom I was already on smiling terms, and two or three single English men. It was a somewhat glum party, standing staring expressionlessly out at the airfield. Were they all as frightened as I was? Perhaps. And as excited? They did not look it, whereas I, though I had not drunk, felt positively intoxicated.

In this new room, the embarrassed man made at once for the bar, where he ordered a whisky. I stood near him. He caught my eye.

'What's yours?' he said.

'Oh, no, thank you very much,' I replied, 'I won't have anything. They have told me a great deal about what we shall be expected to drink on the plane, all of which, by the way, is on one's ticket. So I'll wait, thank you. Moreover I have a rather weak head and cannot take much on an empty stomach. Item and furthermore, I know not how it is, but I already feel a bit tiddly. 'Tis the setting out, I warrant. It does not happen to me every day to set out half across the world. The moment, unlike so many moments, is to me wholly without staleness. You no doubt are an old hand?'

He nodded and took another whisky.

'Steadies you,' he said, apparently feeling some apology was necessary, as he lifted the drink to his lips.

'Going far?' I asked.

'K.L.'

'So am I.'

Then there would be time for his story to unfold. It will become evident that I am nothing if not curious. And why not? *Nihil humani*, etc. I mean, how dull life would be if people did not take an interest in each other, yes even in the dullest—

'—even in the dullest!'

'What?'

'Sorry. I was just talking to myself. It's a thing I do.'

'Flight 248,' said the girl in uniform. 'Will you please follow me.'

We trooped out after her, our B.O.A.C. satchels over our shoulders. The waiting aircraft was only a hundred yards away. Nobody in our party seemed in any hurry to dispute my objective, a seat at a window near the door. So I was the first up the steps and took the seat of my choice. The whisky drinker came up just behind me. Though he had thirty seats to choose from, he took the one next to me.

'You wouldn't,' I said, as I sat down decisively, 'you wouldn't like the window?'

'It's all the same to me,' he said gloomily. I began to suspect that most things were much the same to him.

'Well, it isn't the same to me. From now on, everything, for me, is going to be quite new. Indeed, whatever I may have said just now, it always is. The secret of joy! New every morning is the love . . . And if I talk a certain amount of bosh, you must forgive me. I am rather keyed up.'

When all the passengers had settled themselves, one of the two lovely hostesses, who had welcomed us with such radiant smiles as we came up the steps, faced us from the head of the gangway and made an announcement. She wished us all a very good morning. Her name was Molly Fletcher and she was assisted by June Cartwright and they would be accompanying us as far as Istanbul. Cocktails would be served as soon as we were in the air, followed by luncheon. We were due at Frankfort in about an hour and a half. We must expect to find the time advancing as we went eastwards. Indeed, those who were going the whole way to Singapore would find they had gained, or lost, whichever way you cared to put it, about eight hours. Would we now please adjust our belts for the take-off. Incidentally, we might be interested to know that the pilot had just said to her that it was perfect flying weather. After a smile of heavenly reassurance, she momentarily allowed her lips to close over her teeth.

'*Fermez les guillemets.* Thanks, June,' I said, taking a boiled sweet from a basket which the other girl was offering. The engines meanwhile had started and presently we were moving over the concrete, turning and twisting, a long course, till we came to the beginning of the runway and stopped. A moment of thought, of doubt perhaps. The authorities could still call the whole thing off. Then the greater roaring, the intolerable pressure, the rush forward, and, before I had thought it possible, the roofs hundreds of feet below us. There was an air of relaxation in the sunny aeroplane as we loosed our belts.

'It's your whoreson take-off that's the worst thing. And now, here we are, in another world, the world of our impotence. By which I mean—'

A trolley with drinks had been pushed alongside us. From our position at the back of the plane we were the first to be served. My companion took a whisky.

'And you, sir?'

'A plain Dubonnet. I need no more. Thanks.'

'You can always come back for more,' said enchanting Molly, moving on.

'To continue,' I went on, 'what I was saying. Why this feels so wonderful—you do feel wonderful, don't you?'

He allowed the question, as he was to allow many others, to remain rhetorical.

'It is freedom that makes it so wonderful, the freedom from having to be anybody for two whole days and nights. Or the bondage, if you like, the surrender, the capitulation, the handing over. No outlay of character whatever can be asked of us for this time. We are completely in their power. It is a thing that normally only the arts can do for one. Or am I being controversial?'

Apparently, from his silence, I was not being so.

'The arts, or a war. I believe that many men, weighed down with their peace-time freedom of thought and action, found it, in the last war, immensely restful to be under orders. Responsibility so weighs one down. Here is part of the spell of the church—the handing over. Yes, they have much to account for, Brutus, Bruno, Hampden, Voltaire, Wilkes, Fox and various Russells. No doubt you would care to add to the list?'

He showed no such desire. Indeed I was not sure whether he was listening. Well, if he did not appreciate my conversation, he could always move. He it was who had sat himself down next to me, he was the aggressor. He must take what was coming to him.

'But to you, I gather, flying is just a routine matter. Not for you, the divine extasis, the Kisse of the Spouse.'

He turned and gave me an unhappy look.

'Would you like another cocktail, sir?'

I declined, but my neighbour took another large whisky.

'Steadies you?' I smiled.

'Yes.'

Yes! How pregnant his replies were!

'Now tell me,' I went on, 'you know Malaya, don't you? I am so lucky to have you next me. Tell me all about it, for it will all be new to me. Of course, I've been reading up a certain amount and talking to people who've lived there, but I've never been to the tropics before. Tell me.'

'What is it—what do you want to know?' He had a jerky way of speaking.

'Anything.'

He thought.

'Have you ever seen a peacock wild?' I suggested.

'No.'

'Or a racquet-tailed drongo.'

'What's that?'

'It's a bird out there, with a tail that answers the description.'

'No.'

'Tell me about the flowers. There are of course the flowering trees and shrubs, but the garden flowers—I have the impression that when you have said orchids and cannas you have got near the end of the list?'

'Flowers—I don't know about them.'

Poor chap! Leave that to the wife no doubt? The mistress? The harem?

'Then what do you—I mean, I hope it wouldn't be inquisitive to ask what your job is? But first I'll tell you about mine.'

Let it not be thought that I take without giving. Trays, meanwhile, bearing knives and forks and glasses and condiments and fresh rolls and butter and grapefruit, had been fixed before us, and now Molly was alongside with the drinks.

Would I have white wine or claret or burgundy or champagne or—?

'Miss Flanders, you spoil us! Some Sauternes, please, to start with.'

My companion said he would stick to whisky and had his glass amply refilled. It was becoming clear to me that he was an alcoholic, of a dumb, dreary, soaking kind. What bad luck that I should have been landed with such a neighbour! Well, the more sodden the sod, the higher the requiem. I began to tell him about myself, interrupted almost at once by the passing back to us, from the Indian sitting in front, of a pilot's report, which said that we were now over the North Sea, 21,000 feet above the water, flying at 280 miles an hour. I had, of course, observed our crossing of the English coast and adjusted my imagining to a watery grave. The sea was as calm and blue as could be. There was not a wisp of cloud between it and us. Salmon was being served.

I told the dull man—for so I had christened him—about my fascinating work and the job that was taking me for two months to Malaya. Exhilarated by the inspiring tale, and by the Beaujolais which accompanied the *blanquette de veau*, I extended my confidences, throughout our consumption of *crême caramel*, and *Camembert*, and coffee, until, after we had flown far into Germany and I had seen a lot of dark trees that could hardly yet be the Black Forest, the engines began to relax and the aeroplane to lose height, when I felt I had said enough. It seemed to me that I had very handsomely put my cards on the table. The girls were clearing away the meal.

'Forgive my paean,' I said. 'I hope I haven't been a bore. Now, over to you. You were going to tell me about your job.'

'I'm in irrigation.'

'A steadying job?' I laughed.

There was no answering twinkle. Really, he was too discouraging.

'We are about to land at Frankfort airfield,' announced the hostess. 'Will you please adjust your belts. The local time is five minutes past three. Put out your cigarettes, please.'

We were now falling, banking, circling, diving. Pop went my ears.

Houses and fields came up at us, and there was the airfield. There, man, you've passed it! Presumably the man knew what he was about, but the moment was at hand when we would all suddenly and surely be aware that something was wrong. Then there would be the jar, the crash, the scramble for the jammed door, the flames, immortality. But now our wheels were feeling, ever so delicately, for the asphalt; then we were rolling along securely. O God, thank you once again for giving me another chance. From now on I will try to love my neighbour as myself.

'You must make the best of me,' I said. 'I'm afraid you're thinking you've got next to a terrible bore.'

'Oh no! Most interesting, it's been. It's me, I mean you, you must find me dull, damned dull!'

'On the contrary, on the contrary!'

'I'm damned tired.'

We were directed out of the aeroplane into little motor-buses which drove us to the airport building. As soon as I was on *terra firma*, I became aware, without knowing why, of a fact that I had forgotten. It was Sunday. Here was a measure of our detachment up aloft. For who forgets it is Sunday in the lower air, even on the continent of Europe? Flaubert's instructions to the servant to speak to him but once a week, with the words '*Monsieur, c'est dimanche*', seem to me the most powerful testimony imaginable to the writer's absorption in his work.

Supplied with coupons that would procure us drinks we were led into a restaurant. I needed no more drink. The father of the two children, Mr Martin, and I stood gazing out of the windows.

'Once more in the glasshouse! They have us prisoner, haven't they? Couldn't we perhaps take a little walk out there in the sun?'

To the side of the building there was a length of ornamental water with a fountain playing in it. Ducking under a bar we strolled along beside the water. The other side of it, behind a railing, all Germany seemed to have assembled for its Sunday entertainment. We stared at the Germans staring at us. Then we were called, a man in uniform was after us, waving, we retreated, back within the pen, lambs to the slaughter. We stood there for nearly an hour watching the coming and going of aeroplanes. At one moment, looking behind me into the restaurant, I caught the dull eye of the dull man, who was sitting at a table with a tumbler of the usual before him. Martin, who had observed the good-byes at London airport and seemed even more curious than myself, questioned me about him. So I told him of the nickname I had given my neighbour, of the mystery, almost romance, that nevertheless suffused our relationship owing to his initial forwardness followed by such stolid reserve, and of the ignoble desire to tease that he aroused in me.

'He drinks himself sober. If only I could get him unsteadied by a clear head, he might open up.'

Flight 248 was being called and presently we were in our seats again, sucking sweets, our belts adjusted. Then again, thank you, O Lord, for one more chance. Thank you for so many things. 'There are so many things to be grateful for, are there not? Thank the Lord, for instance, that I am not being broken on the wheel, thank him that I am not watching my grandchildren being tortured until I betray my country. Or is one perhaps not a full man until one has endured these tests? I think often about torture. Do you?'

'Not like that. Not so far-fetched,' said the dull man.

Like what then? But I must not bully.

'Ah, tea!'

A trolley was alongside. My companion declined tea. He did not want anything to eat, and in the matter of drink he would carry on as before.

'Not one of these sandwiches?' I said. 'Freshly cut Gentleman's Relish sandwiches up here—Molly, it's a miracle. How do you manage it?'

'We work miracles,' she laughed melodiously, as she moved on. 'Your whisky in a moment, sir.'

'Do you realise,' I said, looking at the chart as I munched, 'that we do not now, as I had expected, fly over a corner of the Iron Curtain to get to Istanbul? We go down over Venice and along the Adriatic coast to the heel of Italy and then turn at right angles over Greece. By the way, how lucky one is, don't you feel, not to be a writer, not to have to make verbal sense out of experience? To have to produce a travelogue out of a journey, what a constriction, what an impoverishment! You see a thousand butterflies on the wing, you catch a dozen and pin them down. What a magic-reducing thing to have done! Give me the free, elated, wandering thought which is simply the sight of the thing seen, the hearing of the thing heard, as yet un-encased in a straitjacket of language. And, anyhow, words at best are such sloppy approximations. What is language, sir? Language is not to be trusted. Why, consider. You may say, I have caught a very large flea. No, sir, you cannot trust that which ascribes magnitude to what is exiguous *per se*.'

It must now be indeed the Black Forest that I was looking at, but looking through clouds, which became thicker as we approached the mountains. The Alps, in fact, were quite hidden, as was the whole length of Italy. We did not see the ground again that daylight. My companion, who had quaffed his whisky in a single gulp, had now sunk back into sleep, his mouth open. Presently, after the tea had been cleared, one of the pilots came down the gangway, stopping to lean over the seats and talk to the passengers. When he came to us and saw the sleeping man, he decided not to stay and simply smiled at me.

'It's his leave has tired him out,' I said.

'It often does that to them,' he smiled, and passed on.

I glanced at the dull man. Quite chap-fallen. Well, I was not to be silenced. Never have I known such spirits as I had those two days. Now, perhaps, would be a good time to pay off certain scores, to say certain things to or about certain people which I would like to have said but had not thought of in time or had been too decent to say. 'Burtenshaw is so mean,' I said, 'he is the kind of man who keeps his Flanders poppy from one year to the next. He gives his guests invalid wine. I've seen him lift a sixpence from the collection plate.'

Damn braces. For about twenty minutes I had rather a good time.

'Shoe fetichist,' I hissed, and glanced at the sleeper. To my surprise he had an eye open, which was looking at me in a way that made me feel like Jack Ketch. You remember, in Macaulay, the Duke of Monmouth's executioner.

'"Here," said the Duke, "are six guineas for you. Do not hack me as you did my Lord Russell. I have heard that you struck him three or four times. My servant will give you some more gold if you do the work well."

'The hangman addressed himself to his office. But he had been disconcerted by what the Duke had said. The first blow inflicted only a slight wound. The Duke struggled, rose from the block, and looked reproachfully at the executioner.'

Well, that was the sort of look the dull man was giving me.

'Did I speak?' I said. '*J'ai tant à dire, ça se presse comme des flots.* Venice must be down there. Thank God for Otway. What news, I wonder, on the Rialto? If you ever, by the way, wanted to find me in the whole world, look first on that bridge by the east end of the Miracoli. Some imperishable things were once said there. Another time, there was a pigeon in the canal. It was quite water-logged, it could not do anything for itself. A man borrowed my stick and drew it to the side. On the ground it feebly tried to flap its wet wings, but could not fly. Had we left it there on the stones it would have been an easy prey to the cats, so the man tried to lodge it on the cornice of the Miracoli. Twice he threw it up and twice it fell like a stone.'

I stopped speaking. And the third time? For heaven's sake, wasn't he going to ask me what happened the third time? Not he!

'And now Ravenna and Hadria, the Adriatic sea. Let's think of the east coast men, generally an *élite* (yes, I'm a Lincolnshire man), let's think—Byron, Theodoric, Leopardi, Frederick II, Horace—rather a mixed bunch—and, of course, Horace Walpole, talking of whom, paper ho! What, June, you were already bringing it? You anticipate one's slightest whim. I am going to write to my loved ones. What, a pen too? You mean, you're giving me the pen, for keeps? Really, there is something too good to be true about this aeroplane! "Dear loved ones. It is possible that without your restraining influence I become a trifle—"'

The flat blanket of grey cloud that lay so far below had now become a downy quilt that was mounting slowly towards us, every moment more white and more wispy, and that sent up great spouts of unsubstantial vapour which rose in dizzy spirals almost to our wing. The wing itself was in its Indian dancer mood, sending ripples along from shoulder to finger-tips. Presently the spouts were tinged with gold, for the sun, now almost behind us, was sinking with unusual precipitation, as we sped away from it eastwards, discarding the day's unbroached hours along with the empties.

'What, cocktails already? One thing after another! Who says that flying's dull? Just a moment, I'm finishing my letter. "—at length perhaps hear his sad story." There. Dubonnet, please—well, why not?—just a dash of gin, thanks.'

The dinner trays had been fitted over our knees. My companion, who had been heavily asleep, was blinking and yawning.

'Had a good sleep? Look, we are turning. We must be about over Otranto.'

Suddenly it was dark. Then I noticed with alarm a thing not visible by day, the flames of the exhausts spitting backwards over the wing. Was this right? Ought I to tell somebody? Or was it a fact, which, with each moment that we were not burned up, became more probable—yes, by now it must be a fact, that we were, and were meant to be, a chariot of fire.

'Now please, my friend,' I said, 'get even with me. Talk me down. I'll not open my mouth again until at least the end of the *hors d'œuvres*, which I see approaching. Over to you. Irrigation!'

My neighbour accepted the challenge. Diffidently, spasmodically, he talked to me about Malaya. His style was not one of continuous, narrative discourse. The sentences were short, clipped, unfinished, apologetic, yet repetitive withal, like water from a tap, not that has been turned on, but that cannot be properly turned off, squeeze as one may. It was a style that gave a mere synopsis of communicable matter, that was as near not talking as talking very well can be, limp with understatement. The disastrous floods of 1929 were 'a spot of trouble', the second world war was 'the last bit of bother'. It is one of our man-to-man styles and does very well. From what was not said I was able to form a vivid picture of eroding mountain torrents and swirling, muddy rivers, of sudden storms that in a few minutes make a lawn a pond, of the dykes, dams and catchments by which the level of the water is regulated on the paddy fields where, with the slowness of prehistoric time, the water-buffaloes plod before their ploughs, looking infinitely old as they lift their snouts, in imbecile bewilderment, to sniff the first morning of the world. At length, with a decisive squeeze, he had done.

'Thanks. Thanks very much. It's been most interesting. All that water! By the way, why don't you try some of this claret? It's delicious. There's not much wrong with the duck, either. Oh, look, down there, lights! Those are Greek lights. The Good, the True and the Beautiful, how do you think they compare with that other trio, Faith, Hope and Charity? It seems to me that the whole of the latter trinity is comprised in the first person of the former. So the Greeks are the gainers by the True and the Beautiful, by science, that is, and art. Heaven knows I don't want to say anything irreverent about holy writ, but don't you yourself sometimes feel in it a lack, along these lines? Man is not just moral man, time must be filled and it is curiosity as much as love that makes the world go round. Why, even the lilies of the field are only brought in to point a moral. In a word, no botany. And, while we are on the subject, I am saddened that there is to be no marriage in heaven, not even for those of us who like it.'

'You can have it!' said the dull man.

Ah? Ah. I say, you can have that back if you like, or did you mean to throw away your queen? There was a pause while I gave him time either for reconsideration or explanation. He said nothing. It then seemed kinder for me to retreat.

'Harmless curiosity, the great keeper out of mischief. Do you know the Italian for a sedge-warbler? You are in the middle of Blackfriars bridge. Where is the nearest picture by Benjamin West? How can you be bored, and therefore a danger to the community, until you know these things?'

There was a cluster of lights below, a town. Suddenly the aeroplane seemed to catch its breath, a thing it did from time to time, and I caught mine with it.

'I think, don't you, that our end has come when it does that. When one goes out, I believe in instant, unqualified, total, timeless bliss, don't you?'

'It'd be nice,' said the dull man.

'But, as we're still here, perhaps I can enlist your help in doing a competition in this paper. The prize goes to the person who can make the best list of things, of man-made things, that serve a purpose for which they were not intended as well as, or better than, that for which they *were* intended. I've only thought of two so far—an old parchment lease as a lampshade, and the outstretched hand of a statue as a bird-bath. If anything occurs to you, perhaps you'd be so kind. By the way, I wonder what one will happen to be thinking of at the moment of going out. It might be the purple pollen of anemones. No thanks, no more to drink, I've had more than enough. That ham *croûte* was delicious. We must be over Turkey by now. The wife of Bath came this way. She hadde passed many a strange stream. Think of it, three visits by a woman to Jerusalem in the fourteenth century. And how well our travellers keep the tradition going. A cussed lot! The best, in my opinion, are those who tell one, indirectly no doubt, nearly as much about themselves as about the lands visited. One will gladly follow a real card to the most godforsaken places, like Magna Grecia or the Arabian deserts. Am I right or have the engines been turned off a little?'

I was right. The descent to Istanbul had begun. The debris of our dinner was being taken away.

'One gets into the routine, doesn't one? Presently it will be, Put out your cigarettes and fasten your belts, then the Prayer, then the Thanksgiving, the drink coupon, the satchel, the glasshouse, the stretching of the legs, and so on every few hours, as we go round and round the world, the fascinating imponderable each time being the Thanksgiving and what follows.'

So, presently, we stepped out into a brightly starlit night and trooped to the infernal jail where I posted my letter. The air was keen. I would have liked to go for a good country walk. This was out of the question, of course. Mr Martin and I, joined by a man called Walsh, marched briskly up and down in front of the airport. There was no sight of Istanbul. Our fellow-travellers inside, under the bright lights of the waiting-room, were beginning to look worn with travel. The children were fretful. The dull man was sitting, at his usual task, impassively nursing his sorrows—or was it his joy, his joy at having thrown off that harridan at last? I had asked him to join us outside, but he had declined. There he sat, keeping himself to himself, his loneliness emphasized by the manner in which a foreign gentleman, sitting at the same table opposite him, was reading a newspaper, stretched out as though to screen the dull man from his sight.

'Got anything out of him, your dull man?' asked Martin.

'Hardly a thing. He plays a dogged sort of game.'

'You'll have to hurry.'

At length there was a call for Flight 248 and two new hostesses accompanied us to the aeroplane. Belts, prayer, etc.

'I gather it's about 1 a.m. by local time,' I said when we were aloft.

'Goodness, I'm suddenly tired.'

We were working the levers that lowered our seats to the horizontal position.

'For your thing—' he said, 'in there—I thought—for your thing, you know. To clean your nails—I had the idea in there just now—on the edge of a newspaper.'

'The edge of a newspaper, let's say *The Times*, the edge of *The Times* to clean your nails with. Excellent! And so much more effective than the purpose for which the thing was made! Splendid! I *am* grateful to you.'

I chuckled. Really, he was excellent company.

'Good-night.'

'Good-night.'

And the afternoon and evening were the first day.

Mountainous eastern Turkey must be one of the grandest and most desolate regions on the earth. As by a cold bath, I was at once fully awake with astonishment at the wild, abysmal corrugations so far below us in the early light. There was soon a river in a winding channel, the Euphrates presumably, and presently another, the Tigris, and in front there was a mountain peak that I took to be Ararat. Then we turned, almost at right angles, southwards and were over the desert. The sun shone on the faces of passengers the other side of the gangway who were now mostly awake and had drawn back the curtains over their windows. An Indian with a sponge bag passed us to the back of the aeroplane. Early tea was being served.

'This has been one of the most fascinating wakings of my life,' I said.

The dull man, who had observed nothing of our course, did not look as though any waking had ever been fascinating for him. Well, I had not let him spoil yesterday, he should not spoil today. And there, in a loop of the river, was Baghdad.

'It makes one think, doesn't it, this bird's eye view of the world? The passage of history, the armies tramping, now this way, now that, the new top dogs, one after another. There must be a top dog, mustn't there? And now we are moving out, we English, which is all right by me. I don't want to be top dog anywhere, do you—except in the home.' (That was unkind, but 'You'll have to hurry,' Martin had said.)

'Leave the material race to others. It's our turn to become the easterners, the contemplatives, the mystics. By the way, are you interested in space travel? Not before breakfast, maybe. Even on an empty stomach it fascinates me. The theological complications. Another human race perhaps, that has or has not fallen from grace, for whom Christ has or has not died?'

We were losing height. Then Beryl, the hostess, was asking us to fix our belts for the landing at Basra airport, where breakfast would be served. The ground temperature, we should find, would be ninety degrees.

It was indeed. Personally I cannot have it too hot. While we were walking the fifty yards from aeroplane to building, I felt myself opening as wide as the hibiscus that was flowering by the entrance of the airport. There was a forest of palms beyond the airfield, and beside it a wide river, rippled by a hot wind, and across the water more palms. Two veiled women were walking by the river.

'I say, we're getting somewhere. I wonder what there'll be for breakfast.'

In a high room, from the ceiling of which fans were revolving, we were served with porridge and fried eggs, bacon and kidneys and toast and butter and Oxford marmalade and coffee.

'If there's one thing,' I said, 'the British empire will be remembered for with gratitude, it's our food.'

The point was taken up by the young Indian lawyer from Oxford, whose seat was in the front of the plane, and we had an enjoyable set-to. He was humorous and subtle and perfectly beautiful. I quite lost my heart to him. He and I strolled after breakfast beside the great river, in the hot wind. Over there, beyond the palms, was Persia. Thank God I did not have to write all this up!

We were being called.

'What a pity we aren't sitting next to each other!'

'You could move perhaps?'

'No,' I said, 'it would look too rude.'

Our next lap, over the Persian Gulf, was, for me, the climax of the journey, as it were its High Renaissance, still exuberantly forward-looking and unflagging in curiosity, and not yet lowered by the fatigue of too much achievement. Arabia on the right, the Gulf below—it was annoying not to be able to see out to the left. I must at least see Persia. That Far Eastern gentleman would not mind if I went and looked out of his window. I stepped across my neighbour's legs and the gangway.

'Excuse me.'

'Please.'

'May I just look out of your window?'

'Please.'

'I just want to see Persia. You see, I've never seen it and shall probably never see it again.'

'Please.'

'Right, I've seen it now. Thanks.'

'Please.'

'Thanks.'

With a cordial handshake, I broke away and went back to my seat. There was not a vestige of a cloud over the earth or in the sky.

'How is it that "sky" is not a synonym for "heaven" in English as in so many languages? And is this to our advantage? Of course it is. What it amounts to is that they haven't got a word for "heaven".'

On this bright day that I was flying through, however, the two senses seemed hardly to be distinguished; moreover, there was no apparent severance of earth and sky. The Arabian sands were shining white, the water was shining blue, the air was just shining. Brightness was all. A single word would do for everything.

For this great plate of geography set before me, *deo gratias*, and for all those names with their Miltonic echoes, Bushire, Ormuz, Oman, Muscat, and for the feeling of life for once catching up with literature, and me speeding on beyond to Malacca and Alor Star. The moment of ecstasy . . . I think I never took so large a draught of intellectual day.

'Thanks, oh thanks!'

'What for?' said the dull man.

'Oh! Are you still there?' Do you ever feel like taking St Mary-le-Strand home with you for the week-end, and putting it on your knee, and cleaning it properly with bread crumb? A thing I often do is to open the tureen top of the National Gallery, and give a good stir.

Meanwhile, cocktails had been served and, as we came out over the Indian Ocean, there was luncheon. I realised that my journey was now half done. To-morrow's luncheon would be in Kuala Lumpur. The thought that I would so soon be dislodged from my Olympian seat and gathered again into the artifice of time, brought to my meal just the slightest sense of urgency, a sense the utter absence of which had been part of the delight of occupying that seat. These excellent and freely flowing wines that were included in the ticket—let me not forget that life would not always be so. It is possible that I exceeded a little, and that I thereafter slept. At least, when the hostess enjoined us to adjust our belts for the landing at Karachi, it seemed that her words broke in upon a far more exhilarating conversation than any I could be having with the dull man.

'I believe I was asleep.'

'You didn't answer just now.'

'You spoke? Was it something important?'

'No—can't remember—just a spot of tongue-wag—'

Ah, it *had* been important. The *Confessio*—and I had missed it!

The temperature on Karachi airfield must have been well in the hundreds. Stepping through that afternoon heat was very different from slipping through the mild morning air of Basra. For, dry though it was, from its very intensity it enveloped one in a thick and clogging element. Our progress across the tarmac, watched by many pairs of lack-lustre eyes from the glasshouse, was that of goldfish in a bowl of golden syrup set in the sun. And when we had at last floundered to the edge and were ourselves in the airport, behold, the element was the same. We were still within the bowl. There was no way out. Those eyes too were fish eyes. From now on, all life was within the golden bowl. Well, this was what I had come for. Already my gills were adapting themselves and working with a more regular motion. Talking of gills, that poor duke of Clarence! I suppose the manner of his death is one of the half-dozen bits of debris from an expensive education that will remain with any public-school man for a lifetime. Let's try.

'It makes one pant, doesn't it, this heat? One can't get one's breath. It's like being drowned.'

' 'Mm,' the dull man agreed.

'Stuck head downwards in a cask, and drowned.'

'But—wine—in a butt—malmsey—in a butt of malmsey wine—like that fellow.'

'Quite.'

Our party was standing in a queue waiting for direction. Presently we were led to a bus which took us a few hundred yards along a road to a rest-house where we were to spend the hour and a half of our wait. This consisted of an encampment of huts, at the centre of which were a restaurant, bar, reading room and shower-baths. Extending away on either side there were bedrooms for the use of the air staff. Two pilots were exercising themselves on a hard tennis court. Basket chairs were set out for our use on a veranda in front of a patch of parched garden in which a few cannas and a bougainvillaea on a trellis were wilting. It looked as if there were miles of sandy desolation all around. There was no sign of Karachi. Of all the pieces of no-man's land that have been found to set airfields in, this must surely be the most neminal. The real owners were evidently the Indian crows, who busily moved between the telegraph poles, the trellises and the roofs of the bungalows, making the frankest comments on our comings and goings. My spirits, unlike the bougainvillaea, were flagging not at all.

'Blessed heat! I'll have a shower.'

Under the water I was trying to remember something. Yes, of

course. Thanks for that last safe landing. Was I, then, getting so *blasé*?

After the cold shower, I felt a good deal hotter and after a game of ping-pong with Jennifer Martin, hotter still. A stroll then with her father on the deserted road, out into the emptiness. Crows accompanied us along the telegraph wires. At length one of them began to patrol across the road some yards in front of us, as if to say, This is far enough. Very well. We turned back.

News had meanwhile come through that a small repair had to be done to our engine. We probably would not be leaving till about seven. Time began to hang heavy on the children. Various games were tried, as we sat in deckchairs drinking orangeade.

'I spy with my little eye,' said Jennifer, 'something beginning with D.M.' Following her eye, with one voice we exclaimed 'Dull Man'.

There he was, sitting in the bar, apparently in animated conversation with Walsh. To say I felt a pang of jealousy would be an exaggeration. Still, if there was to be any animation, I felt it belonged to me. Presently I joined them. Whatever flow of talk there may have been seemed to have dried up. They looked at me glumly.

'Thought of anything more for my competition?' I said, and explained to Walsh. 'I've thought of an old railway carriage as a poor man's home.'

'Can't think,' said the dull man. 'Tried, but can't think of anything. Think I'll go and have a shower.' He left us.

'Interesting chap that,' I said tentatively.

'D'you think so?' said Walsh. 'I think he's the dumbest person I've ever talked to.'

Now the Indian appeared. He had been on a bed, he said. As the shadows began to lengthen, he and I sauntered up and down the road, until the bus came and took us all back to the airport. Good-bye to the crows, and good-bye, with an exchange of addresses, to the Indian who would be getting out at the next stop. By the time we were in our seats again, it was quite dark. Sad that I should be seeing nothing of India.

No sooner were we aloft than the tray of drinks was pushed alongside.

'So here we are, at it again. I feel as if this journey had been going on for months, don't you? Let's look at the menu—Ah, a curry, I see. That's appropriate. I think I shall have the hock, and probably stick to it throughout the dinner.'

As we ate and drank, Indian lights twinkled beneath and the stars around us.

'This question of artistic inspiration,' I said, 'all the best art is inspired not by nature but by other art, either by emulation (Virgil,

Keats) or reaction (Wordsworth) or simple superiority. Milton reads Salandra, Shakespeare some rotten play about Hamlet or Henry V. I can do better than that, they say, and are provoked to do so. You never find the people who try working straight from nature among the greatest names. D. H. Lawrence, for instance. And what embarrassing turns of phrase he picked up in the school of life! Have you, for example, ever been "crucified into sex"?'

'Yes,' said the dull man, 'I have.'

His words were a slap in my face. I felt at once a great cad, facetious and vulgar.

'I'm so awfully sorry,' I stammered and became silent.

From this moment I was in full retreat from the dull man. I wanted nothing from him. I would have hated to hear his wretched tale now. Fortunately he said no more and left me to look silently out of the window at the stars, and try to recover my self-respect. I had, indeed, other things to think about. The morrow was already with me. I thought about what I should do and say and wear, perused, in my notebook, the list of people to whom I had introductions and, at length, after dinner fell asleep over my Malayan vocabulary.

We were awoken at Calcutta in the middle of the night to troop, like ghosts, to our lighted waiting place. Some local ghosts, at the edge of the darkness, were watching us, a hot breeze stirring the tatters around their legs. In this port I made the acquaintance of those lizards that inhabit the inside walls and ceilings of houses in the tropical East. The alarm they at first inspire quickly turns to affection as one realises that they are the friend of man. Without falling on your head, they clean the ceilings of insects. The newcomer to the East, sitting in his easy chair conversing, keeps his eyes aloft, fascinated to watch them dart, with the speed of light, upon their prey.

Flight 248 was being called. I must have been dozing, my head on my hands on a table. Stiffly, blinking, yawning, we answered the summons back to the aeroplane. Was this indeed still Flight 248, still the same crowded dream? Let me get back into it. Hadn't there been a man . . .? Yes, there he was, settling himself in his seat next to me.

'Next stop Rangoon, I believe?'

'Two hours, about two hours.'

After a short, uneasy sleep, I was looking down, in daylight, on a squared expanse of brown paddy fields towards which we were falling. The next stop after this would be my destination, where we would arrive about midday. Then I would be on the job. It might be a good thing to start the day with a shave at this airport. I was hunting for the razor in my bag as our wheels touched the ground (thanks).

'I'll say good-bye,' said the dull man to my surprise. 'Actually I'm not coming on to K.L. till next week. Job here. Cheerio.'

'Oh, good-bye. Nice to have met you.'

He stepped first out of the aeroplane and walked on ahead of the rest of us.

'So that's good-bye to him,' I said to the Martins.

'Good-bye? Isn't he coming on to K.L.?'

I explained. Ten minutes later, as we were drinking coffee in the airport, we saw him from the window get into a car and drive away.

'So that's him!' I said. 'Not one of my social successes, I'm afraid. Not that there was any ill-feeling, that I'm aware of. Perhaps we simply did not bring out the best in each other. I had certainly begun to find his company rather oppressive. I shall not mind forgetting all about him.'

And that morning I did forget about him entirely, as throughout a five-course breakfast on the aeroplane, served by a Chinese hostess, I gazed down on islands and archipelagos and a glassy sea in which, here and there, the speck of a ship had got caught before the glass solidified, and rocky shores and long beaches edged with palms and paddy fields and at length the mountains of Malaya, upholstered right over their summits with forest.

Nor, in the weeks to come, did the thought of him often cross my mind as I busied myself in the offices of the capital and up and down the peninsula, making so many new acquaintances every day, conferring with so many faces of such various shapes and colours, all so courteous and friendly; travelling occasionally by air, more often by car and whenever possible by the excellent railways; eating Malayan meals, Chinese meals, Indian meals and, at the station hotel in Kuala Lumpur, my base, British meals, about which the intelligent Chinese management has nothing to learn (it knows about mint sauce, bread sauce, caper sauce, horseradish sauce); bathing in the China sea; watching, fascinated, the white liquid latex ooze from the cut bark of the rubber trees; getting involved on the balcony in the evening excitement of the swifts that scream around the station hotel, one of them darting from time to time in through the Moorish arcading to graze the heads of standing drinkers in a lightning circuit of the lounge; calling 'slow! slow!' to the driver of the car as we would approach three Indian women of regal splendour in their long bright draperies, with their bracelets and bangles and jewelled noses, who with one arm each held a sickle which, in a movement of effortless nonchalance, they were swinging around in a full circle to cut the grass by the roadside, the handle of the sickle being so long that no bending was demanded of the royal body, no movement at all apart from the rotation of one arm to disturb the chatter that was issuing from the lovely painted lips of the three queens, the three goddesses; talking, over tea, coffee, lemonade, beer, whisky or port, with well-informed men, voluble, superficial men, tired men, humorous men, impenetrable men, upright, dedicated men, hearing every sort of opinion about the future of that teeming land, where half a dozen civilizations jostle one another; waking each morning to go to the window and greet the myna birds strutting with such importance upon the station roof and look out, towards the mountains, on yet another lovely summer day.

None of these days was happier than the one I spent at the open window of a first-class carriage on the train known as the Golden Blowpipe which took me up to Khota Bharu on the east coast, near the Siamese border. Hour after hour, the engine, it seemed, cut a way for us through the jungle, driving wild beasts, I supposed, into its dark recesses, from which I heard, or fancied I heard, their strange hoots and snarls and squawks. At times we would cross a river or come out upon a clearing, where one of those odd limestone crags would rear its steep bulk, delighting the eye, after all that green cushioning, with a surface of bare rock. At these clear places the sky would open above me, a glorious, interesting, moving sky that was never without clouds and never, except at the quickly passing moments of deluge, quite overcast, but was generally a clean and rain-washed depth of blue across which white shapes were hurrying over the hills to join an infinitely majestic range of cloud mountains above the horizon. That's where you belong, up there, I would say to myself as I realised that there would only be a few days now before I was on my way home.

And, as I drove back down the east coast, the realisation was welcome. For I had been living at great pressure. To lean back in my seat in the aeroplane, and put my feet up, would be exceedingly restful. Then, just as I was about to remember the dull man, I saw the dull man. We had come to one of those ferries over a river. The ferry could hold four cars or two lorries, and took a good ten minutes to cross the broad stream. It would return loaded from the other side. What with waiting your turn in the queue of cars and lorries, and the loadings and unloadings each side, and the crossings, you may well find yourself delayed for two or three hours at one of these ferries. There were fifteen or twenty vehicles in front of mine. I was in for a wait. Getting out of the car, I strolled down to the water's edge. The loaded ferry, which had just left the shore, was straining at the cable which prevented it from racing down stream, as, chugging furiously, it strove to point itself on the diagonal course that it would take across the river. A boy, crouching in the shallow water, was giving a bath to a pet myna, tied by its foot to his wrist. The bird's shrill accompaniment to this operation was undoubtedly happy. So was that of the infant, bathing with its mother, a little further along the shore. She would duck its head, then, as she lifted it out of the water, duck her own, then both heads would disappear, to come up dripping and laughing. This climate, I thought, in which you can stay as long as you like in the water, and let wet things dry on you in the sun, and never a thought of catching cold, I am going to miss it, all this swirling water, this irrigation. . . . To the side of where I was standing there was a little slope, on the top of which was a ramshackle café, in front of which was a dilapidated kitchen table, behind which the dull man was sitting. He caught my eye and beckoned. There was no escape.

'Hullo,' he said, as I joined him, 'what's yours? Stupid question, as a matter of fact, stupid question! It's got to be beer. Only beer in this hole!'

Perhaps it was the unusual drink that had given him an air of expansion, of excitement, that I did not associate with him. I sat beside him, looking out over the river.

'Cheers,' he said, raising his glass to the glass that had been brought to me. 'Quite like old times, isn't it? Thinking of you, as a matter of fact.'

'Me?'

'You. Kept hitting the nail on the head, you did! Didn't mean to, I'm sure!'

'Me?'

''Mm.'

Oh Lord! The ferry was now more than half-way across the river.

'Damned ferry!' he went on. 'Been here an hour already, at least an hour. Mine's the sixth car now. Get on the one after next. 'Nother half-hour. Wanted to talk to someone. Lucky you came. Friendly face. Must talk to someone. In a bloody hole, as a matter of fact. Could you—would you mind'—he took a draught of the heady liquor to give himself courage—'that is, d'you mind if I bore you for a few minutes? Must speak to someone, then you came.'

There seemed no alternative.

'Why, of course. Indeed, it would only be just.'

There was a moment's hesitation during which I thought he might be going to hold himself in. Then he blurted out fiercely 'Damned marriage! My bloody marriage!'

'Quite.'

'It's like this. It may look petty to other people, people like your wife's or husband's, as the case may be, relations, what married people seem to quarrel about, I mean with the people they're married to. It probably isn't.'

'Quite.'

'I mean, people don't bother to quarrel about petty things, do they?'

'Of course not.'

'That is to say, I mean, there's something deep wrong. Oh, can't express myself, can't express myself!'

Deep wrong—that was good.

'You're doing splendidly,' I said and called for more beer.

'Basically, they must be basically right. Top dog, there must be a top dog. What you said.'

I said?

'That is, a word of command, both people, you must both know a word of command when you hear it. No good otherwise, no love. Both top dogs equally, under dogs equally. You must both say, I'll do anything for you. Don't have to go on saying it, once would be enough. After that you'd never want to ask them to do anything. You wouldn't need to. Position of strength. It'd be love. You'd like giving way. They'd like it too. It'd be lovely.'

The ferry had reached the farther shore. The cars had driven off it up a cutting and round a bank out of sight. The new load was coming on.

'But she's never said it, not once. It's not love. So everything's a battle all the time. All the little things. I know they're little things, damn it, but then they're not little things when it's like that, because each one is contempt for me. So everything's spoilt. You wake up in the morning, perhaps for a few seconds forget, then you remember you're in for another day spoilt.'

I was listening unwillingly, but with respect, for there seemed to be nothing second-rate about the dull man's grim communication.

'Gets you down,' he went on, 'day after day like that. Difficult to believe in yourself any more. Cuts the ground under your feet. Makes you damned dull.'

'Oh no! Not that!'

'Yes it does, I know.'

In silence he watched the ferry complete its crossing to our side. There was movement, shouting, waving of arms, as it was beached. A lorry rumbled on board, the queue of cars advanced. Perhaps my companion had finished. But with the arrival of more beer, he began once more, 'Couldn't go on like that for ever—had to come to a head. You got it again.'

'I?'

Oh Lord!

''Mm. It was shoes did it. It was in a London shop. Some awful things she wanted to buy, sort of golf things with a leather flap over the laces, a flap. I said, "Please don't." I'd never meant anything more in my life. She just laughed. Her mother there. She said to her mother, "Now he's sulking. He does get angry about such little things." It was like being trodden on, you know, when the person turns their boot round and round to make a good job of squashing the snail or thing. That's when I decided to clear out. Got weeks of leave still. Decided to come on the next plane I could get a seat on. Left her without any money for a ticket. Get away.'

'Splendid,' I said, 'splendid!'

'She found out at last minute, came to airport, you saw.'

'So here you are. What an escapade! I must congratulate you on what seems to have been a happy escape.'

Yet he did not seem as happy as he should have been. Relapsing into silence, he gazed morosely at the ferry. As the sorry tale seemed to have come to an end, I began to chatter about other things, though he paid no attention to what I was saying. Presently the ferry was once more approaching our bank. The Chinese youth at the wheel of the dull man's car was making signs to us. My companion roused himself. 'Telegraphed to her,' he said. 'Sent her ticket, couldn't get on without her. Coming next week. Bloody!'

He shook my hand and raised desperate eyes to mine.

'So long.'

I watched him get into his car, I watched the car across the water and saw it drive away. That line of Racine had ironically come into my head:

Tous les jours se levaient clairs et sereins pour eux.

And now, in the London street, when I look down from the aeroplane I have heard above the traffic, I perhaps remember the dull man and reflect that

Some are born to sweet delight
Some are born to endless night

and think that among the anxious faces in the crowd quite fifty per cent may belong to the second category, and how fatally easy it may be to slip from the first to the second category, and I walk on a wiser and a—no, I'm damned if I'll be a sadder man for any of them.

That Thoughtful Boy

Leaving my coat on the seat I had found, and putting my bag on the rack, I walked along the corridor into the restaurant car where a few people were already seated, and took a vacant place at a table for two. The seat in front of me had a bag on it. 'Lunch, sir?' a waiter said. 'We serve it as soon as the train starts.' After a glance at the menu, I opened the paper-back volume I had brought with me, *A New Anthology of Twentieth Century Verse*, edited, with an introduction, by Arthur Bland. The book had been much commended by reviewers.

Of course I remembered Bland, 'that thoughtful boy'. By half-term old Tuppy had found an appropriate epithet for most of the boys in his form. There were 'the tall boy', 'the round boy', 'that good boy', 'the happy boy'. A boy called Tower, who was very short, was 'the Eiffel boy'. There were 'the talkative boy', 'that insatiable boy', 'that sinister boy'. The use of 'that' rather than 'the' seemed to imply that in such cases the adjective had been arrived at after particular consideration. Its recipient was probably a more complicated and interesting character than one of the 'the's'. Yes, I had my appellation.

Bland's epithet could not have been more suitable. Ask him the plainest question and you would be aware of having set a turbine of thought revolving. The remotest implications of your question and of any answer he might give, would quickly suggest themselves to him. In a hurried series of half sentences, or perhaps by a sudden, silent, jump, he would move from the particular to the general, giving you an answer heavy with philosophical content, far in excess of what you had asked, and perhaps leaving you at last in doubt about the small fact you wanted to know.

I remember one summer afternoon, while Bullett was standing up construing Virgil with painful slowness, Tuppy suddenly calling out 'Bland! Are you reading a book under the desk?' The question would seem to be one that admitted only the answer Yes or No. Now Bland *was* reading a book under the desk, a novel as it transpired, by Conrad. He did not at once answer Tuppy. The processes that went on in his mind during this moment of silence I take to have been somewhat as follows. He would be imagining the dialogue that impended. 'Yes', he would say. Tuppy would open his eyes wide with that comic look of aggrieved astonishment. 'And what are you reading?' he would ask. 'A novel, sir.' 'A novel?' The eyes would open wider in ever more shocked incredulity. 'What novel?' 'It is by Conrad, sir.' Bland would then expatiate upon the high quality of Conrad's work, expressing opinions which Tuppy must admit were not peculiar to the boy. Quiller Couch indeed had pronounced Conrad the greatest living writer of English prose, and he should know. A word then about Quiller Couch's credentials, culminating in a recently expressed verdict of the headmaster himself. It was at this point in the imagined debate that Bland broke his silence.

'The headmaster, sir, surely knows what he is talking about?'

Tuppy's eyes which, as he waited for the boy to speak, became sadder and sadder until they seemed to be bulging with all the *lacrimae rerum* of offended Virgil, would open no wider, so he shut them and opened his mouth and held his head quite still, a gargoyle exposed to the unpredictable weather of Bland's explanation. He was a born comedian. Bullett meanwhile took his chance and was busy with the crib.

Bland, then, deducing from Tuppy's silence that the infallibility of the headmaster was axiomatic, said that he had heard the headmaster the other day say that Quiller Couch was the greatest living English critic. And Quiller Couch had pronounced Conrad to be the greatest living writer of English prose. In this opinion, of course, he was not alone, and Bland, who was already most knowledgeable about literary matters, named two or three other eminent critics who shared it.

A paper was passed to me. It was addressed to 'Arthur Bland, Esq.' It said, 'Well done. Keep it up. Yours sincerely, Roger Bullett.' I passed it on.

Bland did not need to be asked to keep it up. After quoting others' opinions of Conrad, he gave some of his own. He read some sentences from the book before him to illustrate what he was saying, as he expatiated upon the quality of Conrad's prose. I remember thinking at the time what a good lecturer he would make. Indeed, it was perhaps on that very day that it dawned upon Bland himself what his *métier* was to be. Most of us, I believe, one way or another, discovered ourselves in Tuppy's classroom, accidentally, as it were, during those frequent diversions in which now one of us, now another, would show his hand.

At length, his case, as it seemed to him, conclusively made, Bland stopped speaking. We stared at the gargoyle. What hope was there of its breaking the silence of centuries? Suddenly its eyes opened fiercely and a wind blew through the mouth.

'The book!' it wailed, 'the book!'

'Oh yes, sir. It's by Conrad. A novel called—' and Bland turned the book to read the title on the spine, a gesture known to provoke Tuppy ever since the memorable day on which Pugh had done the same thing and Tuppy had shouted 'You don't even know the name of the book you are reading! Do you know your *own* name?' 'Yes, sir.' 'Tell it to us,' Tuppy had said faintly, the appearance of wrath giving way to that of blank and weary resignation before the injustices inseparable from our human lot which was his normal appearance. Ap Hugh, who was nothing if not a genealogist, spoke for twenty minutes. His performance became the classic diversion. 'Please, sir', we would beg, 'can Pugh tell us his name? It's weeks since he told us.' To return to Bland, 'a novel', he said, 'called *Lord Jim.*'

Let it be understood, by the way, that Bland's long-winded answer, except, of course, that he knew there was no justification for reading anything, even the Bible, under the desk when he ought to have been attending to Virgil, was an ingenuous performance. That is to say, there was, I am sure, no conscious artistry in the way in which he had played upon our curiosity until, at the final moment of his divulging the precise fact of his offence, the title of his illicit book, even Bullett was watching and listening. I am convinced that Bland simply did not realise that he had not yet named his novel.

It hardly needs to be said that none of us who knew our Bland foresaw for him the life of a man of action. He would live, if indeed he contrived at all to keep body and soul together, among books. And so he had. I had noticed in a paper only the other day that he had been appointed professor of poetry in a midland university.

What was now my astonishment when, looking across the carriage and out of the window on the side of the platform, I saw Bland himself! Though I had not seen him for at least thirty years, there could be no doubt about the identity of that gentle, worried face. There he was, standing on the platform by the train in conversation with a young man, trying to see every side of the matter of their talk, trying desperately to be fair. A saintly character, I remembered thinking him. The look on his face told me that, at the moment, he was struggling with some terrible perplexity. Then, all in a flash, a most astonishing thing happened, and at the same time a porter came past shutting the carriage doors, and a few seconds later Bland was lifting the bag off the seat opposite me, debating, with the indecision of one to whom actualities are a torment, whether he should put it on the rack or on the floor. Putting it, at length, on the rack, he sat down; but he did not give me a proper look for some time. His hands were shaking, indeed the whole man seemed to be trembling. I looked away from him as the train moved out of King's Cross station into the daylight, only to be engulfed again, after a few moments, in a tunnel. Meanwhile plates of soup were put before us.

A furtive glance when we came out of the tunnel told me that Bland's eyes were still unseeing, so blinded was he by the unusual violence of his feelings. Well, we had plenty of time, at least a certain amount of time, an hour and ten minutes, to be precise, for I was getting out at the first stop, Peterborough. Perfect conditions for a friendly and uninhibited talk about old times. If, for instance, we had been travelling together to Scotland, we two Englishmen, old friends, with lots to say, and full of curiosity about each other, might well have closed in upon ourselves, thinking, there's plenty of time, a little later we'll open up, anyhow he may have become a terrible bore, I must watch out as he's going to be in Edinburgh while I'm there. We would have funked the intimacy, and only over the hearty handshake of farewell—'It's been wonderful to see you'—at Waverley Station, would we have ventured on Christian names. Bland and I, however, with our not far distant *terminus ad quem* and the unlikelihood, so far as I knew, of our ever meeting again in the normal course of our lives, were well set for a generous exchange of confidences. Even if the thirty and more years did not provide Bland with much matter, it looked as if the last few minutes must have given him something to say. His eye at length fell on his anthology beside my plate and he looked up at me.

'Why—' he said, smiling.

'Yes, it's me. And you, you hardly look a day older.' Indeed, when at that moment his body, which had been gradually recovering its peace, suddenly shuddered, I thought of him as a child who has woken up in the night and is sitting on his mother's knee and seems restored but is shaken again by a memory of the bad dream. Until he should regain his composure, I took charge of the talk, congratulating him on the professorship and on the anthology, and on one or two other books of his that had come my way. I then filled in the gap of time in respect of myself with certain vital statistics concerning profession and domicile, a marriage, three births and now, in that younger generation, a pregnancy.

'My children are all girls', I said. 'In a way they present as much of an educational problem as boys. Have you any daughters?'

'One. She's sixteen.'

We began to talk about female education.

'Which', I said, 'would you sooner teach, at university level, young men or young women?'

Here was a subject on which Bland, now apparently master of himself, could dilate. He dilated. I listened with interest and with just that bit of envy that always comes over me in the presence of a holder forth. These people who give themselves entirely to the subject of their talk are so different from myself. Avid for information and difficult to bore, I yet have a horror of boring, and cannot help keeping an eye on my escape route, with the result that my speech is somewhat staccato, and does not often, I know it, enhance the life around me. We were already among fields when Bland at length reached his conclusion, which was that he hardly distinguished, among his pupils, between the males and the females. If he ever tried to guess whether an examination paper was by a boy or a girl, he was generally wrong.

'I am getting out at Peterborough', I said, as he paused.

'I at Retford.'

'And sons', I ventured, 'have you any sons?' I felt as a dentist must when he has asked, 'Did you feel that?' That my question had provoked feeling in Bland was only too plain. His expression, which had cleared while he discoursed, became troubled again. Searching in his mind on, on, far beyond the monosyllables that would have answered me, he behaved in a manner most characteristic of himself or, as I now remembered we used to call it at school, a Blandular manner. The epithet, whether rightly or wrongly, carried with it the suggestion that Bland's laborious thoughtfulness was due to some glandular excess or deficiency in his constitution, and this was endearing. Bland could not help being Bland (whereas Bullett, for example, could help a great many things). He stared sadly for some time out of the window, his food forgotten.

'Such a good man', he said at length, 'good in the sense of good—so tolerant—the Dean—my father, that is—that was, that is to say.'

I remembered to have heard something about the Dean.

'One reaps as one has sown, that is what I am saying', Bland went on, 'and in his theology the Dean called himself a modernist. I grew up accustomed to having the subject thought and reasoned about. I early found that it does not stand up to thought. We all did, didn't we? And by the age of sixteen, most people's theological position, should they ever have such a thing, gets set for life. So he got an agnostic for a son, which was bitter for him. It needn't have been so bitter, if one had been kinder. Oh, I wish I had been kinder. One used to mock the mumbo-jumbo side of it. I remember once, he had with some difficulty got me a seat in the choir of the cathedral to see the enthronement of a bishop and I simply did not turn up for the occasion, which hurt him a good deal and when he mildly—as so always very mildly—rebuked me, I said—'

At this point I loudly cleared my throat and nodded several times to show that I had fully got his point, being unwilling to hear more about how such a good man had been unkind to such a good man and convinced that Bland's spiritual catharsis needed no further confession.

Bland accordingly broke off, with, I think, gratitude. Presently he started again.

'Once you have allowed the principle of movement, there is no stopping. My father believed himself to have made great advances in enlightenment upon his father, the archdeacon, who as a boy had believed that the world started in 4004 B.C. And the latter, *a fortiori*, in respect of his father. But the process of advance cannot go on for ever. Three or four generations and you walk right out of the whole thing. If you want to stay in it you must stick to 4004 B.C. and the earth being flat and rose petals falling out of the blue sky and the Assumption of the Virgin and all the rest of it, like Roman Catholics. There is no *via media*, alas.'

His look of discouragement was such that I changed the subject. 'Ever meet any of our old chums?' I said. 'I see that Pugh has become Rouge Dragon.'

While we dug up old names and exchanged reminiscences about them, Bland temporarily forgot his worries and we had some good laughs. The train raced along. So did the time. Apple tart and custard were presently being served.

'No custard for me, thanks', Bland said. 'I say, you'll never guess whom I met the other day in an Italian street, much the worse for wear but unmistakeable—Bullett. He holds down the job of British Vice-Consul in Mantua of all places.' At the memory of this most unsatisfactory of boys Bland's face suddenly became serious.

'You asked whether I had a son. I have. But I don't want to bore you—'

'My dear Arthur, you must know, I am unboreable.'

'You are very kind. Perhaps it will do me good to talk. Well then, it's an awful mess. And this morning things reached a climax. And God knows what happens next. I'll tell you.'

Now for some facts. But, of course, nothing of the kind. Bland being Bland, we had to start with airy generalisations.

'Tolerance has always seemed to me one of the major virtues, particularly by the old of the young. I had been lucky to meet with a good deal of it when I was a boy and in my turn I was going to hand it out as it has never been handed before.'

He took a mouthful.

'When ex-rebels succeed to a place in the established hierarchy, they are generally a bit disappointed if they don't have any rebellion from below to deal with. Too docile young seem to them to lack the spirit they once had themselves. This at least has not been my disappointment.' He took another mouthful.

'My faith in toleration has just about evaporated.'

Presenting me, in this statement, with his conclusion upon the whole matter, he began to gaze out of the window and might have relapsed altogether into rumination had I not spoken.

'There's Huntingdon already', I said urgently. 'We're getting on.'

Bland braced himself.

'I have to admit, of course', he said, 'that I have never known a poet or an artist in the flesh. I'm just an academic. I read about them and argue about them and lecture about them, as though I knew. Many's the time I've said that men of genius must not be judged by ordinary moral standards. Byron or D. H. Lawrence must be allowed their overweening egoism. They have their own rules, I have said. I shan't say it again.'

He gazed abstractedly out of the window and I was about to recall him when he continued.

'Yes he's an artist, my son, Peter, that rock. . . . An artist? I suppose so. He certainly pours a great deal of paint over large areas of canvas. Great gobs of it. I haven't a clue what it's all about. When his desire to be a painter first showed itself, of course, I gave him every encouragement. I have always had an amateur's interest in art history, and all sorts of attractive art books have always been available to him on my shelves.'

I remembered that already at school Bland had been proud of his books and had had some first editions of Yeats and Eliot behind glass.

'He treats books abominably,' Bland went on. 'In fact, I think he has now come to regard them positively as enemies. "Knowledge!" he says contemptuously, "Why are you always wanting to know things? You should read Yeats. He says that all knowledge is worth a straw".'

Bland's book on Yeats is generally regarded as a little masterpiece, I believe.

'Two or three years ago, fascinated by the discovery of the painting of the *Seicento* in our times, I had the bright idea of giving him for his birthday a year's subscription to the *Burlington Magazine*. I remember him turning over the pages of the first number to arrive. Ash fell from his cigarette onto the handsome, shiny page, from which it was not blown or shaken as he turned to the next page. After a few moments, "Christ!" he said, an oath which happens, through some quaint atavistic sensibility, to make me wince, "Christ! Who the hell wants to know whether Gaddy-Gaddy or Botty-what-not left a will!" With that he chucked the paper onto the piano, from which it slipped onto the floor, where it remained. You will see that he is neither gracious nor kind. One day he condescended to come with me to the National Gallery, the upshot of which was, he was confirmed in his opinion that I haven't a clue about any painting, not just about his and Grick's.'

'Grick's?'

'You haven't heard of Grick?'

I shook my head.

'Thank God. Perhaps I am not quite so out of touch as I am made to feel. How he mocks me! It's not my ignorance, as a matter of fact, so much as my knowledge, my erudition, that he mocks. He says things like "Bomber"—that, by the way, is his term of endearment for me, deriving from my refusal to sit with him on the ground in Parliament Square in protest against our defence policy—"Bomber", he says, "did Michelangelo belong to the Spanish School?" Which I take in good part, indeed play up to, partly because anything in the nature of a family joke relaxes tension, partly for another reason, which you may regard as masochistic. When he mocks me, I feel that justice is being done. He is paying me in my own coin, for I used to have a term of endearment for my father at least as crude and tasteless as Peter's for me. I used to call—'

'But Grick', I broke in, 'who is Grick?'

Bland insisted.

'I used to call my father "Wizard", in reference to his priestly legerdemain with the sacred elements. Which that good-natured man did his best to take in good part.'

Bland gazed sadly out of the window at the high chimneys of those brick works which are not more than ten minutes away from Peterborough. A whiff of the sour smell of the brick-making came to us in the carriage. The waiter was bringing our bills.

'But Grick', I repeated, 'who is he?'

'He is the hope of English painting, according to Peter. It is not surprising if you have never heard of him, for he has not yet exhibited a picture anywhere. He does not apparently consider that the world at large is yet ready to have the privilege of looking at his work. He is Peter's man of genius. An evil genius. He's ghastly.' Bland paused and his eyes, staring abstractedly out of the window, were taking on a far-away look, and I was beginning to think I had lost him, when he spoke again.

'Sex', he said.

'Yes?' I answered encouragingly, hoping that this was an opening rather than a final pronouncement. 'Does sex play a part in Peter's scheme of things?'

'I suppose', said Bland, 'that most parents, when they see their children becoming of a marriageable age, begin to think with pleasure of the time when they may become grandparents.'

'Of course', I agreed warmly. 'You could not have said anything more apposite to me.'

'There's a girl, Spark', he said, without a hint of pleasure in his expression. 'She's ghastly. But I have said to his mother, she's not the sort of girl he'll marry. And anyhow, tolerance, tolerance, tolerance. We can't expect to be able to choose the people they'll marry. Peter incidentally has often said he disapproves of marriage. He breaks his mother's heart by the things he says, by his stony, unloving ways. Well then, there's Spark.'

Bland paused for cogitation.

'I've always thought', he said, 'that morality would gain rather than lose by the disappearance of religious sanctions. I mean, it is better to be good simply out of love of goodness rather than by hope or fear.'

We had no time for this sort of thing.

'But Spark', I said, 'have you seen her lately?'

'I saw her this morning', he said with distaste. 'Yes, I had to be in London last night for a dinner and this morning I went round to see Peter in his studio. It's a good-sized studio he has, with a little bedroom off it, all of which I pay for. You'd think, wouldn't you, that there'd be an occasional expression of gratitude? It was partly in order to tell him that it's about time he earned some money of his own that I went to see him. I found the studio door slightly open and walked in. He had heard me coming up the stairs and was standing at the other side of the room watching. I was hardly inside the room before I had to stop short in order not to walk on a great picture, or should we say a great area of liquid paint on a canvas, that covered a large part of the floor. Indeed, I had put one foot on a bit of it, it came up so close to the door, and, the paint being wet and thick, I had made a mark on it. "I'm awfully sorry", I said, as I drew back. Peter looked disappointed. "I'd hoped", he said, "that you'd walk across it. Footsteps of irate father striding over masterpiece of delinquent son. It would have been the making of the picture". "But, Peter", I said, "I'm not irate. Let me have a look at it". He stared at me sullenly as I walked round the picture. So far as I could judge the half-dozen crude colours of which the work consisted were of builder's paint poured generously onto half a dozen spots distributed over the canvas. There were disagreeable snaky bands of coagulation where the various pourings met one another. I couldn't think of anything to say. "Which is the right way up?" I asked. "There isn't one", he said, "it's only meant to be looked at from above". Presently I noticed the mark as of a ladder lying diagonally across the paint, which must have been made by the falling or laying of some wooden steps that I saw leaning against the wall of the studio. "Is it called Snakes and Ladders?" I asked good-naturedly. "No", he said coldly. "Then what is it called?"

"Impossible to say at present. It depends whether anything more happens to it while the paint's wet." "Happens to it?" "Happens to it." Peter pointed with a billiard cue at the marks of the steps and I noticed the prints of some bare feet apparently going up the ladder. "That was Spark", he said.

'Then I had an idea. I have mentioned family jokes. I'm rather keen on them. They can, of course, be overdone and become a bore and one certainly shouldn't foist them on people who are not members of the family. But the not too frequent reiteration of things we have all once found funny can make for goodwill, can't it? Well, we once had an odd-job man who was rather a card. Some wistaria had grown right up onto the roof and was blocking the gutter. We had borrowed a long ladder from the farm and put it against the side of the house. It was all bendy. If you shook it, a wriggle seemed to go up it as if along the back of a caterpillar. We were all standing around the base. Ernest, the odd-job man, looked shrewdly up the steps. "You need a good man at the bottom of the ladder", he said, decisively taking up his position at the bottom. His words became for us a proverbial expression and the occasion was one that Peter particularly was happy to remember for he was the hero of the hour. He cannot have been more than twelve at the time. He it was who went up the ladder and cut the creeper.

'"Well", I now said to Peter, "I'll make my footprints here if you like," pointing to the lower end of the step marks, "you need a good man at the bottom of the ladder." He shook his head without a hint of a smile. He wasn't going to move one inch in goodwill towards me.

'"What do you think of it?" he said presently, after an awkward silence, during which I heard movements next door. "I think it's quite, quite brainless", I said. At last he grinned. "Hurrah!" he said. "How perfect! How splendid! My purpose has been achieved". And he gave me a look of amused and ironically benevolent condescension. His words, I take it, primarily meant that he was satisfied to have had from me a verdict that he knew was meant to be depreciatory. Praise from me would, by his values, have been abuse. They may also have sincerely meant that I had hit upon the quality that he regarded as the main virtue of his work.

'At this moment Spark came into the room. She gave me a nod of recognition. She was wearing only a shift and was perfectly filthy from her tousled hair down to the soles of her bare feet which made paint marks on the floor. "What does he think of it?" she said through the cigarette that hung from her mouth. Peter told her. She gave a hoarse laugh that ended in a smoker's cough. The thing I must tell you about her disgusting appearance that had most hit me in the eye was that she was several months gone with child.

'"I expect you'd like to sit down", she said. "I'm afraid there aren't any chairs in here. We could go and sit on the bed." The idea of sitting on a bed with those two, me attempting to talk to Peter about money and—my God—about a good many other things too, did not appeal to me. Anyhow, I'd do it better in writing. So I said it was time for me to go to the station, as indeed it was. To my surprise Peter said he would come with me. So we went together by the underground to King's Cross. As soon as I was alone with him, I broached the question of money. I did this first, because I had prepared what I was going to say on that subject, not because I failed to recognise that Spark and her pregnancy were now problem number one. On that problem I needed time to think and to talk to my wife. His reaction about the money was unexpectedly mild. He didn't argue at all. In fact he hardly seemed interested. He just smiled with impassive condescension. I repeated what I had to say several times, to make quite sure that it was sinking in. He just nodded.

'After that I began to talk about Spark. I was as polite as I could be in my approach, but by the time we were on the platform at the station I was saying that he need not look to me to support his illegitimate children by that filthy and immodest slut. We were standing outside the carriage. Perhaps you saw us?'

I nodded.

'"It's not my child", he said, "it's Grick's." "Grick's", I said. "And she's living with you?" "Yes", he said. "Is he going to marry her?" I asked. "No. He doesn't want to get married at present. Anyhow he can't marry her now. She's married." "Who to?" "Me", he said. "She married me yesterday". At that point—' Bland hesitated.

'At that point,' I said, 'you hit him.' He nodded.

I began to rise from my seat as the train was slowing into Peterborough.

'It's a world of cretins', he said. 'They seem to have eliminated thought itself.'

He too stood up.

'I've got to go back to the carriage and collect my things', I said. 'It's been lovely to see you, Arthur, though I have been harrowed by your story.'

'I do hope I haven't been a bore', said Bland, as we shook hands. 'It has been a relief to me to talk and I could not have been luckier—could I?—in having you as an audience.' He rewarded me with a look of sincere affection. '"That listening boy".'

Tree of Knowledge

The prospect of the garden, seen from a deck chair on the lawn under the beech tree, with its back to the house, was as peaceful as a summer day allows, certainly as most summer days allowed on that lawn. For there was not a human being in sight, save Miss Turberville, sitting over there by the rose bed doing a watercolour of the house. The voices of children could not, for the moment, be heard, even from the distance. The combined age of himself and Miss Turberville, the old man reflected, was a hundred and forty-four. Put him and her end on and you would get back to Shelley.

The distractions, of course, were there for anyone who was ready to be distracted. Watching the wagtail on the grass, during the five minutes in which it would, from time to time, honour our lawn with its tread,—*there* was an occupation which anybody will agree should have precedence over all others; an impeccable excuse for letting one's attention linger. 'I could not leave before Royalty.' Oddly, it always used to come alone. 'Our' wagtail, it was called, though, in truth, all the proprietorship was on the other side. It came and went. Bound to the soil, we were its subjects.

Again, the occasional visits of our green woodpecker were on no account to be missed. Violent in its gold and red plumage, violent in its way of jabbing at the grass, it might stay, if not disturbed, for several minutes busy in one place. When it was back in the shrubbery, one would wait for the violence of its harsh, sarcastic laugh. The lawn might now be left for some time to the thrushes, blackbirds and sparrows, until a troop of unmannerly starlings would invade it, hurrying this way and that, taking possession, like a gang of adolescents at a seaside resort. 'Shoo!' Miss Turberville had been heard to say. 'I don't paint starlings.' In fact, she would not have to wait long before their impatience and roving curiosity had moved them out of the picture.

Somewhere up in the beech tree, above the old man's head, a greenfinch would keep saying 'Squeeze, squeeze', 'Squeeze, squeeze.' He knew that he was most unlikely to be able to see the bird from where he sat, so did not strain his neck by looking up. Anyhow, why strain at his age? The pleasures of disengagement may as well be enjoyed. Just add one more item to the huge, happy, list of things you no longer care to try to do: Looking for a greenfinch in a beech tree that is in full leaf.

Following the movement of a cabbage-white butterfly would involve no strain. To account for its movements, however, was not easy. Drawn by what scents or what attractive brightness would it set out, away from the flower border, to cross the vastness of the lawn, only to lose all direction in that void? As well ask what prompts a hedgehog or a mouse to set out so purposefully across the unpromising surface of a road that it probably cannot see the other side of. As well ask what was going on in the mind of William, the eldest grandchild, who could be seen, deep in thought among the trees, crossing the path that led from the edge of the lawn through the plantation. His parents used to get a bit impatient with the young man and looked forward to the end of 'this wool-gathering phase'. 'But you must give the inoculation time to work', his grandfather would say, 'and once it has taken, it will last for life.' William at present was in a high intellectual fever brought on by the mystical or ecstatic influence of Blake, Wordsworth, Shelley, Crashaw, and Plato.

The grandfather, however, did not mean to surrender to any of these distractions. With the promise of a visit to Italy in the autumn, in the company of William, he was, from a notebook in his hand, improving his Italian vocabulary. It had been his practice for half a century to note in pocket books the words that he did not know which he met in his reading of foreign literature. The older booklets hardly needed perusing any more, as they consisted almost entirely of old friends. The page he was now looking at contained a run of bird names. As often before, he was struck by an inconsistency in his erudition, a putting of the cart before the horse. For what was the logic of knowing the Italian equivalent of an English word, when he did not know what the English word meant? Until he could recognise a woodchat shrike, both by its appearance and its song, and distinguish it confidently from a red-backed shrike, what right had he to qualify himself to drop *averla capirossa* or *averla piccola* knowingly into his conversation with Italians? He had never, as a matter of fact, met the kind of Italians, if they exist, who talk about shrikes. '*Usignolo di padule*', he read, 'Cetti's warbler'. What on earth was that like? Incidentally, you would have expected Cetti's name to appear in the Italian, wouldn't you? For he must have been an Italian. Some eighteenth century naturalist, no doubt. With descendants, perhaps. And the old man allowed his imagination to wander. He and William would be strolling along the terrace of a vineyard above a ravine, when a distinguished gentleman coming towards them would take off his hat, with old-fashioned courtesy.

'*Buona sera.*'

'*Buona sera, signore.*'

He hoped they were not trespassing, the grandfather would say, they were enjoying the calm of the evening and the beauty of the Tuscan landscape, always beautiful but particularly so at this late season, when the leaves were red and gold. They were English, the other would ask? Yes, English. He participated, the Italian would say, in the Englishman's love of nature. Alas, on all sides nature was being destroyed. An agreeable, if conventional, little conversation would follow in the course of which the Italian would inform them that he was the proprietor of that ancient, pink *palazzo* that they had been admiring as they came along the hill side. In a pause in the talk the sound of a bird's twittering would come up from the acacias in the gorge. 'It is, of course, very late in the year, but do I', the grandfather would venture, 'do I hear an *usignolo di padule*?' The Italian, who up to now had been friendly, would open his eyes wide with joy and become positively affectionate. Gripping the grandfather's hand with both of his, he would all but kiss him. 'Cetti's warbler', the latter would add casually, 'that's what we call it in English.' The Italian meanwhile would be feeling for his wallet from which he would take out a visiting card. 'My seven times great-grandfather', he would say. '*Conte* Alessandro Cetti' would be written on the visiting card. Presently the English couple would find themselves dining exquisitely in that pink *palazzo*, with its charming *contessa*, and its very special Chianti, and its generations of portraits, not to speak of its Furinis and Carlo Dolci, and Cetti's own eighteenth century butterfly net. All which would have impressed upon William that Knowledge, precise, meticulous, accurate Knowledge, is power.

Come on, back to the book. Meadow pipit, *pispola*, wood lark, *calandra*—

'Grandpa', said the voice of the five-year-old Philip.

'Hullo, are *you* there, Phil?'

'You didn't know I'd come up behind your chair, did you?'

Grunt.

'Did you?'

'No.'

' 'Cos I was as quiet as when it's night. Grandpa.'

' 'Mm.'

'Are you busy?'

'Yes.'

'I saw you through a little hole in that wooden fence. It was like a window. I pretended I was drawing back the curtains to look out. Then I pretended I was a postman bringing you a letter, when I came across the grass. Here it is.' He handed his grandfather a leaf.

'Aren't you going to read it?'

Tree creeper, *rampichino alpestre*, bullfinch—

'Grandpa, tell me a story.'

'My pipit.' The old man surrendered and shut his book.

Telling stories to Phil was not, in fact, at all an exacting job. You simply had to say 'Once upon a time there was a little boy who went out of the house by the back door and into the wood,' and he was on fire with excitement. He would not want to know what sort of a house it was or what sort of a wood. Everyone knows what a house is like, or a wood. Any baby can draw such things. Most nouns, indeed, that passed through Philip's thought, at least during the periods of imaginative creation—storytelling, for instance, or drawing—(but what periods of Philip's day were not so spent?)—most nouns carried for him simply the Platonic idea of the object for which they were the label. And this for him was wholly satisfying. To clothe them with description, to make them particular, would, if anything, clog the poetical movement with which the slowest and most wooden of monosyllables would be dancing before his mind. The little boy of the story, however, had better have a name and an age.

'The little boy was called Robert.'

'No, Robin.'

'All right, Robin. He was nearly six years old.'

'No, quite six.'

'All right, quite six.'

Phil generally took complete charge of a story before its end.

'Go on,' he said.

'Presently, after he'd been walking for about an hour he thought he'd like to climb a tree. Just in front of him there was a very high tree.'

'Was it very, very high?'

'It was frightfully high. Looking up at it he couldn't see the top.'

'It was so high that it reached the sky. It was billions high. It was the highest tree in the whole world.'

'That's it. It was more than twice as high as the giant who lived in the forest.'

The narrator paused to allow this gigantic fact to have its effect.

'Go on, go on,' said Phil.

'Well, Robin began climbing the tree, and when he was about three-quarters of the way up, he heard a grinding sort of noise below him which was made by the giant who had seen him climbing the tree from a long way off and had brought his saw to cut the tree down and catch Robin that way.'

'Grandpa', called an approaching voice.

Philip's elder brothers, John and Paul, aged eleven and twelve came up to the chair. They had bunches of wild flowers in their hands.

'Grandpa, will you help to tell us what these are, the ones we don't know?'

'Your Granny's much better at flowers than I am.'

'Yes, but she's not back yet.'

'This is tansy, isn't it?'

'Yes, that's tansy.'

'Oh, go away,' said Philip, 'he's telling a story.'

'What about?'

'A little boy who'd climbed three-quarters way up a very high tree that grew right up into the sky.'

'That's silly,' said John. 'Trees don't grow as high as the sky. Anyhow, even if they did, the boy wouldn't be able to breathe at that altitude, unless he had carried up some oxygen. The atmosphere's too thin.'

'And the leaves of the tree couldn't breathe either', Paul added.

'Leaves don't breathe', said Philip.

'Yes they do, silly. It's the chlorophyll in them.'

'It's the chlorophyll', John echoed.

'I tell you what, Phil', said the grandfather, 'let's just go through these flowers with Paul and John, and then we'll carry on with the story.'

'All right', the little boy agreed disconsolately.

'This one', Paul said, 'is it agrimony?'

'Yes', said the grandfather, 'well done, it's hemp agrimony.'

'And this?'

'This—I don't know.'

'And this?'

'Oh, that's tormentil. The next, I don't know for certain.'

'You don't know much, do you?' said John.

'It might be mullein, perhaps', said the old man.

'The leaves are pinnate', said Paul.

'Oh', Philip groaned, 'this is awfully dull. When can we get back to the story about the giant?'

'Story about a giant?' John said. 'That's a baby story. There aren't such things as giants. Don't interrupt, Phil.'

'The leaves are pinnate,' Paul repeated.

There are times, the grandfather thought, when knowledge can be rather a bore.

'I've got an idea,' he said. 'Miss Turberville might be able to help us.'

'But we're not supposed to interrupt Miss Turberville when she's painting.'

'I know, but I'll write her a letter asking her and Phil can be the postman. Will you, Phil?'

'All right.'

So he tore a page out of his diary, wrote on it, twisted it into a triangle and addressed it. Philip ran with it.

'What's this one?' Paul said, holding a yellow flower. 'It was growing in the stream but it's not king-cup.'

'That I know, it's musk. There, she's reading the note, we needn't wait for an answer, you can go now.' So they followed Philip and had presently joined him to lean heavily on Miss Turberville as they criticised the water-colour.

Now, where was he? Meadow pipit, *pispola* (accent on the first), agrimony, *agrimonia* no doubt, but who should say where the accent was? 'There aren't such things as giants.' He ought not to have allowed John to get away with that. He must prepare William for the experience, in a Mediterranean country, of finding himself a giant.

'Oh, hullo William.'

The boy laid his great awkward length along the grass beside the chair, and gazed dreamily up into the tree. Conversation with him was like the utterance at a Quaker meeting. Until somebody had something special to say, communication took the form of an understanding silence.

'I was by the pond', William said at length.

'Yes?'

'A swallow dipped and drank. It was the moment of inspiration.'

'Quite.'

'Life suddenly became literature. Then it was all over.'

'How well I know.'

Philip was running towards them, with a note in his hand.

'From Miss Turberville', he said.

At the bottom of the grandfather's note she had written 'Agrimony and tormentil to you, and I hope they hurt!' Ha! Good old Annie!

'Now will you go on with the story?' Philip said, but at that moment a scrunching on the gravel of the drive at the other side of the house could be heard.

'There they are', he shouted and ran to meet them.

'The inspiration should not come and go', William went on. 'The holiness should be continuous. One should make it so.'

'Quite.'

The grandfather saw his wife walking out onto the lawn and his son and daughter and daughter-in-law with her arm round Philip.

'Here they are', he said.

'Damn!' said William. 'Now there'll be a lot of arrangements.'

Heaving himself onto his feet, he slouched off into the plantation. A splendid chap in his way.

Arrangements! My age-group, thought the old man, has various random uses of a casual nature, and when it comes to arrangements we are positively indispensable.

The Funeral

Kitty's friends had rallied for the occasion. They had come in force, not only from the country but from London, to mourn (or celebrate?) the passing of Jack Fordes. Gerald parked his car, at the directions of a rustic, among many other cars in a paddock next to the church. Stepping out of it, he heard the larks singing. Looking around, he found the Cotswold landscape in the sunshine of this April afternoon no less beautiful than he remembered. And nothing seemed to have been done to spoil the village, the stone walls, the old stone church or the manor house across the road from the churchyard. The place, as always, had that basking look. While he was walking towards the church, the bell began to toll.

The pews in the nave were already largely filled. As he came in, many of the heads turned to look at him. This was evidently a social gathering of some consequence. At a welcoming smile from John and Beryl who were sitting on the outside of the last row but one on the south of the aisle, he stepped over their feet to a vacant seat, made a gesture of prayer, then looked about him. Here again there was no sign of change that he could see since the times he used to come when staying with Jack in his holidays from school. There were the family box pews they used to sit in, the Fordes tombs and tablets on either side of the chancel, the altar frontal woven by William Morris himself. What sort of a monument, Gerald wondered, would they put up to Jack?

'Poor old Jack', whispered Beryl, 'it's a mercy he's gone.'

'It is indeed', answered Gerald.

'What Kitty must have been through!'

'What indeed!'

Beryl could have no idea quite what a mercy it was that Jack was gone. She did not know, no one knew, Jack himself had not had the faintest idea, that his departure would allow two broken lives to be mended. It would reward eighteen years of self-denying virtue with perhaps twenty or thirty years of bliss. Gerald was forty-eight, Kitty a year or two younger.

The organ began to play 'Jesu, joy of man's desiring'. Damn! That moving little tune caught him off his guard. The physical reaction was instantaneous. He wondered how many other strong men in the church were biting their lips to keep back the welling tears. Tears, by the way, that were hardly at all the result of a particular grief, but simply of the music itself, made, no doubt, a little more moving by being played on an occasion dedicated to sorrow; though, as far as that went, if the occasion had been a happy one, a marriage, for instance, the welling would have been just the same. Let us simply say then, on an occasion. Reasoning thus with himself and biting hard, Gerald turned off the gas flame. The milk that had foamed almost up to the edge of the saucepan began to go down. He had mastered himself. After all, the mastering of emotion had been his life's work, had it not? With the aid of a facetious thought he was fully himself again. I wonder, he thought, what my halo looks like to the row behind.

Now Kitty was coming into the church on the arm of Paul, her eldest son, the second son and the daughter following. Reaching the box pew, they disappeared from sight on to their knees for a few moments, to reappear standing, Paul on the outside, then Kitty, then Rose, then Stephen—ah, Stephen! Gerald looked at the last with intense curiosity and saw a fine head of wavy black hair, that was certainly most unlike the trim blond covering of the elder brother. Then his eyes rested upon Kitty. The curls, now a little grey, over the back of the neck, the adorable ears, the incomparable carriage of the head—everything was still there and seemed to hold a message of fulfilment. Let the decencies first be observed (and what did he and Kitty not know about observing the decencies?) and all would be well. Bless that hallowed head, haloed if ever there was one. Now the congregation was standing up. The coffin was being brought in.

When It, the Thing in the box, that had once broken the school record for high jump, had been placed on the trestle, the clergyman began to speak. 'I said, I will take heed unto my ways that I offend not in my tongue.' Goodness, the heed that they had taken unto their ways! They had been as certain as they could be that neither Jack nor anybody else had had an inkling of what they were about. It was the strain of taking heed, together with a growing revulsion at the deceit, which at length had made them decide to terminate, so abruptly and so heroically, the course of true love. So, all in a moment, from being the bad, they had become the good. Never had anybody been the recipient of such Christian love and forbearance as Jack had. And he had not had the least idea of the fact. Rather a pity? No, one could not go that far and wish he should know all. For who could suppose that a knowledge of the bad would be cancelled, and more than cancelled, by a knowledge of the good they had done him?

Anyhow, now he would never know, and it was a great relief to have the anxiety out of the way. For, though the years had much diminished its attacks, there was still at times the dread in the middle of the night that some clue Jack might catch had been unhappily left about. The only fear now seemed to be from the questioning young. 'How was it,' they might ask, 'that father's best man went right out of his life?' 'Well,' Kitty would answer, 'he was posted abroad for some years, and then we gave up living in London when we came into this place on your grandfather's death, and so, one way and another, they drifted apart. I believe they still used to meet at times in London clubs.' Which statement would be entirely correct. 'And did you know him well?' They would persist. 'What's he like?' She would be equal to the question, except in one respect. She never had been able to control a blush. 'It all seems a bit mysterious', they would say, keeping the question open, 'if there was no quarrel or anything, his just disappearing like that.' So a certain minor worry would remain.

The major anxiety, however, was now gone for good. Jack would never know; or rather, would never have known. For Jack was now extinct, a Jack-in-the-box whose jumping days were over. Dear Jack. Gerald felt much affection towards the memory of his old friend, particularly the further back the memory went; for by the time of his marriage a distressing pompousness had been already setting in. Gerald remembered most exactly standing with Jack in the chancel there, being shown the monuments. He and Jack could not have been more than fifteen years old at the time.

'Do you believe in an after-life?' Jack had said.

'Er—I don't want to be rude to all these ancestors of yours—'

'Never mind them.'

'Well—of course—'

'Of course what?'

'Of course I don't.'

'Thank God. I was afraid you might', said Jack with a laugh, taking Gerald's arm and leading him out of the church.

This pact of more than thirty years ago was not one that Gerald had ever been tempted to break. So Jack was now, in every possible sense of the word, extinct. Looking around the church, Gerald wondered how many people present believed in the immortality of the soul. Perhaps half a dozen among the old, the old women that is, for he had never met an old man in a club who had the slightest use for the idea.

They were now singing a psalm. 'I will lift up mine eyes unto the hills from whence cometh my help.' Gerald's surname was Hill. Kitty must have chosen the words and music for this service. Was it possible that there was a deliberate pun here, a message back to him from the box pew?

Yes, he felt nothing but benevolence towards the deceased. Did not La Rochefoucauld say something about liking those you have treated well better than those you have treated badly? Or was it the other way round? Whichever it was, Gerald, who had treated Jack both badly and well, had La Rochefoucauld's support for liking him. And now, most likeably, he had disappeared, and there had been no broken house through Gerald's doing, no smirch on the Fordes family, nothing discreditable to that clan but what Jack himself had brought upon it. There was, it was true, one living lie, but as nobody had known about this except Kitty and himself, nor would, now, ever know, it could be discounted. And now the good conscience was going to have its reward. Gerald, his eyes on the box pew, gave himself over to the warmth that was tingling into his numbed spirit.

Of course, he knew nothing of Kitty's state of mind. He simply trusted. No word, spoken or written, had passed between them since that day, eighteen years ago, when, with a decisive blow, they had put out their flame. Knowing how fatally easy its re-lighting would be, they had contrived, according to plan, whenever chance occasionally brought them together in a room, to avoid one another or at most to exchange a polite smile. This would have caused no remark from anyone, for they had never been known to be friends. Discretion had guided them from the first. Throughout all these years, then, he had trusted hopelessly. Now he did so, with every hope. He was quite sure that Kitty was now wooing him in the church as excitedly as he was wooing her.

The congregation sat down while the parson gave a short address. He did not say that Jack Fordes should be a warning to those with plenty of money and not enough to do, to those who have inherited a comfortable position but have not character equal to their comfort. He did not say that he was a bore and a snob, who was quite unworthy of his angel wife. He did not say that the alcoholism of ancestors is no excuse and that when, driving under the influence, he had broken himself to pieces, he had only got what he deserved. He did say that life is short while eternity is more than long. That it is not for us to assess the moral performance of others. Before which of our neighbours would we care to open our whole souls? That 'our brother', carrying with him our love and our prayers, had now gone to a place where all human perplexities were resolved. Escaping quickly back from the particular to the general, the preacher finished his four minutes' discourse with an exhortation to prepare for the long rather than to snatch at the short.

'Rather a tactful performance', whispered Gerald.

'Or an opportunity missed?' smiled Beryl.

During the long separation Gerald had been informed of the way Kitty's married life had gone by various common friends. When the accident had taken place, and Jack was lying between life and death in the nursing-home, he had sent a message by one of the friends—his first communication with her since the parting—to ask whether it would be a good thing if he went to see Jack. The answer had come back, 'Thank you, no.' For weeks after that Jack had hung on. It was even being suggested that he might live for years, though terribly maimed and not right in the head. Then there had been the announcement in the paper, and now here they all were at this relaxed, happy funeral.

After some prayers, they stood and sang a hymn. What a lot he and Kitty were going to have to talk about, filling in the gap of time. On his side there would be little of consequence to tell, for he had had no lively relationship with anybody in those years. The two or three miserable attempts to find a substitute for Kitty were hardly worth mentioning. It would simply not be the very interesting tale of official Gerald, servant of the Crown in peace and war, who awoke each morning with a frozen heart. The interesting story would come from her side. For whereas he had, as it were, ceased to live, she, with husband and children, had had to go on living, however unnaturally. What mental and emotional travail she had been through in doing this, he had no idea. But there was one matter about which he was sure. In classical drama, the action is generally built around various amorous certainties. A loves B, who loves C, who loves D, who loves A, but nobody loves his lover. Or A loves B and B loves A, but duty intervenes. In the drama in which he and Kitty were the principal actors, Gerald was certain that, whatever might happen, Gerald loved Kitty, Kitty loved Gerald.

Now they were on their knees again, or rather, decently inclined forward, and the heads in the box pew had disappeared once more. Now they were standing while the strong men in black moved to lift the coffin. Remembering that film with the funny men carrying the grand piano, Gerald thought how Jack would have laughed at it, if he ever saw it, for he had had a simple sense of humour that kept breaking through. It was perhaps the best thing about him. Sharing this laugh with the deceased, Gerald felt he had made his final peace with Jack. Really, this was being the pleasantest of funerals.

As the faces of the bereaved, following the coffin, had to meet the eyes of the congregation, Gerald, for all his curiosity, looked away. Then, confound it, that tune struck up again. Not again, Kitty? There was a disagreeable hint of genuine emotion about its repetition. 'His favourite tune' or something of the kind. Angry at his own physical weakness, Gerald was constrained once again to bite back the welling, helped by the thought that, of course, Jack had had no favourite tune. His total lack of music had indeed been one of the many things that had made him so unworthy of the musical Kitty. The laughable incongruity of Bach making one weep for Jack! Come, come! Slowly the people walked out into the sunshine.

It might have been supposed that the dead of so proudly an armigerous family would have been put in a private vault under the church. The procession, however, followed the coffin to a corner of the churchyard where Jack was to be laid in the earth. The grass was dry, and towny, black shoes left the path and moved among the mounds to place themselves about the new grave. The larks were singing for all they were worth. Stephen was now the other side of the grave opposite Gerald, who let his eyes rest a moment upon him. What a sensitive unFordesy face! 'Man that is born of a woman,' read the clergyman, 'hath but a short time to live . . .' Mind that piano! Jack was lowered out of sight. 'Earth to earth, ashes to ashes, dust to dust.'

Free! Free! Gerald remembered the ending of that chapter in *The Count of Monte Cristo*, when the prisoner has escaped from the dungeon. '*Libre! Libre! Libre!*' Burtenshaw, in the desk next his, had been construing. 'A book! A book! A book!', he had said.

The family, after a look into the hole, began to move away. The people slowly followed them. 'Give me cremation every time,' whispered Beryl, 'it's a tidier job.' 'And yet,' answered Gerald, 'there's a suggestion of the phoenix about flames, of the whole blessed thing starting up again. This is somehow more satisfactorily final.' 'That's true.'

Paul, leaving his mother's arm, turned back among the people, moving from group to group. 'My mother says she hopes you'll come back to the house for some tea, anybody who would like to. All of you, please, all of you.' Gerald sensed that the company did not need pressing. Having got into those togs, and come all that way, they would, no doubt, have been disappointed not to have the opportunity of discreetly showing Kitty by their words and the expressions of their faces, how much they shared the happiness of her delivery. Moreover, there was probably not one of them who did not much look forward to a cup of tea. With the song of the larks in his soul, Gerald sauntered towards the house amidst the dry-mouthed and dry-eyed throng.

The procession wheeled to the right after coming out of the churchyard gate, moved about fifty yards along the road, then turned into the drive of the manor house on the left. It made no concession to an approaching car, the driver of which stopped and switched off his engine with the patience of one accustomed to meeting sheep on the highways. Once out of the churchyard on to the road, tongues had been loosened and voices raised. The party had begun. Primroses were growing on the grassy banks beneath the walls on either side of the road.

'A primrose path,' said Beryl.

'For a flock of "black sheep",' said Gerald, as they were directed into the drive. Beryl giggled.

'I say, it's a gem, *Château* Fordes,' John observed concerning the house before them. 'I bet the National Trust would like to have it. Do you know if they will be able to afford to go on living here?'

The question brought Gerald down, or rather a little of the long way he had to go down, to earth. The romantic coming together of himself and Kitty would indeed involve many practical adjustments. He certainly did not see himself staying, even for one night, in this house with which his only association would be best limited, as it now was, to the time before his first Kitty period. The time after that period would be one that they would both wish to forget as they made their new life well away from their places of endurance. There would be much, too, to consider with regard to the children. He had learned that Paul, who would come of age next year, was at an agricultural college. Stephen, the clever one (naturally), had been one term at Oxford. Sixteen-year-old Rose he understood to be in love with a horse. They were reported to be particularly nice children, who adored their mother and had made the best of their father. Perhaps, thought Gerald, in a few years, when they were all married, they could be let into some secrets.

The company followed Kitty into the house and up the stairs to the long gallery on the first floor. Here, on a side table beneath the portraits, there were three urns of tea and plates of sandwiches and cakes. Kitty herself moved to the far end of the room, discreetly, no doubt, not wishing to give a too convivial handshake to her guests as they came in. Opposite the portraits, at the other side of the gallery, there were distorted views through greenish leaded panes of lawn and yew hedges. Above the heads of the guests, geometrical patterns were woven in a plaster ceiling. The coat of arms appeared in the corner of several of the portraits, and was to be found, Gerald remembered, all over the place, along with the motto 'Mine is Mine,' in paint, plaster, wood, and iron.

Gerald was one of the last to come up the stairs into the gallery. He was in no hurry, sauntering along the primrose path towards Kitty. There were various faces from the past, and some from the present, he would have a word with before he came to her. He stood by the tea table, with a cup in his hand.

'Why, Gerald.'

'Reggie!'

'Still lying abroad for your country?'

'Consummately. At home, actually, for the moment. And you, still breaking wind?' Reggie was a distinguished organist.

'Vigorously. Dear Gerald, it's lovely to see you. Why don't we see each other oftener? Let's have dinner.'

They made an engagement for Wednesday week at the Travellers.

'Madge!'

'Gerald!'

'Let me pass you one of these sandwiches. Enjoy the funeral?'

'I always enjoy funerals. They're generally such a relief to everybody. You know the worst. At a wedding the worst is still to come.'

'Quite. I imagine this occasion must be a pretty happy one for all concerned. Do you ever see Kitty, by the way?'

'Hardly at all, for years. She was so stuck down here, devoting herself to that lout, and her family, and lots of good works, I believe. She's a good woman if ever there was one.'

'Indeed she is.' Madge could have no conception how good she was.

'Unlike a good many of these wives, I'll bet,' said Madge, surveying the row of portraits. 'What a ghastly motto to marry into! Enough to make one run off at the first opportunity! I must say, if I'd been Kitty, I'd have cleared out long ago, family or no family. What puzzles me a bit is that, living with her, he should have got worse rather than better. I mean, he was all right at first.'

'Hereditary.'

'Yes, but his father was not a drunk. I believe that you've got to go back to a great uncle. It's a tiny bit mysterious to me.'

The mystery, if it existed, was one that Gerald, in his present mood, did not care to explore.

'The poor chap!' he simply said, with unaffected generosity, as he took her empty cup and put it on the table.

'Hullo, Madge,' someone said, and she moved away.

Gerald found himself facing a tall man he did not know. They smiled at one another.

'I'm an old friend of the family, from London,' said Gerald. 'Do you live hereabouts?'

'Yes, just over there. If you could see through these rotten windows, I'd show you.'

Gerald thought that this was the sort of green half light in which Shakespeare must have worked. Indeed, there was a local legend associating the poet with this house. Gerald had often thought, by the way, that neither Shakespeare nor any other dramatist that he knew of had hit upon just the plot of the drama that he and Kitty had been acting in.

'I'm the local doctor,' the tall man went on.

'Oh, are you? Then you must have known Jack Fordes pretty well?'

'I did. At least, so far as it was possible to know him. He kept himself very much to himself.'

'It was a pity he went to pieces like that.'

'A great pity. I can't fully explain it. It was as though there was something gnawing him.'

'Thirst?'

'Partly. I was meaning something on his mind.'

'But there can't have been that,' said Gerald, almost crossly.

'I know, it's difficult to believe, especially when he had such a devoted family.'

'Gerald!' A hand was put on Gerald's shoulder.

'Glad to have met you,' he said to the doctor, and turned to his acquaintance.

So, with a smile here and an exchange of words there, he advanced slowly along the gallery. Rose passed in front of him at one moment, carrying a plate of sandwiches, looking exactly as Kitty must have looked at her age. Then suddenly he was face to face with Stephen. The boy's bright eyes looked at him questioningly.

'I must introduce myself,' said Gerald. 'My name is Gerald Hill. I used to know your father when we were boys.'

'I know. I'd have recognised you from the photographs. You were his best man.'

'That is so.'

'You have always been a bit of a mystery to us. Father always stalled when we asked him about you.'

To his surprise and distress Gerald found himself blushing.

'I want to tell you,' he said, 'how very sorry I am about your father.'

'Thanks. Not that there seems much reason for sorrow.'

'Er—in a sense no, perhaps—'

'It all depends what you think about an after-life, doesn't it?'

Gerald blinked. He had had little experience of talking with people of Stephen's age since he had been of that age himself. He now supposed that once upon a time he himself may have said things like that, long, long, ago, before he became smooth.

'But, your generation, of course—' Stephen went on.

'My generation?'

'Well, you mostly seem to be non-starters on this subject. Mother's an exception.'

'You run me off my feet. And what does your generation think?'

'I think they are very close.'

'They?'

'The dead.'

'Oh yes, the dead.'

'Mother thinks so too. She says it's like having him continually in the room, as real or more real, because sober, than in real life.'

'She says that, does she?'

'And then they know what you're thinking.'

'Ah.'

'They know everything, at least a great deal, both of the past and the future. Spiritualistic experience helps to prove that. And they remain tremendously interested in everything that is going on here.'

'Tremendously.'

'Which doesn't necessarily mean that they are at once happier.'

'No, no.'

'What they now know may in fact make them very sad indeed. But they are happier than we are in being one stage further on.'

'Quite.'

There was a pause.

'Mother hoped there wouldn't be a great party like this,' Stephen said, 'but we kept her to it. We said it was the least we could do if people turned up at the church. She hoped lots of people from far away wouldn't come. She particularly hoped that you would not think it necessary to turn up. She said so.'

'Oh, it's—it's nothing.'

It had begun to seem to Gerald stiflingly hot in this green gallery.

'What are you all going to do?' he said.

'It seems to be laid on by Mr Charteris that we can all go on living here. He's the lawyer, by the way. He's wizard. Then, if Paul gets married, there's a little house in the village Mother has her eye on. She says she'd hate to leave the neighbourhood. And then she's got all her jobs. She'll never give up sitting on the bench, if she can help it. She's a great one against sexual offences under hedges.'

Gerald interpreted this last sentence (correctly) as a brave attempt to put an embarrassed elder at his ease. The attempt was wholly unsuccessful.

'And of course,' Stephen went on, 'she'll never marry again. She has as good as promised that.'

'She has?'

With each blow the boy dealt him Gerald felt himself being forced backwards on to the ropes.

'And your—your father,' he asked faintly, 'how was he at the end?'

'Pretty sad. Of course, he didn't know how to laugh, not properly.

Never did. At least, I never heard him. When he was in the nursing home, he got delirious. The last thing he said to me was "You damned bastard!" Funny; it wasn't one of his words.'

Gerald backed from the bright eyes that were upon him. Luckily, at that moment, with an 'excuse me', a body passed between him and Stephen. He drew away into the crowd and back through the gallery the way he had come, and down the stairs, and out into the drive and the road. Gerald, you poor fool, you damned, dumb, miserable fool! So Jack too had known and been keeping the secret? For how long? And how much did Stephen know? Sorry, Jack, I'm sorry, sorry, sorry.

Gerald walked hurriedly, but aimlessly, into the churchyard. His conversation with Stephen had made him very uncomfortable indeed. For the moment, in fact, he had no wish whatever to go on being alive.

Fourth Centenary

Martin was the first of the house party to come down to the library, where drinks were taken before dinner. He had a purpose. It seemed to him that he had once seen on the shelves there such a work as he was seeking. Putting on his spectacles, he followed a row of books until—yes, here it was, a *Dictionary of Provincial and Obsolete Words*, in two volumes. Taking out the second of the volumes he stood consulting it, with his back to the room. 'Snowze', he read 'to pry into.' H'm. It was as bad as he had feared. He turned the page. Absorbed in his quest, and in the sombre thoughts it occasioned, he was unaware that his host had come into the room.

Philip stood a moment at the door, entranced by the sight of his library. The room in its structure, decoration and most of its furniture was the work of Robert Adam. The brick and russet tones that, in the lamplight, glowed from painted surfaces and the leather tops of tables and desks, and from the backs of the books, combined with the elegant geometry of the ceiling, of the pilasters of the bookcases and the lunettes above them and of the library ladder stationed in a rounded alcove, to produce an effect of intellectual warmth as inviting as a glass of Madeira. And there, beneath a lamp, under the invigilation of blind, marble, Homer, a man of learning was standing, reading. This, Philip thought proudly, is civilisation.

He tiptoed up to his guest and took him by the arm.

'Martin.'

'Philip.'

Committing to memory the entry relating to 'snudge', Martin shut the book and looked at his friend. It must have been evident, even to Homer, that the two of them were glad to see one another. Their friendship, indeed, of long standing, was one that had steadily ripened in spite of some testing facts. The first of these was an immense disparity of income. Martin, who sometimes felt that Philip must be the proprietor of half England, frankly did not have an acre or a tenant. Another was that Martin was in Philip's employment. Another, and subtler matter was that—however much he (Martin) might now disclaim it—Martin, during the war, had saved Philip's life. When all around was turmoil, he had, by coolly manipulating the pressure points and improvising a bandage, prevented his friend from bleeding to death, then laboriously lugged him, at great danger to himself, to a place of safety. The episode might have been fatal to friendship, but Philip, unlike Monsieur Perrichon, did not resent his saviour. 'Oh shut up!' Martin would say, if ever the subject seemed to be coming to the surface, and in fact it was now a banned topic between them.

'He's really a man of action,' Philip would say to others. 'You'd never think it, would you? Such a quiet chap.'

The job that Martin did was indeed a quiet one. He was engaged on making a catalogue of the archives in Philip's muniment room. Not long after the war, and a few weeks after Philip had succeeded his father, Martin had paid him a visit. Philip was intoxicated with his new possessions. There was so much to look at, and it was not till the afternoon of the second day that they had reached the muniment room. Philip had inherited from his father a middle-aged gentleman, known as the archivist-librarian, a Mr Beecham.

'I warn you,' said Philip, 'he's rather a bore, but he's a kind of institution. Of course, I'm sure he's good at the stuff. My father loved him. I find him a social blight. I'd welcome anything you have to say about the way he's doing things, as it's your line of country.'

They walked up a steep staircase to what was called the turret room, where the archivist worked. An iron door opened from this chamber into the muniment room. They could be heard coming and when they went into the archivist's sanctum Mr Beecham was at his desk, bent over an ancient parchment deed. He lingered just three seconds over his work after their entry before he looked up. Philip introduced his guest.

'My friend is in your way of business,' he explained. 'What have we got to show him? Is there anything special you'd like to see, Martin?'

Martin had been looking around the place. The first thing he had noticed on coming in was that Mr Beecham was smoking a pipe. He was the kind of pipe smoker who fills his pipe to overflowing so that, when he lights it, sparks fall out from the bowl. Mr Beecham's pipe had evidently been lit only shortly before their entry. As he rose to shake hands, he brushed aside sparks off his desk, and off the manuscript that lay upon it. The smoke from his pipe and from the log fire that was crackling in the hearth made a haze through which Martin deciphered the cardboard labels, yellow with smoke and curling at the edges, which were tacked on the tops of the bookshelves that lined the walls. On these were written, in fading ink, in a pseudo lombardic script, HISTORY, LOCAL HISTORY, GENEALOGY, ARCHIVES, etc. The room was exceedingly warm and snug.

'I'd like to see the Gautby cartulary,' Martin said.

Mr Beecham laughed genially.

'I might have guessed you'd say that! If only I'd had notice of your coming! I'll have it for you tomorrow morning, if you're going to be here. It happens to be across at my place.'

Philip frowned. He had been told the other day that this lovely manuscript would fetch five, if not six, figures at Sotheby's.

'At your place?'

'Don't worry, don't worry. It's as safe as houses in my hands. Let's look at this instead.' And he directed Martin's attention to the parchment on the desk.

'Early thirteenth century, but I don't have to tell you that. As a matter of fact,' he went on, one professional to another, Philip excluded, 'there's a little word here that stumps me. Perhaps you could read it for me. "*Ac*"—something.'

Martin bent over the document and followed Mr Beecham's pointing finger.

'It looks to me like '*acecia*", said the latter helpfully, 'but I can't find such a word in the dictionary.'

'I haven't the least idea,' Martin said, giving up with a speed that surprised both Philip and Mr Beecham.

'Then I'm not such a fool,' the archivist said with a chuckle that should have sounded complacent but actually sounded a bit uneasy.

Philip was looking at Martin's face. It had taken on the look he had learned to expect from it at moments of danger or crisis, a look of masterful, disciplinary, control, that pressure-point look, as he called it.

To break the silence that had followed Martin's last words, Mr Beecham began a lecture on the Star Chamber. Philip, catching Martin's eye, tried to indicate his apologies and after a few minutes cut in.

'I'm afraid we're in a bit of a hurry, Beecham. Could you just let us have a look into the muniment room?'

'By all means.'

To move from the archivist's room into the repository was like stepping from a hot hall out into a winter's night.

'Phew!' said Philip, with a shudder.

'How's the place heated?' Martin inquired.

'It isn't heated,' Mr Beecham answered. 'I don't believe in heating. I'm old fashioned. I say that the documents got on very well for several centuries without heating. In fact they survived and here they are. Has it ever occurred to anyone that the conditions suited them? Oh, I know I'm not in the mode.' He puffed his pipe with self-satisfaction. 'Go on,' he said, as Martin stretched out a hand, 'take down anything that interests you.'

Martin took down at random a parchment covered volume of accounts of the period of Charles I. The outer sides of the cover were furry with mildew, as were the insides, as, when he looked into it, was the inside of the spine, while the paper pages of the book were blotched with damp stains and could not be turned without disturbing the lump of decaying sponge into which their lower two inches were coagulated and from which fragments fell even at Martin's gentle touch. Before putting the book back he examined the next one in the series on the shelf, and the next, and the next. All were in a similar condition. At length he put the first one back, gave Mr Beecham a look and remarked to Philip that he was afraid they would catch their death of cold if they stayed longer in the muniment room. Philip was in complete agreement with him on this.

'Thank you, Beecham,' he said.

'Thank you,' said Martin, and leaving the archivist in his smoky den they came down the stairs.

'Well?' Philip said, when they were out of possible earshot.

'He must go. He's a humbug.'

'I've always suspected it.'

'He doesn't know the first principles of his profession.'

'Taking that cartulary over to his cottage, without asking me is pretty cool, isn't it?'

'It's deplorable, for every reason. Do you know what that word was he couldn't read? It was *ac etiam* or, as they used to write it in the Middle Ages, *eciam*, meaning 'and also'. They used to run the words together, *aceciam*, a very common expression indeed in a mediaeval document. He seems to have taken it as the accusative of a noun, *acecia*, which he could not find in the dictionary!'

'And the Star Chamber?'

'He seems quite unaware of the advances made by scholarship since he was at school. And then all that damp and mildew! You soon won't have any archives left at that rate of decay! And smoking like that over the records! One way and another his offences nearly add up to the archival sin against the Holy Ghost.'

'And what is that?'

'Actually to use the documents as spills.'

So Beecham went. He was replaced by Miss Davies who was principally librarian, having no training in archives. The responsibility for the custody of the records was given to her, however. In the now well heated (but not over heated) muniment room she would each morning study the instrument which registered the relative humidity of the air and adjust the ventilation accordingly. She would produce for any serious student who had had the owner's permission such records as he or she wished to see, and she would answer such letters as she was able to answer. Questions that were beyond her were referred to the new part-time archivist, who was no other than Martin. Here it must be stated, in parenthesis, that Martin's strictures upon his predecessor had had no ulterior motive whatever, nor did Philip ever suppose that they had had. Martin, in fact, had needed some persuading to add this job to his various other jobs of a similar nature.

He was mainly responsible for continuing the catalogue of the records where Beecham's predecessor had left off. (During Beecham's twenty years almost no progress had been made on the catalogue.) Boxes and tins and bundles and bundles of estate records lay unexplored, tied up in packets or loosely massed as the steward's clerks had put them away one, two, three, four centuries ago. Martin would come for a fortnight, three or four times a year, take his seat in the turret room and work his way through the bundles and tins and boxes, arranging, numbering and listing. His descriptive lists, arranged estate by estate, within a topographical framework, numbered chronologically and rounded off by an alphabetical index of persons and places, were typed and bound. Already half a dozen buckram-covered volumes could be seen on a shelf to the right of his desk. Blissful, boring, alphabetical, numerical, topographical, chronological, work. Not always so boring . . .

He was now staying for one of his fortnights. The family had been away the evening before, when he had arrived, and had not returned until today, so that their encounter in the library before dinner had been his first meeting with Philip on this visit.

'Had a good day up there?' the latter asked.

'Of course.'

Martin adored his days in the turret room. No household noises ever found their way up that remote, steep stair; while the window looked over an area of the park through which no traffic passed either to the front or the back doors. The silence in the room was broken only by such sounds as he himself chose to make and in winter by the crackling of the fire and the occasional contented creak with which old furniture responds to warmth. The hush, like the parchments under his hands, took him out of this raucous age and placed him, like St Jerome in a primitive picture, in timeless fixity at his desk. The only interruptions to his work came upon him now and then unawares as, looking up from his manuscript and gazing out at the park, generally by way of the left side of the heavy stone mullion that divided his window into two, so that his eyes went directly up the centre of the lime avenue to the distant temple, he presently realised that his thoughts had been wandering. He remembered reading somewhere that St John of the Cross was happiest looking out of a window at the top of a tower, scouring the horizon for some celestial vision. He was neither St John of the Cross nor St Jerome, but sometimes, he felt, not far off.

This day had begun normally and well. Everything was set. The fire was bright as he entered the room about 9 a.m.; the day's supply of logs was in the basket. His work awaited him on the floor beside the desk and consisted of the next of many unexamined black tin boxes, measuring about three feet all ways, on the side of which was printed in white paint WARWICKSHIRE ESTATES 3.

Opening it he saw the familiar jumble of parchments and papers, some of them rolls, some of them packets tied with string, lying as they had been emptied out of some sack or off some shelf into this tin box perhaps a hundred years ago. Tudor or Stuart, the lot of them, he said to himself as he turned them gently over.

Ah, the Great Seal of James I. He lifted out a disk of bronze wax, about six inches in diameter, attached by pink silk threads to a sheet of parchment. It was the King's first seal too, not at all a common one to meet with, for James, by royal warrant, had soon had it replaced because 'the canopy over the picture of our face is so low imbossed that the Seal in that place doth easily bruise and take disgrace.' Yet, on this particular impression, 'our face', though dangerously prominent, had been not a whit bruised. Interesting. Perhaps worth an article. He laid the object back in the box and drew out a folded letter that allured him, but put it back before he had even read the name and address with which it was endorsed. Stop skimming off the cream, he rebuked himself. Manners! Take the one nearest you first, and observe your own rules.

At the same moment he had an access of that feeling of regret that sometimes comes over the archivist as it does over the archaeologist, the explorer and anyone who deflowers. Keep out! Leave things as they are for heaven's sake! It's not too late to call the whole business off.

Also of that unnerving sense of the great destructive power he had towards the defenceless objects beneath his hands, such as can be aroused by a baby in a pram or a picture in a gallery. How fatally easy, should one's reason slip for ten seconds, to smash the precious, vulnerable thing!

Overcoming both these habitual sentiments, he had set to work. For what he was about to receive might the Lord make him truly thankful.

'You find it quiet enough up there?' Philip continued.

'I found it as wonderfully quiet as ever. The rest is din.'

This rather cryptic answer, together with a familiar something about Martin's manner, caused Philip to look closely at his friend. Yes, the pressure was there. Martin had taken up his action station. To find out what it was all about must, however, wait, for other guests were coming into the library. In addition to various neighbours and their wives and two personages of the first importance from London, these included the mayor of a nearby town in which a repertory theatre was to be opened in a few weeks, and the first director of the said theatre, with his actress wife. Philip had taken much interest in the latter project. His donation had, in fact, made the scheme possible. And what more auspicious way of opening a theatre than with *Romeo and Juliet* in April of the year of the fourth centenary of Shakespeare's birth?

The fact of this much publicised anniversary, and of the recent appearance of various books about the national bard, and of many reviews of those books, together with the presence of the theatrical people and the imminence of the opening of their theatre, accounted for the phenomenon that as the company walked into dinner, they were all, one way or another, talking about Shakespeare. All that is to say, except Martin, who walked alone. Usually a sherry man, he had this evening, as Philip noticed, taken a strong cocktail. Assuredly something was afoot.

The moment of silence after the company had sat down to table was broken by a declaration from one of the important personages that he found Shakespeare's plays tedious to read and insufferable to watch, that all that killing on the stage was intolerably barbarous and the humour intolerably crude, and that the plays were clearly written to order, as were the sonnets, by a servile and go-getting snob. The devil's advocate having said his say, the process of beatification began. Almost every voice joined loudly in the chorus of praise. It was like the singing of the Hallelujah Chorus, Philip thought, a national event in miniature. One of the guests actually began to rise instinctively to his feet. The praise shifted after some minutes from the works to the man. Each was as lovely as the other. For Shakespeare, it was agreed, is our English saint, the self-effacing mirror of mankind, the most altruistic lover of his friend, the well-mannered, the sympathetic, the sweet-tempered, the gentle one, the gentleman of all time. To all of which the important personage simply raised his eyebrows and answered 'H'm.'

The talk then, while remaining general, shifted to the identity of Mr W. H. and the dating of the sonnets and various other things such as the emendation of 'a table of green fields', and Bardolph in the Chronicle, and the books that would have been used at Stratford grammar school, on which matters various people made a show of erudition. It is time, Philip thought, that we changed the subject. But first, 'Martin,' he said, 'you haven't spoken yet. Do you think it necessary that the author of the works should have had a university education, should have been abroad?' He had the impression of calling his friend back from a long way away.

'No,' said Martin. 'A university would surely have spoiled him. A person of his intelligence could not but have become a great scholar. He would have lost the common touch. He would have become a theologian, a philosopher, a Bacon, perhaps. I have always thought that if we had no information whatever about the authorship of the works of Shakespeare, we should look for just such a person as William Shakespeare of Stratford. Yes, "the Stratford man" is incontestably their author.' The company waited a moment or two to see if this was all he had to say. 'Alas!' Martin added.

Cryptic again! Why 'alas', Philip asked himself, turning to the lady on his right, the wife of the mayor, and broaching a quite new subject, a matter of local politics. On his other side was the actress and beyond her Martin, who now began to pull his social weight. 'I adored your Hedda', Philip heard him say and saw her gleam back at him. It occurred to Philip that a few years ago she would now have been listening to a lecture from Mr Beecham on the Black Death.

So successful was Martin with his neighbour that when Philip thought he had done his duty by the mayoress, and turned to his left, he had some difficulty in gaining the attention of the charming lady. Once gained, however, he did not let her go until the end of the dinner, not minding in the least the obligation he was imposing upon the personage on the mayoress' right. Let him sing for his supper! Let him atone for his facetious irreverence! It occurred with pleasure to Philip that his importance held the office once held by Francis Bacon. Let him pay for it!

'Would you care to move up to this end of the table?' Philip said, when the ladies had left the room. Port and brandy were passed around and Philip noticed that Martin, who hardly ever touched spirits, helped himself generously to brandy.

'Martin,' he said, leaving the other guests to talk among themselves, 'now that I've got you here, I want to pick your brains. These people have been talking to me about the opening of the theatre. They want a ceremony. They want me to make a speech. Well, what am I to say? On the theatre itself I shall be all right, but obviously there will have to be some mention of Shakespeare. I don't want to be banal.

Can you give me some factual tit-bits, something biographical if possible, the fruits of the latest research?'

'I am no Shakespearian scholar.'

'Perhaps not one of the three or four world experts. But knowing you, I don't mind betting that you know a great deal more than, for instance, anyone at this table, plus a bit more.'

Plus a bit more, Martin repeated sadly to himself.

'In Shakespeare's infinite book of secrecy,' he said, 'a little I can read.'

'Stop making cryptic oracular pronouncements and stop being modest, and try to be some help to me. What I want is a little-known biographical fact or two, which illuminates Shakespeare's character. Some contemporary opinion of the man, if such exists.'

'That is just what everyone has always been hoping in vain to find. Certain external facts suggest certain negative things about the character. For example, he was clearly no martyr to a political or religious cause. He was one who rendered unto Ceasar. Again there is that thing about his storing corn to sell at a profit which might be taken to suggest that he was a sharp-fisted businessman. But as to his charm, his laugh, the sound of his voice, his temper, his eating and drinking habits, his way with children and with his neighbours, next to nothing yet has been' (and between that word and the next there was the faintest pause) 'divulged.'

'What's that about the corn?' said Philip.

'A thing in the records at Stratford. And, by the way, this is not a fruit of the latest research, it has been known for years. In the middle 1590's there had been some very bad harvests. The price of grain had gone right up. At length in 1598 the Privy Council was compelled to take action against "engrossing" and "forestalling", that is to say, hoarding of corn and malt. In a list drawn up by the Justices of the Peace at Stratford-on-Avon, the name of William Shakespeare appears as one of the principal engrossers and forestallers. Another Shakespearian item a few years later, is related to the same thing. Shakespeare brought an action in the Borough Court against one Philip Rogers, an apothecary, who also sold ale and tobacco, for the recovery of a debt for malt supplied. The registers of the Court do not survive for the relevant year. All they have at Stratford is Shakespeare's plea, so nothing more has been found there about the outcome of the case. I'll let you have a note of these items, if you like, not that they get you anywhere much.'

'Interesting, however. Thank you. Perhaps I can work them in. Would you say that these are the most nearly disagreeable pieces of information that have up to now been found in records about

Shakespeare?'

'I have to repeat that I am no expert, but so far as I know, up to now, they are, perhaps, as you say, the most nearly disagreeable—up to now.'

'Well, if these are the worst things that can be found, which, it seems to me, are not even necessarily susceptible of an unpleasant interpretation at all, in fact they may simply show that he was behaving, as he should, like a Wise Virgin—it is clear that no Achilles' Heel has been found for Shakespeare—let this be the theme of what I say in my speech—has been found for Shakespeare either by the curiosity of archivists or the malice—'

'We are not curious,' Martin broke in, 'we just can't help finding things every now and then.'

'When are you going to find something important in my archives, by the way? I say, I think we ought to speak a few moments to these people before joining the ladies. Let's have a good talk tomorrow, Martin, I've lots to tell you, and lots, I'm sure, to hear.'

He turned from Martin and rallied his guests, passing the decanter.

Sleep on it, Martin had said to himself. The words, however, were a mockery. He passed a sleepless night, in spite of the unusual amount of drink he had taken in the hope of fuddling his head. His brain, indeed, was only the more active, worrying at the problem, or rather at the facts before him. For there was no problem. He had known from the first few minutes what he meant to do. The night, then, was simply so much time that had to be spent, in sorrow certainly, but not in doubt. It was the kind of night that is spent in the condemned cell.

How often, Martin reflected, momentous deeds are done, after sleepless nights, by those who must be almost too tired to know what they are doing. Who had a good night before Waterloo? He remembered himself being almost too blind with fatigue to see what he was doing with that blessed bandage, let alone to care much about his danger. Executions and torture must generally have been undergone by men exhausted by sleepless nights, by men, that is to say, who cannot 'appreciate' what is being done to them, quite as it would be 'appreciated' by the comfortable fireside reader about such things, supposing he were suddenly to be lifted from his chair and put in their place.

If Martin had hoped to find his sensibilities blunted in the morning he was disappointed. He seemed to be watching his own movements with quite unusual alertness and those movements had been rehearsed many times during the night. Entering the turret room, he had looked first at the fire and put two logs on it. Then, taking out his key ring from his hip-pocket, he had unlocked a drawer of his desk and taken out the large key to the muniment room, with which he unlocked the iron door. It gave its usual clanking shudder, and there was the usual rush of air, as he pulled it away from its close frame. Slowly, for it was heavy, he opened it wide enough to allow the passage of his tin box which he then dragged through into his room. From the open drawer of his desk, from which he had taken the key of the muniment room, he now took a smaller key with which he opened the tin box, putting the lid right back. He then took from the box a little roll of documents, some papers with a piece of parchment rolled round them, tied together with pink tape. He put this little bundle in the middle of the fire. Kneeling before the grate and manipulating the bellows, he watched the records burn away. When no flame any longer came from them, with the point of the bellows he knocked the charred remains into ashes.

Then he stood up and gazed sadly out of the window. He had no hope whatever of seeing the Lamb of God this morning out in the park. For he had just committed an act of complicated sin, by which he had deceived a friend, robbed an employer, betrayed his profession and cancelled the truth. And all to what end?

In order that nobody should ever know more than they already knew about the action for debt brought by William Shakespeare against Philip Rogers, apothecary of Stratford-on-Avon. Particularly in order that they should never read the testimony of Kate Warren, spinster, aged twenty two years, who upon her oath, deposed that for four years or thereabouts she had been maid-servant to the said Mr Rogers, the defendant, and that she knew Mr Shakespeare, the plaintiff, well for three years or more ever since 'hee hadde so cunninglie intanglid her goode master'. That the said Rogers had already paid much of his debt so that there was but 35 shillings outstanding which he would surely have paid soon had the said Shakespeare shown any kindly forbearance 'but hee ye said Shakespeare who is notoriowselye niggardish and a maliciowse bumfidler[1] who rejoyces in ye misfortunes of hys poore neighboures hadde noe compassion on hir goode master and one daie shee ye saide Kate lookinge from ye wyndowe sawe ye saide Rogers walkinge homewardes on ye roade and as hee was lame and frale hee walkid with a stikke, and sodenly alle unawares Mr Shakespeare came behind hym and kikked hym in ye backe and by reason of hys fralenesse hee fell to ye grownde where as hee was lyinge on ye roade hee ye sayde Shakespeare kykkyd hym moste pitifullye agayne and agayne at whiche ye said Kate ranne owte to helpe hir master and two or three wommen hir neighboures ranne

[1] Bumfidler: busybody.

owte alsoe showtinge "ye coward rogue, gette gonne clunchfist, ye snowzinge snudge[2] snowt", and soche like angrye wordes and at laste thay drove hym away after he hadde grivouslye kikked them all, for he disdained not to kikke a woman, and alle ye whyles he scremyd "I'll have mye bonde! I'll have mye bonde!" Another tyme, whanne ye saide Kate hadde browghte to ye saide Master Shakespeare at hys howse, ye Newe Place, som parte of ye money owyd bye hir master Rogers, hee receyved ye said money but whanne he sawe that yt was not ye fulle amounte hee jumpyd sodenlye from his chair for hys temper was vilanous quicke and blowrie[3] and chasyd ye said Kate who hadde fledde for shee feared hys bloudie entent whanne shee sawe hym snatche upp a bodkyn. . . .'

[2] Snudge, snutch: mean.

[3] Blowry: disordered. (*Warw.*)

Professor Needham

Professor Needham strode forth towards the park, evidently a man in a hurry. If a friend had met him and said 'What's the hurry?' Needham would have had a ready answer. He was a busy man, who believed in hurry. He had a goal to reach and time was short. 'Yes, but' the friend might have said, 'this walk is your afternoon's recreation. Why not relax the pressure a little?' 'The sooner I reach the Albert Memorial, my regular turning point,' Needham would have answered, 'the sooner I am back.'

If the insistent friend—but then Needham had no insistent friend—had urged the matter and said 'Are you quite sure you are hurrying towards something and not away from something', the professor (at least until today) would have answered confidently, 'Towards, without doubt, towards'. He believed that, were he to turn his head over his shoulder, the spectre behind him, called Boredom, Woolgathering, Dithering, or by whatever name was suitable to its abject moral state, had been so far outstripped that it would be invisible.

Making the circuit of the Albert Memorial, in the opposite sense to that in which he had made it the day before, for such was his practice, he turned homewards towards Bayswater. During the last week spring had come to London in torrents. Cherry blossom was littering the flower beds and forming in pink and white drifts against the grass edges to be kicked by children where, so very recently it seemed, they had been kicking the snow. But it was not the spring that had unsettled Professor Needham today. With the purposefulness of Lot he pressed forward.

Ask the bank about that deed of covenant. Remember to tell the boy's mother that he had seen Willie's cap under the sideboard. (Willie was his grandson. On the days he took Willie for a walk delays were permitted around the statues on the Memorial.) Put out the food for the gulls. Ask F. to sew up the hole in the pocket of the brown coat. Ring the B.M. about those photostats for that Swede. Fix a time to go with the others to the Town Hall about the dustbin protest. Cut out that thing about Galla Placidia and send it to Hargreaves.

As Professor Needham was walking under a pink cherry tree, suddenly, coming from nowhere, like a thought into a vacant mind, a gust of wind hit the tree and shot a spray of pink petals into his face. Too sudden to be avoided, the discharge was so well aimed that it was hardly possible not to feel that there had been an intention behind it. To Needham it seemed to be Nature's derisory comment upon his attempt to pretend that this time today was just like this time yesterday. As at a word of command, he gave up the pretence and allowed himself to live over again the experience of yesterday evening.

Unwilling, yet curious, he had opened the box covered in faded green buckram and began fingering those old letters. 'Giles, my dear,' the first one started, in a hand that was incontestably his own, 'cultivate *Ennui*, the prerequisite of all artistic inspiration. . . .' What tosh! With fascinated incredulity he had read on.

The contents of the green box, at which he had not looked for nearly fifty years, were the result of a compact between himself and three other undergraduates. Forming themselves, like Gray, Walpole, West, and Ashton, into a Quadruple Alliance, they had kept up a correspondence with each other for three or four years until the parting of their ways had loosened the bond. With the death of Giles soon after, and the return to their writers of his collection of letters, the epistolary alliance had dissolved. Nor in fact, except for a few accidental meetings, had Needham had any contact whatever from that day with the other two surviving allies, Roger and Philip.

During this half century the green box, which could now more properly be called a yellow box, had followed Needham in his various changes of domicile, the decision, at each change, to preserve it being based on no renewed reassessment of its intrinsic value—indeed, almost from the first he was sure that if he were to re-read the contents of the box he would find them to be silly stuff which he had quite outgrown—but perhaps at the beginning for no better reason than to justify his having bought the box and put them away so tidily in it, and later simply from a scholar's piety towards an archive which, merely by the passage of time, was becoming venerable. Venerable, it must be repeated, not interesting. For it was not part of Professor Needham's system to be interested in himself. A nostalgic backward glance at his own past was quite alien to him. The editor of the cartulary of St Michael's looked only outwards and forwards.

The task of editing this great document, which he had undertaken on his retirement from the chair of history, would have daunted a lesser man. The two fat volumes, compiled in the reign of Henry IV, contained copies of over a thousand deeds relating to the property of the hospital, tightly written upon large parchment folios. To transcribe all these deeds, to translate them, to locate as far as possible the properties mentioned in them, to identify the witnesses to the deeds where this could be done from the Close and Patent Rolls and other publications of mediaeval records, to analyze the place-names, and to make an exhaustive index *nominum, locorum* and *rerum* to the whole book—here indeed was a breathless undertaking for one's declining years. Only a man of Needham's energy and healthy expectation of life would have been offered the job, and would have taken it, at his age. No wonder he was in a hurry.

It is interesting how one seems more and more pressed for time as one grows older. It is not merely a question of finishing certain allotted tasks before one dies. There is such a daily pressure also of minor agenda. Get the chisel and scrape off that annoying little dab of white which the painter left on the glass of the study window. Check on Gilbert's birthday. Make sure the licence is still under the socks. Find when the Revocation of the Edict of Nantes was revoked.

To the suggestion occasionally made to him that his editorial work must be rather dry stuff, Needham was ready with his answer. London topography, and the land of the hospital was mainly in the London area, is full of human interest. From your daily intercourse with ancient deeds you begin to feel at home in the noisy mediaeval crowd that jostles you along the stinking alleys of the city. Set Needham down, seven hundred years ago, in the taproom of the Blue Boar over against St Alphege in Gutter Lane, and he could have addressed the publican by name. The other day his cartulary had introduced him to no less a person than Geoffrey Chaucer, occupant of one moiety of a messuage on London Bridge for which the rent was much in arrears.

Some of the ground his afternoon walk took him over had once belonged to the hospital. On that slope the other side of the pond, where a boy was now vainly trying to get his kite into the air, there had been a bloody scuffle among some apprentices one summer evening in 1401, that is vividly described in the Assize Rolls.

Yet it was not in fact the random passages of human interest that kept the professor to his task. The urge was wholly prosaic. Simply, the old must have work. They do not demand that it shall be interesting. Indeed, they perhaps no longer find one thing much more, or less, interesting than another. It must merely fill the vacuum their nature abhors. So long as they can stoop, gardening at its most pedestrian, does very well. The planting out of things in rows, the cutting of dead heads—there are always more rows, more heads. You are racing against time. You are absorbed. By definition, you must be happy.

So, for Professor Needham, the charm of his work was that it provided him with an unending series of little, next, things to do. There would always, or at least for long enough to see him out, be another line to transcribe, another name to index. Running into Chaucer like that had not, therefore, in that it disturbed the routine by suddenly requiring him to dispose of one dead head in quite a different manner from all the others, been particularly welcome. For any new reference to this poet would certainly be of much general interest. Needham would then have to follow up the matter of that messuage. To have found that Chaucer was living just there, just then, might well revolutionise Chaucer studies. It would certainly add lustre to the distinguished name of Needham. Pah! That was an infirmity he had long grown out of.

Did he, on making this unexpected meeting with the poet, take down his Chaucer and dip into it for a few moments, to get the flavour? He did not. It was a long time indeed since Professor Needham had read anything for its flavour.

Poetry is for the very young. Needham had had his period of reading and, yes, of writing it. Then there had been the stage of novel reading. Novels are about private life. Presently you get married and then you know about private life. Needham's marriage had been most satisfactory. There had been certain emendations and adjustments to be made in the proof stage, but the final text, established now so very many years ago, had been beyond reproach.

So novels become tedious. You can then with a good conscience devote yourself wholly to scholarship, to history, biography, books of fact. In these, Needham's reading had been prodigious. He was exceedingly learned. He had also written various books, two at least of which were regarded as standard works, and countless articles in learned periodicals. The older he grew, however, the less did he care to put pen to paper. For he was well aware that it is hardly possible to write a sentence without creating, or failing to create, an imaginative world. Whichever was the issue, he had begun to find his sentences as soft as wool, in the latter case because of the failure, and in the former—who was he to let his imagination play with the facts, to take sides in manners of opinion, to put forward the 'Needham view' of history? In recent years he had far preferred the honest research that went into a book to the writing of it.

So, in the fullness of time, he had become an editor. Here, at last, was work that could be judged by an absolute standard. You either got the thing right or wrong, and that was that.

What an intellectual odyssey it had been from his first to his second Chaucer period! A tale of progress, was it not, of steady mental purification? Was it not?

Then, yesterday morning, he had received a letter that had made him blink. For he had recognised the handwriting at once as Philip's, grown somewhat larger with the passage of time, unlike most handwritings, still, unquestionably that of the moving spirit in the Quadruple Alliance. Needham was aware that Philip had, as might have been expected, made a name for himself in the world of letters. Here now was the elderly literary man asking whether Needham had kept any of those old letters. He had been unpardonably careless, he said, with his own collection, but re-reading what he had the other day he had found them absorbing. Would Needham be prepared to lend him any that he might chance to have?

Needham, with, as always a firm hand on himself, had not, as soon as he was in his study after breakfast, at once gone to the letters. He had done his usual good day's work, four hours in the morning and three between tea and dinner, not, however, without an occasional glance up at the green box on top of its bookcase, almost touching the ceiling. There must by now be a good layer of dust on it; for the professor was most unwilling to allow any dusting to be done in his study. He suspected that when his wife did succeed in getting in with a duster she never got as high as the green box. Most unusually today a line of poetry came into his head, that of Sappho about the apple at the top of the tree forgotten by the pickers. 'No, they did not forget it, but they could not reach it.' At length, after his dinner, at the period allocated for reading learned books and reviews, he took down the box, blew the dust off it out of the window and opened it. Within a few minutes he too had become absorbed.

For every *a priori* reason the letters, of course, were most uncongenial to him. As has been said, he did not care at all about his own dead selves and the further back he went the more embarrassing they became. Then to one quite unaccustomed to reading literature, the literary quality of these outpourings was most distasteful. And they were exceedingly literary. Precious, affected rubbish! Some of the letters, both his own and the others', consisted almost entirely of quotations. They were, indeed, of their time, for the period of his adolescence had been one in which esteemed English poems might well consist of nothing but quotations (or misquotations) from the poetry of foreign languages, alive and dead, cemented by quotations from English poetry. 'Silent for nearly a month, my dear Philip, your voice is as hoarse as Vergil's to Dante, *che per lungo silenzio parea fioco* . . .' Arrogant literary tosh! Pretentious, adolescent tripe, Needham growled, as he read on avidly, placing without hesitation the forgotten tags. 'O saisons, o châteaux, it is irremediably donne. . . .' An exasperating thing about these youngsters was the way they seemed to assume for themselves, simply by unavowed quotation, the romantic status of the big names from whom they quoted.

Then he had come upon a whole verse, frankly acknowledged, from a poem called 'The Scholars'.

> They'll cough in the ink to the world's end;
> Wear out the carpet with their shoes
> Earning respect; have no strange friend;
> If they have sinned nobody knows.
> Lord, what would they say
> Should their Catullus walk that way?

On reading this, Needham had got up and walked about the room, reflecting upon his own slight output of friendship and of sin, until realising that it was a carpet upon which his eyes were fixed, he had sat down again and read on. And on. It would be tedious to follow him as he dipped into the several bundles, each marked with the name of an Ally and drew out the letters. Let it suffice to say that he read enough to come to the conclusion to which he wished to come, namely that, whereas Philip, in these literary exercises, had been finding himself, the other three, the deeper they plunged, had been losing themselves. Giles had been right to become a soldier, Roger a colonial servant and himself a scholar.

At length, in a letter of his own, he had come upon the sentence, 'I believe in my conscience I intercept many a thought which heaven intended for another man.' Like a reading passenger who has forgotten that he is in an aeroplane and looks up from his book and then down through his porthole at the ground for re-assurance, so Professor Needham had looked up from the letter, and then at the clock. Heavens! It was after midnight. Folding the paper before him, he had put it back in its envelope and replaced that in the packet to which it belonged in the box. With a corrugated wrapper, brown paper and adhesive tape he had then prepared the box as a parcel, before he went to bed, and first thing the next morning he had taken it to the post office, pleased with his decisiveness.

Now, on his afternoon walk, he kept saying to himself, 'You might have given yourself another evening or two. You hadn't read half of them!' Then he remembered and said over to himself that gay, airborne sentence, which came drifting down towards him, like a parachutist, in a leisurely pirouette, random, undisciplined, naughty, and quite unlike the phrases normally admitted to his territory. Enough! As he reached the park gates, he declared to himself that the episode of the green box was, for him, closed. Such, in fact, was the substance of a note he had sent with the box. Philip could keep it and do what he liked with it.

Out on the pavement Needham pulled himself together. Get a new book of stamps. Tell them not to send that beastly Sunday paper any more. Tell Latham to correct 'wound' to 'would' in his copy. Ask F. if she ever found out what Clarence can have meant. Test all picture cords.

The scholar's progress seems to consist in the elimination of ideas and their attendant uneasiness. Ever more matter of fact, your mind has no room for them, for the mechanism of your work increasingly absorbs you. At length perhaps you will spend your days simply sharpening pencils, cutting the pages of learned books. You approach life's greatest and final anxiety without hope or fear, or, indeed, much interest.

It was only a short walk from the park to the Victorian building, on the third floor of which Professor and Mrs Needham had a flat. His tea was awaiting him and by five o'clock the professor was back in his study; for the three hours between tea and dinner were the most sacred working hours of his day. He had not been long in there when the telephone sounded in the hall. His wife answered. It was Alice asking about Willie's cap. Putting up the receiver, Mrs Needham began to hunt for the missing object which at length she found in the dining room.

Though he had been the last person seen with it, she had not cared to go in and ask her husband about the cap, not between five and eight. It was remarkable how forgetful he was, he who had in some respects such a prodigious memory. For things immediately under his nose, he was no good at all. The penalty of having a great brain, no doubt.

Had she gone into his room, she would have found him gazing out over the roofs at the sunset. 'Penobscot', he was saying to himself. 'Penobscot'. There was no reason whatever why he should be saying this. A word, like a tune, will just come into your head, when you are off your guard. 'Guadalquivir', you may find yourself saying just after you have woken up in the morning, 'Guadalquivir'. There had been a period perhaps of several minutes of inattention to his work during which 'Penobscot' had been circling like a bat within his head. Having a room with a view was certainly a mistake for his kind of work, particularly now with these lengthening summer evenings. You gathered Penobscots and a great deal of other wool from over those roofs. He must talk to F. about moving his study to the other side.

In the hope of driving out the annoying syllables, he turned over the pages of his mediaeval Latin dictionary. *Amburbala*, he read, an expiatory procession, *dindymus*, secret, mysterious, *porretum*, a leek, *podagrice*, goutily, *vaciniensis*, of or for whortleberry. *Dindymus*, he said aloud, *dindymus, dindymus, dindymus*. . . .

Presently his wife in the kitchen heard him come out of the study and go into the dining-room, looking no doubt for a book in the shelves there. Then he was in the hall, the walls of which were also covered with books. Then he came into the kitchen.

'We don't seem to have a Catullus, I mean a Chaucer, in the house,' he said. 'You don't know of one, do you?'

'I'm afraid I don't,' she said.

He lingered, staring in an unseeing manner at what she was doing. She looked curiously at him. He did not seem to be himself.

'You won't get your dinner just yet, you know,' she said at length to break the silence. 'It's not much after seven.'

He then said quite the most surprising thing he had said to her for many a year.

'Fanny,' he said, 'I'm bored.'

The Regans

Fifty or sixty years ago, when summers were long and hot, when honeymoons, at least among the middle orders, did not take place till after marriage, when a great deal that would now be said was left unsaid, and there was widespread ignorance of the facts of life, when the country clergy had unlimited time for contemplation and when boys had to make much use of their imagination to amuse themselves, an eleven-year-old boy called Percy set out from the rectory with a packet of parish magazines to be delivered round the village. One of Percy's amusements was to carry on a dialogue with himself in French. '*Sanguineux paroisse magasins,*' he was saying as he approached his first objective, Walnut House, where the nearest neighbours to the rectory, lived, the Regans.

It must not be supposed that Percy was at all disgruntled or in the least bit resented the errand on which his father had sent him. He liked spying out the land. Those who are old enough to remember that children's board game, *L'Attaque,* dating from the time when the French were our enemies and therefore at least from before the *Entente Cordiale* of 1904, will remember that while the English and French soldiers were easily distinguished by their uniforms, the spy (who alone was able to capture the enemy's Commander-in-Chief) looked the same on each side, a sinister black-hatted figure, watching silently through a hole in a hedge. Percy liked to identify himself with that spy. He believed himself to be a master of furtive movement. '*Sanguineux chaud,*' he murmured in reference to the temperature of the day, as he turned his steps into the Regans' drive, which curved within a yew hedge round to their front door.

There was a noise of clipping and a voice, and there, as he came round the curve, was Mr Regan, his back towards Percy, chopping furiously at the hedge, littering the drive with the cut shoots. As he jabbed, he hissed 'She's—' and again and again he declared what she was. 'Grrr! Grrr!' he growled and then again 'She's—!'

It must here be noted in parenthesis that, in those distant days, the spectacle of a gentleman cutting his own hedge was unusual. His borrowing the shears from his gardener implied at least that he had a great deal of energy which more conventional occupations had failed to exhaust.

Percy, keeping on the other side of the drive, was now near enough to Mr Regan to scent the vapours of alcohol. How soon would the man turn and see the boy? In fact, he never saw Percy, for it happened that Mr Regan slowly turned as the boy passed him, keeping his back always towards him. It seemed to Percy almost as though he (Percy) had willed him so to move. Reaching the porch, Percy saw that the door was open. As was the custom in that village when a front door was open, he stepped inside without knocking and found himself face to face with pretty Mrs Regan who, when she saw him, at once turned about and was gone, but not before he had observed that she had a black eye. Taking one of the magazines from his packet, he put it on the hall table, then tip-toed from the house and escaped along the other half of the drive. Out on the road again, he began to whistle. '*Très intéressant, très,*' he said to himself. '*Mais il est prépostoire, n'est-ce pas?*'

Meanwhile Percy's father, in the silence of his study, had just succeeded in banishing from his mind the Regans and the disagreeable duty they presented to him. The ringing in his ears of that angry voice from their bedroom window, which had violated the stillness of the summer night, had momentarily ceased as he became absorbed by an article in *The Times* stretched out on the desk before him. It was concerned with space travel, a subject which H. G. Wells had recently been bringing into people's minds by his scientific fiction. The author of the article the rector was reading claimed that the matter would not always remain a subject for fiction, that, if the advance of scientific knowledge continued at its present rate, there was no reason why man should not find a way of reaching the moon, perhaps two or three centuries hence. And what might he not find on the other side of the moon? A further century or two and he would be on Mars, where almost certainly he would find vegetable, if not animal, life, perhaps even sentient beings like himself. And then all the stars. It was most unlikely that a race like our own should not have come into being on some of them.

This last thought had often been in the rector's mind and occasionally figured in his sermons, though never as anything but an academic speculation. Now, it seemed, a way might be about to open towards the most exciting revelations of God's purposes in the universe. Suppose, for example, it were to be found that Christ had been crucified also on Sirius and Aldebaran. Or had not been. In either case, here indeed would be food for thought. Questions of prodigious immensity were about to be asked and about to be answered. With the conquest of Space, might we not also be near the rolling up of Time?

Might not the end of the universe be at hand?

He remembered reading somewhere that, as history approached the year A.D. 1000, the belief that the end would then come was so generally held that no new buildings of any importance, not even churches, were put up for a generation or two before that date. If now a promise of the real end was appearing above the horizon, another such lull would come upon the spirit of mankind, a period of theological *non possumus* in which the imminence of revelation would make nonsense of the slow movement of private spiritual endeavour towards the Truth. The thought that such a lull would now not only be permitted but imposed by one's whole intelligence brought comfort to the rector. For, in honesty, he had to confess to himself that his own spiritual movements, looked back upon, were those of a man marking time rather than of one climbing a mountain.

He was a pastor, a teacher. A teacher is one in possession of some knowledge to be imparted to those who do not possess it. He was continually worried by the thought that he did not possess any such knowledge. He could, of course, recommend to his parishioners Hope and Faith rather than Despair, but then anybody could do that. He was no nearer *knowing,* at forty-eight, that he was on the winning side than he had been at eighteen.

The stationary condition of his soul was not due to any want of trying to get it on the move, though he had always been cautious of any vulgar 'seeking after a sign'. Spiritualism, for instance, was no part of his programme. Dean Inge had said about the mysticism of Plotinus that there was no occultism about it. 'There is no "mystical faculty",' he had said, 'only the spiritual sense which all possess but few use. There is continuity of development from sense-perception up to the vision of the One.' For some maybe, but not for me, thought the rector as he had often thought, acquiescing in the conclusion this time with a better conscience than he had ever done so before, thanks to that astronomical article.

His eye happening to fix itself upon the door handle of the study, he noticed that it was slowing turning. Presently the door was opened silently and Percy showed his head.

'*Vous disturbe-je?*'

'Come in, Percy.'

The boy advanced and stood in front of his father's desk.

'The Regans,' he said. He then danced on his toes, making the gestures of a boxer.

The matrimonial discord of the new people who had become their neighbours had forced itself upon the notice of Percy's parents, while Percy himself, whose turret room commanded a view of their house and garden, had been aware of it from the afternoon of their arrival. A lively description of the incident he had then seen could have been read in his diary by anyone who had found that ingeniously hidden pocket book, and who had mastered the cypher. The rector had called upon the Regans in the early days and had thought her as nice as she was pretty and had admired her blooming baby in its pram. Mrs Regan, moreover, came to church. She was certainly an addition to the village. With her husband, however, he felt that he probably would not get much further. He felt him to be an enemy, that unattractive thing a 'man of the world', selfish, self-indulgent and material-minded. He no doubt was the kind of man who thought that religion was all right for the women and children. He had an ill-tempered face and certainly drank too much. The evident tension between him and his wife was surely his fault. It might be guessed that he did not observe the precepts of Christian marriage, that he had a contempt not just for the general principles of Christian behaviour, sweet reasonableness, patience, turning the other cheek and so on, but also for those special rules that appertain to matrimony. God in his bounty, the rector argued, has, for the man and the man only, associated pleasure with the act of generation. His clear intention is, however, that generation, not pleasure, is the purpose, the only purpose, for which the act should be performed. We ought then to be grateful for the bonus attached thereto and not complain that it is no greater. The rector had had one child, Percy. After that difficult birth, the doctor had said that Percy's mother ought not to attempt to have another child.

'*Madame Regan,*' Percy said, after a savage upper cut, '*a un noir oeil.*'

His father stood up. Now was as good a time as any. He knew that Mrs Regan might be expected to be out, helping with the decoration of the church. He would go straight away, before his courage failed him, and talk to that beast. What on earth was he to say?

In the hall he put on his cassock, which indeed he often wore when visiting in the village, in marked distinction to some of his free and easy modernistic colleagues, who seemed to believe in breaking down what one of them was continually pleased to call 'the sartorial barrier' between themselves and their parishioners. It was particularly important that he should be seen to be making this visit not just as a neighbour but as a priest.

In his parishioner's drive he had a few words with Stacey, the gardener, who was clearing up the yew cuttings into a large wooden wheelbarrow. Though he found the Regans' door ajar, the rector knocked and waited, determined to be correct in every way. As the maid showed him into the hall, Mr Regan appeared.

'Good morning,' said the rector.

'Good morning.'

'Stacey tells me you've been having a go at that hedge. I'll bet it was hot work.'

'It was indeed. Come in here, won't you?'

'Well, thanks, if you have a minute to speak to me.'

Mr Regan led the way into the dining-room where a tumbler of whisky and soda, evidently just replenished, was fizzing on the sideboard.

'Have a drink?' said Mr Regan.

'No thanks.'

From the window, out at the far end of the lawn in the shade, under the walnut tree, the rector saw Mrs Regan sitting with her baby on the grass. Presumably she had not cared to show her black eye to the village.

'Take a seat,' said Mr Regan.

They sat facing one another across the shining mahogany table.

'Now what can I do for you, rector?'

'In the first place I must ask you to forgive my—my intrusion. The last thing I want to do is to stick my nose into other people's private affairs. But when—when—' He lifted his eyes for help to Mr Regan's, which were loaded and pointing straight at him. He lost his nerve.

'Perhaps,' he said weakly, '*you* could speak to *me*.'

The victim was giving the firing squad the order to shoot. To his surprise the other's face suddenly became quite pleasant, almost smiled.

'I'll accept that invitation,' Mr Regan said. 'As a matter of fact I rather badly needed someone to talk to. Here, do have a drink, won't you?'

'No, no, really, thanks.'

Thinking over this conversation afterwards, the rector was much to regret his refusal of that drink. He knew, it was true, how silly whisky made him. He knew that by drinking whisky with Mr Regan—and so indecently early in the day—he would seem to be condoning the vice, which was no doubt the cause of all Mr Regan's troubles. Moreover, he resented the look of astonishment on the faces of men of the world when they found you would not conform to their 'fast' habits. Loitering about in the dining-room in the morning drinking whisky was, in his opinion, 'fast' behaviour. Still, he felt that the hand of friendship had been held out to him and he had rejected it, just at the moment when he was beginning to think that Mr Regan was not such a beast after all.

'Yes,' said the latter, leaving the glass for which he had been reaching towards the sideboard, 'I think I can guess what has brought you here. You may have heard or seen things that make you think all is not going well on this side of the hedge. Well, you're right, it isn't. I know I lose control at times and make a row. Well, I'm sorry. God knows, I'm sorry.'

The rector noticed with satisfaction the use of the word God. This was being much easier than he had expected, for Mr Regan was doing all the work. He need now only deliver his prepared phrases, duty would be done and he could leave.

'Please don't think,' he said, 'that I have come here in order to be critical, still less inquisitive. I just thought that a word of sympathy from an older married man might be helpful. Heaven knows that marriage, Christian marriage, is not all plain sailing. It has its ups and downs. There has to be give and take. Now one side has to give, now the other. And so with habits of mildness and unselfishness, and with God's blessing, we may build up an atmosphere of sweet reasonableness that will carry us over even the most difficult periods. One's got to have patience, patience and self-restraint. It's often hard I know, but it's worth it and it gets less and less hard as time goes on.'

Mr Regan waited a moment. When it was apparent that the rector had finished, he began to speak.

'Give and take, you say. I quite agree. And a proper man isn't much interested in taking. What he wants to do is to give, to share, wouldn't you agree?'

'Er, yes, but of course.'

'Well then, the damnable thing is when they're not interested in taking what you want to give them, isn't it?'

'Er—' The rector did not know what he was being asked to agree to.

'When you are always made to feel that it is you who are the one who is asking for something, the child whining for a sweet and they're oh ever so calm and adult and wise and cool and collected, disposing of their favours, damn them, and not for one moment going to lose their control and with absolutely no heart for the frustration they can see they're putting you in while they tread you out as if you were a slug with their contempt or the damned patience with which they put up with your childish tantrums. It isn't that one wants them to give. One wants them to take, to want to take. That damned incuriosity!'

The rector had lowered his eyes. He had no idea what all this was about.

'I say, I must ask you to excuse my language,' said Mr Regan, 'but it has all become rather more than I can bear, this daily running my head into a brick wall.'

Mr Regan paused, and when there was no comment forthcoming

from the rector, went on, 'I see that the problem of my marriage is not one that you have been bothered with. I congratulate you. I most sincerely envy you.'

The idea of being envied by Mr Regan was so surprising to the rector, and in a sort of way so flattering, that he was tempted to open his heart to him and say that, though his own marriage had been the smoothest thing in the world, yet he had his worries. Lifting Mr Regan out of the trivial actualities which he took so hard, and which, incidentally, the rector found quite incomprehensible—how was it possible that sweet girl should be such a heartless villain as Mr Regan described her?—he would give him a vision of the higher Realities and then concede that even in that world of endeavour there were humiliation and frustrations and brick walls. The adventure, however, of making such a confession to such a person as Mr Regan seemed to him *a priori* so rash that he held himself back. One reason, also, for doing so was that in the exchange of confidences he might seem to have had much less to give than the other. The impact of Mr Regan's head against his wall was so much more violent than that of the rector's against his.

Mr Regan was gazing down towards the far end of the lawn. 'And it might all have been lovely,' he said, 'so lovely.' His voice and his eyes were tender and sad and vanquished. All the fizz had gone out of him.

Neither of the two men could think of anything more to say. Presently the rector stood up.

'Well, I could only repeat what I've said already, which I won't do. I'll just say that I hope you will manage to overcome your troubles. You will have my prayers, and, of course, if you ever wanted to talk to me again, I shall be delighted to see you.'

'Thank you, rector, it was good of you to look in.'

Conscious that his mission had not been an unqualified success, the rector, as he walked away, enumerated to himself those parts of it that certainly had been successful. There was that glass of whisky on the sideboard that had remained untouched during his stay. There was the mention of 'God', and the apology for the use of the word 'damn', and Mr Regan's envy of himself. There was the gentleness of which Mr Regan had shown himself capable at the end. All these points were good. What was bad was that the rector felt he had perhaps come quite near to rescuing a lost sheep, and had funked it. And to have come away without discovering what it could be that was making a grown man so angry, was surely a failure. Yet, was it his business to uncover heaven knows what embarrassing beastliness, perhaps? No, on the whole he had not done at all badly. He had been into a lion's den and come out alive again and without suffering any disrespect to his cloth, and having said his say.

His wife, to whom he described the interview, was as mystified as he was. 'Such a sweet girl,' she said, 'she's much too good for him.' They were again discussing the problem of the Regans that afternoon over cups of tea in the study. They agreed not to talk about the matter in front of Percy and not to send him with messages to their house or in any way encourage his interest in the Regans. The boy was already far too inquisitive.

The rector observed the slow turning of the door handle and the opening of the door.

'*Peux-je?*'

'What is it, Percy?'

'The Regans.'

He pointed upwards with one finger to indicate his bedroom, and then sideways to indicate the view from his window of the Regans' house and garden.

'*Quel tohu-bohu!*' He raised his eyes to heaven.

'Percy,' said his mother, 'I'm not going to have you spying on people!'

'Do you know what it's all about?' the boy asked.

'It's none of our business, Percy.'

'Well, I do know,' the boy said. 'I heard him say it this morning. It's all because she's frigid, frigid—grrr—frigid—grrr—frigid, frigid!' The violence of the utterance shocked Percy's parents and the rather odd word puzzled them. What were they to make of it all? Their sentiments were, as a matter of fact, accurately expressed by Percy in his summing up of the whole business.

'*Dans le très chaud temps nous avons, il semble prépostoire complaindre d'une personne étant froide, hein?*'